LADY

MW00330796

by

Christopher S. Rubel

Cover by
Joel Cinnamon

Edited by
Veronica Castle

Published by
Crimson Cloak Publishing

ISBN 13: 978-1-68160-066-6
ISBN 10: 1-68160-066-8

Published in 2016
Crimson Cloak Publishing
P.O. Box 36
Pilot Knob, MO. 63663

Publishers Publication in Data

Rubel, Christopher S.
Lady of the Deep
P. 438

1. Fiction 2. Stories 3. Sea 4. Native Americans
5. Romance 6. Sailing 7. Marine Archeology

.

Acknowledgements:

Lady of the Deep *would not have come to publication without the help of others. I am grateful to those who answered questions, edited, criticized, and in their way added to the finished high quality of this novel. The couple, Carolyn Shadle and John Meyer, both Ph.Ds., living in La Jolla, California, performed an early edit of the manuscript. Katherine Hauser Rubel, my wife and encouraging, even though always objective, supporter, edited and shaped the manuscript in ways I could not have done alone. Thank you, Katherine.*

Professional artist, Joel Cinnamon, Claremont, California, created the cover art. Anyone who has published knows how often a new book is judged by its cover. Thank you, Joel.

Novelist and multi-talented friend, Chuck Kelly, who lives in Long Beach, California, introduced me to Crimson Cloak Publishing, the company that publishes his novels, including his most recent gripping novel, Sammy. Thank you, Chuck, for introducing me to Carly McCracken and Crimson Cloak Publishing. What a positive experience this has been, which is unusual in the writing and publishing game.

Thank you, each and every one of you.
Chris Rubel
Claremont, California
16 June 2015

Dedication:

This novel is dedicated to the countless Native Americans and indigenous Californians who have survived the coming of the Europeans to this continent and especially to California.

Chapter One

Jon Scott had left his home slip dispirited and fatigued. He could not face society for another day. Work no longer energized him. Discouraged with relentless grief, he was sinking, feeling guilty, too, spreading gloom upon his friends, his clients, and parishioners. Waves of grief from Miriam's death three years ago still enveloped him. Jon thrived with their marriage. He plummeted into dark emotions losing her to a dreadful cancer.

With the restorative balm of sailing, being alone, salty air, sounds of a strong bow wave, and the rhythmic motion of a fine craft plowing ahead, Jon's grief decreased. In evening twilight the *Daimon* approached the rock-rimmed bay, her skipper's inner knots loosening with each passing nautical mile. This was his therapy.

Jon caught a good wind while sailing down the rugged southern side of the island and arrived early enough to linger there in a dusky light. The dark, steep cliff off his port beam soon loomed close, as he turned to port.

He recognized the silhouetted rocks ahead. Four years had passed since his last sail to the island in November 1980. Two warning buoys off his starboard quarter marked the reef dangerously close to the surface. Clear of that hazard the anchorage was near. Vigilantly watching the decreasing depth on his fathometer he crept further into the bay. The plan was to drop the stern anchor at about thirty feet in the current tide, still quite low. He noticed some kelp ahead, a possible hazard that he didn't remember.

Jon thought, *Maybe I was here at high tide before.* At high tide maybe the kelp seemed less.

A light evening breeze kept the *Daimon* slowly moving toward an anchorage. He struck the main sail and coasted gently, with only the genoa sail pulling. No other boats occupied the small bay. The chart showed that the deep water became shallow enough for anchoring in another 200 yards. The fathometer confirmed it.

Suddenly the *Daimon* stopped dead on course. The light wind died. Not a thread moved. He had hit nothing firm, no rocks, but still the boat's forward movement halted. Jon didn't want to start the two-cylinder diesel, but had no choice. He didn't want the current to carry him into the rocks.

The engine started easily, as it always did. Two spins with the Farymann and off it thumped, *pum-pum-pum-pum.* Jon put the propeller in gear and the boat moved a few feet forward. But seconds later the diesel nearly lugged to a stop. Quickly Jon disengaged the prop and let the engine idle. Grabbing the flashlight, he shined its beam into the water. A mass of kelp entangled the boat. With the water as clear as gin, a school of small fish glistened through the dense, green kelp forest.

Once Jon got under the hull, his work would be cut out for him. In the morning he would slice away the thick, lush weed. This required strength and endurance. He was too tired now. Besides, it was too dark to do it this evening.

Fourteen hours of sailing were enough for one day, Jon thought.

On Monday morning he had sailed out of Alamitos Bay, Long Beach, in a damp fog. His destination was the Isthmus, near the west end of Catalina Island. After an overnight stay, he sailed around to Cat Harbor and took the day to relax, swim, and clean his boat. In the pre-dawn hours of the next morning he left Cat Harbor, following the coast of Catalina, moving southeast toward Farnsworth Bank to round the San Clemente Island's west end.

The rock formations on the weather-beaten side of the Catalina Island intrigued him. The colorfully contrasted pressured rock strata swirled and twisted as evidence of the dramatic geologic history of southern California.

He had eaten breakfast at the helm as the sun rose, while a fair breeze moved the boat well along the rocky coast. He had barely finished his coffee when he entered the Catalina Basin, one of those exciting places where the ocean floor is nearly four-thousand feet below. As he continued along to the west end of San Clemente island, the westerly breeze averaged eight to eleven knots. On a beam reach the *Daimon* was very happy moving along at nearly seven knots.

Now, at this darkening time, he sought an anchorage with minimal light. In the middle of November, days are short and nights come quickly, dropping a dark shroud over the water. Sailing about a mile off the island, he first spotted the rocks of China Point at about 1700 hours. That gave him a dead-reckoning course. But the west wind strengthened about 1930 hours. That caused him to overshoot the bay. He had to tack back. Nearly to his anticipated anchorage, the boat stopped abruptly, gripped in kelp. Jon was caught. He assessed his choices:

I'm in a fix; tired, stuck in thick kelp, and I just hope the kelp keeps me here until morning. It's going to be a restless night, watching for drift.

Stars shimmered in the ink-dark heavens. The quarter moon hung faintly above the west horizon. The fuzzy cluster of stars, the Horsehead nebula in Orion, seemed to be winking at him, and Venus won the brightness prize. He heard a splash astern. A large fish rippled the water's surface, reflecting the stars in dancing pinpoints of light. A gentle temperate breeze ventilated the bay, wafting across his deck as he relaxed in shirt sleeves. Tonight, the crescent moon would soon disappear and Jupiter and Saturn would be rising, somewhat less bright than Venus.

He heard another splash, then others, and he wondered if fish had jumped or maybe a seal was close by. There would be little sleep. Every few minutes, he lifted his head just enough to see the dark outlines of the rocks and his other markers, to keep a check on his position. He remained stuck fast. But, when the tide came in, it might lift the *Daimon* above the kelp and set him adrift. He hoped to be free of the kelp, but wary that he could possibly drift into the rocks.

By first light the tide rose, but not enough for him to power the *Daimon* out of the kelp. He fixed breakfast and savored the moment in this harbor, delaying his dive for a while. Two seals peered at him from the midst of the kelp. He imitated their bark and watched them look at one another. One barked back in response. He wondered what he'd said. Even in his predicament, he felt better being there.

This journey is working. I don't feel nearly so wrapped up in my dark cloud.

Seldom did other boats wander into this bay, this less-than popular cove. Fine with Jon. He needed more time alone, away from everything and everyone. He cleaned up from breakfast, checked other items to make things shipshape, and then turned to the task at hand. He prepared to snorkel for the job of cutting kelp.

A row of seagulls lined along the cliff and shared his enjoyment of the warmth of early sunlight. Every so often one or two would compete for a surfacing fish that flashed in the waters below. Often a hovering pelican swooped down and snatched the prey, the seagulls fought for whatever morsels dropped from the victors.

Jon tugged on his rubber fins and adjusted the face plate and snorkel. By the transom ladder he lowered himself into the calm sea water. With no one around, he felt free and soothed at the same time as he moved naked through the kelp. It brushed his skin, feeling very good. He pulled himself through soft, slippery leaves and branches. He ducked below to see the propeller entangled by thick, green strands of kelp, tightly twisted around the blades and shaft.

Cutting kelp is like trimming a dense underwater hedge. Fortunately, his long, sharp knife sliced easily through the tender vines. Severed pieces drifted about as he cut, some sank, others floated. They had to be cut into small segments or they would seize the rudder and propeller again.

Small fish crowded around and nibbled on the cut fragments with almost microscopic sea life attached to them. The process took longer than he had expected. When he finally finished he was relieved and tired. Before he surfaced, he swam around the boat to survey the hull. When everything checked out, he reached for the stern ladder to climb aboard and try to back the boat out of its green, slippery berth.

Something below caught his eye. What he saw startled him. He surfaced and washed off the mask. He pulled it back on and pushed himself down from the stern for another look. No doubt about it. It seemed to be a body partially buried in the mud. The lumps in the sea bottom looked like a head and a sandy hump beside it where the shoulders could be. His heart thumped; he was transfixed. With no current, no drift, everything in this watery world seemed to exist in an eerie silence. The kelp bed waved slowly from its mud-anchored roots. Some thirty-five feet below, the swaying kelp, resembling tropical palms in a gentle wind, almost obscured the image of the body. He had to do something, but he could only stare, expecting it to move. To investigate he had to secure the boat and prepare for a dive.

Out of the murk crawled a lobster, a careful, easy grab for his evening meal. He climbed aboard and dropped the lobster into the cockpit. Then he went below and took a gallon milk container from the ice box, unscrewed the cap, swigged the last few gulps, and replaced the cap. Back in the cockpit, he opened a lazarette, reached into a collection of lines, selected one, and measured out fifty feet from knot to knot. He tied one end to the small dinghy anchor and the other end to the plastic milk container, slipped back into the water, and swam to a depth of about fifteen feet. He dropped the anchor through the kelp, near what seemed to be a body, watching it sink to the sea floor. A cloud of mud puffed around it. He needed breath so he surfaced. He was satisfied that the visible plastic bottle marked the spot clearly.

The engine kicked over and in reverse, very slowly, he guided the *Daimon*'s sleek thirty-six-foot hull free from the kelp bed. Although wet, nude, and chilled in the early morning air, Jon was relieved to be free. The boat again moved in open water. He calmed himself about the possibility of a body beneath him. There was no urgency. A drowned body in the mud wasn't going to go anywhere. The priority now was to drop anchor. At the helm, wrapped in a large towel, with early sunlight on the water, he found a clear waterway around the kelp to a viable anchorage. A pelican crash-dived a few feet off the bow as he slowly powered forward. Then it bobbed to the surface. The pelican gripped a thrashing fish, nearly as long as its beak.

Jon cut the engine and drifted slowly forward. He threw out the stern anchor and played out the line as the *Daimon* moved forward. Then he planted the bow anchor and slowly powered back to secure it with adequate scope. The calm water assured him he would not drag the anchors. Unless a storm came in from the southeast, he could relax slightly knowing the boat was secure.

Everything happened as planned, but he remained disturbed by the image of a body in the mud.

There's always something to disturb my peace. Such is life.

He began gathering the gear needed for the dive. The seagulls on the cliff took this moment to screech and fly, all of them changing places in a manner so organized that only genetics could explain it. The racket jarred the air, a fitting accompaniment to the unsettling anticipation of what he might find below.

He struggled into the wetsuit, imagining and preparing for possible hazards. A lone seal, not far from the starboard quarter, barked three times. He wondered if this might be an omen.

Three barks, the number three, the Trinity.

Jon had two scuba tanks. The one with just enough air for a brief dive he put into the dinghy with the faceplate and breathing regulator. Lowering himself down the stern ladder, he climbed into the dinghy and untied it from the stern cleat. He rowed toward the plastic bottle. The inflatable dinghy glided over the top of the kelp. With each pull on the oars he had to wiggle green plant strands off the blades. He tied the dinghy's bowline to the anchored milk-bottle line and swung himself into the water. The seagulls seemed to laugh and he wondered if they knew more than he. He checked that the regulator worked, cleared his mask, and dived.

As he descended, his heart thumped wildly and he felt his pulse beating against the tight straps of the faceplate. When he reached the sea floor, he maneuvered closer to the anchor. With air being quickly depleted, he had to act efficiently. Approaching what seemed to be a human head, covered with sea growth, he reached out and swished away the vegetation.

It was a woman, a wooden woman. She stared at him with large, opaque eyes. She appeared to be black, her features sculpted and fine. He rubbed the vegetation from her face. Excitedly brushing away more mud, he saw a magnificent torso, complete with full, round breasts. Using every ounce of strength, he stood her upright in the mud, her feet still buried. She seemed at least five feet tall. Below her hips protruded a large chunk of carved wood, that looked like a fine, prominent rear end with a carved flowing dress. Broken fasteners protruded from the wood. Four remnants of large bolts and pegs must have once secured her to a proud craft. Splinters of heavy, black wood still clung to them.

He wondered where the rest of her ship could be. As he looked along the muddy floor he found no sign of anything structurally resembling a ship. Fifty feet away, in deeper, murky water, loomed an outcrop of jagged rocks. They appeared to be no hazard to most small boats, peaking ten feet below the surface at low tide. He could see nothing else but kelp and mud.

A chill ran through him. He felt uneasy in this deep place. Rising slowly to the surface, he reached into the dinghy and grasped the long line. If he worked fast he had enough air to descend again. Working his way down through the kelp and using a few slip knots and a bowline knot, Jon managed to secure the line around her. He studied her with the line tied and ready to lift, a phrase came to him which he said to himself, *A Lady of the Deep.*

Now he must see if he could get her to the surface. He brought the dinghy anchor up with him. Later on he would use it and the plastic bottle to mark the new location of the form on the sea floor. He hoped he could drag the figure closer to the *Daimon.*

Back in the dinghy, he rowed hard, dragging her along the bottom. Straining powerfully on the oars, he pulled his submerged burden to within forty feet abeam of his anchored sailboat, dropped the anchor, and left the milk bottle on the surface as a marker.

Aboard the *Daimon*, Jon adjusted the fore and aft anchor lines to maneuver the boat nearly above his Lady. He used the main boom as his crane, extending it beyond the port beam of the boat. With a couple of blocks and the largest port winch, he prepared to lift her - or hoped to lift her - onto the deck. He had no idea how much this water-logged wooden figurehead weighed. When raised above the water, he wondered if he could manage to lift her aboard the boat. He cranked the winch slowly and carefully, as she rose from the depths.

When she broke free of the water, her dull, dark eyes seemed fixed on him and he thought of the line:

Each turned his face with a ghastly pang,
And cursed me with his eye.

Strange to think of the *Ancient Mariner* poem now. There was no curse nor ghastly pang in her face. Still, he felt uneasy. He had disturbed a fine relic that carried a spirit, perhaps the very woman herself in her wooden form.

He left her there, suspended mostly above the water, as he cleared the scum and debris with a stiff hull brush. As the grime and barnacles disappeared, he stared at the detail of her black skin, full lips, and a damaged regal nose. Her eyes, opaque and dark, seemed to look through him. For a moment he wished he could close them gently and let her sleep.

Her weight from the boom caused the sailboat to list to port. He guessed she was close to 300 pounds. Struggling to wrestle her aboard, using the rigging of the boat, he laid her gently on the foredeck. The calm bay helped him. Had there been swells she surely would have damaged the hull or, swinging freely, become a hazard.

He positioned her on her side and padded her with spare cushions and several life jackets to give added protection to her and the deck. Tying her securely, Jon used every lifeline stanchion and cleat within reach. Despite his efforts he knew that carrying her to home port without incident would require good weather and some luck.

He imagined her serene and powerful face, staring down from her ship's prow, taking great waves head-on or observing starlight reflected in calm waters. What were her ports of call? What had she witnessed? Who carved her? What bow had she graced?

He could not look at her simply as a marine salvager would, calculating the worth of a water-logged chunk of lumber. This ancient, rustic woman was imbued with a spirit, of that he was certain.

Chapter Two

On the second day in the quiet island cove, late afternoon clouds gathered. The sea turned gray. A growing swell rocked the *Daimon* a few degrees in rhythm side to side. Jon swam and walked on the narrow beach, getting some exercise. Later, he sat and tried to read in the cockpit with a glass of Syrah, but he could not concentrate.

His interest wandered to his found treasure. He could only think of the figure-head, his Lady. Questions consumed him. Researching her history would be his next adventure. He went to the foredeck, and stretched out alongside her, his hand on her shoulder. The well-carved voluptuous breasts revealed a cleavage that disappeared into a dress that appeared to flow in the wind, maybe once on the prow of a square rigger. The dress still looked as if it were flying. Some of its wispy tips were broken off, damaged from rough waves, or perhaps from a violent misfortune.

As he lay there, staring at his prize, Jon was unaware of a growing affection that was stirring inside him. It was a feeling of love that a child slowly develops for a strange and large wooden doll like Pinocchio or for a rag doll that becomes the child's constant companion.

He studied her and imagined how she might have been painted. The tip of her nose was gone, but nothing diminished her elegance. Her long hair fanned out as if in flight. and flowed into that part of wood once attached to the ship. Her bare feet were tight together. Her toes gripped the wood. The very dark color of the whole figure made him wonder if she had originally been all black. This seemed unlikely. He had only seen fair-skinned figureheads.

I wonder if she's been in a fire?

Everything about her intrigued him. Now, on deck and in the bright sun, he could see nothing sinister in this figure. She struck him as determined and brave, her countenance reflecting a steadfast grace and femininity. With arms and hands swept back, her face and bosom met any oncoming seas.

Why had she come to rest so close to the rocks? Where were the remains of her ship? Had her ship been a bark, frigate, clipper, or schooner? So much to learn about her and how she came to be here.

Pushing slack lines aside, he leaned against her and watched the birds, the water, and the reflected light on rocky cliffs rising 300 yards to port. A healing warmth and a deepening peace slowly rose within him, this journey had become even more the medicine he needed.

The afternoon dimmed to dusk, time to prepare a small meal and turn in. Tomorrow would be a long sailing day and he could not be sure how the boat would handle the extra bow weight, especially if the swells became choppy. The prevailing wind would be just right, on a port beam reach, the *Daimon*'s favorite breeze in any sea. With luck, the swells would be mostly off the port quarter and they might give him some surfing seas. It would be a fine trip home. Jon's sense of peace deepened.

He poured one more glass of the Syrah, to enhance his lobster feast. Jon prayed for its soul and thanked his creator for providing him with this bounty, but the crustacean just wiggled his long, probing feelers and curled and uncurled his tail as it slid into the boiling water.

Before turning in, he listened to the NOAA weather forecast. The news remained good for tomorrow's sail. Twenty-four hours from now he'd be in home port. The log book had been neglected, so Jon took this time to make it current. He added detailed comments about finding and raising the figurehead and securing it on the foredeck.

Jon swam and walked on the narrow beach for exercise. He felt at peace with himself, much more relaxed. The ghosts of his otherwise anxious, working self had vaporized in the salty air of this cove. Then, out of nowhere, he began to cry.

Thoughts tumbled over themselves as he allowed himself to feel the pain of the losses he'd tried hard to escape. The tears helped. Overwhelmed with a dark, heavy feeling, he let it happen. Gradually it drained into the sand and the bay at his feet as he gave in to it. He sobbed for several minutes. Releasing, purifying, it struck him that his tears were nearly the same saline solution as this ocean. *Thank you, Lord!* He repeated several times. The cloudy quiet of the bay, the gentle swells, with his Lady on the foredeck, safe and at rest: he felt as close to heaven as he'd been in a long time. So many thoughts and a rush of memories with Miriam flooded his mind.

Miriam... he now saw that his Lady and Miriam were somehow linked. It didn't matter how, but he knew they were connected, at least in spirit. When his weeping ended, he felt cleansed and thought again of where he had been. Another verse of Coleridge bubbled through his mind:

Alone, alone, all, all alone,
Alone on a wide wide sea!
And never a saint took pity on
His soul in agony.

Interesting how in a time of healing and peace the memory of loss and months of aloneness would affect him so deeply. He felt as though this whole voyage had brought him to this instant.

Edging into his mind, like an approaching fog bank, grew a memory and a longing. He didn't want this now, but it would not go away. Miriam's face, her body, her voice, her fragrance, everything about her flooded into him and became a deep ache. He entered an occupied zone, taken by a storm front, and the memory of the woman he had adored blew a mighty wind within him. Three years since losing her seemed no time at all.

Why her, now? This whole journey was about being within myself, escaping, and getting away from work and from all the pain and loss. What muse brought Miriam to me now?

The whole scene came back. He hovered over her, holding her as she lay dying, gently moistening her lips with the small sponge; he talked to her, told her how he loved her, how he would never forget her, promising he would come to her in eternity. Only twice did she stir during those long hours, perhaps understanding. Once, she seemed to squeeze his fingers, ever so slightly. She died that terrible night, peacefully, at three in the morning, the time of the Holy Spirit.

A seal's bark jarred him into present time. He did his seal imitation and was rewarded by an answer. They exchanged barks several times. In the mild night air, under high clouds, he stretched out on the cockpit cushion and lapsed into a deep sleep.

Dreams rolled through his night theater in rapid succession, flooding him with images, feelings, memories. Spaces that had been closed a long time were opening and he pictured an ancient sea chest, with a broken, massive lock, its lid creaking open and revealing relics from an era long past. Gold coins, ancient scrolls, paintings, jewelry, lace, a pair of shoes from the 18th Century, a three-cornered hat and a belt buckle made of gold still attached to a wide, black, leather belt just his size. He wrapped it around his waist. In the dark, starless night, moving side to side with the gentle rolling of the *Daimon*, the dream spell broke.

That night he slept, the best sleep since departing his home slip.

<u>Chapter Three</u>

This was his dreamboat, the *Daimon*. She was an Angelman South Coaster, a rare ketch, thirty-six feet on deck. She had been a sister to the one designed for Lana Turner. That delighted him, knowing that his boat matched the one that had intrigued the beautiful actress. He also enjoyed her name, Angelman, after her designer.

Somehow, it seemed a blessing to think of a boat, always referred to in the feminine, being named an 'Angel Man.' He was not sure of the gender of angels, but maybe, just maybe, if he sailed long enough in this craft, he would learn more about them.

The *Daimon*'s design would go well on any tack. A schooner prow and bowsprit, along with an exquisite sheer line gave this classic wooden boat an appearance unequaled by most sailboats. She had balance and grace in nearly every sea or wind. She always sailed well, but especially beating she could point high into the wind. When on a reach, her hull speed averaged about eight-point-two knots; she did that easily even in a ten-knot wind. Living aboard enabled him to do the continual maintenance a wooden craft requires.

For Jon to varnish, paint, and clean such a beautiful vessel was therapeutic. Rigged by him to his specifications he could single-hand her in most all conditions. In fact, she held his confidence in nearly any blow or sea because of her strength and oversized rigging. Often, under sail and at the helm, he felt enchanted with his craft.

Along the west coast of California unmanageable conditions were rare. And when the seas got rough, there were many places to hide among the Channel Islands. One only needed to know enough navigation to find the protected harbors and to have the skill or luck to reach them.

The trick with any boat is to know how to run with the weather. His worst time happened in one of southern California's major Santana winds, those ferocious seasonal northeast winds. Nearly overpowered, he ran for two days and nights, ending up beyond the blow, nearly 100 miles south southwest of Catalina Island. He ran with just a storm jib, the boat endured well through heavy seas at hull speed, seas that mounded into twenty-foot breaking waves. He would never forget that treacherous storm. More times than he could count, the waves lifted the transom, aiming the bow down into its trough and then the wave would break just astern or amidship. During those memorable forty-eight hours, the cockpit was half-filled with water much of the time. Without the sea anchor creating drag astern, the boat would have broached.

I guess we only risk these things because we know life is a lottery and often enough the odds are in our favor.

He rehearsed every sailor's prayer:

Lord, your ocean is so big and my boat is so small. Have mercy, Lord.

That stormy trip taught him well. It took four days to sail back to Long Beach, but luckily his radio worked well. It enabled him to let the Coast Guard Radio in Long Beach know he was safe enough and to give his probable location.

The Coast Guard informed him that several people had called to check on him.

As if out of a reverie from memories of long-ago journeys and times past Jon returned to his present moment and his pleasant anchorage. Dawn arrived and the rocks just ahead caught the early light. Although still cloudy on this quiet morning in this island cove, the rising sun shined beneath the clouds to the east. The swells had grown. The pressure against the hull from an increasing breeze strained the anchor lines. Weather conditions were rapidly changing. He was pressed to get underway.

Jon raised the stern anchor. The boat swung on the bow anchor like a weather vane, into the wind. The early morning breeze on his bow made it necessary to power out through the waterway to clear the reef, the rocks to the west, and the edge of the kelp to starboard. He needed to do this hastily, as the weather front increased. The radio forecast announced a detected low to the southeast, moving northwest. This meant he ran the risk of sailing directly into the weather, which included rain and light fog. He noted seas were forecast to become swells out of the southeast, rising to perhaps six feet by noon. If he approached the coast, he would be taking the swells on his starboard quarter or abeam. For now, however, the swells were on his port beam. His Lady would have a smooth ride, with no bow-pounding seas. To make things easier, he would adjust his course and take advantage of the swells, which put him west of his home port, over seventy nautical miles from this San Clemente cove.

Noting the time, he stowed the bow anchor and headed homeward. He hoisted the main, unfurled the genoa, raised the mizzen, stopped the diesel, and began a comfortable northwesterly sail. He headed on a broad beam reach with a choppy, following sea. It all felt fine for now.

Setting the self-steering, he went below to fix poached eggs, bacon, orange juice, and coffee. Gradually leaving the island's Pyramid Point and the peaceful cove astern, he thought about his Lady from the deep, wondered how many years she had been mired at the bottom of the ocean. Were there adventures to come? He had a lot to learn about her. Falling in love with an ancient figurehead might be a lot safer than one of those real-life women. Besides, how could he ever love a woman after loving and losing Miriam?

No woman could begin to capture my interest or heart after being with her.

He thought of a familiar song that fit his current reflections: something about a paper doll to call one's own ...

By noon, he had covered twenty-five nautical miles. If they kept moving this well in even choppier seas, his Lady and he might be in Long Beach by late evening, entering the channel in the dark. When the wind strengthened, surprisingly, it came more dead ahead. He had to head up to starboard, changing his course more toward shore sooner than he had planned. The forecast had not included this. Point Fermin lay distant off his bow, Saddleback Mountain was to starboard, but by early afternoon the haze obscured the coastal landmarks.

Along with the charted lights and horns, he had enough experience to recognize points along this coast and, other than fog, usually he had no problems sailing into Alamitos Bay. The light towers of the Edison Company plant made for clear markers, along with the oil rigs in the Catalina channel. Polaris, when visible, could be a great help on this particular course, but cloudy skies obscured the heavens and tonight's increasing clouds would render Polaris useless. As always, he trusted most his little Raytheon Radio Direction Finder (RDF), his best navigational friend.

Dolphins crossed his bow about 500 yards off, probably fifty of them. Counting jumping dolphins is a difficult exercise. They circled, jumped, and played.

Sometimes, especially at night, they were attracted by the wake of a boat as they frolicked in the phosphorescent trail. The dolphin light show frequently enhanced night sailing. Whales, too, made spectacular leaps at night, a massive explosion in the dark of blue-yellow-white phosphorous sprays. He wanted his Lady to share them with him. He wondered if she remembered the years of being at sea on the prow of a great ship, the first one to see ahead as the bow wave thundered beneath her. If only she could tell him her tales!

The mild chop and the large swells now off his port quarter kept him busy steering, but he felt satisfied as the boat moved well. Cloudy skies and a light fog made the water look almost gray, but the temperature felt pleasant. His attention wandered to naming. Calling her his Lady of the deep sounded corny. She deserved a better name.

By now they had a personal relationship and he talked – yelled - to her up front, as she lay on the foredeck.

Then his memory returned to Miriam, the woman he'd loved for so long. Perhaps he had retrieved his beloved from the depth of his unconscious in the form of a figure-head. But, no, Miriam never left his thoughts and feelings. Since her death, he had not been able to imagine another relationship. He swore he'd never be in love again.

Miriam's talents and interests included scholarship in history and art, along with her artistry on the piano and violin. He could not imagine any woman as interesting and as complicated. He had come to appreciate her moods, passions, and sensitivities, which she willingly shared. Her dying at forty-four infuriated him, especially such a lively forty-four. Her death seemed like a bad trick, a warp in God's judgment. Miriam's ease made everything seem right and okay. She embodied an eagerness in living, going after every scrap of life she could find, maybe anticipating how it might be snatched from her too soon.

She must have sensed it, intuition being her strong suit. Sometimes she just knew what they had going on between them. She could read situations with a clarity that lived up to her name. Named after the sister of Moses, it was Miriam, the prophetess, who watched her infant brother in the basket. He said it over and over to himself, 'Miriam. Miriam'.

The wind shifted. He lowered his heading five degrees and trimmed the sails. Even with increased choppy seas from an approaching weather front, the boat moved better now, freer, and with less helm.

No matter the weather, the afternoon was for him beautiful. He began to feel quiet in the simple task of sailing on a course to his port, what a treasure! It gave him such joy and memories of Miriam stirred what Charlie Brown called 'good grief'. After all, could he not feel joy along with the grief?

Here I am at the helm of a boat I love, after a wonderful week of sailing, crying over my lost Miriam.

Cabernet! He startled himself as he announced the name. It had come to him from a glance into the cabin, through the companionway to the wine rack. The light caught one bottle of dark wine and his Lady was suddenly christened Cabernet. The dark wine color went with her complexion, certainly the dark of her eyes. But why would a figurehead be dark?

Jon had read a lot about the Black Madonna and questions suddenly came to him.

Research had to be done in order to put all this to rest. He became obsessed with this Lady from the deep, Cabernet. Just as the *Daimon* held steady on course, the name also stuck, at least for a while. He knew no one would ever hear him speak her name, so there would never be a need to explain. Of course there would be interest in her, maybe even trouble should there be a law about relics from the sea.

But, slowly, another name crept into his view. Thinking of his Lady and this adventure, giving him time to think of Miriam, he thought of the name Meri. From seminary days, when he studied scriptures, he knew the Egyptian name for the goddess Isis. Meri, the Egyptian plural being Merti, eventually became Meri. Meri, or, the Latin form, Mare, or later, Mary; mare, the sea being the primitive source of all life. His mind circled through these obscure thoughts, as the bow wave's rhythm and the hum of the wind in the rigging soothed him.

Meri. I'll call her Meri. She's from the sea and Meri has such a deep sea meaning. The name is related to the sea, the source of life, along with the sun. This Lady from the depths of the sea brings back so many feelings and memories of Miriam, my love. They seem related. Cabernet is a wine and I could do symbolic ramblings about that name, too, but Meri is closer to Miriam. Meri. I like that name.

He took the storm jib out of its sail bag and wrapped it around Meri, doing his best to make her look like a rolled-up sail on the foredeck. He lashed her down well and inspected her new shapelessness. Seeing this new form made him feel calmer, and she would be less obvious to the curious eyes they would encounter between here and his slip in Long Beach.

Chapter Four

Off his starboard bow a small sailboat appeared from time to time on the swells. He noticed it as he ate lunch and cruised toward home. Suddenly, he observed that its mast had broken halfway up. Swells rocked the sloop. Loose rigging knocked about on the deck. The portion of the mainsail that wasn't in the water flapped uselessly. As he got close, he saw that the sailboat was definitely floundering.

Adrenalin kicked in and his relaxed mood flipped to vigilance. The wind blew at twelve knots and, judging from the white caps, it blew stronger ahead, where the small craft pitched and rolled. The cockpit looked empty, with no one steering, but when the boat crested, he noticed some movement aboard. He changed course, turning off the wind about ten degrees and coming closer. Less than a quarter mile away, his pulse raced. The boat was definitely in trouble. He glanced at his watch and noted the time: 1510 hours.

The disabled craft, an old Cal-20 from the sixties, had lost its rudder. Now he saw the movement in the cockpit was a frantic dog. The boat disappeared in the troughs with the upper part of its mast and loose sails dragging and flapping above the crests. The boom swung wildly as the Cal-20 was tossed about.

He eased his main and genoa, slowed, and shouted *Ahoy!* The dog barked as he approached. Then Jon saw what looked like a body in the cockpit.

"Ahoy, Cal Twenty!" He yelled louder, but the only response came from the barking black spaniel. He let out the sails even more and nudged his boat closer. The broken mast of the disabled boat ranged back and forth in the swells. Watching to stay clear of the shrouds and lines dragging in the water, he reached down and turned the key to *Start*. The engine idled, thumping out of gear. Coming abreast of the boat, he gained a view into the cockpit and saw a body nearly covered by a dark blue blanket.

He shouted again and the dog barked with greater frenzy. Suddenly, its tail began to wag and the dog began hopping frantically from one side of the cockpit to the other. The person appeared motionless. Jon put the engine in gear, let the sails luff, and took a turn around the Cal-20. On the transom he read, *Zephyr-Marina del Rey,* painted in blue letters. He prepared a line for taking her in tow. Alone in these seas, he knew it would be too hazardous to bring her alongside. Moving precariously close to the bow of the hapless sailboat, Jon flipped the line over and over again until it caught around the starboard bow cleat. He pulled the line tightly enough to secure a slip knot, played out twenty feet of it, and fastened the other end to his starboard stern cleat.

He worried that there might be more than one person on the boat, perhaps someone below in the cabin, but the seas were too rough to check. The *Daimon* was underway with the impaired boat safely in tow, following well in his wake. He called the Coast Guard and headed toward Los Alamitos bay.

"Coast Guard Radio Long Beach, *Daimon* calling."

Without hesitation, he heard, *Daimon, Coast Guard Radio Long Beach.*

"Coast Guard Radio Long Beach, *Daimon*, bearing 310 degrees, about fifteen miles off Laguna Beach, swells running six feet, a Cal-20 in distress with an unconscious or dead person aboard her. Need immediate assistance. No way to know the condition of the person. ETA Long Beach, Alamitos Bay, in current wind conditions, is 2200 hours. Winds are out of the west-southwest, at eleven to thirteen knots."

Daimon, stand by and wait for instructions.

"Roger. *Daimon* standing by." He hung the microphone where he could reach it from the helm.

All he could do was to hold his course and wait. Glancing back, he saw the spaniel's head pop up from time to time. He could do nothing else in these rolling seas without creating a problem for either boat, his or the Cal-20.

The radio crackled: *Daimon, Coast Guard Radio Long Beach. Maintain current heading and report any changes in sea conditions, your speed, or ETA. Dispatching Coast Guard to your position at this time. Present weather forecast, light rain and partial obscuration in your vicinity by 1600 hours.*

"Roger, Coast Guard, thank you. *Daimon* remaining on frequency."

The Coast Guard must have had a launch out to sea, because one appeared quickly, throwing an impressive bow wave and heading in his direction. She moved at high speed towards his port bow. He calculated that she must have been at the east end of Catalina, or somewhere very near that point when summoned. He glanced across the water and saw only a distant ketch in the haze; his was the only sailboat within miles.

The swells were so high that he kept losing sight of the Coast Guard launch in the troughs. Every time he rose to the crest, the launch appeared larger and more powerful.

When it was within shouting distance, a uniformed woman appeared on the bridge. Using a megaphone, she commanded that he slow on course so they could come alongside. He yelled back that they should come along his starboard side and put someone aboard the disabled craft while she was in tow. Jon thought they'd have less trouble with the swells on his starboard and more control underway. Surprisingly, they did as he suggested.

The launch swung around him in a large arc and came alongside, its bow twenty feet off his starboard quarter and adjacent to the Cal-20. Someone, presumptively a paramedic, climbed down a ladder to its cockpit. The wind pressed the small sailboat against the hull of the launch. This made boarding easier. The broken mast and rigging in the water dragged to port, presenting no hazard for the launch. Within seconds, the Coast Guard paramedic assessed the emergency and a basket stretcher was positioned on deck.

With the help of a second sailor, the two strapped a person into the basket and raised the basket deftly aboard the lifeboat. He heard the dog barking furiously as its master was taken away. The basket descended again. The paramedics wrapped the dog in a blanket and strapped it in. Suddenly, the whole contraption jerked upward as the paramedics straddled the basket, controlling the dog. In moments, they were secure on the deck of the launch.

The rescue was a graceful ballet. In minutes it was over without a hitch. Jon held his course with not the slightest variation; his knot meter read six-point-eight knots.

Nothing was said to him during the operation, but afterward, a voice on a megaphone called out an order: "When reaching port, contact Coast Guard immediately. We have your CF numbers and your slip location in Alamitos Bay. Leave the Cal-20 at the Harbor Master's dock."

"Roger. Wilco!" he shouted back.

The Coast Guard's twin diesels thundered up to maximum power. The big launch dug its stern into the water and left him in a great mound of propeller wash that threw the *Daimon* at least ten degrees to port. Rescue or not, he would report that dangerous and rude seamanship.

A few moments later, a radio call from the same voice that had hailed him with the megaphone announced, *Daimon, the party is alive and unconscious, dehydrated and sunburned. She's lucky you came along. Coast Guard off.* Before he could respond, another commanding voice said, *Repeat. Report to the Coast Guard or the Alamitos Bay Harbor Master immediately upon reaching your destination. We expect your call by 2400 hours. Coast Guard off to the Daimon..*

He responded: "I repeat! I'll report upon entering the harbor. Thank you for the news, Coast Guard. *Daimon* will remain on frequency until arriving in Alamitos Bay." He felt accused of something, when all he had done was to bring in a boat in distress.

The *Daimon* maintained nearly her hull speed in twelve to fifteen knot winds with storm swells building astern to help propel him home. Darkness came about eight miles off Huntington Beach in light rain. The lights of the city were visible, which helped him navigate. His radio direction finder picked up the Long Beach jetty signal. He was on the last stretch home, with the hapless Cal-20 following well.

I've got a lot more to put in the log when I get back. Better do that before I forget some of the details of this adventure.

Chapter Five

About 2050 he rounded the jetty into Alamitos Bay. The wind had all but died. Swells ran high from out of the south at four to six feet, combining with a westerly swell and making for a choppy sea. Inside the jetty channel, however, the sea calmed. He started the diesel and took in the sails as he slowly powered inside the channel toward the Harbor Master's dock to drop off the towed boat.

Wish I didn't have to deal with the authorities. Sure like to get to my slip. But what a fine time I've had!

Up ahead he could see the Harbor Master's office and he sang to himself:

Eternal Father, strong to save,
Whose arm hath bound the restless wave,
Who bids't the mighty ocean deep its own
Appointed limits keep.
O hear us when we cry to thee for those
In peril on the sea.

"Good old hymn 608," he mumbled, grateful for this safe arrival. Before long, he would glide into his own slip, all lines secured, the dockside electricity in, and his ketch would be home once again. But first he had to obey Coast Guard orders.

What the heck! This shouldn't take too long.

Or, so he thought.

A bright beam caught him midway down the channel. The light glared, blinding him for an instant, and then a familiar amplified voice commanded him to follow a craft that materialized just ahead, out of nowhere. The patrol boat made a fast u-turn not more than fifty feet ahead of him. It caused a rolling wave to splash against his hull and toss the disabled towed sailboat astern from side to side. Above the cabin of the offending boat, a twirling light suddenly blazed and, next to it, a strobe flashed brightly.

Following the patrol boat, he came alongside the lighted dock at the Harbor Master's office where two police officers awaited him. One of them took a line and slipped it over his bow cleat, the other hooked the stern. Together they pulled his yacht to dockside and tied off the lines. They didn't know how to secure the dock lines properly, but he asked only for time to put his bumpers down. Whatever the problem, he wouldn't let them scar his boat. When the bumpers were in place, he stepped onto the dock and raised his arms as ordered. They frisked him, checking for weapons.

"What's this about?"

"The Coast Guard asked us to detain you for questioning about an incident at sea," responded an officer. "We've also been ordered not to let you move beyond this point without finding out who or what you have tied on your foredeck."

"That isn't a person and it's no one's business," he countered.

"The Coast Guard will determine that," he replied. "Coast Guard and Customs will be here soon."

"Yes sir," Jon replied, hostile at first, then shifting to a milder tone. "Would you like to come aboard?"

"We'll stay here," one officer said, almost politely. At the same time, his partner shined his flashlight around the boat and into the cabin ports. The floodlights on the Harbor Master's dock illumined the *Daimon* well enough, but he kept looking into the boat.

"Are you looking for something?"

"Just checking," he replied. "Anyone else on board?"

He told him that he'd been alone and in great peace for the last five days of cruising, until this very moment.

"Am I under arrest?"

"No," said the officer with the flashlight.

"Then, I presume I can get aboard my boat and go to my slip. The Coast Guard can question me there just as well as here." He moved toward his boat.

"Stay put!" commanded the one closest to him.

"Then, I am under arrest," he said. "In that case, I'd like to make a phone call."

At that moment a harbor patrolman came down the gangway onto the dock, greeting him.

"Hey, Jon, what've you done?"

Frank Martinez walked past the officers. He usually patrolled Basin Four, where Jon had his slip and where he'd been living for the last three years, since Miriam's death. His friendly face relieved Jon.

"Am I glad to see you, Frank. What took you so long?"

Frank stood just a few inches shorter than Jon. At six feet, his square jaw and muscles presented an impressive figure, especially in uniform. With his dark, Indian features and Jon's blond hair and blue eyes, they obviously came from different worlds.

Frank and Jon liked each other from their very first meeting. But, tonight Frank was professional, cautious suspicion being a part of his personality and a part of his work as a patrolman. Even though they were almost instant friends at first meeting, Frank maintained a cautious distance for quite some time. Eventually Jon passed his tests, including the physical ones. One evening, they playfully arm wrestled several times. It took that evening for Frank to finally become trusting and open with Jon.

Jon could take him once or twice, but his resolve, aided by shorter and stronger arms that had the advantage, gave Frank the leverage. He never allowed Jon a third victory. He could always control situations with his expressive, bushy, black eyebrows and monotone words, emanating from his substantial belly. When Frank spoke, his dark eyes penetrated. When things got tough, because of his bearing and obvious strength, he could readily handle almost any situation.

"Frank, would you please explain to these officers that I'm a sailing bum, a psychotherapist, an Episcopal priest, and a good citizen?" He moved toward Frank to shake his hand.

The officer closest to Jon said, "Stay put, sailor!"

Frank focused on the policeman. "Officer, he's okay. I know him well. When you give him an order, I suggest you treat him with respect." Frank pulled out a cigarette and lighted it.

"We don't know him from Pancho Villa," responded the officer. "And we don't know you either." As an afterthought, he added, "Better not light up here."

That set Frank off. "Chuck, don't fuck with me!" he growled. "You know me and you're in my territory. Whatever's going down here is over. Jon and I are going aboard his boat to have some coffee and wait for the Coast Guard to show up. If you guys want to waste more of your time, be my guests, but you don't treat Jon like a prisoner unless you have a charge against him." Frank leaned closer to the officer, appearing taller than his six-foot stature. For emphasis, he stuck his thumb under his badge. "You got a charge?"

The officers huddled briefly and the one with the flashlight said, "Okay, you handle this. All we have to do is record it. He's right. We're in your jurisdiction, and I'm hungry."

Frank offered a hearty second to that with, "Yeah, Chuck, take your buddy to the café. You're at the end of your shifts. I've got this handled. Remember," he added, with a big grin, "the doughnut shop isn't open yet."

Chuck nodded. "He's all yours, but you better have him right here when the Guard comes. We're informing them that you're holding him."

Jon turned to Frank. "Since I'm your prisoner, you should put the cuffs on me before these fellows leave. That'll keep them happy."

Frank smiled mischievously, "Don't push your luck, Jon. You don't want to piss off the Long Beach Police. They get paid the big bucks to rule by intimidation."

"That's enough, Frank," snapped Chuck. "We're out of here. You're in charge." With a nod, the two officers walked up the gangway to their police car.

The Harbor Patrol boat had long been in its slip, arriving just ahead of the *Daimon*, with two harbor officers on board obviously listening to the exchanges. When the policemen left, the two men in the boat approached Jon and Frank.

"So, where's our coffee?" asked the shorter man.

Jon offered to prepare his great instant brew, but they were distracted by the arrival of a white Coast Guard vehicle, its light bar blinking. It pulled into a parking space next to the gangway and one of the passengers came down the ramp. A familiar female voice called, "*Daimon* skipper?"

"I'm the skipper. Come aboard." Frank followed Jon as he slid the hatch open to climb down into the cabin.

"Just wait there! We'll be right with you," ordered the same voice. The low tide made the gangway steep. Frank and Jon stepped back onto the dock and waited, smelling the pungent fragrance of the sea wall life. Small crabs scurried back and forth when the gangway moved under the weight of the approaching Coast Guard officers. A large starfish just below the piling next to the gangway reflected the floodlights. He detected a shimmering under water orange star. Schools of small, glistening fish darted here and there.

Questions began the minute the Coast Guard arrived. The woman officer looked like a child next to Frank, but her military uniform and manner conveyed authority.

"What's on the bow of your boat?"

Thinking fast, Jon replied, "I bought an antique and I'm taking it home."

"Mind if we look?"

He stepped aside and gestured permission. "Watch the lines. Don't trip," he cautioned.

The ensign climbed aboard, flashlight in hand, and walked along the rail to the large sail-covered lump on the foredeck. She bent over it, lifting a corner of the sail, inspected the exposed part of the figurehead. Turning to Jon, still bent over it, she asked in a demanding tone, "Where'd you get this?"

"I bought it from a salvage yard," Jon said. He decided to lie, not sure why and hoping for a pass.

"Do you have a bill for it?"

"They're going to mail one to me. We're still unsure of the price and they're supposed to do some research first."

I better keep track of this story I'm weaving.

He did not want to give her more than she asked, otherwise his story would get entangled and suspicions would be aroused. If he were asked about this again, he would have to produce documentation. He hoped the understaffed Coast Guard would forget about this. Later, when he had the time, he needed to enter this into his log book, keeping track of what he'd told her.

"What happened out there yesterday afternoon?" she asked. "You know, with that sailboat you're towing and the woman we rescued?" As she spoke, she shined her light in his face.

Jon shielded his eyes and asked her to turn off the light. "How about some coffee?" he suggested. "We can sit down and I'll tell you the whole thing."

She said nothing. He hastily added, "Listen. I called you people as soon as I saw the sailboat was in trouble and there was someone aboard."

Jon had a moment to reflect. He wondered why he had not told the truth, as he always did. Something inside him made him feel strangely possessive, a little afraid and somewhat insecure. He wanted to share his record catch as a proud fisherman does with a weigh-in photo. However, a deeper-seated fear of loss, a fear that others might take his prize away to claim as theirs, not his, welled up inside him. Could the gods be angry with him for taking her, like a mermaid, from her rightful place in the sea? Why lie? Why this need to cover her up? Was she a lifetime catch out of season? Was he feeling some primal urge?

Frank spoke up, declaring Jon to be trustworthy and respectable. "It's very late. Couldn't we do this tomorrow, after the skipper here gets some rest?" He added, "Is there a charge or crime?"

The officer thought about this for a long moment and then said, "Fine, we can take care of this tomorrow morning, but don't leave your slip until you check in with us." Reaching into her pocket, she pulled out a small folder that had her badge attached, and produced a card. "Call this number tomorrow morning. I'll be there after 0900 (9:00 AM). Ask for me, Ensign Shabro. They'll page me. Leave everything tied on your boat just the way it is now. Do you understand?"

"Of course I understand," he told her, working hard to keep his voice down. "I was going to go to church in the morning, but I'm sure the Lord will understand that the Coast Guard comes first." He could not help some sarcasm, but she paid no attention. "I've got no reason to do anything but cooperate," Jon added. "My Coast Guard safety certification is aboard and I'm registered with you in this marina." He suddenly felt exhausted. "May I go to my slip now?"

She nodded permission and turned toward the car. Frank and Jon stood on the dock for a moment. Jon asked him for a rain check on the coffee invitation.

"How about breakfast early on Tuesday?" Frank asked. His broad, comforting smile helped to ease Jon's fatigue and anger.

"You got a date. I'll call you when I get back from my swim. And Frank, thanks for showing up at my trial tonight."

Frank took the tow line attached to the Cal-20, walked it around the end of the dock, and tied the boat up in one of the Harbor Master's slips. "We'll keep this wreck here. You don't want to have to deal with it. Anyway, it should be officially impounded."

Jon was relieved to see the three of them walk up the gangway together. Left alone, he started the diesel, dropped the dock lines, and headed for his slip.

I wonder if I ought to just stay here, dockside. No. It will feel good to be home, get a shower, and climb into my bunk, in my own slip. My Lady and I will go home. Seems like a ticket to heaven.

Chapter Six

He slept restlessly, awaking when someone knocked on the hull of his boat at 0830. After he slid back the hatch, he poked his sleepy head out into an early morning fog. A young girl stood on the dock wearing shorts and a sweat shirt reading 'No Fear'. She seemed to be about sixteen years old.

"I'm looking for Dr. Scott. Are you Dr. Scott?"

"Well that depends on who's asking," he responded.

She seemed shy, but determined; a woman with bearing and presence. He stared at her long, black hair and dark, almond eyes and stood still, posing, waiting. She took him in, watching him as he watched her.

"The Coast Guard told me you found my mother, so I thought I'd come meet you. They wouldn't tell me much, but I nagged enough for them to tell me your name. They said your boat had a big thing tied on the deck. I couldn't miss your boat with that thing there. What is it?" she asked. Then without waiting for an answer, she said, "I found you through the marina office. I know it's Sunday morning and maybe not a good time, but ..." She shrugged and offered a slight smile.

"I'm usually gone by now. But the Coast Guard changed that." With a quick smile, he added, "Jon Scott at your service."

"I'm Krystal Fitzpatrick," she responded. "When Mother went out for an afternoon sail and never came back, we were scared. Everyone was searching for her. You found her." She started to cry softly.

"Do you want to come aboard?" He stepped into the cockpit from the cabin steps and offered a hand, explaining that he would go below and put on water for coffee. He wanted answers, and this seemed like a good time and probably the right person to ask. He went below. Krystal stepped aboard and made herself comfortable on the cockpit bench. The seat cushion was still wet with dew, but she didn't seem to mind. With the cabin door ajar, he couldn't see her, but that didn't keep her quiet.

"Finally, Mother's asleep, so I came to find you. She was unconscious until late last night." She hesitated. "They thought she might be in a coma, but she was just unconscious. Schwartz, our dog, went crazy when she saw me. She's a love. The poor dog was really thirsty, too, but it didn't stop her from running around, turning circles, and jumping up on me. The security guard at the hospital kept her all night. Isn't that a nice thing to do? I mean she fed Schwartz and talked to her, and she wasn't even sure if her owner would live or not. She could've called Animal Control or dumped her on the police, but she kept her all night. Really nice."

Krystal fell silent. It struck him that she might be counting her blessings.

"Now, finding you ..." she went on. "I'm so glad for what you did."

He emerged from the cabin, having listened to her rapid-fire soliloquy with great interest.

"Water's heating. We'll have coffee or, if you'd rather, tea in a few minutes."

He could see that she'd been awake for hours, probably running on adrenalin. Caffeine wouldn't be the best choice, but when he handed her a cup of strong instant coffee, she took it eagerly and asked for sugar.

The morning fog had thinned and the sun's rays bounced off every surface; what moisture remained made everything glisten.

"Isn't this a beautiful morning!" he declared. "A good day to know your mother is okay, to be sure. Meeting you makes it special for me, too. Of course, I haven't met your mother, but the Coast Guard radioed me that the woman they rescued was alive. It seems the Coast Guard believes I had something to do with your mother's near catastrophe. I'm supposed to call them about that soon, about 0900. I got a hostile reception when I came into the bay last night. In fact," he added, "I'm late making the required phone call. Relax for a few minutes."

Krystal nodded, then suddenly remembered: "Oh! I was supposed to tell you not to call Ensign Shabro. She was at the hospital early this morning talking to my mother. When Mother went to sleep, I told the woman I was going to come find you." Her mouth twisted a bit. "She was really thoughtless, asking all those stupid questions when Mom's practically delirious. Mom was awake, but she seemed confused. She didn't answer some of the questions right, I guess. That woman kept asking them over and over, taking notes, and she told me to tell you not to call her. She said they'll get in touch with you."

Krystal set off on another talking jag, barely taking time to drink her coffee.

"Ms Shabro was very different to me after coming out of Mother's room. She wouldn't let me stay in the room, but I kept going back in. I told her she was my mother. She gave up and I stayed most of the time, except I had to go to the bathroom a lot. My stomach's been upset. I got really scared. I tried not to think of my mother dead or drowning. I had a couple of terrible dreams when I tried to sleep."

When she stopped to catch her breath, Jon said, "You know what I'd like right now? I'd like you to feel the morning. Just take in the peace of this marina. Notice how all the boats are washed off by a good rain, waiting for their captains and crews to come aboard and enjoy a Sunday outing. I'd like you to know that your mother's going to be fine, and so are you and the dog. And, if all of this isn't luck, perhaps God has found a way for just the right things to happen for you and your mother." Sometimes he preached on Sundays. Maybe he had just delivered this morning's sermon.

Krystal sat quietly for a few minutes and looked around, as he had asked her to do. "Please come meet my mother," she said, excitement in her voice. "I want you to meet her, and I think it would help her. She isn't that far away, only a half hour, and I can take you in my car. It's small, but I think you'll fit. You're taller than anyone in my family, but the seat goes back and ..."

He shushed her with a smile and a raised hand. "Of course I'll come," he said. "I want to meet Schwartz, too. And I imagine that your mother is worried about her boat. I left it tied up at the Harbor Master's dock, but I should call and make sure it's still there. It can't sail, you know. It doesn't have a rudder, the mast is broken, and the main sail is ripped to shreds, and I don't know what happened to the jib." An expression on her face brought his explanation to an abrupt close.

"I hate that boat. Mother loves it, but it's given her problems ever since her husband - Robert, that's his name -

left it for her in the divorce." The look of scorn on her face expressed her contempt. "Robert and Mother adopted me, but I don't claim him. Mother and I don't look alike, so don't act surprised when you see her. She's really pretty and I always have to explain I'm adopted when people see us together." She paused and smoothed the long, black hair back from her face. "Robert bought a big boat and gave her the reject. If you ask me, I think he wanted her to die trying to sail that little boat in the ocean. She's a better sailor than he ever thought of being and knows boats better than anyone, but everything's wrong with it and she had no business taking it out to sea." He heard her scorn shift to anger.

When she fell silent, with tears in her eyes, she turned away from him and stared into the distance. "Let me finish a few phone calls," he said. "Stretch out here in the sun, while I check my exchange for messages. It might take a while, because I've been gone for five days." He stepped down the ladder and closed the cabin door.

He was relieved having had his colleague cover for him while he sailed. Barbara always did an excellent job with his emergencies, and he happily returned the favor whenever she took off. Sometimes their clients teased them, pitting one against the other, making comments about how much better they felt talking to the other therapist. They enjoyed the game during their nine years of practicing together.

He copied eleven messages. All of them could wait. One message was Barbara's, telling him that three of his people had consulted with her during the week. The last message came from Ensign Shabro, the Coast Guard officer with the tight, white uniform. Her message offered good and bad news. For the good news, she informed him that her investigation into the Cal-20 incident might back up his story. For the bad news, she announced, "We still have serious business over the so-called antique. Customs has questions for you. Call me Monday and be prepared to hand over paperwork on that chunk of wood. You've got my card and number." His body stiffened with her order to call. He took some deep breaths, told himself to relax, and felt suddenly famished.

He emerged from the cabin to find Krystal sound asleep. Clearly, the girl was exhausted, overwrought with everything that had happened during the past forty-eight hours. He was glad that she felt safe and comfortable enough to sleep on his boat.

His stomach growled, leaving no doubt what would be the next step. He hadn't eaten since yesterday afternoon, except for granola bars and a large orange juice. Just then Krystal stirred, sitting bolt upright, looking right at him. She seemed disoriented for a moment, but then smiled a modest and beautiful smile.

They watched a great blue heron landing on the end of the dock, close to the stern of the next boat slip. Its great wings slowly opened effortlessly as it went after a fish that jumped not twenty feet away. The heron gulped the fish, landed near the tied boats across from them and remained there for a time. Several seagulls lined up nearby for possible leftovers, if the heron fished again.

Krystal looked back at him. "Five! I was five when Robert left the first time, when they started their battles. He stomped out of our house over and over, once he even broke the front door off its hinges. He even backed his big Mercedes into the side of Mother's T-Bird, her baby. After that, I didn't see him for two years, and then he came back to start it all over again." She paused, twisting strands of hair around her finger. "I'm upset. I don't know why I got into all this here, with you." She took a few jerky breaths, and asked, "Who are you, anyway? I'm telling you all this and I don't even know you."

He smiled. He wanted to put her mind at ease. "I'm Jon Scott, a psychotherapist, and I'm always getting into trouble for going where I don't belong. I'm sorry if I stumbled into your privacy. But, you apparently need to talk about this."

"I've got a good shrink, thank you, but we don't get into this stuff anymore," she said. "We used to talk about this over and over, until I told her I'd had enough, and we stopped. Now, here it is all again, just like it used to be. I'm talking about it again. Does this junk ever get better?" Before he could respond, she quickly added, "Do you know that horrible man has been fighting about the divorce settlement for the last five years? He even threatened to kill my mother if she didn't stop suing him for back child support. Big deal for him. He's got lots of money! He's got a motor home, a new BMW, a fancy, dumb blonde, and his big sailboat. So I ask you, therapist, does this crap ever get better?"

He was used to this question coming from clients and sidestepped it with, "Should we get a bite to eat and then go meet your mother? We don't have to say another word about this personal stuff." He wanted nothing more than simple cordiality with this young woman. After all, she wasn't five. She said she was seventeen and drove her own 1976 Datsun 280Z. It looked brand-new, and she drove as if it were a Porsche Speedster.

He followed her in his Chevrolet pickup, barely able to keep up. She turned down his offer of breakfast and didn't seem to notice or care that he was hungry. She insisted they go directly to her mother's bedside.

Chapter Seven

Jon parked the pickup in the CLERGY space of Memorial Hospital and waited for her at the front entrance. As a minister, he had been to this hospital many times to visit parishioners and friends. His memories of this place were too numerous to sort out. He rarely came here unless a parishioner, patient, or family member requested a visit. It occurred to him that, had he lost Krystal, he wouldn't have known the name of the patient he had come to visit. Fitzpatrick was Krystal's last name, but being adopted she might have a different name than her mother's.

Seven months earlier, his good sailing friend, Clyde, died here of cardiac arrest. He saw Clyde twice that night, but he died in the early morning. Jon doubted Clyde even knew him, but he was able to have prayers with him and Marilyn, his companion. After Clyde's funeral, he took the ashes to sea. Marilyn came with him and, in the quiet of early morning. They slowly spread Clyde's ashes. In silence they watched them float and drift. Marilyn clearly didn't want to leave the place where the ashes floated. He remembered a flying fish passed directly over the spot where the ashes lingered on top. Marilyn considered this an omen. Jon thought often of Marilyn, wondering how she was doing. They had sailed with him several times. Clyde adored her. He was amazed to finally find a woman who loved to sail with him.

Krystal interrupted his thoughts.

"Are you coming?" She stood nearby, hands on her hips. He did not see her walk up. "You aren't even here, are you?" she said in a harsh tone. "Maybe you're not interested in meeting my mother. She asked me to find you. She wants to meet you. Remember? That's why we're here." Frowning eyebrows emphasized her sarcastic lecture.

He was hungry and getting impatient. She could tell by the set of his jaw.

"Come on, Dr. Scott." She held out her hand to him, breaking the frost between them. In the lobby of the hospital, Krystal took the initiative, "We're here to see Sky Rowan, in room 325."

The woman at the desk scratched out a sticker with "325" on it. The volunteer looked up and said, "Father Scott! I didn't recognize you in those clothes and on a Sunday morning, too. Are you with this girl?"

"Good morning, Betty. Yes, I am with her. We're here to see her mother. Is it clear for us to go in?" he asked, acknowledging hospital protocol.

"I've never seen anyone stop you from visiting any patient you wanted to see, Father. Here's a clergy badge."

He could barely keep up with Krystal, who already had the door to elevator number Four open. "I'm hungry," he couldn't help but say, almost whining.

"We won't be long with Mother. We're not supposed to stay more than a few minutes, according to the bitchy nurse who kicked me out early this morning. I had to remind her this patient was my mother. She said I didn't look anything like her. So, I said, 'I'm adopted, if it means anything to you.'" Krystal leaned back against the elevator bulkhead and sighed. She said, "You're hungry, but I'm too tired. Just like a man, thinking of eating at the wrong time!" Before he could counter, the door opened onto the third floor.

Prior to going into the room, he stopped Krystal and looked intently into her eyes.

"Krystal, I want the two of us to be friends, if possible. We've had an interesting beginning, but I must tell you, I don't take sarcasm or criticism well. I want us to be very much at peace before we enter this room. I never go into a hospital room carrying emotional junk. It gets in the way of connecting with people. I won't let you do that either. Ready?" He paused, waiting for his comment to sink in.

She made no response, but gently took his arm. "Thank you, Dr Scott. I'm sorry for dumping something on you that has nothing to do with you. You've been nothing but nice to me. I guess I'm nervous. With men I just have so much junk. Okay? I'm sorry. And, by the way, thank you for saving Schwartz, too," she added.

Again, she looked tearful and it took a full minute for her to regain composure.

He said, almost in a whisper, "You'll be okay, Krystal."

Krystal reacted by tightening her arm around his as she knocked gently and slowly pushed open the door with "325" stamped on a metal plate, just below the little window.

They entered the room. The open blinds revealed tall buildings in the distance. Far to the north stood the San Gabriel mountains, wonderfully clear this morning. One vase of flowers on the window sill gave added color to the light green walls. In a big chair by the bed sat a book Krystal had been reading during the night, while her mother regained strength and consciousness. Krystal went to her mother's side, stroking her hair gently. Her mother smiled a weak smile and raised her left hand just enough for him to see, as if to say, *Hi*. He quietly moved to stand beside Krystal and gazed down into the face of an unusually beautiful woman. The three of them were silent for a few minutes while Krystal stroked her mother's soft, rich hair. Krystal's straight, black hair was a stark contrast to her mother's light brown waves. They didn't know how to begin talking. He broke the awkward silence, not waiting for the introduction he had expected.

"Ms. Rowan, I'm Jon Scott. I'm the skipper who came upon your Cal-20 about fifteen miles off Laguna yesterday afternoon. Your boat is okay. It is ..."

She interrupted him in a surprising rush of temper: "I don't want to see that boat again. Take it out to sea and blow it to smithereens. If anything floats, bring me some fragments for proof." Suddenly, she seemed embarrassed, took a few deep breaths, and settled down. Her face relaxed and her pleasant, soft smile returned.

"Sorry for the outburst. I'm very glad to meet you. I'm more grateful than you can imagine. Thank you, Krystal for finding Mr. Scott and bribing him to come here."

She lightly squeezed his hand. Krystal put her hand on theirs, joining the three of them.

"Mother, Dr. Scott and I had a talk about lots of things this morning. He has a way. I just started talking about things I only talk about in sessions. We're not supposed to stay long. That bossy nurse Ratchet told me not to tire you out."

"Doctor? Are you a doctor?"

"Not a real doctor. I'm a therapist-type doctor - all talk."

"I better watch what I say." A slight smile softened her comment.

"Ms. Rowan, I'm so thankful you're okay. I've been told there are no accidents. This is one of those times I believe that," and he gave a gentle press to her soft hand before he placed it back on the blue blanket.

Krystal said, "Mother's a doctor, too. She's a professor. So, are you two going to just call one another doctor all the time? Why not pretend you're just people?"

"She's right. How should I address you?" Jon asked.

"How about just using my name, Sky?" She looked tired, but still smiled.

"Then, it is Jon for me, Sky." He moved back, ready to leave the room.

"Please come back, Jon. Come back soon. I want to hear how you found me. An officer from the Coast Guard thinks you caused my problem at sea. She could not persuade me. It didn't feel right, her saying that," she said, still smiling and closing her eyes for a moment. "I'm getting tired. I'm sorry."

"I'll leave you and your daughter alone for now. Krystal, I check for messages several times a day." Turning back to Sky, he said, "I hope I haven't tired you out."

"Hey," said Krystal. "You just got back from not checking messages for a week and you're telling me you check them several times a day? Give me a break." She frowned for emphasis.

"Remember, Krystal, we had an agreement."

She looked uncomfortable, stepping closer to her mother and watching him.

"I'll see both of you soon. God bless," he said as he backed to the door. A nurse entered the room as he left. She looked at him with recognition and greeted him.

"Father Scott! Remember me?"

"Sarah. Sarah Brownell. Right?" he said, taking a chance.

"Amazing. It's been at least four years. I was at Hoag Hospital the last time I saw you. Remember that fellow in the coma, Charles? You came and read the paper to him every week. His whole family didn't come to see him as often as you did."

"I'd forgotten Charles, but, yes you're right. What a good friend! He died at Hoag. I thought he would come through that trauma. He'd been in a fire. I remember that terrible story." Jon stood back, looking at her.

"I'll never forget him. He'd been in that terrible tanker truck fire. He was in coma for months, and you kept coming to see him."

"Sarah, it's so good to see you! Are you Ms. Rowan's nurse, the one who ran her daughter off this morning?"

"No. That would be Wilma Burns. She was the duty nurse when Sky Rowan came up from the ER. Wilma's a good nurse, but she's hard on anyone in her way, and she enforces all the no-visitation rules. She hates talking to families who are emotional and upset. She often tells me, 'Get rid of the people and the patients, and this would be a good job.' Of course, she acts like she's joking, but I think she really feels that way."

Syringes in hand, Sarah gave him her big smile and made her move to the door.

"Good seeing you, Father."

Too hungry to wait any longer, he hurried to the hospital cafeteria. Staff and visitors gathered at the lunch counter, some already lining up at the register. Impatiently, he grabbed a few things within easy reach, not caring what they were. Four burritos remained in the pan. He took one, got orange juice and a small cup of coffee. This would tide him over for a while.

He paid and went to a table in the corner. Sunday's paper was strewn over the table and, like the terrible news on the front page, it was a mess. He straightened it out as best he could and perused assorted columns while munching on the lukewarm burrito.

I think this would have been quite good about three hours ago.

The newspaper stories were dreadful, all of them, from the murders to the atrocities in South Africa to the scandals with a local church. Even the 1984 Olympics had scandalous news. He quickly looked for the funnies. Funnies? Reading those confronted him with even more hostility and sarcasm, and he could find not a trace of humor, except for the Peanuts cartoon.

Maybe I'm just in a bad mood.

Even the movie selection seemed filled with rage and violence. One absurd animation movie looked intriguing; a Disney facsimile. A French movie enticed him.

He read the commentary, finding it to be the only film of interest. It had a plot of romance and a well-known French cast along with subtitles. He chose this film for later. But first, he had a boat to clean and a nap to take. A nap sounded very good to him.

Chapter Eight

As Jon drove back to the marina he could not stop thinking of Krystal and her mother. He kept feeling Sky's soft hand in his with Krystal's hands gently resting on theirs. He visualized Sky's sleepy, lovely, brown eyes. Was this love at first sight? Impossible. Jon didn't believe in it, at least not for him. However, that moment deepened for him as a warm space for all three of them, a bonding moment.

What a special time for me! Am I making more out of our meeting than I should?

About 4:00 he awoke from a fine nap. His first thought upon waking was his mysterious Lady on the deck, wrapped in her temporary, plastic shroud. The figurehead seemed safe enough for now, but anyone could easily come aboard to nose around. He decided to take the chance and go to the movie. The marina theater was just a few minutes away and he had time to fix a salad. Everything seemed like a distraction from his desire to talk to Sky and Krystal. The artfully done movie, well-directed, with the glorious leading woman - feminine, beautiful, and yet very strong - managed to eclipse his concerns for a while. Her sensuous hands reminded him of Sky's.

As he walked over the bridge back to the boat later that evening, carrying the mood of the movie with him, Long Beach felt like France, perhaps Antibes. He imagined an accordion playing in the distance, maybe Gene Kelly or Leslie Caron about to dance across the bridge toward him. The peaceful marina was beautiful, with the lights reflecting in the water and myriad masts, like upward-reaching wish-sticks, praying for a good sailing day.

Monday morning came all too soon. The movie had stayed on his mind, stimulating interesting dreams. He wrote them in his journal before leaving the boat. He felt he needed to work on the symbolism on at least one of them soon, or he would lose its fine points. But, for now, he had to get to his office.

What a gift, to be able to walk four blocks from my boat home to my work! I feel so grateful for this place, especially on a fine November morning.

As he walked into the sunlit office, he felt good, glad to be there. He gave the dry plants water and turned them a few degrees to catch a different light angle. The blinking on the message machine light caught his attention. Thirteen messages greeted him from the weekend, several of which he had already returned having gotten them from his pager. He listened to the usual ones: people wanting to know their appointment times, some changing times, and three clients requiring his attention. Of course, having been gone for a week intensified some of the calls. He had enough time before his first client to return the more pressing ones. To his surprise and delight, two of the messages were from Sky Rowan, calling from her hospital bed.

"Hello Father, or is it Doctor? I mean, Jon. This is Sky and I just want to thank you for coming to see me. I'm hoping we will stay in touch. Call, if you feel like it."

The first call came last evening, while he was at the movie. The second one came in at 5:20 this morning. It especially intrigued him.

"Jon, please call or come see me as soon as you have some time. I'm getting out of the hospital today, probably this afternoon. Krystal gave you our home phone number. Please do call." Her mellow voice made a request that could not be ignored.

"May I have 325, Sky Rowan's room, please?" Sky answered pleasantly. A welcoming voice at this time of morning was a gift. A nurse's visit interrupted their brief chat. He told her he'd call again a little after noon.

He could scarcely wait to talk with her again, but he had clients to see and chores to do. With difficulty, trying not to think of Sky, he paid attention in his first two morning sessions. Between them, he thought, *I'm feeling like I did at fourteen, over forty years ago, when I fell head over heels for Becky in eighth grade.*

At noon he called Sky's room. The hospital operator informed him that Sky had been discharged. He called the home number Krystal had left with him and got her recording, then the tone. He left a message, hoping to sound poised and formal.

"Hello, Krystal. This is Jon. I am returning your mother's message. By the time I returned her call, she'd been discharged. That is very good news. Please let her know I called. I'm at my office number. Anytime you call, I'll be paged. I hope all's well with both of you."

His pulse quickened, but he felt satisfied with his message, although it might have been more honest if he had said to her machine, "Krystal. I desperately want to talk with your mother. Please call me the moment that is possible." But, he managed to be cool for now. Krystal probably could see through him, but he hoped Sky couldn't, at least not yet.

He wanted to be fully present with his clients, but the re-entry from vacation, the discovery of his Lady, and the real-life Sky challenged his attention. He rationalized that his sessions were usually productive, even when he was not well or not quite with it.

What an ego you have, doctor!

He cautioned himself, as he barely knew this woman, Sky, that these feelings were immature and premature. It didn't help. In the midst of these thoughts, the phone rang, and he listened as he let the answering machine take it.

"Dr. Scott, this is Sandra Wells. I'm a reporter with the Long Beach Press Telegram following up on a story from last weekend. I have some questions. Please call me as soon as possible." The voice left a phone number, insisting he call her back soon, since the story was going to run in the morning edition.

An hour later, he had time to call. Her first question was a shock. "You are suspected of having a collision with a sailboat this weekend. That collision caused a woman to be hospitalized. Could you explain what happened?"

Jarred and defensive, all he could say was, "Where did you get this kind of information? It is false, you know?" Why did he feel defensive? He'd done nothing but help a fellow seafarer in trouble, someone who might have suffered more exposure and even death. He was a helpful person and resented the accusation. Besides, he thought all this was cleared up.

"I got the story from Saturday's Coast Guard log," was the reporter's retort. "We publish it every weekend here at the Press. Shall I mail the log entry to you? I'd be glad to do that or I could read it to you." The pause must have been a bit too long. "Dr. Scott, are you there? Did you hear what I said?"

"Yes, Ms. Wells, I heard what you said. I'm interested, but I don't have time now. I'm expecting another call. Suffice to say, for your story, I returned from a splendid sailing vacation and came across a rudderless Cal-20, with a broken mast, a black and white dog, and a person prone in a cockpit seat. I took the craft in tow, radioed the Coast Guard, and gave my position. Officers boarded the craft, picked up the injured woman and took her to the hospital in Long Beach. The Coast Guard has dropped their investigation." He said this without taking a breath.

"That would be Long Beach Memorial, Dr. Scott?" she asked. He responded affirmatively. She continued, "Also, I understand you had some kind of contraband on your sailboat. What was it?"

"Ms. Wells, I had no contraband on my boat. I picked up an artifact. How I acquired it is not public information. I don't wish to discuss it until I learn more about it and document it in my own log." Wanting to escape this inquiry, he threw her bait for a future story, "What if, when I learn more about this artifact, I call you with details? It might be worth a story."

She took the bait, and asked several more questions about the artifact. He obviously had aroused her curiosity. His Lady from the depths now had someone else wondering about her, although he doubted her image and presence would affect anyone like it affected him.

He didn't recall saying *goodbye*, but the figurehead lying on the foredeck of the Daimon suddenly consumed his thoughts, which were interrupted by a call from Sky Rowan. He nearly dropped the phone as he swung around in his desk chair. "Ms. Rowan, so glad to hear your voice. I've been wondering when we'd talk today. I'm also very pleased to learn you've been released from the hospital and -"

"Dr. Scott. Please take a breath. Are you okay?" It took him by surprise. She seemed so much in command, not like someone who had been under medical observation four hours ago.

"Yes. I'm okay. Well, maybe not quite okay. Would you mind if I said something honest and quite personal, something I'm embarrassed to say?"

"No. I don't mind at all, Dr. Scott. I'm listening."

The words rushed out. "Ever since your call early this morning I've thought of little else other than our next talk, our next meeting. I don't understand why it's so important, but it is. There! I said some of it and my face is red and I want now to hang up and get control of myself."

Light laughter came from her end of the line. He could hear her breathing, teasing him with a long silence. But, she was serious and sincere when she responded.

"Dr. Scott. You came to the hospital, held my hand and talked with me. With Krystal's intuition about you, along with all that has happened the last couple of days, I feel good energy with you. I wanted you to stay, Dr. Scott - I mean, Jon, I look forward to our getting to know one another enough."

"What do you mean, 'enough?'"

"I'm not sure, maybe just some time together talking, so I will know who this person is who saved my life."

"Ms. Rowan, I mean, Sky, I'm sure you're right. You name the time and place and I'll be there. I'll need a little time to re-schedule some clients." It was a very different response. Most often, he told the other person when he was available and set the venue for any meetings or dates.

I immediately accommodated her, willing to meet her on her terms and wherever she wished. I'm a gone goose.

"I'm an early morning person, Jon. Are you?"

"I certainly am. I live at the marina and swim about six in the morning. I could meet you tomorrow after a brief meeting with a friend. I could be anywhere local to Long Beach."

"I wish I felt up to swimming. Sounds like a wonderful way to start a day. I still feel a bit unbalanced, maybe even a little unsure of myself." She paused. He heard a teapot whistling in the background. Sky continued, "Just a minute, let me turn the stove down."

She put the phone down. He heard a cupboard door close, the singing teapot pitch dropping, and the sound of crockery being moved about.

"Here I am again. Let's meet in the marina, at the coffee shop near the marine hardware store. Say, eight or eight-thirty? Will that give you enough time?"

"I'll be there, but I'm not sure I'll recognize you without all that hospital hardware, Ms. Rowan."

"Jon, this Ms. Rowan stuff has to stop now, please." She paused. "If we are going to be formal, you'll have to address me as doctor, too. We both have doctorates, but let's not compete. Furthermore, I'm not sure I'll sleep all that well thinking about our meeting. Now I am embarrassed, so we're even."

"Sky, I can't wait to meet you. If I could, I would argue you into seeing me this evening. I have only one more appointment, but you need a night's rest."

"You're so considerate. I do think I'd better get to bed early. Krystal has gone for Chinese takeout. She's convinced that we need to eat something. Krystal can be quite as bossy as her mother sometimes."

He chuckled. "You don't seem bossy, Sky, but how would I know from a ten-minute phone call? Now I'll be bossy and insist on your getting all the rest you can get tonight. Take your time, please. I'm not a medical doctor, but I do know something about trauma, and you will feel some disorientation at least for several days, possibly for a few weeks. You're especially vulnerable right now, so take care. In the morning, if you don't feel up to getting together, please call me and let me know. We can meet another time, when you're better."

"Not on your life, Jon! You aren't getting out of this breakfast. How much time will you have?"

"I have to cancel a breakfast engagement with Frank Martinez. You met him. He'll understand, I'm sure. My first appointments don't begin until ten o'clock. We'll have time. Besides, who knows? We may not find that much to discuss," he said, with another chuckle.

"I'll see you in the morning. Oh, that felt good. I'm going to say it again to hear myself. I'll see you in the morning," she repeated.

The rest of the evening was quiet. After finishing with his last client, he walked to the boat and secured the storm jib covering the figurehead. It had blown away just enough to reveal one dark foot. He knew that no one must see her, but he didn't know what to expect next for her or between them. He pressure-cooked an artichoke, a piece of fresh salmon, and asparagus spears, with, of course, some Cabernet. The wine and his Lady shared the same color. He folded the boom tent back for the view and sat in the cockpit, thinking about the past week.

The masts surrounding him swayed gently back and forth. Some of the lines flapped against their masts, clinking in rhythm with the gentle swells in the boat harbor. The harbor seemed very peaceful and the lights along with a few stars reflected in the water.

"The peace of God which passeth all understanding," he recited to himself.

His dreams that night brought images from the last week. For a time he thought he could hear Meri, his Lady, moaning in the water near the boat. He felt he had to dive to save her from drowning. In the twilight of the dream, he thought about swimming to the moaning wooden figurehead in water too deep for him.

Then, Miriam was with him, smiling, snuggled up against him, spooning. Suddenly, he was somewhat aware, hugging his pillow. That dream came about three in the morning, the time he usually walked the gangway to use the head. Longing for Miriam, he awakened enough from the dream to actually get up and walk to the head.

A small crab scurried across the dock, glistening in the dock's overhead light. Back aboard the boat, he snuggled back into bed, listening to the crackling of the mussels on the pilings close to the boat, a crackling sound he rarely paid attention to anymore. The sounds lulled him back to sleep and he did not awaken until five-thirty.

Chapter Nine

Brahms on the clock radio awakened him. Not yet fully awake, he pulled on his swim suit and opened the cabin door, sensing the morning in the darkness. He climbed down the stern ladder into the water and gasped with the sudden rush of cold. When the bay was this frigid he had to swim vigorously. His usual course took him around the yacht club to the first canal and back in thirty minutes. This morning, he got back to the boat eight minutes faster. In the cabin he was changing out of his trunks when three loud thumps on the hull startled him. The clock read 6:17, barely light, and he was anxious to meet Sky on time. He suddenly remembered his meeting with Frank at 7:30. But, after that, he could meet Sky.

I'll call Sky. I've got to see Frank for a few minutes, then I can meet Sky. She'll understand, I hope.

Ensign Shabro's authoritative voice addressed him. "Dr. Scott? Dr. Scott? Coast Guard, Dr. Scott." She thumped the hull again with her rubberized flashlight.

He put on his robe. He unzipped the boom tent and poked his head out to growl a response. Shabro stood beside a harbor patrolman, who, unfortunately, was not his friend, Frank.

The ensign offered no polite formalities. "I need to ask you two questions. If there is any hesitancy in answering these, you may want an attorney present."

"Am I under arrest or something equally stupid?" he grumbled. "I have an important engagement in a few minutes, so please be brief."

Ensign Shabro stood rigidly straight in her starched, white uniform. Her otherwise attractive face looked dour. She looked him in the eyes and asked, "Are you guilty of smuggling anything?" She gestured with her head to the covered object on the foredeck.

He laughed. "No."

"It isn't a joke, Dr. Scott. We are considering charges for colliding with a small craft owned by a Dr. Sky Rowan and for smuggling contraband aboard your boat."

"This is harassment! I was told that this matter has been settled, at least the suspicion of my hitting her boat. I'm about to have breakfast with Dr. Rowan and you are free to join us. The relic on the foredeck of my boat is my own discovery. I claim it as salvage and not something stolen or smuggled. I haven't yet done the paperwork, so please back off until I can explain and clarify things." He tightened the cincture of his robe. "If you will, come to the marina coffee shop. I'm meeting Dr. Rowan there. But, I don't want you to cause her further stress. As you know, she was released from the hospital just a short time ago."

The ensign informed him she had met Sky in the hospital, warned him she might show up, and promised that he soon would definitely hear more about this. Finally, she said something of interest. "Dr. Rowan was hit by a sailboat about the length of this one. She said that she didn't get a good look at the boat, but it looked familiar." Shabro watched him intently as she reported this.

This information shook him. He could not imagine anyone colliding with another boat and not stopping to rescue the lone occupant and her craft. No matter what stories he heard about rotten people at sea, he refused to accept that sailors would be anything less than honorable, good sports at the very least. No good seaman abandoned a threatened boat in any hazardous situation at sea.

Ensign Shabro said, "Dr. Scott? Are you thinking about these charges? Are you seriously thinking about what you've done? Is there something you want to admit?"

"Yes, of course, I'm thinking about it! I'm also furious at anyone striking Dr. Rowan's boat and not bringing her in safely. This news shakes me, Ensign Shabro. I want to help you find this hit-and-run skipper." His voice sounded hollow, like he'd been hit in the stomach. Then it occurred to him Sky could not possibly be familiar with his boat, and he mentioned that.

"Thank you, Dr. Scott," she said. "But you are still a suspect in this incident."

"Ensign Shabro, look carefully at my boat. If you find any marks on her, I can tell you the date and time I bumped a dock too hard without my bumpers. You will find no new marks on this boat, no rips in my sails, no places where the rigging has touched anything that might have left a trace. I know my boat like I know my own body. Please, be my guest and look her over carefully and then come have breakfast with Dr. Rowan and myself. I must get dressed or I'll be late." Ignoring any response, he went below.

He heard their feet retreat as he dressed. Wishing he had nothing to do prior to seeing her, he took comfort in thinking soon he would meet Dr. Sky Rowan. Despite the complications, nothing could quell his anticipation. Did she suspect him striking her at sea? No! He was sure she did not. The feeling between them on the phone would have been very different had that been the case.

<u>Chapter Ten</u>

Jon stood beside the railing of the café while waiting for a table in outside seating. It was nearly 8:15, their arranged time. The sun warmed the patio dining area and a Mexican man began to open the umbrellas at each table. Boats in the marina reflected the morning light, making the harbor a maze of glistening masts, gleaming windows, and dew-covered decks. Masthead wind vanes moved gently, oscillating with the morning's soft drafts. Joggers went by on the walkway below him, one pushed a three-wheeled stroller carrying two warmly bundled babies. A frenzied dog sniffed and pulled on his long leash which slowed and frustrated one woman of the foursome.

He watched a man try to rig a thirty-foot sloop several slips down the dock below him. His jib lines were tangled, something a sailor does not allow. He wanted to help him, but waiting for Sky was his priority. To humble himself, he recalled his early days of sailing and how he learned by countless mistakes, some embarrassing, some serious.

"Jon." He wheeled around to face a stunning woman. She wore white slacks, a blue and white striped blouse, and white sandals. They were nearly close enough to hug. She took his hands and looked up at him with smiling, brown eyes. Her light auburn hair was in a bun, tied with a thin blue ribbon. Small, gold earrings set off her face, untouched by makeup.

"Well, do I pass inspection?"

"Do you ever! Sky, I can't tell you how goofy I've become this morning looking forward to meeting you here. I met with Frank a while ago and he said I was too preoccupied and he'd see me later. It all started last night when ..."

Sky interrupted: "When we were attempting to end our phone conversation? Both of us had a hard time hanging up. We've got a lot to talk about. I think I've gotten you into something that isn't fair to you. I need to help and I need to explain."

"I don't need any explanations. Really, I don't," he said.

"No, Jon. I do need to talk about a possible problem before we go any further."

"Whatever it is, Sky, let's get to it. But, first, sit down here, in the shade of the umbrella. I'll order whatever you want to drink. Then let's order breakfast."

"Hot chocolate with just a little whipped cream on it. I'll warm it up with coffee later, if there is a later. I think we'll at least make it through the hot chocolate," she said, looking seriously thoughtful.

They were distracted for a moment as the waitress took their orders. Then they looked at one another, absorbed in their impressions. Sky broke the silence.

"There is an officer with the Coast Guard who thinks you are the one responsible for my collision. I don't know what to say, Jon. I only got a few minutes' look at the oncoming sailboat and could not get out of the way. It was a big sailboat. It had CF numbers on the bow, but it all happened so fast, I can't recall the numbers. I might, if I saw them again. I have a pretty good memory. The sailboat hit my boat hard, tore my stays and ripped the mast down from just above the spreaders. I knew I was in trouble. I got knocked down." She paused for a moment, her hand on her forehead as though reliving the experience. "The collision threw me down into the cabin. I hit my head hard. I thought for sure my boat would sink. Something caught up above. I guess the rigging got caught on the other boat. My boat whirled around. Yes. I'm sure my loose rigging caught on the boat that hit me. I tried to get up, but I was thrown again, this time against the cabin's port bulkhead. Schwartz, my dog, was thrown, too. I don't remember anything after I hit the bulkhead. Somehow I got back into the cockpit, because that's where the Coast Guard or you found us, isn't it?"

Her eyes searched for his response. Her outstretched hand gripped his arm. He imagined every moment of what she described. She did not let go of his arm until she finished her story.

Sky leaned back and sipped her hot chocolate. "Jon, I'm so sorry about this. You couldn't have been the skipper on the boat that hit me. In the hospital, I told the ensign I was sure your boat wasn't the one that hit me, but I couldn't know for sure, could I? With just the glance I got, I remember that skipper was heavy set and a woman was at the helm. I couldn't believe it was happening. I yelled at them, but she just kept coming at me. I must have yelled 'Starboard' four or five times. I could see them over their cabin top as they came down a swell towards me just before the collision."

At that moment he wanted to take her into his arms and hold her. He wanted this breakfast to go on forever.

"Sky, you could have died out there. Thank God you're alive!"

Just then, Ensign Shabro came toward them, shattering their intimate moment.

"Should I come back later?" she asked in a surprising display of sensitivity.

"I invited you. Please join us. I understand you and Dr. Rowan have met."

Sky gestured for the ensign to have a seat and began a nonstop monologue.

"This isn't the skipper of the boat that struck mine on Saturday afternoon, Ensign Shabro. I'm embarrassed if you got the impression I thought it could have been Dr. Scott's boat. There was a woman at the helm of the sailboat that hit me and I might be able to recognize her. She had long, blonde hair. There was a fat man. I couldn't see his hair, because of his yellow slicker hat. He had a gray beard. The boat was a sloop, too. You said Jon's boat is a ketch. That boat was a sloop and it had a CQR anchor on the bow. I've seen that boat before somewhere." She fell silent for a moment with closed eyes. "I'll never forget that bow coming at me."

"Sky, how could you be sure it was a sloop?" Jon asked. The ensign echoed his question.

"I saw nearly the whole boat at one point, as it scraped by, just before the rigging caught my stay. It was a sloop. It had only one mast. I even saw some of their cockpit. Ya'know? My ex bought a sloop like that one. He got it after the divorce. I never saw his new boat, but I've seen pictures of it. Krystal showed me a snapshot of it a long time ago. The woman at the helm just kept the boat coming dead ahead, right at me, as if she were obeying strict orders from Captain Bligh or maybe she wanted to sink me," she said.

Ensign Shabro ordered coffee and turned to Jon. "Dr. Scott, you told me you'd help find the skipper of that boat. Will you?" Her tone had become almost friendly, but she returned to her usual harsh, clipped voice to remind him of the other matter at hand.

"You realize you're still suspected of smuggling." She studied Sky, as if she expected a reaction from her.

Instead, Sky calmly told her, "I heard from my daughter about the salvage Dr. Scott has on his boat. She was very curious about it, but didn't seem to know really what it was. As a professor and archeologist, I suspect it is a significant piece. I am already working to identify it. Dr. Scott and I will handle it professionally, protecting our research until everything is legally registered. I assure you, this salvage is not stolen. No salvage laws have been broken. You can take Dr. Scott off your 'most wanted' list." She stared at Ensign Shabro like a professor correcting a slow-witted student.

The ensign finished her coffee and backed away from the table just a bit.

"I believe you can leave us now," Sky said. "I'm sure the Coast Guard has more important matters with the drug war and illegal aliens. The CG always complains about being over-worked and under-staffed."

Ensign Shabro straightened her back, trying to regain her authority. "We'll see about this. Dr. Scott, you told me originally that you had bought what you're now calling salvage. Better get your stories straight. A full report is required to complete our investigation. We can't forget the incidents in question. Dr. Rowan, you are very convincing about the sailboat that struck yours. Given your position on Saturday, it is unlikely Dr. Scott's sailboat could have been anywhere nearby at the time of the collision. You must have been hit about three or four miles out, not long after you left King Harbor. From the time you left King Harbor, you couldn't have gotten much farther than that. Can you recall anything during those twenty hours you drifted?" The ensign looked out at the harbor for a moment before continuing.

"I have some recall, but it is all jumbled up. Maybe I could unscramble what I think I experienced, but all I remember is that it was awful and I was really frightened."

"Don't fret about this, Dr. Rowan. We'll piece things together somehow, I'm sure."

Officer Shabro was attractive when she relaxed and especially when she wasn't accusing Jon of something. "But, the so-called salvage on the deck of your boat is still questionable, Dr. Scott. We will require a report soon."

She excused herself, dropped her business cards on the table and reminded them she would be in touch soon. "Dr. Rowan, you do realize you have made yourself a party to whatever Dr. Scott has done." And, with that, she walked to a white Dodge van with the Coast Guard seal on the door.

"So much for a romantic beginning to our breakfast! I had a different plan for our first social time together, Sky. I'm sorry this happened."

"I'm glad we got this stuff on the table, Jon. It's okay and we'll work this out together. I'm excited about the prospects of how we do that."

They were quiet for a time. Then Sky gave him a mischievous grin; leaning back smugly in her chair, she said, "The Coast Guard has attached me to you." She fondled her coffee cup and watched him with a slight smile.

"You're a sporting woman to get involved this way," he said. "In fact, I'm delighted we've been thrust under the same blanket of suspicion, so to speak." He imitated her smug posture and focused expression.

After breakfast the waitress came with more coffee. They thanked her and declined. As she left the bill, both of them grabbed for it, but Jon won. Sky said, "Okay this time, but next time I'm buying. Remember, you've already proven yourself to me. You saved my life. Did you know there are cultures where, if you save someone's life, you're responsible for them for the rest of their lives?" She resumed her fun and affected serious expression. Then, as he twisted the napkin through his fingers, she reached out and took his hand again. "Look at me a moment. I'm going to say something to you. I only want you to think about it and not say anything back to me. Okay?" Her gaze focused intently, penetrating him. What else could he do but give his consent?

"Right this minute, you are completely in control. I don't want you to disappear, Jon. Something has happened between us. I have no expectations, but please be honest, communicate with me, and do not just disappear. Okay?"

She stared out at the harbor for some moments.

"You have my word. No conditions. I would ask you the same, to be honest and not disappear. Okay?"

"You got it!" she affirmed, and began to rise from the table. "If you'll pardon me, I need to excuse myself for a few minutes. Don't go away." She rose and turned away from her plastic chair. She glanced back over her shoulder at him as she walked toward the women's room.

He paid the bill and left a tip that reflected the importance of this breakfast meeting. When Sky returned, they walked to her car and hugged politely. She got into her gleaming red and white T-Bird convertible. As the engine started he commented on her well-kept car.

"Those pipes sound good, too."

"I love this car," she said.

It was pristine with white upholstery, the white hardtop; his favorite top, because of the porthole windows. There was not a blemish on the car and the red body sparkled, obviously blessed with a recent waxing. The baby moon hubcaps gleamed.

"One more thing, Sky. When I say 'goodbye,' I affirm the true meaning of that word. Do you recall the true meaning of 'goodbye'?"

"God be with you, too. I know what it means. I must admit, I have a hard time with religious stuff. I'm embarrassed to tell you that, but I must confess." She smiled so sweetly that he gave her a kidding absolution gesture. They took one more moment to look at one another, letting the feelings of the moment sink in.

Chapter Eleven

Jon made arrangements with the Marina Shipyard people to lift the figurehead off his foredeck with their stinger, the dock-mounted crane for light-duty work. On Wednesday afternoon he powered his boat over to the shipyard, just across the channel from his slip. Butch, the crane operator, walked to the old crane and called to the *Daimon* as it approached the slip. Butch knew Jon's boat because he had helped paint the boat bottom just three months ago.

The *Daimon* coasted into the shipyard slip, just below the crane's angled boom. An electric motor whined when Butch worked the levers of the crane. The crane's long arm swung toward Jon's foredeck even before Jon secured the dock lines. Earlier in the day he had left his pickup with a rented trailer there to haul the figure-head. The trailer was necessary, because he might need to use the pickup before unloading Meri. He put an old mattress in the bed of the trailer. His Lady, Meri, would be taken to a dry bed for the first time in her life. This would be her mobile home for the trip to his storage unit, or so he thought.

As the hook dropped, Sky surprised him by showing up. She gave him a warm smile as she stood next to Butch. *Beauty and the Beast*, he thought. She introduced herself to Butch. He was helpful, friendly, and always making people laugh with his crude humor. His beer habit had swollen his mid-section and gave his red face big, puffy cheeks. The steering wheel of his Datsun pickup left black marks across his bulging t-shirt.

Jon stood on the foredeck of the *Daimon* and reached for the hook as it came down. He worked two webbed slings under Meri, preparing to receive the hook, and turned to look at Sky. The swinging hook nearly hit him in the head. Butch braked the cable, and shouted at him. "Heads up, Jon! Just about conked you on the dome! And close your mouth while you're gawking at Dr. Rowan. Pay a mind to what we're doing. I'll take care of Dr. Rowan." He gave an exaggerated wink Jon could not miss from the deck ten feet below.

"Sky, I didn't expect you to be here for this. I just told you about it to keep you informed. But, I'm really glad you've come," Jon shouted to her from his deck.

"Wouldn't have missed this," she yelled above the noises of the crane's creaking frame, the cables moaning in the blocks, and the whine of the motor. "My assistant took my class so I could celebrate this time with you and your figurehead. I called and Butch let me know when and where so I could be here for the happening." She reached up and affectionately touched his burly arm. "I'm taking pictures." She held up her camera.

The hook fit firmly into the slings' eyes. Jon motioned to Butch to take up the slack. The bow of the boat lifted several inches, as the crane took the weight of the carved, water-logged wood. The upward motion stopped as the figurehead cleared the deck by a few inches and hung there, gently swinging. Butch called to Jon. "Two hundred fifty-seven pounds, according to my crane scale, Jon. That includes all the water in the thing, too."

The crane swung the Lady to the dock and Butch lowered her onto the old mattress in the trailer. Sky hopped in with Meri; tracing the carved features with her fingers. As Jon climbed the gangway to the dock, she said, "Let's take it to my workshop. It is well-protected. It will be right at home with other sea relics. My shop is about twenty minutes from here."

"Just tell me where it is, Sky. I need to pay the shipyard, move the pickup and trailer out of here, and put the boat back in her slip. Then, I could meet you."

A voice from behind blurted out "Let me go with you, Dr. Scott." As Krystal approached them, she added, "I'll meet you over by your slip. We can go to mother's workshop together." The whole time of that the figurehead was being retrieved she had watched from a distance. She greeted Jon with her hand outstretched. Krystal's braids cascaded to her waist. She wore sandals, blue denim shorts, and a white blouse, tied in a knot just below her breasts.

"Krystal, glad to see you. Your help is most appreciated. I'm in a bit of a hurry to finish this. I want to get this stuff done in time to get to my therapy group this evening," he said.

"Looks like I've got competition." Sky paused. "You know, Krystal, you could drive my car and I could go with Jon," she said, tilting her head to one side, speaking with a teasing tone of voice.

The matter got settled. They walked toward their cars on the far side of the shipyard. Sky reached over and threw Krystal's right braid back, playfully, and Krystal bumped her mother's hip with hers as they walked. He didn't know who would show up, but was confident the two of them would work it out. He was pleased. Meri would have a safe place to rest and he'd have more excuses to see Sky.

He had covered up Meri with a blue, plastic tarpaulin, afraid someone would get curious. He didn't want to answer more questions. When he cut the engine and glided his boat into her slip, Krystal was right there to greet him and help with the dock lines on the bow.

"Is this the way you do it, Dr. Scott?" she asked as she ran the line's loop under the cleat and hooked it back on itself.

"You've got it, Krystal. But, please, no more 'doctor' for us. I know I'm old enough to be your father, but Jon will please me more," he said. "You've learned how to handle a dock line. Are you as good a sailor as your mother?"

"I do okay. I grew up around sailboats. Both my lousy father and my wonderful mother loved sailing. They had a Columbia 36 when I came along. He's got a bigger boat now. Can't pay child support, but he can own a big boat and a new BMW. Sailing and arguing about me were the only two things those two had in common. Even when they sailed he shouted at her all the time." Krystal twisted her long braid as she spoke.

Jon drove his pickup pulling the trailer. As he drove the flood gate opened again as Krystal told more of her story, occasionally she interrupted herself to give him directions to the shop.

A gripping tale flowed out of her. She had been orphaned in Vietnam and had escaped through Saigon's fire and terror in 1975, when the U.S. abandoned South Vietnam. Her family had been lost during the war years, her mother killed in 1969, her father in 1970, when she was three. Her brothers and sisters were either lost or killed. She thought they were killed. The sister closest to her was with her in the orphanage, but as they were being evacuated in buses, the bus ahead of hers, the one carrying her sister, was hit by machine-gun fire and exploded. Then the helicopter that took off just before hers, with many of the other evacuated orphans, exploded. Rockets and gunfire flashed all around. Krystal had nightmares for years, usually with her sister's bus exploding. Once, she even saw vividly in the dream as her sister flew above her. She wore a blue and white dress which flowed in the wind. Her sister waved to her as though everything were just fine. That was the last of her dreams of that terrible day. She was eight in 1975, the fall of Saigon. Now, at nearly seventeen, she felt grateful every day to have been adopted by Sky Rowan.

"I never liked mother's husband and refused to call him 'father' to his face. He was always mad about something. I was scared of him. Always scared. When we first met, I was nine, and I could tell he didn't like me. I didn't know much English, mostly French and Vietnamese. He taught me English, and I am grateful for that, but he called me 'stupid' and I hated that." She was quiet for a moment. "Turn left here. Mother's place is down the next alley, on the right."

They stopped beside a high chain-link fence with a wide gate, partially opened to a small parking lot. A sign on the gate had a caricature of a snarling, fierce German Shepherd, with the big letters, *Beware of the Dog!* Schwartz bounded out of the open workshop door, barking and wagging her tail. Just beyond, an opened garage door revealed a spacious workshop, probably large enough to hold five or six cars. Jon could see some tools and a clutter of relics, the most obvious was a barnacle-encrusted brass ship's lantern. He noticed a ceiling-mounted I-beam with a chain hoist on rollers, which he soon would use to lift Meri out of the trailer.

Sky's Thunderbird was parked to the north side of the building, and he could hear a radio playing Coltraine from the local FM station in Long Beach. He couldn't see Sky yet, but soon she came around the corner. She wore rubber gloves and carried a wire brush in one hand and a magnifying glass in the other. Her Oshkosh overalls fit well over a blue t-shirt. A pair of worn, paint-splattered running shoes adorned her feet, and a yellow bandana held back her hair.

"Back the trailer over here, Jon, just below the chain hoist."

She and Krystal watched him back the trailer, which he did in one motion. He enjoyed showing off skills from his earlier life as a truck driver.

"Well done!" Sky exclaimed.

"Thank you," he said, faking modesty. "The shorter the trailer, the harder it is to back. This one's really short."

Sky pulled the chain-lift to the end of the I-beam, directly over the trailer. It rolled easily and was well-maintained. She flipped the ratchet lever to let the hook down. She positioned it directly over the covered figurehead. Jon peeled the plastic tarpaulin back and secured the web straps to the hook. With some effort, they slowly lifted Meri and pulled the rolling chain block into the workshop. Jon laid the old mattress from the trailer on the floor to give Meri a bed.

"It will be safe and out of the way here," said Sky. Krystal smoothed the pad and they lowered Meri. "I'd like it facing up, if possible. I want some pictures and need good light on the face and that fine body. This figurehead is well endowed."

She stroked the carved breasts with her rubber-gloved finger tips and caressed Meri's forehead.

"I'm reacting to your calling this figurehead an 'It.' Her name is Meri. Maybe you could humor me and think of her at least as a wooden woman?"

"Blessings, dear lady," she said with a tone of sarcasm. "Welcome to Sky's workshop. You'll be at home here." She talked to Meri as a good teacher to a respected student.

Jon said, "Those iron pins sticking out of her back end will keep her upright, I think. Let's try rolling her into that position. Give us a hand, Krystal. Be careful, it seems solid, but it may be really quite fragile. Is she ever heavy!"

He slipped the web straps out from under the figure. Then he bundled them and put them into the bed of his pickup.

"I wish I could stay for a tour, but I've got to return the straps and the trailer, then make it to therapy by 7:00 o'clock."

"So when do we meet next?" Sky asked.

"I'll call around nine-thirty, after my group, if that isn't too late."

"It's never too late or too early," she said, gently touching his arm.

"She only sleeps when there's nothing else to do," Krystal said. "Sleeping and eating are just necessities for Mother. Sometimes, I feel guilty relaxing when she's home," she added. "I wonder if the two of you are alike; all the time places to go and things to do. Do you ever rest, Jon?" Krystal asked. Then she added, "I noticed nobody had time for lunch today."

"Sure, I'm a modified Type 'A' now, not like in my younger years." He opened the door to the pickup. "I'll call after my group," he repeated. "Krystal, I'm sorry about your missed lunch. You might have said something." He looked at the two of them standing close to one another, their arms hooked together. They were becoming a good trio.

Chapter Twelve

The group that night went unusually well, with several of the seven members sharing a deep well of feelings. A young woman had broken up with a man the whole group had come to dislike. She was grieving for the broken relationship, but relieved, too, that she felt she could finally let him go. Tonight, along with the sadness and fear of being alone, she expressed confidence in herself and relief the door had shut and a new one would open for her. The group supported her and mirrored her self-confidence.

Another member, a young sheriff's deputy, was able to face his father's recent illness and death. The group members grew close, working hard. When Jon ended the group, he felt a hearty respect for them, along with feeling lucky and pleased with his work. "What a privilege it is to know people with your courage and depth of caring for one another!" he told them.

Soon after, at 9:40, he called Sky. She answered on the second ring. During their hour-long talk they covered many subjects, some light and easy, and a few more tender and difficult.

At one point, Krystal came on the phone to thank him for the talk earlier in the day. After Sky took the phone from Krystal, she said, "You've made yourself indispensable. What are you going to do about that, Dr. Scott?"

"First of all, Sky, I'm going to remember I'm not Dr. Scott when it comes to you two. That will relieve me of an attitude of clinical responsibility. Also, I will insist on being just my usual self. I'll have to remember not to scratch and burp, because I'll be so relaxed around the two of you."

The conversation ended with their setting a date, beginning early afternoon on Saturday, with no definite plans after that. She already had some information and some historical possibilities in regard to the figurehead.

"I may have identified the shipwreck itself, Jon, although it's too early to know for sure. If I'm right, you've found a relic from the mysterious disappearance of a ship about 1849."

The possible identification of the ship itself excited him. He could think of little else that night, as he cooked a late, light supper. The whole story - from his vacation, to finding the figurehead, then the ordeal with the Cal-20, and meeting Sky and Krystal - seemed to tumble out of an inner closet of treasures. A couple of glasses of wine helped mix the events of last week into a mellow inner voyage. The evening's Santana, the strong northeast wind rocking the *Daimon*, caused her to strain against the dock lines. Halyards on masts of adjacent boats in their slips slapped in their various rhythms. If the gusts didn't get too strong, he would be gently rocked to sleep.

Jon felt blessed beyond measure and peacefully slept very well until first light. He arose around six for his swim. Invigorated and dripping salt water, he carried his towel, clothes, and shaving kit, and walked up the gangway to the head in the marina parking lot. A blue heron stood alert to watch him from a couple of slips away. He stopped to observe this poised, regal bird. They studied each other. With only his swimming trunks on, he wondered if she thought of him as a featherless biped - the definition of a human being - which took him back to his philosophy days of Socrates, Diogenes, and the plucked chicken joke. One more step in the big bird's direction and the great wings opened. The heron lifted into the air only to land on the next gangway beside the stern of a forty-foot powerboat.

The clear Thursday morning was unusually warm for November. It was one of those southern California days when the Santana winds cleared the air and ventilated the Los Angeles basin. On a morning like this, he could see every detail at Avalon, about twenty miles across the channel. To the north, the crystal clear mountains rimmed the view. Later in the day, of course, the wind would whip the sand and dust into the air from inland. He rehearsed a lecture he could give on these winds: *These winds typically run a three-day cycle and can grow to nearly 100 miles per hour downslope from the San Gabriel and San Bernardino mountains. By the time they reached the coast, their velocity usually diminished, but they could be very hazardous and unpredictable out to sea.*

To mark these events the Marine authorities flew two triangular red flags warning mariners of unsafe wind conditions. But, at this moment, early in the morning, not a breath of air stirred. Every sailboat's wind-guide was motionless.

The heron got a fish and flew low across to the other side of the marina, making the only ripples in the water. He thought to himself how God provides. A feeling of centered peacefulness welled up within him.

As he walked up the steep gangway to the head, a Coast Guard messenger stopped him: "Dr. Scott, I have an envelope for you. I need you to sign for it."

"It's good timing. I was feeling fine about this beautiful morning." He reached for the clipboard to sign for the envelope.

The courier showed no expression. Having performed his duty, he returned to the van. Jon went to the head with his dressing gear and an envelope from the Coast Guard. He decided not to open it until after he fixed breakfast. He hoped to prolong the peace of this otherwise blessed Thursday morning.

Chapter Thirteen

A very depressed man showed up for his first appointment. He recently learned he had prostate cancer. Jon and he had worked together through his wife's long illness and death in June. Now this. He spent much of the session staring silently at the marine painting, with its turbulent waves and the rocks of Point Mendocino. Quiet sessions take more listening than those when the client is talking nonstop. When people keep quiet in their sessions, every nuance, sigh, and utterance counts. Even a couple of sentences could express more in depth than when people chattered on. When his client left, he was tearful, but seemed in control. He welcomed a hug and assured Jon he looked forward to their Monday appointment.

After a day crowded with appointments and calls, Jon tackled the envelope. The contents had been mixed: There were no charges. This whole matter was just a formality, but there were also demands for information that would either indict him or end the suspicions. The essence of the form letter demanded a report on his voyage - the course, the times and events logged - ending on Saturday night, 3 November, 1984. Along with his log book entries, he was to give a full description of the cargo aboard his vessel upon entering the Alamitos Bay Marina, that Saturday night. In his mind he had not broken any laws. He was very angry about this nonsense and figured there must be someone higher up than Ensign Shabro.

A Congressman did owe him a favor, but it wouldn't be ethical, because one of his family had been a client, so Jon couldn't ask for a favor. He had no way out except to spend a few hours writing up a detailed report, but he would tell them more than anyone wanted to know, including what kind of toothpaste he used on the trip and how many revolutions before his Farymann diesel started.

It was nearly midnight when he finished typing in his office. He felt both satisfied and exhausted. His vacation, the sailing, and many of the events he had so enjoyed were now contaminated, not really his own anymore. He felt sorry for himself, then guilty for feeling sorry for himself, and then angry about his feeling guilty and ashamed about feeling sorry and angry with himself. Hungry, angry, lonely, and tired met all the criteria of the *halt* condition, the time when a person should do nothing at all.

He felt better just walking the several blocks to the boat, breathing the night's ocean air, and to looking at the brighter stars; bright enough to show above the lights of Long Beach. As he unzipped the boom tent and stepped aboard into the dark cockpit, he noticed a letter stuck in the hatch. The script read, 'Dr. Jon, I miss you!'

He poured a glass of sherry and opened the crackers and cheese and placed them on the galley table, with the map of a South Pacific island laminated on the surface. He held the unopened letter under his arm all the while. He liked to sit at the table sometimes and track the trails, coves, and the many symbols on this old military Naval south-sea-island map embedded on his galley table.

Sometimes, when he had guests, they would study the map and make up stories about being anchored this place or that. They imagined hiking on a hill or trail. Perhaps over on this side they'd be able to see out to sea. There were two little churches, depicted by their particular symbols on the map, one on the south coast and one on the east. He wondered about these churches and what denominations they might have been, who they served, and what languages were used. Once in a while he thought of researching this island by going to find and to explore it. It was not too far from the Philippine Islands, perhaps one of them.

He sipped the sherry and munched a cracker with brie cheese; he opened the envelope. He sensed a fragrance to the handmade paper. The handwriting was unfamiliar to him, but quickly he knew who had written the note.

Dear Jon,

Twice this evening I drove by your building and saw a light still on in the office on the third floor. I think that's your office. I dropped off a small package earlier this afternoon. I didn't want to disturb you, but hoped we might have time to walk and talk. I'm thinking of you, your figurehead, and us. By the way, I think your figurehead came from one of two boats that went down close to San Clemente, one in 1849 and another in 1861. Both of these are noted in American Squadron naval logs, from Monterey's historical archives.

Frank, the marina guard, told me which boat was yours. Hope that was okay.

Yours truly, Sky.

Jon felt touched by Sky's letter and her finding his boat. In moments he slid into sleep. His last thoughts were about calling her in the morning, a more polite time than now. He slept fitfully. The dreams he recorded were barely understandable. He listened to his mumbling on the slow speed of the micro-cassette. But, one of them perhaps anticipated the events to transpire later at San Clemente Island. It took place under water with his ex-colleague, Dr. Jim Marsh, who had drowned in a fishing accident ten years ago.

In the dream, Jim sat on a hatch of a sunken boat, smiling at him. Jon looked through a glass window or porthole at him. Inside a dry room on the ocean floor, like being in an aquarium, they recognized one another. He gestured and grinned as he held up a large model clipper ship. The model clipper was a tangled mess, masts broken, sails and rigging torn and tangled. Jim let it drop to the mud below his feet and then stamped on it, still grinning. After he crushed it to pieces in the mud, he leaned down and picked up a wooden figure, perhaps like the Lady from the depths, and put it in his vest pocket. Then he turned his back to Jon. That was the dream's end.

He had not dreamed of his good friend for a long time. It left him very curious and in a nostalgic mood, missing Jim and remembering the terrible days after losing him. Such a good friend! He thought of the book they were writing, wondered if he still had it somewhere. He put on the tea kettle while thinking he might someday be able to finish the book on his own.

The tea kettle's shrill whistle blew just as his ship's clock rang six bells. Thus began his Friday morning. The dream left him in a reflective mood. He stared out the cabin porthole to the adjacent boat, he thought of old times, the fights, laughter, the women they had known together, and then, Jim's drowning. It didn't help that they didn't find his body for many months. Jon lived with the images of Jim's going down in forty-four degree water. Jon swam and ate, the dream remained vivid while he went through his early-morning routines. The phone rang and jolted him into the present.

Sky's excited voice started without a greeting or hesitation. "Jon, I know the boat! I'm sure of it. In the archives I have found a record and some letters about the ship that went down. There is an entry in a ship's log about the name of the vessel, the *Madonna*. She originally carried a French name, but was given another by the crew who stole or bought her in 1841. Let's find a time to go over some of this material. It's fascinating."

"Sky, it is so good to hear from you. I didn't even get a chance to say 'hello.'" Her enthusiasm was contagious. "What about tonight, Sky? I'm finished at seven-thirty."

"Tonight it is. How about the Japanese restaurant on Pacific Coast Highway? You know, that one in the shopping area that serves sushi and those other scrumptious Japanese delicacies. I've been wanting to try it."

They agreed on 7:45 at the Shogun Maru restaurant. Not only did they have exotic food, it also provided a good place to talk. His everyday routine - the sessions, phone calls, and processing some of his necessary paperwork - went better, as he looked forward to the evening with Sky.

Chapter Fourteen

Sky arrived early, already in a booth, waiting for him. Several large books and a small pile of papers covered the table. He watched her undetected for a few seconds. She read, thumbed through loose papers, and sipped tea. Then, as she sensed his presence, she looked up and smiled. She wore a lush, brown sweater with a large collar, and her hair flowed around her face cascading nearly to her breasts. Her right hand held the pen she used to make notes as she read. Her left hand swished her hair back as she continued to look at him. The whole scene probably took ten seconds, but for Jon, time stood still.

"Come look at this. Oh, by the way, hello."

He moved to sit across from her, but she stopped him.

"Sit here, next to me. We need to be able to look at some of this material together and sushi is just the right food, because what we're discussing is on the ocean floor."

He slid in next to her, breathing in her now familiar scent. He moved closer to share the menu.

"Perhaps we should have some sake to start and then a salmon-skin hand roll as an appetizer?"

"Sounds delicious," she said. She flipped over a copy of a ship painting for him to see. "Your figurehead came from the sister vessel to this one. At least I'm quite sure of this.

We won't know for sure until we find the rest of the sunken vessel, but that can't be too far from where you found your Meri."

The waitress took their order and suggested evening specials from the sushi bar.

The spicy green mussels sounded good, along with several of the *maki* rolls. She brought the sake, the soup, and the salads, to get them started, while they perused the papers and Jon thumbed through a marine history book. It was a large, thick book, filled with reprints of documents and painted reproductions of vessels from the middle of the1800s through the early 1900s; tall ships, brigantines, barks, frigates, steamers, and many smaller boats, dories, captain's gigs, and others used to service the larger vessels.

"Where did you find this marvelous volume, Sky?"

"I asked our research librarian at Cal State to gather some materials and, like magic, the next day this appeared. I also asked her to look up names of sailing vessels known to be in California or west coast waters in the last 200 years. You can't believe the list of hundreds of boats, especially during the 1800s. We saw one from the late 1840s, the *Madonna*, and when we looked into that one, the sister ship, the *Apostle*, showed up. Originally French, an Englishman bought the boats and renamed both of them about 1845, maybe earlier.

"The dates are confusing, because they are different in the sources we have. I don't know their French names, which maybe could help us. They were spice, tea, and cloth traders, and they also collected hides for a Boston company. Both were owned by the same trader. The *Madonna* was the second one built in Boston to nearly identical specifications as the *Apostle*. There is no mention of their figureheads, but, if you look carefully at the painting of the bow of the

Apostle you can make out a figurehead that could easily be the same size as yours. The *Apostle*'s figurehead or bow ornament looks more ornate and it seems to me to be a male figure. It's not that clear in the painting." She studied the print in the book using a magnifying glass.

"I'm amazed you found this," he said, gaining respect for her scholarship. Also, her expressing an interest in his Lady flattered him. When he remarked on that, Sky covered his hand with hers and said, "I'm excited finding out about this. The work I'm supposed to be doing seems dull and tedious at the moment, but this gets me going. There's life and mystery in this work, don't you agree?" Then, hesitating, she added, "But, Jon, I need to ask a question and you must be honest with me."

"Go for it!"

"I may be stealing something away from you by my enthusiasm about this. I sometimes get so involved that I might be jumping far ahead of what you wanted me to do. Maybe you like being in charge. I don't want to take this project away from you."

Touched by her concern and her interest, he said, "I think she led me into your life from the very first moment her muddy head attracted me. One thing for sure. Meri has opened a whole new chapter for me and maybe for us. I think so."

After the sake and sushi, their talk slowed. They enjoyed the silences. She squeezed his hand and they shared their first kiss. The message in the kiss expressed the fullness of their being together; very together just at this moment. Her brown eyes teared just a little.

"Sky, are you okay?"

"I haven't had a total warmth throughout my entire body nor a feeling of deep emotional connection like this, it seems, ever, Jon." She looked away, seemingly embarrassed.

"No, don't look away. We have just met, but so much has happened in the few hours we've known one another, I think we're entitled to have these shared feelings. But, let's remember that the intensity of how we've begun may sweep us away too quickly. Let's just be sure to stay honest, as honest as possible, even about our uncertainties. I've lived at the beach too long, Sky. People here move fast, slamming into one another, getting sexual from the starting gun, and then, whammo! they usually implode and shatter." He paused. "Let's not let that happen," he said. He looked intently into her still tearful eyes.

He paid the bill. They gathered up all the books and papers scattered among the empty dishes on the table and walked out of the Shogun Maru. Her arm was through his to help guide him to her car. She unlocked the driver's door. She took the pile of books and papers from him, placed them on the passenger seat, and fastened the seat belt over them. He watched her move across the seats to do this, every motion effortless, efficient, and sensual. When she straightened up she leaned against the car door facing him. He put his arms around her waist. For a while they simply looked at one another under the sodium vapor parking lot light. He noticed her red lips looked almost blue in this light and her eyes seemed black.

"You look strange, Sky. How come your lips are blue?"

"You look strange, too. Your face is a yellowish color with blue dots on it, if I look at the light and then suddenly back at you. It's psychedelic. With the magic of what we're experiencing with one another, I'm sure things between us will often seem strange."

She burrowed her head into his chest and they breathed together and then shared another lingering kiss.

"It is very difficult to say goodnight to you, but let's meet tomorrow afternoon," he said.

"Right now tomorrow afternoon seems a long way off."

She gradually slid her arms from around him and took hold of his hands. He watched her slide into her T-Bird, smiling a goodbye. He closed the door and she pulled away into the night. He wanted nothing to take away from the mood of their time together.

He slept well that night even though he retained several good dreams. The phone jarred him awake. As reflex he answered on the first tone. A woman's upset voice uttered brittle, clipped words. "Jon, I'm suddenly aware of being too vulnerable with you. You are a very complex man. I'm not sure how far I should allow this relationship to go," said a voice he barely recognized. It sounded strangely familiar.

"Who is this?" he asked, still groggy.

"If you don't know who this is, we're in more trouble than I thought. Who do you think this is? It's Sky Rowan."

"Sky, you don't sound yourself. What's wrong? What's happened? Talk to me."

"The figurehead is too important to you. It's just an old block of water-soaked wood; nothing to be excited about. Get it out of my workshop as soon as possible. I don't want it here, and, don't refer to it as Meri or your Lady!"

"Sky. What the heck is going on? Clearly, this is a crisis!" His hands began to shake, then his arms and shoulders. His bare feet hit the sole of the boat and he began to pace, trying to think what to say. He sat down at his galley table and fumbled with the gold-braided cord hanging from the ship's lamp above the table. "I need to see you. I could be there within a half hour."

"It is best if I don't see you for a while." Then, silence, just her breathing.

"Something has happened. Tell me what's happened," he demanded.

She struggled to breathe and then to talk. "This figurehead ... it's possessed or something. After I left you last night I stopped by the shop. I walked by the thing and tripped and fell. I never fall down. I swear it tripped me. On the floor my eyes suddenly looked into its glass eyes. They were opaque at first ... dirty, I guess. When I rubbed the crust off of them, the glass eyes stared back like the thing's alive. It kept staring at me. I'm sure of it. It won't let me rest until I get the message. This thing has some kind of message, some information or something." Her voice cracked, and she breathed heavily, unevenly, obviously upset, maybe afraid.

"Calm yourself, Sky. Drink some water. Take deep breaths. I'll come right away. I can be over there before my first appointment. Are you at the workshop?"

"No, I'm at home. I don't want you here. You care much more about that figurehead than anything, including me."

He tried to calm her with his best therapist's voice. "We both care about the figurehead. It is an archeological discovery. That's what it is. An artifact. An interesting artifact, but an artifact. Yes, it is marvelously carved and preserved well, but it's just a relic, an important relic. Let's talk about this. Come on, Sky. You're used to relics. Try to relax and I'll be there at the shop right away. Meet me." As he spoke, he remembered the feelings he had when he first discussed and named Meri. Was he lying to Sky and himself?

"If you insist, Jon. But, this is strictly business now, a matter of research. We won't have another evening like last night. I'm a professor and an archeologist. You're a therapist and a minister, and we have nothing personal between us. If you can remember that, I'll meet you at the shop in a half hour. Otherwise, just get that damned chunk of wood out of my shop. We'll have no further reason to talk."

He felt flattened, as if one of his old Peterbilt tractors had run over him. He would meet her right away. Thoughts of her hand in his, her kiss, faded. He felt his defensive self take over, clinical and removed. She sounded like she needed therapy, not a friend. He thought of Miriam, suddenly longing for her again. He felt he had somehow betrayed her with last night's flood of feelings and desire for Sky.

Maybe this is all wrong. Maybe I'm not meant to have a new life with another woman.

No matter what, he had to play this out. He drove to the shop determined to see it through. Sky had parked her car in front of the open gate, and through the door of the workshop he could see her standing next to a work bench. She had a metal piece, a large metal candlestick, clamped in the vise. He knew she had seen him, but she pretended to be engrossed in her work. She wore a full-face protective plastic shield, not wanting to get any splattered solvent or particles in her eyes as she scrubbed with a stiff brush. A colorful blue bandana wrapped her hair and she wore a yellow t-shirt under the coveralls. When she spoke, her voice was now normal, no longer cold and clipped. Had she been caught in a waking nightmare when she called?

"Jon, I've only been here a few minutes and I already feel creepy with that thing. Get down on the floor and look at the eyes."

He peeled back the blue, plastic cover. He knelt and looked at Meri's face. He squinted, but saw nothing but darkness. He went to his pickup for a flashlight, returned, and knelt down again. He shined the light through one eye and looking into the other, he could see what looked like a rolled up document, perhaps a scroll. He could make out just the top of it spooled around a small stick. He called to Sky. "Look into this eye while I shine the flashlight in the other one."

"No," she said. "This thing is haunted. You're obsessed with it. You need to get it out of here."

He thought about Sky's fear and the mysterious dark eyes of the figurehead. He had to appeal to her professionalism.

"You're an archeologist and we'll have a professional relationship. I'm willing to pay your fee to treat this artifact as an artifact. Please look into the left eye as I shine the light into the right eye. You're right. There is a mystery here. I don't need a romance with you. I want to cherish this discovery, the solving of this mystery. You're an inquisitive archeologist. Look - really look - at this log on your shop floor." His irritation became anger as he spoke to her.

"Jon, I'm scared of this thing. I've been inside pyramids, graves of all kinds. I've unwrapped mummies with tweezers, spending countless hours alone in a laboratory. I've never had a reaction like this." She slowly approached the figurehead on the floor and took the flashlight, looking up at him for reassurance.

"I'm right here. I think the Lady 'knows' that her secret or message will be discovered. She knows that she's in the right hands."

"Don't call this log Lady. It's just a relic. You wouldn't believe my nightmare involving this possessed figurehead."

"Let's talk about those dreams," he said, sounding like a therapist. "What do you recall from your dreams last night?"

"How can you be so clinical?" she demanded. She slowly bent down to look into the eye as she held the flashlight to shine in the other. This illuminated the interior of the hollowed skull.

"Jon," she said, her voice changing again, this time with excitement. "There's some kind of scroll inside this thing." She looked up at him with the first sign of forgiveness, then went to work and examined the head of the figure. With the brush she'd been using on the artifact in the vise Sky gently removed the loose crust from the figurehead.

He didn't have much time left, but he didn't want to stop her work.

"Sky, I hate to leave, but I've got an appointment in about forty-five minutes."

"Well, just go on then," she said, sounding more like her seventeen-year-old daughter then her adult self. "Ignore all the problems I've admitted to you this morning. Your clients are obviously more important than this work."

Her hostility stabbed him.

"Sky, if you had a class to teach right now, you'd be off to teach it. That's your work. Meeting appointments and showing up for clients are my work. If we're going to stay on a professional level now I expect you to keep your opinions to yourself about my coming and going."

She looked at him as though she wasn't used to people talking to her that way.

"You're right. Go to your appointment. I'm curious now. It's one of my curses - curiosity." She lowered the protective face shield, stood up, and went back to work on the clamped object.

Jon drove to his office. He felt confused and hurt. He had to focus during the therapy hour coming up and the two more after that. Usually, he could block out nearly all his own turmoil while attending to clients. At the moment, he wasn't sure how he would get through the morning's therapy sessions. He could cancel his sessions, but no, he never did that and wouldn't start now.

There's more going on with Sky than I've seen before, but maybe it is worth getting to know her and maybe we'll get through these times. I hope so.

In years of doing therapy he had missed very few sessions. He'd missed one the morning his mother died, another four days when Miriam was dying, and two the night he crashed his motorcycle on Highway 395.

But, this morning's emotional turmoil, after getting a taste of possibly a paranoid side of Sky, had been a whole new scenario for him. This was especially so after their closeness the night before.

Then it hit him: *That's the clue! That's what this episode is all about. I actually have gotten through her defenses. Perhaps it happened all too fast. That's it! She's not used to intimacy of any kind. I just need to slow down and give her time.*

Although he didn't know her entire history, he knew her alcoholic husband's affair and his abuse had ended their marriage. In defense Sky had sworn off men forever after that; forever until their sudden connection.

He wished his 9:30 appointment would cancel or at least be late, but she arrived on time. Luckily, this first client had done enough of her own work not to rely on him. After a few minutes, he got into the session and began to concentrate, relieved to be involved. The session went well, intense and productive, despite his emotional state.

Often the best therapy occurred when he was upset or distressed about something. That mystified him, but also confirmed important things happened not because of him and his expertise. He cherished and sometimes romanticized the ongoing mystery of true dialogue. He valued highly how healing dialogue and relationship could and should be. He cherished the mystery of the therapeutic process .

The next two sessions were uneventful, but reassuring. He could easily release his clients when he knew they were processing things well. When they integrated thinking and feeling, kept journals, and stayed mindful of their work in the sessions, his work as their therapist was easy. This morning's clients were like that. He knew they would do their homework between sessions and next appointments.

Then the phone rang.

"Dr. Scott?"

"This is Dr. Scott."

"This is Krystal. I need to say something about mother. I know it's none of my business, but I overheard her call this morning and I'm worried about how you might have taken that."

"It's kind of you to be concerned. I was upset by her call. Guess I had presumed too much." He hesitated, wondering how much he should reveal to her.

He thought: *She's only seventeen, but like some other teenagers, she seems wise beyond her years.*

After a pause, he added, "Maybe I had been swept along too fast with her, Krystal."

"That's exactly the problem." She paused. "Mother really opened up with whatever you two shared last night at dinner. She came home singing. I hardly ever hear her sing. But, about three-thirty this morning, I heard her crying. She really sobbed - for a long time. Then, she threw a book across her bedroom. It broke her dresser mirror. When I heard the crash, I ran to her room. I was scared. I was afraid someone was in the house with us. She was standing on her bed. She looked like a wild woman."

"What did you do, Krystal?"

"I grabbed her and we fell down on the bed together. She cried for a long time. She kept repeating things I couldn't understand. I wanted to call you or nine-one-one. I was real scared. I haven't seen her like that since that scene when Robert finally left. Remember? I talked to you about some of that. What a terrible time! A terrible time for both of us! Mother swore she'd never get involved with another man. No man was ever going to take advantage of her." Krystal paused again, breathing heavily. After several sighs, she went on. "Whatever happened between you two last night, she got scared and out of control. Maybe there's something you can figure out about this. Know what I think? I think she fell in love with you. I think she's terrified about that. She's vulnerable again. I had a crush on someone once and know how scary it can be. But, maybe it's worse for adults. Could that be?"

"Krystal, you're seventeen. Where'd you get all this insight?"

"You forget! I grew up with a drunk alcoholic bastard. I've spent a lot of time in support groups for teenagers of alcoholic parents. I'm not stupid. Sometimes I sense things about my mother before she talks to me about them. Sometimes I feel like the mother. But, she's been so good to me. She never had a childhood. Her parents died when she was young. Maybe we're connected with similar histories. I lost my parents. I'm an orphan and she adopted me. I told you some of this. She didn't have parents then, either. Does any of this make sense? Maybe talking this way you'll treat me like one of your clients." He felt a smile in her voice.

"I can't believe you're a seventeen-year-old, Krystal. But, then, you told me so much about your escape from Vietnam as a little girl, I'm sure you're probably grown up beyond your years in many ways."

"I wish I weren't. I go to school with all these people who seem like children. I have to pretend I'm just like them, constantly acting like I care about all their stupid stuff. They're stupid and immature, it seems to me. Guess they can't help it. But, I have to remember, especially with my friends who haven't been through anything. My life would be just weird to them, if they knew," Krystal said. Another pause followed. Maybe she was crying. He couldn't tell for sure.

Then she said the words he'd hoped for. "Jon, don't be put off by mother's anger this morning. It's just her being afraid, that's all. I didn't want her to call you feeling like that, but she wouldn't listen to me. She said she had to stop anything that might get out of control."

"Thank you, Krystal. I'll remember what you've told me. I want nothing but the right things with your mom, whatever that might be. She's gotten through my defenses, too, you know."

The phone call ended well, with both of them somehow reassuring one another.

He suggested that she call him as soon as she was ready to talk again. He hung up and he knew Krystal and Sky were a rare combination. He said a brief prayer for both of them. He felt thankful for Krystal's interpretation of the morning's turmoil and her own thoughtful, courageous call.

Chapter Fifteen

The rest of his office day went well enough. Jon had several sessions and then he worked on the next Sunday's sermon. He preached seldom, but when he did he devoted lots of time and study to his message. Throughout the day he was distracted by thoughts of what seemed to be a scroll hidden inside Meri's head. Mostly, he yearned to see Sky.

If it's a scroll, it may have symbolic meaning. It's like Meri's conscious and the scroll is what's on her mind.

He'd risk calling Sky.

Maybe she'll let me into the shop again. Maybe her mood's changed. There must be a way to retrieve whatever we see in there without damaging the figurehead.

He had forgotten to eat lunch. Now, at nearly seven in the evening, he went to the coffee shop in the marina and ordered split pea soup, crackers, and half of a sandwich. Along with the quick dinner, a glass of the house Chardonnay helped soothe him.

Becky, his favorite waitress, took his order. At every opportunity, while serving other patrons, she talked to him in short installments about her boyfriend.

"We're getting married in May. Would you do the ceremony?"

"We'd have to talk about that, Becky, the three of us. There's more to a marriage than a ceremony."

"I know that. Is it expensive to talk to you about marrying us? It isn't like we don't know each other. Roy and I've been living together for six years. If we had problems, we'd sure as heck know about them by now."

She accomplished this conversation while waiting on at least fifteen others. By the end of dinner, as Jon paid the bill, she had an appointment time for herself and Roy for pre-marital counseling. From that evening's dinner and Becky's talk with him, both Becky and her growing family became a part of Jon's life.

Becky was about thirty, twice married, with an eleven-year-old daughter. Her father was a Long Beach policeman. Her mother was a bartender in Huntington Beach.

Becky had little contact with them. She knew her previous two marriages were mistakes and had waited nearly seven years to be sure Roy was different from the first two men. She'd married at sixteen, already pregnant, and then lost the baby. After ending that marriage at eighteen, she'd married again at twenty-two, to a cocaine addict. That only lasted six months, was filled with chaos and abuse, and ended with her in the hospital after almost being killed. Roy, now a policeman, earned her trust, after several years; which was not an easy thing to do. She tested him often. Jon had met and liked him, although usually he was suspicious of police people in personal relationships. Too often they were involved in violence at work and became violent at home. However, Roy had passed all her tests. Roy's brother, Brian Callahan, a Roman Catholic priest, would not consider performing their ceremony, but as he and Jon got better acquainted he warmed to Jon, and was relieved Jon would do the nuptials.

Fr. Callahan and Jon got to know one another and talked at length. They had dinner at a local restaurant, drank good wine, and conversed in depth about theology and Christology and their views on ministry until the place closed down. Brian consented to blessing the marriage if Jon would perform the ceremony. Becky, Roy, her parents, Brian, and Jon had already had one meeting over lunch to discuss this wedding. That dinner conversation - while she waited on him the evening of the split pea soup and half sandwich - had turned into a rich chapter in his life.

The next day, he impatiently wanted to talk with Sky. He drove to her shop that Sunday afternoon. Through the partially opened door he saw her pacing back and forth.

"Sky, it's Jon," he called, hoping not to startle her.

"Come in. I've got something to show you." Her friendly voice disarmed him, slightly. Both of them seemed somewhat protected. She looked sexy in her coveralls, blue denim shirt, paint-spattered running shoes, and her hair tied back with the familiar bandana. She held the little scroll. She'd actually, carefully freed it from the skull of the figurehead.

"We're going to have problems with this scroll. If we try unrolling it, it'll be like a roll of fossilized toilet paper. But, I know someone at the Huntington Library who may be able to help. She's successfully opened books that looked like bricks. They were so caked with mud, their pages were stuck together. It isn't easy, takes a lot of time, but she knows how to do it. I'm sure I could get her to help with this scroll."

"How'd you get it out, Sky?"

"Look here, on the top of the head." She gestured for him to look where she was pointing. She had removed a small block of rectangular wood, like some kind of trephining for a lobotomy. The removed piece sat on the stomach of the figurehead. He fitted the small, rectangular block gently into the hole in the head, impressed with the precision fit.

"I can't imagine how you got this out or even how you found it would come out."

"Once I got the surfaces clean enough I found the fine lines where the block had been cut to fit perfectly - what craftsmanship! The top of the head, this carved-out place, is only about one-half inch thick. How the empty space in the head kept from leaking water I'll never understand. If the thing had been in deeper water, I'm sure the pressure would have forced water into the empty space, utterly ruining this scroll. The clear glass eyeballs and the block of wood in the head were sealed in with tar or pitch. Whoever did this really knew his craft."

Jon felt a strange surgery had been done on his Lady. He stood looking at the opening in her skull and for a few seconds became angry at Sky for doing this deed, mostly angry that they had not done it together.

Sky went on, oblivious of his feelings. "There's very little moisture in that hollowed area; just the dampness of the wood itself. The scroll did absorb some salt water, but at least salt offers some degree of preservation.

She pointed out the scroll's layers of rolled paper or parchment. "I can't wait to see it unrolled!" She nudged Jon in the stomach with her elbow, almost gleefully, with no apparent memory of what she'd said to him earlier that morning or how he felt about the surgery on his Lady. Jon swallowed his irritation about Sky's going ahead without him. He realized they were making progress and they agreed to see what Sky's friend at the Huntington Library could do with the scroll.

It took some doing to reach Sky's friend, but she persisted. Sky and Jon began to relax with one another as they waited to hear from the Huntington Library.

Finally, three days later Sky received a call from the woman at the Huntington Library in Pasadena. She arranged for the scroll to be delivered. But, both Sky and Jon sensed they had to learn more about the scroll and what it might reveal. They waited with anticipation for four more days. They called Dr. Theresa Fortner's office everyday in hopes she had succeeded. Several times Jon expressed his frustration awaiting the findings. Finally, the news came on Monday evening.

Sky called Jon and played the message from her answering machine so Jon could hear it.

"Dr. Rowan, this is Theresa, Theresa Fortner. I have good news about your scroll. It had no mold, which means there was very little damage from dampness. I think the paper was a fine paper for the time, probably from France. The salt water environment helped protect it. I x-rayed it first, then put it through a series of baths. After soaking it for twenty-four hours in my favorite milky concoction, it unrolled much more easily than I had anticipated. Then, I dried it slowly on the spool dryer in my lab. It is completely unrolled, except for three inches or so at the very bottom. The writing on the scroll is mostly intact. I think you'll find the text interesting, to say the least." Her message ended with an invitation to call with a meeting time.

Sky made an appointment for Wednesday, without consulting Jon, assuring him that she would bring back the scroll along with Dr. Fortner's results. They would talk over dinner Friday evening. Once again Jon was disappointed and frustrated at being left behind.

I need to talk to Sky about how we proceed together on this. I really don't like being left out of her decisions. Maybe we've got a problem.

Also, complications from possible legalities worried him. Whatever might be revealed from the scroll also might add to the complications. They had a lot to consider, it seemed to him, but Sky was swept up in the excitement of discovery and could not be restrained, no matter how worried he might be.

The next message that evening was from The Press Telegram newspaper reporter. "Dr. Scott, this is Sandra Wells following up on my story. I'm the reporter who called you a while ago about the relic you found. It has become an item of great interest, especially to my editor. I need more information to finish up Saturday's issue. Please give me a call as soon as you can."

This was disturbing. Jon didn't want anything in the news about the figurehead, but, it seemed unavoidable. The reporter already had a story and perhaps she merely wanted clarification. Had Sky talked to her? He would have to talk with her, but not tonight. Things were getting out of control.

What's going on? Maybe this is just piling up with my feelings about Sky, the tensions and changes we've had. But this reporter's call reminds me of the Coast Guard insinuations, accusations, and the possible charges against me for bringing home this figurehead.

At least he was no longer suspected of hitting Sky Rowan's boat. He needed to talk to Sky and get their stories straight before he talked to the reporter.

Jon phoned Sky and she agreed that they should only give vague information about the figurehead, not much description, and certainly nothing speculative about its history nor the location of where he found it. Ms. Wells was not satisfied with what he gave her, but he again assured her he would follow up with an exclusive story as soon as he knew something certain and publishable. She assured him that she would only write what she knew so far, things that would keep the story alive. In fact, it seemed to him the newspaper article would be useless and premature. Nevertheless, she insisted she would have something in Saturday's paper about his discovering the distressed Cal-20, along with Dr. Sky Rowan and her dog, Schwartz. An added news item would be about his return from a sailing vacation during which he retrieved an antique figurehead, possibly from a mysterious shipwreck.

He cautioned her about sharing that information, because they had no idea from where this figurehead had come. He even suggested to her it might be a leftover from an old movie shot in the ocean, having no value whatsoever. With that possibility, Sandra became quiet. She agreed to play down the find, but she would mention it and wanted a photograph of it, which he refused to provide. Neither Jon nor Sky would tell her where the figurehead was stowed. But, Jon knew Sandra could easily figure out where it was if she learned Sky Rowan was into oceanography and had her own shop.

He had made reservations at the Long Beach Yacht Club for 6:30, but he arrived early to relax, read, and watch the boats in the marina. This would be a shared, special meal in his favorite place for entertaining, the club. Living aboard made it difficult to have a formal meal on the *Daimon*. There was always too much clutter. Being a member of the Long Beach Yacht Club made it possible for him to have a slip there, in Basin Four, a place close by to socialize, plus a fine Olympic-sized pool. He felt at home at the club, even though most of the members were politically conservative. The good weather helped make it a fine evening. The marina would be very busy, lots of boaters out for time on the water this entire weekend. Sky and Krystal arrived for dinner. Both of them seemed glad to see him. Krystal surprised him with a hug, while Sky offered her hand. The waiter set another place for Krystal. When Sky and Krystal were seated, Bruce unfolded their napkins and placed them in their laps. He paraded about. He acted very gay and reeked with affectation. He always kidded Jon when attempting to put the napkin in his lap.

"Cool it, Bruce!"

"Am I making you nervous, Sir?" Bruce said with a wry, teasing smile.

Bruce arranged the glasses and showed Jon the wine. He smiled at him the whole time he poured it. Jon thought sure he would spill it. Bruce had practiced this many times, pouring the wine while seeming not to watch what he was doing. This part of his act had become one of his trademark antics.

Sky was remote, but pleasant. Krystal sat next to her. Jon sat across from both of them. Once they ordered, they began the business meeting. Sky had learned more about the sunken ship, *Madonna*. She had been built in Boston, launched about 1838, along with a sister ship, the *Apostle*. Both of them had French names when built, being first sailed by a French company. They were sold to an American company, a Winfield Stith or Styth, in 1845, who took both ships around Cape Horn to California, Oregon, Washington, and possibly to Alaska.

Sky was convinced there were archived logs that pertained to these ships, because they had been used to transport the Russians as they were removed from the west coast. Many Russians had retreated to the Alaska territory. Others stayed put, changed their names and businesses, as

Fort Ross (the Anglicized name for *Rossiya*) surrendered to the Mexicans and Americans, beginning about 1839. During a later conflict, about 1849, the *Madonna* came into the history of this southern California coast. "What happened aboard the *Madonna* would make a good movie," Sky said, finishing her dissertation.

For a while, Krystal looked interested. Growing impatient with the details coming from her mother, she interrupted. "Are you going to pretend being here now is only about history, Russians, and old boats? C'mon, you two!"

Sky and Jon looked at one another, surprised, and then Sky surprised Jon by taking his hand in hers.

"Jon, I owe you an apology. I owe you one, too, Krystal," Sky said. She looked away from both of them and then continued. "I consider myself to be very honest, but I wasn't honest with you and I handled things very badly when I got scared. Krystal's right. We have to talk. Right now, just know that I appreciate the way you've responded to my craziness. Krystal, take a lesson from your goofy mother." She put her arm around her daughter, gently brushing back Krystal's long hair from her face.

Jon thought he should leave the two of them alone, but Sky took his hand again.

"Just be patient with me," she said. "These last two weeks have been whoppers for me. I need a good shrink or at least a good drink."

He took his hand from under hers and put it on top. "All I want for now is a place in your lives. I would like to get to know both of you. I've been protected long enough, living like a zombie. I feel like I'm coming back to life with you, both of you."

The three of them became quiet until Sky broke the spell, raising her glass of wine and toasting Krystal and Jon, chiming the rim of her glass against theirs.

"All that matters to me is we're here, back in touch with one another and on friendly terms. I'll toast that with you," Jon said.

Krystal raised her cup of tea and said, "A toast to both of you. Mother, you've found someone, finally, who has a heart and a brain."

They finished the evening with a three-way hug. Sky and Jon set a date for further talk about the scroll, now unrolled and readable. The mystery of the *Madonna* was unraveling before them. Even Krystal caught the fever. The scroll was the next item for investigation. The only moth in the butter was their worry about the article coming out in tomorrow's newspaper about Meri.

"Sky, I know you've got a lot to do and so do I. I've been neglecting several tasks, especially my paperwork. For the next few days, let's at least be in touch on the phone."

"If we catch up, we'll feel a lot freer. Let's get together this weekend. This evening has been so special, Jon."

Krystal moved aside so the two of them could hug goodbye. Jon looked at Krystal, still holding Sky, and said, "Take care of each other. See you soon." They slipped their hands apart and walked down the stairs to the parking lot.

Chapter Sixteen

A smiling waitress greeted Jon at the counter of The Omelette House. She handed him a section of Saturday's newspaper. On the front page, there it was, *Local Therapist Discovers Sea Relic, by Sandra Wells.* A photograph of a generic figurehead topped the article. Pictured was a man's carved upper body, sporting a rich mustache. It looked refinished, perhaps a museum piece. Under the photograph, the comment read, *Pictured here is an ancient ship's figurehead, like the one found by Dr. Jon Scott. Dr. Scott's figurehead is unavailable for this edition. Reportedly it is a voluptuous woman with long hair and a flowing skirt.*

Some of the details were nearly correct, but misleading, for which Jon gave thanks. The less known the better. San Clemente Island was not mentioned, however it did report the figurehead had been found in shallow water at a local island. Ms. Wells also divulged a few words about his having *rescued oceanographic archeology professor on the faculty of California State University Long Beach, Dr. Sky Rowan, from a damaged sailboat. Also on board was Dr. Rowan's dog. They had drifted for several days after a collision at sea. Upon rescue the Coast Guard airlifted the victim to Long Beach Memorial Hospital for life-saving measures.* The last paragraph disclosed that research was progressing on the figurehead and, *It is thought the sunken ship to which it belonged is close to where Dr. Scott found it. Dr. Rowan speculated this unique figurehead came from a large 19th Century sailing ship.*

Jon wondered what else Sky had told the reporter. As he re-read the article, little else could be deduced from the information Ms. Wells revealed. He was most embarrassed by the statement that he had rescued Sky Rowan. He had only called the Coast Guard when he found her boat. They rescued Sky Rowan. He just towed the boat back to Alamitos Harbor. Nothing about any of this seemed heroic to him. Boating people do these things every day, towing hapless boats and helping one another at sea.

He put down the newspaper and finished his coffee. Julia, the waitress, asked if he wanted a refill. She said, "Dr. Scott, you're a celebrity. I saw the morning paper."

"Julia, I am hardly a celebrity. Would that have made a difference a couple of months ago, when I asked you to go to dinner?"

"Maybe," she said, with a coy expression as she poured him more coffee and topped off another customer's cup.

Julia and Jon had been teasing one another for a couple of years. Only a few months ago, however, he learned she was the single mother of three children, working two jobs. She fled from an abusive husband, saving her life and the lives of her children. She borrowed a car and drove nearly straight through, from New Hampshire to California. Jon learned of her past when she became ill. She required medical attention and had no means for anything. Several customers who frequented the restaurant in the morning put a fund-raising effort together, inviting two country-western singers to come to the local VFW hall. To Julia's embarrassment and eternal gratitude, they raised $11,000 that night. That gift enabled her to have health insurance, the surgery she needed, and it took care of some of the expenses during her recuperation.

Jon folded the newspaper and said goodbye to Julia as well as to the man beside him at the counter. He left the money on the counter and turned to leave. The man quickly swivelled in his counter chair. "So, you're the Dr. Scott in that article? What a coincidence meeting you! I just read the paper. Julia gave it to me when I came in. She told me she knew you."

Jon thought few people read newspapers, but here two people at breakfast referred to the article. His question startled Jon. "Yes, I am," Jon confessed.

"I know someone who will be very interested in what you found out there in the ocean. He lives in Dana Point. His name is Carlos Diaz. We both belong to a skeet-shooting group. He gave a talk to the club about a year ago about his great-great-grandfather." Then, he introduced himself. "I'm Clyde Maxon. I own the hardware store on Second Street. I've seen you in my store from time to time, but didn't know who you were. Glad to meet you." They shook hands. Jon felt as though he were signing some kind of agreement with him.

Julia took the money from the counter and smiled at him. "This will teach you to go around rescuing damsels in distress," she said.

Jon gave his card to Mr. Maxon, left, and walked the four blocks back to his boat. The early morning sun glistened on the dew-covered boats. He unzipped the boom tent to step aboard. A slight morning breeze came from the northeast and the seasonal Santana winds were increasing. The wind vane at the top of his mast swung around several times and then settled firmly on the northeast, confirming his forecast. Usually, Santanas last about three days. In the marina, they generate lots of noise. Halyards slap masts, docks creak with roughened water, and boats strain at their dock lines. The gusty northeast winds increase, sometimes to fifty and sixty knots or more.

To see dew on the boats while a Santana wind is brewing was unusual. The mountains to the north, Mt. Baldy especially, were clearly visible, appearing closer than their thirty-or-so-miles' distance. Snow billowed on the top of Mt. Baldy, swirls rising high in the air. Sometimes these winds became destructive, but usually they just caused clamor and dust. Once in a while a boat broke lose from its moorings. The damage to the wind-driven boat, loose in a marina, was one part of the story, but many other boats could be damaged substantially too, as a loose boat collided with the exposed sterns of boat after boat. An old adage advises, *When the winds are strong, be out to sea or safely moored in a leeward cove.*

Not having clients this weekend and his sermon written for this Sunday, he felt free to dwell on the questions that gathered in his mind. The unrolled scroll called to him. In the afternoon he phoned Sky and left a message on her machine. He inquired about a time they could look at the scroll. He relaxed aboard, trying to read. It was noisy as the wind whistled, halyards and lines clanged against masts. His ketch vibrated and ranged back and forth on her lines. Along with the din a Brahms tape played on his stereo. Even with all this going on, it was still one of his favorite places to be.

He interrupted himself for a few minutes to walk the dock, checking the other boats on his gangway to be sure their lines were secure. On the boat next to his the lines slapped too hard for his peace of mind. They required attention. He tied them together, away from the mast. The banging, clanging halyards on other boats were not close enough to disturb him. He returned to his settee in the womb of the *Daimon* to read, just in time to hear the phone ring, adding to the cacophony.

"Hello." He paused.

"Is this Jon?"

"Yes."

"Jon, this is Sky."

"I know."

"Is something wrong? Did I call at a bad time?"

"No. Why do you ask?"

"You seem so professional, so cold."

"Well, Sky, I'm just hoping we can talk some things over. I've not been very direct with you on several occasions and I need to clean things up. I'm still a bit gun shy from our last conversation. I know we've worked things out, but I'm a bit hesitant. Sorry. But, I'm really glad to hear your voice."

"I'm feeling suddenly very awkward. I'm returning your call, Jon. Is this a game?"

Jon paused as a thought came to him. *Maybe I'm more angry at Sky than I realized. She should not have talked so much about the figurehead to the reporter. I thought we agreed to keep the details to herself, especially because we don't know enough yet to reveal the little we do know.*

"Okay. You're right. I did call you and I've been hoping you'd call, but I'm unsure how things are between us. I don't like asking for reassurance. Guess I need some clues from you as to where we are. I guess I should apologize about still feeling a bit cautious. I also have an issue we need to discuss when we get together. It can wait until then."

Sky paused. "I told you I was sorry. Don't make this any more difficult for me. I know we need some time to talk. Krystal opened the whole thing up last night. I guess she did me a favor, but I felt very embarrassed by what she did."

"Let's get together, Sky. Where are you? I'm here in a strong wind, listening to Brahms, sort of reading, having a glass of good sherry, with the heater going. Can you hear the halyards banging in the background? This marina becomes a Stravinsky symphony in strong winds. In fact, I've thought of having a musician come and record the sounds of a marina on days like this. It would be composed of all kinds of sounds, from creaking gangways and squeaking ramps to the squeals and groans of straining boats. Along with all that would be the chimes of lines slapping against masts. I think it would make for a marvelous cacophonic symphony," he said, attempting to lighten up the moment.

"That's a very intriguing idea. I think I know the person who would take you up on doing such a thing. He's got the recording equipment and the musical ability. Let's really talk about doing that," she said, obviously relieved. Then she added, "I'm at my shop. Anytime, the rest of the afternoon, I'll be right here. I've got the scroll, too. It's fascinating. Having it unrolled, I put it on a long piece of plywood. I've smoothed it enough to hold it down by a piece of clear plastic. It's really well preserved. Jon, you've got to see this!"

"I'll be there as soon as I can. It will take me about thirty minutes to button up here and drive over. Do you want me to stop and get refreshments?"

"Just come as soon as you can."

He heard acceptance, perhaps even desire in her voice.

As he entered the shop he called her name. A muffled, "Hello" came from the head. "I'll be out in a minute."

Spread out on a sheet of plywood under clear plastic, just as she had described, the scroll grabbed his attention. Sky had moved an assortment of projects aside to make room. He could not tell, for sure, but the scroll looked like old, brown paper, suggesting wrapping paper or thick parchment. The black ink script was clear through the whole text. A few smudge spots blurred the text and there were three or four small random holes in the paper where letters once were. Edges of the scroll were roughly cut, probably with a dull knife. It averaged five and one-half inches in width. The writing became clearer down from the top of the scroll about four inches, leaving the rest of the length, about twenty-two inches in all, easier to read. The script was in a beautiful hand with letters crowded together and flourishes here and there. He counted the lines, about sixty-six from top to bottom.

Sky came out of the bathroom and greeted him as she dried her hands. Her bib overalls had splotches of rusty stains and, here and there, streaks of white denim where she had spilled bleach or solvent. Her yellow bandana completely covered her hair. Only a few strands fell around her face. It reminded him of how her hair looked when down and free, falling over her shoulders. She walked directly to him and kissed him on the cheek as she nudged him gently with her shoulder.

"I could hardly wait for you to get here. I would like to think it's because I'm excited about this scroll, but I think I'm excited just to see you. I might as well admit it. Again, I apologize for that awful phone call. I guess I dumped on you because I felt so frightened. I am still very embarrassed. I'm sorry, Jon," she said.

"We've discussed all that and I'm pleased and, yes, excited too. Thank you for your honesty. It really helps. I'm still a bit wary, but I'm better. I'm hoping we can just be ourselves again, without any expectations or reservations."

They turned their attention to the scroll. Sky pulled a swiveled spotlight over to the scroll, adjusting it to minimize glare. She sat down in her chair. Jon pulled a paint-spattered stool up beside her. They agreed to type it as close to the scroll's format as possible, but punctuation was often missing. They would have to be imaginative with some of the phrases.

"Read to me what you can make out, Jon. I'll type it out as you read," she said, pulling the portable Olympia into position.

"Okay? Here goes," he said. "I'll fill in what seems to be missing and we can put my additions in brackets when we type it again."

December 2nd 1849 Madonna took first gold [fro]m the Indian. Last night 27 Indians came aboard. Master Brooks Mr. Thompson Mr Hedge and three new crew agreed on the gold Indians agred [agreed] on southern course We drank ru[m] all of us. Indians bring more gold aboard. Six bells and all gold below More than promised No time to weigh or count. The secret is [safe] with us.

33 will make the voyage south Madonna all ours when Indians are free in Mexico I am Madonna's carpenter Wilfred Cramer.

Captain Styth First Mate Scoggins and landing crew left for gold fields Madonna abandoned 14 ships abandoned near Madonna.

Apostle arriving this week.

December 4th, Night and fog covered us. 3 boats 6 manned oars in each boat Indians pulled Madonna two miles beyond north mountain at bay entrance 5 hours st[eady] work Sea flat Some tide

No wind Drifted southward during daylight past Yerba Buena entrance Monterey larboard on horizon Wind WSW Indians aloft Mr. Hedge teaching Unfurled 6 sails No reefs

Madonna 5 knots by 8 bells first afternoon w Main and Fore upper topsls Mainsl and Foresl Outer jib and spanker readied.

December 5th, Madonna under sail five knots Indians afraid aloft.

Indian fight at 4 bells 1 Indian unable seaman and 2 Indians in forecastle Some Indians cannot eat Madonna's food yet. Mr. Brooks at helm watch Standing 2 watches.

December 6th, Santa Cruz Island larboard beam 10 miles north Madonna bearing southeast. Mr Hedge took sun at noon, 119deg 41' N 33 deg. 43' W

December 7th, 6 bells Second watch Sail ho 15 miles astern 8 bells sail ho 10 miles astern. Mr. Hedge aloft 8 Indians

Top sails unf[urled] all three masts. Jibs drawing 7 knots at 2 bells. Sail astern 10 miles. Mr. Thompson made alarm Mr. Brooks spied Spanish flag atop Ordered watches on deck Made stations for each Indian and the 3 crew. 2 canon prepared. Mr. Thompson Mr. Hedge and 2 crew fired 4 trial shots.

Mr. Thompson confident Madonna holds distance into night. 7 knots at 8 bells Dusk at sea. Fog at distance. Sail astern out of sight. No lights astern No lights aboard Madonna

December 8th,, Madonna 5 miles larboard Santa Catalina Island Sail Ho 8 miles astern. Full sail. Madonna no studding sails, no top gallant on mizen [mizzen].

Indian died. 3 Indians in forecastle. Others now eat Madonna's food. Big Indian talks to me every watch. Shuka his name. He killed Vallejo and took other Indians to Yerba Buena in 4 days walking.

Gold on 4 mules. 4 Indians leaving Sutter Mill shot by Mexicans and miners. Wives and children shot by miners.

Shuka saw 2 children raped by miners and killed. Killed Vallejo.

Shuka and 5 Indians took ingot gold from Stone and Kelsey place and burned the houses.

December 9th Madonna 10 miles north Santa Clemente Island off larboard bows. Sail ho 4 miles astern. American brig. 4 knots

Brig fast More sail More length.

December 10th Last writing here. Madonna aground and holed doubling island. Stowing this writing in figurehead sealing it into secret place. Maybe someone will find it. No way to save this log on shore of Island.

Sail h[o] 2 miles. Sun down. Burning Madonna All ablaz[e] Gig and long boats away 18 Indians 2 crew Mr. Thompson Hedge Brooks Cramer aboard boats to pull north. Three dead 2 awash Some lost. Night and fog to larboard No sight of mainland Many miles to mainland. Wind southeast 10 knots Madonna stern full afire Breaking. Mizen [mizzen] in sea Main sails burning Tar burning on aft deck thick black smoke I stand at head stowing scroll in figurehead Heat strong from fire Astern Brig hove to close astern in dark night Pray we escape

Make the journey to north

All furled Brig standing starboard 1 mile Must seal scroll before I swim

Dark dark God help us all. I, Wilfred Cramer, will swim to last boat God help us all. W. C. Madonna

Sky re-read what she'd typed from his halting reading. She had a hard time reading some of the text. Jon had filled in at least four whole words for clarity, but it seemed true to the original. They sat silently for a time. Then both of them commented about the log's drama.

Jon said, "I'd really like to have known this Wilfred Cramer fellow. His words seemed like a Patrick O'Brian story or something out of Richard Dana's wonderful saga, *Two Years Before the Mast*. This is amazing, this whole discovery. So much detail. He must have written this under a lot of pressure, considering their situation, being pursued and all. He had to be a really cool fellow to have done this.

"Sky, let's have some dinner. I'll buy. You've accomplished a major feat getting this scroll out, unrolled, and preserved here. I don't know where this takes us, but it sure does give the figurehead a rich history."

Jon cleaned his glasses and gently wiped the plastic covering the scroll. His moist fingerprints had smudged it as he compressed the plastic firmly to read the difficult script.

"Let's go to the yacht club again, if you're buying. That waiter has his eye on you and I like how he struts his stuff when he sees you," she said, whimsically. "But, I can't go like this. How 'bout I meet you at the boat in an hour or so?"

"You look just terrific to me, but you're right. There are some snobs at the club, especially on a Saturday night. By the way, they have a small dance band there about eight o'clock, if you'd like to see if you and I can dance." He took her hand. He gently kissed it.

"You've been taking your romance pills. Perhaps you've overdosed." She blushed and left her hand in his. "I'll work on staying brave and healthy about all this, Jon. But I must admit, I still feel some of the fear I felt yesterday morning. Please be patient with me."

"That's no problem. You'll certainly have your chances for practicing patience with me." He became focused and serious. "There's just one thing I need to clear with you. I've not wanted to deal with it, but I have to. We agreed not to talk to anyone about the figurehead until we knew more. But, that reporter had lots of information and I think she got it from you. Am I right?"

"I'm sorry, Jon. I just felt so at ease with her and we got to talking and I just blabbed what we'd found. I don't think I gave her too much to disclose in an article, but I felt lousy that I didn't clear it with you before talking to her. I'm really sorry. I hope no harm has been done."

"It's too late, if so, but in reflection, nothing bad has come of it and eventually everything will be public, or nearly everything. It's okay, Sky. It took me a while to realize I was upset by what she knew and upset at you for telling her about Meri."

He took both of her hands and kissed her forehead. They timidly embraced for a moment. Then she stepped back and smiled. She removed her bandana. Her hair tumbled down over her shoulders. She wagged her head back and forth, her hair flying freely.

"About six-thirty, then, at your boat?" she asked.

"It's a date."

Then she added, "Jon, when you leave, please pull the gate closed for me and lock it. I'll go out the side gate. Oh boy! Dinner at a yacht club with a good-looking man.

Maybe I've died and gone to heaven," she said, wiggling in a happy dance.

As it turned out, they did dance well together. There were some slow dances and several fast ones, where she let go and they whirled around. Between dances, they could not help talking about the scroll and *Madonna*'s carpenter, Wilfred Cramer, a new person in their lives. This added to their evening. Jon could, in his mind's eye, watch them having a good time together. He could see and feel their dancing, letting her come and go from his touch and various cradles. The slow dances he liked the best, because they fit together just right. By about ten o'clock, they were both mellow. She broke the spell.

"Time for me to fold up my tent and go home. I've had such a fine time. Our conversation flowed and I only became afraid a few times. You just stayed right with me, though, and I feel safer now. Not safe, but safer," she added for emphasis.

Jon signed the tab and bade Bruce, his waiter in waiting, goodnight. They walked down the broad, carpeted stairs to the parking lot. Near his gangway her car gleamed in the overhead lights.

"Sky, I do want to hold and kiss you goodnight, but I'm a little wary of doing that unless you're feeling safe and not just safer. I wish I were more confident."

"I'll take the holding and the kiss. I'll give myself the lecture later on how careful I need to be. I'll be okay, Jon. Something about us has changed for me."

After a mutual embrace, breathing in the fragrance of her hair, he tucked her into her Thunderbird. She cranked the window down. He leaned inside and gave her one more kiss for the road.

Chapter Seventeen

Sunday's service went well. The compliments about Jon's sermon helped quiet his inner critic. One couple wanted to talk about the homily, so they made a breakfast date for Wednesday. They had met for discussions before, so he looked forward to the Wednesday time with them.

What a gift to have someone hear a sermon and actually want to discuss it!

Ryan was a school principal. Linda worked as an attorney. Together they attended a theological graduate school part time simply because they shared an interest in the related subjects. When the rector of the church first introduced them to Jon, she mentioned they would have lots to talk about as they became better acquainted. She was right!

Jon parked the pickup and walked toward his gangway. A car drove up beside him and Clyde Maxon, the man he'd met at The Omelette House, put down the window and called to him. He had a companion. Jon walked to the passenger side of the car to say hello.

Mr. Maxon said, "I've brought my Dana Point friend with me to talk to you. This may not be a convenient time. I see you're all dressed up like a priest this afternoon and maybe my timing isn't good. I forgot about people who went to church on Sunday." He chuckled at his own joke. His passenger sat quietly, not looking at Jon nor offering a greeting.

"Mr. Maxon, I need to change clothes and then I'd very much like to talk for a while. Do you want to wait here or would you like to go to the yacht club bar and have a drink on my tab? If you'd like to do that, I'll join you in about twenty minutes?" he said, as graciously as possible.

"That bar idea sounds great. We'll meet you there. I know where it is. I sail with Dick Brophe on his sloop and know that bar well. Take your time. We'll look forward to seeing you there soon."

This wasn't the way Jon wanted to spend his afternoon. He felt preoccupied with the log from the scroll and wanted to see Sky. He had awakened about 3:00 AM and could not get the log nor Sky out of his mind. Even though he had to preach his sermon twice that morning, Wilfred Cramer's log took much of his concentration. In the homily he had managed to put in an analogy of finding soul messages in new and surprising places in our lives. He thought of the scroll and how Cramer had sequestered it within the hollowed head of the figurehead - a desperate thing to do probably as his ship is burning, but also a very clever thing to do. Jon imagined that this hiding place might be the only part of the ship that wouldn't be destroyed. Also, maybe he assumed the figurehead would draw attention and be worthy of salvage when everything else disappeared. Figureheads attracted a lot of interest in those days of square-rigged ships. They were the icons for ships' builders, captains, and crews. Figureheads were the finishing touch of wood-carved art to ships where everything else had a function, from the keel to the top of the masts.

In his sport clothes and deck shoes, he felt relaxed and ready for a drink and conversation at the yacht club. The afternoon was just right, with a slight breeze moving the palm fronds rhythmically back and forth. A few clouds to the north, near the San Gabriel Mountains, made the blue sky even more interesting. The bar had a view of boats, water, and palm trees. Being on the second story, there were places one could see beyond the peninsula into the Catalina Channel, to the southeast.

Perhaps it will be an interesting meeting. If not, who could complain about the peacefulness and charm of our venue?

"Dr. Scott, or is it Father Scott on Sundays? Word got out that you're a priest," Mr. Maxon quipped with a laugh. Not waiting for clarification, he said, "Let me introduce my friend, Carlos Diaz. We've known one another for at least ten years and he's told me some tales that might interest you. Carlos, this is Father Jon Scott. Carlos and I've been skeet-shooting for years. He doesn't miss and enjoys putting me to shame."

Jon greeted him and then ordered a drink to catch up with them. He also suggested they get on a first-name basis. Carlos was not at ease yet, having seen Jon in a priest's collar just a half hour ago. But he soon relaxed. A Roman Catholic, he told Jon he had been an acolyte as a boy. He now served as a volunteer docent at the San Juan Capistrano Mission and also was a Eucharistic minister at a church in San Clemente. Clyde Maxon bragged about his escaping the church and he said that he didn't miss it at all. He watched Jon for a reaction, but Jon remained poker-faced, not rising to the bait.

Once Jon had a dry Rob Roy in his hand, with two onions, he remembered Miriam and that they shared onions from drinks. Then the three of them got to the subject that brought them together. Carlos seemed fascinated that Jon had a ship's figurehead. He understood it had been found near one of the local islands. Twice he asked Jon which island.

Twice Jon refused to say which island, only that he had found the figurehead near one of the Channel Islands. He thought that might divert Carlos, because San Clemente Island is not usually considered a Channel Island. Even so, he stressed to both of them that this detail was very confidential for now. They both assured him they would not tell anyone. Carlos expressed excitement just hearing that it was found near an island.

As if launched on a wave, Carlos began to open up. "I suspected as much. I am very interested in this, Father, because of my great-great grandfather. He left a long story behind that has been shared with each generation since he died in 1866. When I was a kid, my father and his father told me stories about how we came to southern California. I don't know how much is true, but much of it seems to be. My great-great-grandfather was named Shuka. He may also have been known as Harik. Harik was the name used in great-grandfather's written story about the ancestral saga, but 'Harik' means 'his father' in Kashaya. So, I call him Shuka. He was a Kashaya Pomo Indian, from one of the tribes in what's now northern California. His family was enslaved by the Russians. They lived or were kept at Clearlake, near Fort Ross, until the Russians left in 1840. Then the family was held in servitude by two white men who took over the fort and the Indian families belonging to it." Carlos took a drink from his beer bottle, resting for a moment before continuing.

"When Marshall discovered gold and the fever took over around Sutter's mill, Shuka and others of his tribe were forced to work the gold prospects. What a time! Not that long ago, either. I have the whole tale and it is both tragic and fascinating. I've used it in lectures as a docent at the San Juan Capistrano Mission and have done some writing about it, too.

"Wouldn't it be something if your figurehead came from the same boat that brought him here?" he said, taking another long swallow of his Dos Equis. "Shuka had a lot of gold when he found the ship, the one they used to escape. No telling how much, but that's part of the story I was told." He pulled out a pouch of tobacco and a packet of cigarette papers.

"Mr. Diaz, the timing of meeting you today is not surprising to me, because many things in my life happen this way, but I am very interested in what you've told me. I'll explain more about that later. There is another person, a Dr. Rowan, who will be very interested in your story, too. By the way, the management discourages smoking in the Long Beach Yacht Club. It's a new thing for us. Feel free to step out onto the balcony over there any time you need to smoke, though. You can take your beer with you," Jon said.

Clyde Maxon had been quiet, listening to Diaz - leaning forward, showing interest, not interrupting, which was a difficult thing for him. Mr. Diaz fingered his papers and pouch, deftly rolling a cigarette. He excused himself to have a smoke. The instant he got beyond hearing, Clyde turned to Jon. He wanted acknowledgment for bringing Carlos Diaz to meet him. Being honestly appreciative, Jon thanked him. Their having met at The Omelette House was a gift. This whole sequence fit into many times in his life that seemed to be coincidental events. But, he had learned that there are no accidents and coincidences are more co-incidences. Two things became clear for Jon. First, Mr. Diaz would be interested in whatever might be found in the water near San

Clemente. Second, Jon did not quite yet trust him, nor others, and would keep playing his cards close to his vest for now. Later when they discussed it, Sky Rowan agreed with him about this. She expressed relief that Jon had not disclosed the San Clemente Island location, but admitted they would have found out which one soon enough. Currently there was too much unknown and still up in the air. Mostly, the matter with the Coast Guard wasn't yet completely put to rest. He knew they would be in touch with him soon to request more information.

Carlos Diaz came back to the table. He was a big man, with a handsome, almost square face, punctuated by large, dark eyes. He wore cowboy boots and denim jeans and a red tartan Pendleton shirt. He appeared to be in his fifties. He tied his salt and pepper hair back in a long braid. In the center of his chest a single long white tooth hung on a leather thong from around his neck. Jon could see the Native American heritage in his rugged features. The more he talked, the more Jon learned. He was exceptionally well educated, having a Master's in business, with a strong background in history.

Clyde and Carlos said they would need to be leaving soon, but perhaps just one more drink. Jon ordered a round for them and they finished the conversation with observations about the football game on the bar television, the history of the marina and the yacht club. Clyde and Carlos talked about this once being marshland. Clyde ended the conversation by telling a couple of stories about racing on Brophe's sloop. Then, he said, "Wouldn't that be something if we found a lot of gold? How about that! This is getting even more interesting."

"Don't count on anything being true, Clyde. Remember this is all story, so far. We don't really know anything. And, besides, you promised to keep this stuff between the three of us. Keep that promise, Clyde," Jon said, without the hint of a smile.

Then, at the last minute, Jon suggested that Carlos Diaz, Sky Rowan, and he to get together soon. They had a good deal to discuss. He affirmed Dr. Rowan would want to learn as much as possible about his great-great grandfather, Shuka. The subject of possible sunken treasure did not come up. But, from what Carlos Diaz revealed, along with the information given by Wilfred Cramer's scroll, there could easily be gold in a sunken hull, if and when they could find anything at all.

Clyde looked dejected. He said, "I guess I'm not included. Looks like I'm out of the picture."

"Clyde, your bringing Carlos into this is a real gift. I owe you a lunch soon, but I think there are some difficult and sensitive things the three of us, Sky, Carlos, and I, need to talk over in order to figure out what to do next. I hope you understand," Jon said.

"No problem. I've got work to do anyhow. But, if and when you can, fill me in on what's happening. This is more interesting than anything I've got going," Clyde said, extending his hand for a goodbye shake.

They parted in the parking lot about 4:30. Jon walked to the boat to call Sky. It was Sunday afternoon. Jon figured she would be either at her home or the workshop.

Chapter Eighteen

Someone had been on the boat while he'd been gone, the boom tent left unzipped. He peeked inside. He always zipped up the boom tent, securing the cockpit. To his surprise and pleasure, there sat Sky, reading, smiling up at him.

"I hope you don't mind."

"I'm so glad you're here. I'm glad you felt you could come and enjoy the boat. These afternoons are so peaceful. I'd planned on calling you just as soon as I got here. I knew you would be excited along with me. I've had a fascinating meeting with a man whose great-great grandfather was aboard the *Madonna*. I'm sure of it, Sky," he said, hardly taking a breath.

Sky leaned back on the cockpit cushion, looking very attentive. Her hair flowed over her shoulders. Even though she never wore makeup, her face glowed in the half-light of the late afternoon. She wore gray slacks and a lavender turtle-neck sweater. Her eyes stayed intently with his. He leaned over and kissed her, very lightly, on the lips.

"I liked that very much," she said, smiling. "Perhaps we could do that again soon." She pulled just a little on his shirt sleeve for emphasis. "I've had such a nice time sitting here, reading, meditating, and feeling envious you have this for your home."

"Mi casa es su casa!"

"Gracias."

After Jon told her more about Carlos, they talked about going to dinner and how to decide what to do next about the figurehead and searching for the *Madonna*. They felt confident about finding the sunken vessel and almost certain that they knew just where to look. Perhaps it might be simple. After all, the figurehead could not have been far from the shipwreck itself. They speculated the vessel had to be close by, in the mud adjacent to the figurehead.

But, it wasn't quite that simple. It would be a few weeks before they could really know what truly had happened to the *Madonna*. How much of the ship had burned before sinking? What could be left? The information from Carlos Diaz would become very valuable.

Jon had no time to pursue matters about the *Madonna* for the next three days. Neither did Sky. They were frustrated being delayed. She had a full calendar of classes and faculty meetings. He had three full days of clients, including several emergencies and the hospitalization of a suicidal client. Of course, days go by fast, especially when one is responding to the needs of others. Being too busy, Jon had to cancel the luncheon he so wanted with the couple from church.

Such is life, he sighed.

By Thursday evening Sky and Jon managed to arrange a meeting with Mr. Diaz.

They made a date with him for an 8:00 Saturday breakfast at The Omelette House. He felt relieved learning that Maxon could not join them. It seemed a relief to Carlos, too. He specifically suggested to Jon they should just keep this between the three of them, knowing Dr. Rowan would be coming to the breakfast. He was enthusiastic about moving ahead on this adventure, as though he had opened up a gold mine of possibilities.

Excited, the three of them arrived early for that meeting. They greeted one another and Jon introduced Sky. Carlos, having only sketchy information, began right away with questions about what they knew and were willing to share. Quickly, they turned the subject back to Carlos, asking what he might know about a ship that sank years ago, perhaps around 1849, off a southern California island. They kept things vague on purpose. Carlos pulled on his eyebrow and had other nervous mannerisms Jon hadn't seen at the yacht club. He had dressed up, too, sporting a white shirt, open at the collar, and slacks instead of the jeans he had worn when Jon first met him. Sky, too, had spruced up. She wore a dark brown skirt and light blue soft sweater, an unusual and striking combination. Jon could not recall having seen her in anything so feminine. She looked stunning, with a small, bright blue and brown silk scarf tied around her neck and her hair up in a well-done bun.

Mr. Diaz became reflective. He said, "Do you mind if I get some pages of a story? It will interest both of you." He opened a brown leather briefcase while ordering a southwest omelette, hash browns, and toast. Sky ordered a short stack of blueberry pancakes with apple sauce and tea. Jon had his usual, the boring oatmeal and a side of crisp bacon. In a struggle to cut down on caffeine, he ordered decaffeinated coffee.

Julia was working this morning, which made the atmosphere more pleasant for Jon. They always enjoyed one another, or, at least, she made serving him seem enjoyable. Sky watched as Julia and Jon traded greetings and Julia affirmed that everything was going well. Seeing a question in Sky's eyes, Jon said to her, "I'll tell you a bit about Julia later. She has an interesting history." Then he introduced Mr. Diaz and Dr. Sky Rowan to Julia, while she brought the tea and coffees. Catching bits of their conversation, she realized they were talking about the figurehead article that had been in the paper.

Once they felt more comfortable with one another, Mr. Diaz began to tell the story of his great-great grandfather, Shuka, and how he had come to southern California. Sky took notes. From the introduction they had at the yacht club, Jon had heard some of the story before, however, it was all fresh for Sky.

He told them his great-great grandfather had told his children about coming to southern California on a square-rigger. Carlos's great-grandfather had written the story in great detail. It had been preserved and copied since the late1800s. Shuka and twenty-six Indians, most of them from his tribe, the Kashaya Pomo tribe, had escaped brutality and slavery under a Jesús Vallejo, who worked for two cruel men, Stone and Kelsey.

These two men had taken over Fort Ross, which they called *Rossiya*, when the Russians left and abandoned the settlement to the Mexicans in 1839 or so. The Russians had captured and held hostage hundreds of Indians, using them as slave labor, to work and for their sexual gratification or entertainment. They committed atrocious acts upon the Kashaya Pomos and other tribes in northern California and Northwest Territory.

The climax of this slavery of the Pomo Indians came in 1851 or 1852, when the American Army decimated hundreds of them in several tribal communities, mostly in California's Clearlake region. His great-great grandfather revealed having seen his sisters being raped several times.

Shuka's father had been beaten to death by a Russian in 1837, when Shuka was 12. They made his mother a housemaid and sex slave. Shuka didn't see her much at all after 14 years of age. His mother had three babies by one of the Russians and one baby by Kelsey, later on. Two of the babies died, but the one baby from Kelsey lived.

Mr. Diaz paused, taking some bites and sipping his coffee. His hands shook and his voice quavered as he continued with this tale. He apologized for being upset and told how he could never tell this story without getting angry and depressed. He had written about aspects of it, which were published in various historical articles. Also, he had kept a personal journal with many of the details, having researched the history through reliable sources. He assured them everything Shuka had passed on seemed to be true. He apologized to Sky for the graphic ugliness in the story.

He pulled nervously on his salt and pepper eyebrow and looked out the front window of The Omelette House for a few seconds, regaining his composure. Sky and Jon were completely absorbed in the story. It seemed the three of them had created an immediate bond. This was different for Jon than doing therapy. He could not remain objective. He was personally involved, somehow feeling they truly shared this history with one another. Carlos took a few more bites of his omelette, sipped his coffee, then he continued the tale.

Shuka remained afraid his whole life, because he and two of the other Indians with him had killed Jesús Vallejo. Vallejo had beaten an Indian boy for stealing some of the gold he was forced to mine at Woodrow Creek, in 1848. Vallejo whipped the Indian so severely, the boy died. Shuka and the others decided this was too much for them to bear. That night, after the boy's death, they broke into Vallejo's house, killed him, and took as much gold as they could carry on four mules - ingots, coins, nuggets, and bagged dust.

They burned Vallejo's house, hoping to distract anyone around from noticing their escape. They headed westerly from Sutter's Mill, not knowing where they were going. The small band walked and hid for nearly a week, fearing the whole time that they were being pursued. Shuka had explained that four of the fleeing Indians became separated from their tribesmen. Those four were shot by two miners and a vigilante who worked for John Marshall's outfit. Shuka saw them get shot. He watched from a hiding place as they were also knifed by the shooters.

When Shuka and the other Indians with him got to Yerba Buena, they found lots of ships abandoned in the bay. Carlos explained that about 1847, the name for the area, Yerba Buena - a tribute to the area's lush, green foliage - began to give way to the new name, after St. Francis of Assisi, San Francisco. The crews had abandoned their ships and gone to the gold fields to strike it rich. Shuka told his children how everyone was crazy with gold fever. Not only the able-bodied seaman, but also owners of ships, even captains and officers, deserted their ships to go to the gold fields in 1848 and 1849. Mr. Diaz confirmed that at one time in the bay around Yerba Buena, there were countless abandoned ships tied up one to another. Some were anchored, others, that had not been properly moored, drifted into shallow water of the bay, and careened aground at low tide. He told how there were ships tangled up in one another's rigging, when the winds of the bay had caused them to collide. Shuka discovered some men aboard one of the ships, one tied near a dock alongside others. He paid them a portion of the gold they had stolen from Vallejo to help them escape. They had more gold than they could weigh. Four heavily burdened mules labored to carry their treasure during the week-long journey from Sacramento to Yerba Buena bay.

Diaz thought that Shuka led the group. The story goes that no one knew how to sail the ship, except the four or five crew members on board and several others who signed on, figuring they would be paid later in gold. The captain and first mate had abandoned the ship. But, one of the men on board, a man named Brooks, knew navigation. Between the others, they knew enough to sail the ship and could teach the Indians to crew - climbing aloft, unfurling sails, learning to tack and gybe as needed. Rowing dories with tow lines tied to the bow of the big ship, the Indians slowly pulled the big square-rigger in the dark to the entrance of the bay. They rowed most of the night pulling the ship to sea. Once beyond the entrance of the bay they found enough wind to sail south.

Shuka told his children that the Indians didn't know anything about sailing and at first they could not eat the food. They had been sick during the whole trip and one of the Indians died. The ship's crew members helped. They figured they would get their gold when they got the Indians safely to Mexico. Shuka had two Indians guard the gold. They had weapons and knew how to use them.

A couple of days into the trip south, having gone by coastal islands, they spied an American ship, a frigate, chasing them. They realized they would be no match for the Americans. They also knew, if captured, they would be killed or worse.

Mr. Diaz added, "A Commodore, John Sloat, had been sent to Monterey about that time to police and control the Pacific Coast. He had armed ships under his command with trained gunnery sailors and lots of cannons. The increased transport of gold from the west coast south to Cape Horn and up the Atlantic coast, required much more protection of the ships. West coast ships doing commerce via the Panama Railroad's harbor railhead needed security, too." Clearly, Carlos Diaz had done his homework.

The end of the story became more exciting. It was indeed a hero's journey. Sky and Jon were transfixed and their breakfast sat ignored after eating about half of it. Mr. Diaz filled in his own details here and there, clarifying certain vague aspects of the story that had been handed down through four generations.

He said, "Shuka and the crew on board the ship could not sail well enough to outrun the American ship. For three or four days, the American ship gained on them. They had trouble trying to tack around an island, maybe Catalina, but I think more likely San Clemente. They hit rocks and the ship began to sink. In order to escape, they set the ship on fire and rowed in the darkness to the north. They knew land was not too far off in that direction. The desperados hoped they could make it there to escape the pursuing Americans. The ship burned easily. When the fire reached the gunpowder and other explosives in the hold, it exploded. They were too far away in the darkness to see what happened to the ship, but after it exploded, the fire disappeared. By the time darkness fell, the story goes, the American frigate was quite near.

"They rowed all night and day, taking turns, Indians and the crew, in three long boats, probably the same dories they'd used to pull their ship to the open sea. When daylight came, they could still see the island astern. On the horizon lay the American frigate; no sails could be seen, just the masts. They were less afraid, thinking the frigate's crew hadn't seen them escape; she wasn't coming after them. Now the mainland became visible. This gave them more hope and they rowed hard toward landfall.

"They got to San Juan beach in the darkness the next night. They all separated, running and hiding for several days. Shuka told how he never saw his tribesmen again, except for four of them. He saw the ship's carpenter some months later. Shuka found a way to survive in San Juan. He worked for a man named Villaseñor and another man named Montgomery. At times, he felt safe hiding among others at the local Mission.

"He told his children he had a good life from the time he got to San Juan, but he never got over his fear that he would be caught by the Americans. He changed his name to Salvador Diaz. He had a friend by that name in Bodega Bay when he was a boy.

"He married a white woman in 1853. They had seven children. My great-grandfather, José Diaz, was one of his seven children. Neither the ship nor the gold were ever found. That's why, when I read the story about your discovery of the figurehead, it occurred to me that you might know where this ship sank, whatever might be left of her. I did some research and know she was either the *Madonna* or the *Apostle*. Both of those ships were on this coast at that time. Both were lost in 1849, according to the records from the Monterey Authority. The same company owned the two ships, but I don't know the name of that company," Carlos said. He finished, looking intently at them. Sky and Jon remained silent, still thoroughly engrossed in this tale.

He leaned back, visibly worn out. After a long sigh, he said, "I think I need a smoke, if you two don't mind." He asked to be excused for a few minutes. "I need some air." He stood up, towering over them.

They assured him they would be waiting. They needed time to soak up his story. Jon thanked him for what he had shared and for the trust he showed in telling them about his great-great grandfather. Carlos walked slowly away for his smoke. His shoulders were a bit hunched. At that moment he seemed tender and vulnerable.

Sky and Jon watched him walk through the door; his big frame filled the doorway. He leaned against a palm tree on the sidewalk. He pulled out a bag of tobacco and rolled his cigarette. He did it all with three fingers of one hand, pulling the bag closed, drew the string tight with his teeth, and tucked the bag back in his pocket in a single, continuous motion. Their table near the window provided this theater. Both of them kept quiet as they watched Carlos and his handmade cigarette, while the story deepened inside them.

"He is a very interesting man," Sky said. "I trust him and think we ought to include him in what we're doing. What do you think, Jon? Do you see any reason not to include him?"

"I just like him. There is something so authentic about him, so unpretentious. Yes, I think he could add not only some energy to our research, he also might help us attract the people we're going to need to find this sunken vessel."

They discussed several options of what to do next. They came to the decision to arrange a dive soon, to see what they could find. Jon knew three divers, including Frank Martinez, his marina patrolman friend, who was a veteran diver. Frank could organize this dive and gather all the necessary credentials and insurance. He also had access to a dive boat he used in his side business. Jon got enthusiastic having a plan gel so quickly. Sky, too, became excited about this next step. She felt unsure about how easy it would be for her to be on a boat again so soon after her trauma. But, she assured

Jon she could adjust. Finding the ship, if they could find her, would be worth everything. Sky would arrange for a few days off from teaching and wondered if Jon could so soon take a few days off from the practice. He had some complications in the next two weeks: one sermon next week and then two weeks of seeing clients. After that he could take at least three days off. It would take at least two weeks to arrange the details for their expedition.

He could chart the area, gather data that would assist in locating the sunken vessel. He had to figure the tides for the dive week and track the weather forecasts. Even into December was usually a good time to be on the ocean near southern California's Channel Islands, however the weather still must be monitored. They needed no extra hazards. No use wasting a trip with three or four divers, the cost of the dive boat, and all of them taking their own good time to do this. Going to the eastern end of San Clemente Island from Alamitos Bay would take, probably, four to six hours. He needed to allow for added time for unusual swells, winds, or surprises. If they left the marina by 2:00 AM, they should be at the dive site by 8:00 or earlier. That would give them enough daylight time for, perhaps, two days of exploring.

The water ranged in depth from thirty to about 400 feet. Perhaps they would be lucky enough not to have to dive too deeply. If the vessel had hit the rocks off China Point, which makes sense from the story they had heard, it could lie in depths of about forty to 300 or so feet of water. Judging from the location of the figurehead, Jon hoped the shipwreck was in the shallower water. That would help them a lot.

Mr. Diaz came back to the table. He sat down, heavily, with a sigh as he pinched off the stub of his cigarette with his bare fingers. He looked relaxed and expectant. Jon responded to his expectancy. "Mr. Diaz, Dr. Rowan and I are very appreciative of your sharing this story with us this morning. We want you to help us. We want you to be an active partner in our finding this sunken vessel. Of course, this is a complicated adventure. Your history with this ship will be very useful, if you're willing to come in with us on this expedition. Are you?"

Without hesitation, he affirmed his interest and offered to do anything he could to help find the ship. He clinked his coffee cup against both of theirs, answering with a broad smile. Then he reached over with his hand, even larger than Jon's, and they shook as if making a deal. The three of them were on the brink of a new project. Of course, it might be dangerous, but certainly exciting and filled with mystery.

Sky assured them she had some budgeted money for this kind of exploration, but she would have to write a proposal. She could do that this weekend. She added her requests had never been denied in her sixteen years as an archeologist at Cal State Long Beach. She was quite certain there would be sufficient funds.

"Also," she added, "I think it is best we only go for the vessel because of its attraction as a relic. No mention of any secondary gain, like possible buried treasure, should be made in this proposal. Do you both agree to that?" They agreed.

Mr. Diaz said, "We have no knowledge of any gold there, of course. There is mention of it in the family myth passed down from Shuka or Harik, but we don't know anything more than that. Wouldn't it be something if we did find some gold in the vessel, assuming we can even find the vessel!" He leaned back in his chair, rested his head against the wall, and took a long drink from the last of his nearly cold coffee.

The hours sped by, with mundane tasks; cleaning the boat, doing paperwork in his office, and then the high point would be to visit Sky in her workshop on that Saturday afternoon. The evening ended with their going to dinner with Krystal. Krystal had shown up at the shop with a boyfriend driving her Datsun. Sky scolded her, because she was not supposed to let anyone other than herself drive her car. Jon watched the two of them, the boyfriend, Sean, standing beside him. For the first time, Jon saw a mother-daughter confrontation. They handled it well. Krystal quietly agreed she had made a mistake and she would not let anyone drive her car unless they bought an insurance policy for the trip - Krystal's way of making light of an embarrassing situation.

"Dr. Scott, I begged Krystal to let me drive her car. She didn't want me to, but gave in. I didn't mean to get her in trouble," Sean lamented.

"Well, Sean, I hope she doesn't give in to everything you beg for. Don't think you can have your way with her. She's a tough cookie."

Sean was shy and took Jon's teasing comment with a red-faced smile. He was tall and with spiked hair he seemed taller. He had an earring in his left ear and wore jeans low, but not as low as was the fashion back when Jon was a senior in high school.

Jon never truly went in for the fads and fashions in school. He thought himself to be above all that. He might have been seen as a 'geek' in those days, a word not then in use. Sean and Jon chatted about this and other light matters for a few minutes. Gradually, as they talked, Sean relaxed.

Sky and Krystal returned to where Sean and Jon sat on a bench, beside the figurehead. The blue plastic shroud cover protected Meri from dust and prying eyes. They discussed going to dinner together, but Sean said he had a previous commitment, which surprised Krystal. She offered to drive him home and he accepted the offer. Before parting, Sky and Krystal discussed meeting to drive to dinner. Krystal and Sean purred off in the blue Datsun.

Jon, Sky, and Krystal met at an Italian Restaurant in downtown Long Beach. It was a popular place with writing on the walls, sawdust on the floor, and good, inexpensive food. The menu listed pizzas, thick and thin crusts, a variety of pastas, antipastos, lasagna, and a superb *cioppino*. The three of them enjoyed the food and conversation. The level of discussion they shared impressed Jon. He had not been around teenagers socially for a long time. He noticed the maturity and awareness Krystal possessed on one subject after another. Sky and he had a couple of glasses of the Chianti poured from a whicker-wrapped bottle and Krystal had a Coke. With each bite of pizza, Sky and Krystal, with closed eyes, moaned together in feigned ecstasy, having fun, savoring each mouthful. They got silly. Mother and daughter became more verbal, indulging their quick wits as the meal progressed.

The time came to pay the check and depart. Before getting up, Sky mentioned having had breakfast with Carlos Diaz. She told Krystal about his great-great-grand-father and the likelihood that he had been on the figurehead's ship. Krystal grew very excited. Quickly, she made sure she would be included in the dive-boat trip. Sky protested in vain for a few rounds, but Krystal won, claiming she would learn more in an adventure like this than she would in a whole semester of high school. Sky could not refute that. They left the restaurant in good spirits, the two of them leaving in Sky's T-Bird. Jon drove slowly to the marina in his pickup.

Suddenly, he was surprised by how intensely he missed Miriam. Moments ago with Sky Miriam's image popped into his mind, confusing him. He thought as he began to feel closer to Sky, perhaps he was awakening repressed love and grief for Miriam. Then his thoughts came back into the present. Jon realized, as he drove away, he had hoped for something more with Sky that evening, especially being a Saturday night. His feelings roiled. He was not aware how much he would miss her after such a sudden and casual departure.

Of course. We've spent the entire day together. We've had such a good time. Why wouldn't I miss her? That's a good sign to me - a very good sign.

Chapter Nineteen

Rain started about three in the morning, coming down hard. Jon felt he'd stepped into a cold shower as he emerged from the boat on Sunday morning. The snug, warm boat, with the pelting rain on the deck above made for very deep, sound sleep. Lightning and thunder started by daybreak, with gusty winds out of the southeast. Boats rocked, halyards slapped and clanked against their aluminum masts.

When he walked to the head in the rain and wind, he awakened rapidly. The low tide made for a steep gangway up to the sidewalk. Wind-driven rain raked him at an angle. He'd left his raincoat in the pickup, just a few parking spaces from the head. He retrieved it. The walk back to the boat would be much more pleasant. By the time he reached the shower, he was already soaked and cold.

Preparing for his shower, he let the water heat up before stepping into it. Frank Martinez, his Harbor Patrol friend, entered the tiled shower room.

"Jon, fancy meeting you here! I didn't recognize you with your clothes off," he said.

"Frank, you're just the man I want to see, but I didn't expect to see you in here this morning. I undressed for my shower, Frank, not for you. Are you going to be on duty this morning for a while?"

"I'm on until 4:00 PM today. I'll be watching this basin and parking lot for an hour or so. I'm supposed to meet my lieutenant at the marina office at 9:00 this morning."

"I'll make quick work of my shower, Frank. I'll come find you in the parking lot, if I don't drown looking for you."

"It's been raining steady ever since I came on duty. Really a gully washer at times. Had some hail earlier. I'll be in the patrol car right next to the head, waiting. Want some coffee?"

"You've pulled this coffee thing on me before, Frank. That coffee thermos of yours hasn't been washed in years. Your coffee would keep a narcoleptic alert for a month. But, we could go to the yacht club. I'll get us some coffee there, if you want," Jon offered.

"Here I make a generous offer and you complain. I was even going to buy the coffee. I'll be right outside, Jon. I'm curious about what you want. See you in a few minutes."

Jon took a three-minute shower, did his partial shave, trimmed his reddish goatee and mustache, and dried off. He put on enough clothes to be sociable, covered with the raincoat, then stepped quickly from the head facility just a few paces right into the patrol car. Frank had backed into the parking space, thoughtfully putting the passenger door close to the sidewalk for Jon. He started the Ford Crown Victoria and slowly drove through the parking lot to the yacht club.

Once inside, they poured their coffees from the pot upstairs in the bar. Jon invited Frank to sit down just for a few minutes. Frank refused a muffin, patting his slightly bulging stomach. He was in his forties, in good condition, but he had to work at it. So did Jon.

Jon had a proposition he knew would interest Frank. He stayed glued to what Jon outlined, Frank's feet shuffling from time to time, as he struggled to save his questions for the end. After Jon told him some of the story, he reminded him of the figurehead and all of the problems he had coming back from his vacation a couple of weeks ago. Then Jon opened the proposition. "How would you like to be hired for a dive, Frank? I'm thinking soon, perhaps, when you can take two or three days off. We're going to be looking for a sunken ship, an old square-rigger, a ship that sank in 1849 or 1850."

"Sounds like just our meat, Jon. Where is it?"

"I really don't know, except for the vicinity. If I tell you, Frank, you've got to keep this confidential. There are only four people in on this adventure, five now, if you know."

"No problem with that. Why would I destroy our chances of being first on a scene by blabbing it? Give me some credit, Jon." He leaned back and sipped his coffee.

Jon thought his asking for confidentiality on this subject might have hurt Frank's feelings, but Frank assured him quickly, "I keep things confidential all the time. Being on patrol in a marina like this, I know stuff no one would suspect I know and I don't gossip or tell anyone anything. That would only make my job harder. I'd lose what friends I have around here. But, I understand your caution, especially if this is a valuable discovery you're going after. If you don't want me to know where it is yet, that's okay." He paused, giving Jon time to think about this. "You know, Jon, I'd get my butt in a sling for not reporting where you got this figurehead. I've really stuck my neck out for you, but, so far no one has asked me any questions and I haven't had to tell the truth, what little of that I know. You owe me, Jon. Keeping my mouth shut is good for at least a breakfast."

"Are you suggesting I bribe an officer of the law?" Jon asked with a smirk. "It's off the east end of San Clemente Island. I have no idea how deep the wreck is. It may be too deep to dive to, but I hope not. My guess is the depth is less then 200 feet, judging from the chart for that area. It could be deeper, but it isn't likely, especially if it is at all close to where the figurehead was buried. She was in about thirty-five feet of water," Jon said.

"She? What do you mean, she? Oh, I get it, the figurehead is a woman." Frank smiled and took a drink of the good coffee. "Diving to find this could be a piece of cake. Just a thought, Jon, am I doing this for peanuts or is there some money in it?"

"We certainly can pay your bill on this, Frank. Besides your expert help, I think you would want your familiar crew, the other two or three divers you usually have. Plus, we will pay you for the cost of the dive-boat." He said all this as he wondered if they could actually afford this adventure.

"I'll get out my charts. I know that area somewhat. It's a great place to dive, if it is where I'm thinking it is. I'd be surprised if there's something there that hasn't already been found, though. There is a small bay at the southeast end of San Clemente about a half mile wide, if even that, from my recollection. If it's in that area, it certainly must be known."

"I think it is just outside, a bit southeast of the anchoring area, having struck rocks rounding China Point, or, at least, that's what Sky and I think happened. There might not be much left of the ship. It burned and exploded before it sank, as far as we know. And, while you're down there, you can bring back enough lobster for all of us to have a great dinner."

"I've got to admit, this grabs me. The sooner the better! When can we do the dive?" Frank asked, rubbing his big hands together. A radio call interrupted them. Pulling his radio from its leather holster he answered, "Martinez." Watching Jon and grinning as he took the message, he responded, "Ten four." Frank was for sure excited about doing this dive.

"I've got to get going, but count me in. I'll work up an estimate of what it will take and talk to one or two of my dive-boat friends. Let's talk tomorrow or Tuesday, if that's okay with you. I'll look at the schedule and see when I can take time off." He stood up and adjusted his belt with all the enforcement devices hanging on it; radio, handcuffs, the night stick/flashlight combination, and a formidable 9mm. weapon. "Thanks for the coffee."

With his good looks, a touch of gray hair at the temples, and the uniform, he made a very impressive presentation. He rarely had a problem with anyone, because of his size and bearing. As he turned to leave, they shook hands. With a big smile, he gave Jon a thumbs up before starting down the stairs to the lobby of the club.

Frank and Jon became friends through the years that Jon had lived on his boat in the marina. Sometimes, usually in the evening or late at night, when Frank walked the gangways on patrol, they sat and talked or they walked the beat together, having long conversations. With pride, he told Jon about his family, his wife, Lupe, and his four kids. His father had been a mayor in Mexico and had been killed by the Mexican Mafia when Frank was nine years old. He and his five brothers and sisters made it to the US. His mother came later.

He could tell fascinating stories. He knew that he had a captive audience in Jon, since one of Jon's interests was people's stories. Their friendship added to their forthcoming exploration to find the *Madonna*. But, for now, Jon had to leave for church or he'd be late.

Jon followed on Frank's heels, then waved goodbye to him as he drove from the parking lot. Rain had started in the early morning and was coming down hard now. He hurried to the boat to change into his clericals for the 11:00 A.M. service.

It's my morning to assist at the Eucharist and being late isn't an option. I want to call Sky, but I guess there's not enough time. I'll call her this afternoon.

Suddenly, she consumed his thoughts. He felt glad to have had this conversation with Frank, but he did not like to hurry, especially on Sunday mornings. And, as usual, he made it to St. Paul's Episcopal Church on time, with ten minutes to spare for vesting.

Billowy clouds added drama to the Sunday afternoon sky. The rain had cleansed everything: boats gleamed in the sun. Often a cumulus cloud eclipsed the sun, the light changing from bright to shade added to Jon's variety of moods. He felt very nourished after experiencing an inspiriting Eucharist and sermon. As he anticipated looking for the *Madonna* Jon became excited. He tried to imagine the adventure ahead and that kept his thoughts swirling.

I must talk to Sky and tell her about Frank.

Sky had told Jon there were financial resources for just this sort of exploration, because she had recently received a grant renewal for oceanographic archeology in southern California waters. She had earned a reputation delivering two papers on artifacts found from the Civil War at the

Isthmus at Catalina Island. This gained her recognition for her work there. She was pleased they renewed her grant.

They could not know yet what this exploratory dive-boat trip would cost, but Sky assured him there would be adequate money, unless they ran into some major problems. There needed to be enough for the trip's insurance, the divers and passengers, and much of this must be paid up front.

Chapter Twenty

He changed his clothes, put on khaki pants, his Topsider boat shoes, and a long-sleeved, dark-blue shirt. The phone rang just as he fastened his belt. "Hello," he answered.

"Is this Jon?" the woman's voice asked.

"Yes, this is Jon."

"Jon, this is Krystal. Is mother with you?" she asked without waiting for him to respond. "I haven't seen her since she left the house early this morning. I expected her back for brunch at ten. We had plans for brunch. She knew you were going to church, and told me she would be free until early afternoon. Then she planned on seeing you," Krystal said. Her voice was choked with emotion..

"Krystal, you sound upset. I know it isn't like Sky to stand you up. Could she have gotten involved in something at her shop?"

"I've called the workshop a dozen times, but there's no answer. I'm afraid to leave here, because this is where we were supposed to meet. If I leave and she calls, I'll miss her call. I don't know what to do."

"Okay, Krystal, now I'm worried, too. I'll go to the shop. I agree, you stay there in case she calls or comes home."

"I'll be here. If you learn anything at the shop, please call me right away," Krystal said, starting to cry.

"I'm sure she's okay, Krystal. Don't start imagining problems. We don't know anything, yet. I'll call you just as soon as I get there. You may have heard from her by then," he said.

Sky's Thunderbird sat in its parking place, with the driver's door unlocked and not fully closed. The unlocked gate was pulled so Schwartz could not get out. As he opened it, Schwartz came running, barking a half-hearted bark and wagging her tail with her entire body. He scanned the area as he petted her and then went to the workshop. He slid the door open enough to see inside. He heard a muffled sound. Cautiously, he entered the workshop and listened. The muffled sound came again, from the bathroom, in the far corner of the workshop. Opening the door, there sat Sky, scrunched up on the toilet, wrists bound to her ankles with duct tape and duct tape over her mouth. He reeled backward at the sight of her. Her clothes were torn and she had scratches on her face. There were several small cuts on her throat. Her frightened eyes riveted on him.

Easing the tape off her face made her scream with the pain. Not knowing what else to say in his helplessness, he asked, "What happened?"

"Oh God, I've been through a nightmare!" She burst into tears, shaking all over as he peeled the duct tape off her wrists and ankles, being as careful as possible to minimize the pain of the tape pulling her skin. As best he could, he wrapped his arms around her and lifted her off the toilet, carrying her to the old couch in the workshop.

"Sky, whatever has happened, you've been through something unthinkable. Please. Tell me everything. I must call Krystal, though. She's worried sick not knowing where you are," he said, smoothing her hair back and kissing her on the forehead. "Also, I need to call the police. I want to hold you and let you sob or scream or something, but I must at least call Krystal."

"How can you call Krystal? Do you know where she is?"

"She's at home, Sky, worried sick about you."

"Yes, you've got to call Krystal, if you know where she is. They said they had her," she said, taking deep, jerky breaths, with definite relief in her voice. "I'm afraid of your calling the police. What if those thugs get even with us for calling them? Besides, I don't want the police or anyone to know about the *Madonna* yet. If you must, please at least wait to call them until I can tell you what happened. There can't be any hurry now," she said. Then, grasping his hand firmly, she added, "I'm sorry. I didn't say anything about your wanting to hold me. I want you to hold me, but call Krystal. Can you do both at once?"

"Yes, I can do both. Krystal is safe. She's at home, scared to death not having heard from you."

Punching in the numbers, Krystal answered on the first ring. He told her where they were. He explained nothing, except to tell her Sky was okay and he would bring her home soon.

"What happened? I'm coming over there right now. Don't leave," she said.

"Krystal, If you're coming, bring some juice, perhaps a banana or some yogurt. We'll wait for you. Do come soon, though. And Krystal, be careful and don't talk to anyone."

Sky was able to talk to her, which seemed to soothe her. He hung up the phone.

"I've been terrified. They told me they had her. They demanded I keep my mouth shut and tell them where to find the boat and if I didn't do what they told me, they'd kill Krystal. I'm so relieved we've talked to her," she said, trembling. "I'm so glad you're here. I know the police need to be called, too, but I want you to know first what happened. We've got to agree about what they wanted and took. The cops are going to want to know all that. It involves our project. It might get even more ugly than what happened this morning. These men mean business. They took all my papers, Jon, all my research. They missed the scroll, thank God! I don't know how they missed it, but they didn't take it. One of them kept telling me they had Krystal, so I'd be stupid not to do what they wanted. I now know that was a lie. What a relief!" she said, pausing to sip from a paper cup of water.

Jon dabbed her scratches with hydrogen peroxide as she talked. Sitting beside her, he could feel her trembling and her uneven breathing made talking difficult.

"Especially with threats like that, the police need to be in on this right away. I'm going to call them. As soon as they've come, we've got to get you home. But, you're right. We need to have our stories straight for them. Let's just tell them they took all your research on several projects, including the stuff about the figurehead. That isn't a lie," he said.

"That's good enough. I'll just tell them exactly that. But, what about their coming back and getting revenge on us for calling the police? Do you think they'll do that?"

"We need to report their threats to the police and insist they take it seriously. I'll be alert to whatever they might do. I know you're afraid. You have reason to be. But, we have to have the police in on this. But, remember when talking to

162

the police, don't offer anything that they don't ask about. The less they know about our research, the better," Jon insisted.

Jon took a warm, damp washcloth and gently wiped her face, neck, arms, and hands. She liked that, gently giving pleasureful moans and smiling at him. But, her smile changed to wincing when he added a little more of the peroxide.

"You need food and a good, warm bath. I'm just so glad you're alive, dear one. I've got to tell you. Yes, now's the time. I don't know what I would do if anything happened to you or Krystal. How quickly you've become a huge part of my life. I love you. I just love you. I don't know at all what that means for us, but I have to tell you. To think that this figurehead and what we've stumbled upon could bring harm to you or Krystal is horrible," he said.

Sky's eyes filled with tears and she wrapped her arms around his right arm, burrowing her head into his shoulder. Very quietly, she said, "As afraid of those words as I am, what you just said to me made my entire body warm and at this moment, nothing is wrong. I'm going to work on letting your words in. I do believe you, by the way. You don't know what that's like for me - just to believe you."

He called the Long Beach Police Department. The dispatcher answered right away, being a Sunday afternoon and probably a quiet time for the police. He gave the address of the workshop and described his red and black Chevrolet pickup, which was parked by the gate. He told the dispatcher that the situation is resolved, but a report must be made. He stressed that there was good reason to believe that the people involved were dangerous.

Krystal arrived before the police. She came running into the workshop, dropping to her knees next to her mother on the couch, hugging her carefully. The two of them cried together for a few moments. Schwartz sat on the couch, snuggled next to Sky, tail wagging and licking Krystal's face. Jon watched, wishing this moment were on film.

Krystal took the juice out of the brown bag, and he handed her a paper cup from the cooler. She poured the drink. Sky sat up, swallowed the nectar, and then held the cup out for a refill. Krystal looked at Jon a couple of times, anguish on her face.

"Jon, what about those scratches? Should they be washed out or something?"

"I've already used some hydrogen peroxide on them, Krystal. They look to be very surface, but we'll keep an eye on them. If they redden, we'll take her to emergency. I don't know what caused them," he said.

Sky told them she had fought with two of the men as they grabbed her when she got out of her car. "Before I could scream, a hand clamped hard over my mouth. It hurt," she said. She thought a car had followed her when she left the house at seven this morning, but couldn't be sure and, being preoccupied, she hadn't paid much attention. Sky saw the car again when she turned into the alley toward the workshop. She thought it was an old, blue Honda. It was close behind her, but she still had no thought of danger.

"When they grabbed me, one of them, a big, young man, who smelled sour, really smelly, put his hand over my mouth. I could barely breathe. He held a knife to my throat and forced me, grabbed my arm, bent my wrist painfully, it still hurts. He ordered me to open the gate to the workshop and then the door. I wanted to scream or fight, but the one holding the knife to my throat terrified me. I did everything they told me to do. I think he cut my neck at least some, or it felt like he did," she said. She paused, catching her breath.

"I was so scared!" At least, even though terrified, Sky got a good look at all three of them.

She paused and continued."They told me over and over they had Krystal and for me to do what they told me or Krystal would die. I obeyed. They wanted all the information about the sunken vessel. Especially they demanded I tell them where it was. They ordered me to forget about going after it. They told me it was all theirs. They said if I went after it, they'd finish the job on us.

"I gave them the stack of paperwork about the figurehead. They took the whole pile. Remember, Jon, the papers I brought to the restaurant? They took all those, plus others I hadn't even looked at yet. They kept demanding to know the location of the ship. Finally, knowing it was no use to hold back, I told them exactly where to find it. That's all they wanted. They finished with me and I heard their car leave, Schwartz barking and barking for some time afterward," she said, taking several deep breaths. "I don't think they have much that will help them, but they know more than I wanted anyone to know about this."

She took several more deep, jerky breaths and allowed Jon to hold her. Krystal and Schwartz snuggled next to her.

"I was terrified. They threw me on the floor. One of them said, 'Hold her down, Luís, I'm going to get some of this.' Another one stopped him. He said, 'We gotta get out of here!'" She paused, looking at Jon, her eyes filled with fright. "The one who said that grabbed my ankles and wrists and just wrapped and wrapped the roll of tape around and around. Someone taped my mouth shut with the same tape. I must have fainted. I don't remember their putting me in the bathroom where you found me. I remember scratching at someone before they could get my wrists taped down. I think I got one of them really good. He slapped me really hard and maybe that's when I blacked out."

"Sky, that's enough for now. You and Krystal stay put on the couch. While we're waiting, I'll make you some tea."

He put on water and turned the heat up on the hot plate. It occurred to him Sky couldn't know where the *Madonna* was, so how could she have told them its location? He wondered if she were thinking clearly. He had to check this out with her.

"How could you tell them how to find the sunken ship? You don't really know where it is."

"That's simple. I just told them it was at the northwest end of Catalina Island in 150 feet of water, between Ship Rock and the west end," she said, smiling.

"At least that gives them some place to think about. What's taking the cops so long? They should be here by now," Jon said.

A moment later, the police arrived. They drove past the gate down the alley. Jon saw them go by, so he ran out of the shop and hailed them. They backed up. "This is the place, officers!"

They parked and came through the gate, two of them. One was in plain clothes, a Detective Aubry, and the other, a patrolman, Officer Williams. In their business-like manner, very polite and professional, they took down the whole story, asking lots of questions about identities, description of the car the 'dirt bags' were driving, and they wondered if she could pick the men out in a line up. The detective looked around the workshop, uncovered the figurehead and asked about it. Detective Aubry was curious about everything there. He walked around the shop and the yard. He wanted to know exactly where the suspects had left their car. He noted the details she could supply. Sky gave them much more than most victims could have recalled. She mentioned the blue Honda, their descriptions; her skills of observation and lucidity were exceptional.

"One of them, the Mexican, they called Luís. The other two were Caucasians. I didn't hear any other names. One, the short one, kept spitting chewing tobacco. I'll never forget the smell of the one who muscled me around. He had me in a tight grip with his knife at my throat."

The time with the police took about an hour. Officer Williams wrote down everything he could on a small notebook, straining to keep up with Sky's report. They prepared to leave, having obtained more information than they could use.

Detective Aubry said, "We can't be certain what will come of all this information, but thank you for your clarity and help. One thing I will guarantee you is that we'll do whatever is necessary to find these goons. I'll personally keep you up to date, Dr. Rowan."

Some fresh oil drops remained where Sky thought their car had been, which might be analyzed and become evidence, but that wouldn't help much. Something had fallen from the pocket of one of them, the shortest one. She remembered seeing something fall from his left, front pocket when he took a jackknife from it. Officer Williams found a small piece of paper with writing on it, one of the numbers contained Sky's house address.

Detective Aubry said, "If he had that in his left, front pocket, he might be left-handed." Officer Williams put the piece of paper in a plastic envelope. The two of them said goodbye, left business cards and, again, Aubry assured Sky they would be in touch with her soon. It seemed Schwartz knew they were friendly, vigorously wagging, begging to be petted by both of them as they walked to the gate. Officer Williams took a few seconds to pet her. Aubry opened the passenger door of their cruiser and called back to them, "We'll be in touch very soon."

Sky and Jon talked about her fear of going home. Maybe she and Krystal would be okay, especially if the three men were greedily eager to get to their treasure hunt.

"I can't just let you go home, you and Krystal, after all you've been through. I'll go with you, Sky. I think you're safe enough, but you've got to be scared. After what both of you have been through, so much threat and rough stuff you've experienced, you've got to be scared."

"Jon, we'll be okay now. You've helped soothe us and it seems the cops are really paying attention. Maybe you could give us a call in a while, after I get home, just to be in touch? Okay?"

"I'll give you time to get home. Then I'll call. You can call me any time, too. Don't hesitate, Sky. Just call me and I'll be there."

They parted with a long, solid hug. Jon assured her again that he would phone her within the hour. Reluctantly, he let her go.

Chapter Twenty-One

The clear Monday morning had few signs of the Sunday storm. Jon swam an especially long time, nearly an hour, which felt very good. After he showered and tidied up the boat enough to tolerate his mess, and after a quick reassuring call to Sky, he walked to The Omelette House for breakfast. He greeted Julia. She reminded him he had forgotten her birthday. She had hoped for at least a Porsche. He apologized for forgetting. "If you're very nice to me, I'll get the Porsche for you next year, Julia," he promised, showing her his fingers were crossed.

"It won't be worth being nice all year. Forget It. I'll stay with my Nova. That way I don't have to be nice. I thought you were different than all the other guys," she said, warming his coffee.

"I am different, but maybe not different enough to be special."

"Remember the saying, 'Nice girls stay home; bad girls go everywhere?' Well, I haven't been anywhere in a couple of years." She pouted, faking deep disappointment.

Another customer drew her attention. She slid the newspaper in front of him, turning to attend to the man who had come in. It was just after seven-thirty, a little early for the beach crowd on a Monday morning. The surfers were the only ones up by five or so in this neighborhood. The new customer and Jon chatted about the weather, the price of gasoline, and he complained about having to drive to Los Angeles this morning. He asked Jon where he worked. Jon said, "Four blocks from home." Jon could see the envy on the other man's face. They finished the chat with comments on the newspaper headline story. Their breakfasts arrived and they began to read and eat quietly.

Julia busily handed Jon the bill with a friendly smile. He left the money on the table, telling her and the conversational customer goodbye, wishing them a good day. The day ahead occupied his thoughts. He needed to be in the office in less than an hour for his first appointment. He had to check the exchange for new messages and there were phone calls to be made. He felt refreshed and ready to jump into his therapeutic personage for the day. He had time to drive to the Union Oil station on Pacific Coast Highway and get fuel. Then, he would leave the pickup at the marina parking lot and walk back to his office for his first appointment. As usual, life is what happens while one makes plans. The event at the station changed his morning radically.

As he pulled into the station he saw a blue Honda, perhaps a 1979, in the island across from him. Having heard Sky talk about a car that might have followed her being a blue Honda, he noticed it immediately. He stayed in his pickup and studied the car. A man sat in the passenger seat. Another man tended the nozzle. The one outside looked to be a Mexican and the other, the one inside, was a Caucasian, but Jon could not see him well enough to be sure. The car had no front license plate. He started his pickup and drove around the station, coming into the island beside them. He took down the number from their back plate, and got a good look at the one finishing filling the tank. He got gas and went up to the station window to pay his bill with cash. The suspected man was only about ten feet away from Jon when he paid. Jon felt positive, intuitively, this was the car and these were two of the ones who had attacked Sky. Of course, he thought how wrong he might be, but he could not ignore his strong hunch.

He put his quarter in the pay phone at the side of the station and asked the operator for the Long Beach Police Department. The Honda pulled out and headed toward Seal Beach. He could do nothing more than leave a message for Officer Williams or Detective Aubry, which he did. In the message, he identified himself and gave them the license number of a car he thought might have been the one at Dr. Sky Rowan's workshop yesterday afternoon. He left his office phone number. He drove to the marina parking lot and parked in a space he considered his. Walking hurriedly to his office, he got there with only two minutes to spare. As he unlocked his door the phone began to ring.

"Yes, Detective Aubry, the Union Oil station on Second and Pacific Coast Highway. The license number was 4ELHO54. After they left, I looked at the driveway where they were parked and there were two fresh oil spots where they had been. When they left, they went toward Seal Beach on PCH. I wanted to follow them, but thought better of that, calling you instead. I know this may not mean anything, but I believe these were two of the jerks who attacked Dr. Rowan."

"Thank you, Dr. Scott. Can't be sure it's the same guys. Not sure what to do with this info, but, if you're right, it says they're still in the neighborhood. I'd watch yourself, too. If they knew about Dr. Rowan and her daughter, they must know something about you. One thing Officer Williams and I wondered about is how come they didn't come after you? Maybe they think a woman is an easier take? They knew your name from the newspaper article and you would be easier to target than Dr. Rowan, it seemed to us. Thanks for this, Dr. Scott. I want you to know this is not just being handled as a routine complaint. We'll be on it. It's priority. We agree they are dangerous. Be careful," he said.

They said goodbye and hung up. For a second, Jon sat at the phone and took inventory of the whole situation. No extra time remained before his first appointment. His first client sat impatiently in the waiting room. Because Jon was rarely late for any appointments, she began to wonder if she had the right time. He assured her she did and he invited her into the consultation room. From the third story picture window, part of the marina and the edge of the harbor could be seen. Sometimes Catalina Island was visible. He loved this office.

His client made tea from the hot water side of the cooler. She asked him if he wanted a cup. He said yes and thanked her for her thoughtfulness. Then their session began.

A few minutes into their time, she stopped herself, and asked him if he were okay. His attention had not been thoroughly with her and she knew it. That brought him back to focus and the rest of the session got intense and useful, thanks to her candor. They had been working for a couple of years. She knew him well, not in any of the details of his life, but she certainly knew whether or not they were connecting. The rest of the day's sessions went well, despite his concerns about the safety of Sky and Krystal, and some concerns about his own. By three in the afternoon some of his concerns were quieted by a call from Detective Aubry.

"We tracked that Honda to a Huntington Beach address, Dr. Scott. Also, an officer in San Pedro spotted the car in a parking lot near Ports O'Call. That's all we have except for a possible lead on one of the occupants of the car who propositioned a woman not too far from where the car was parked. She made a police report about the guy, because she told the officer she felt afraid of him. He was threatening and pushy. She indicated the man who had scared her had gotten out of that Honda. I'm going down there now. I'll be in touch, if I learn anything," he said.

"Detective Aubry, I appreciate your response and keeping me in the loop on this. I'll relay this information to Dr. Rowan as you make progress. Thank you." Jon hung up.

Two more sessions to go. When he called Sky, Krystal told him she was taking a nap. He didn't want to disturb her. Krystal took his quick report and he said he would call when he got through about seven that evening.

Chapter Twenty-Two

That evening, Sky and Jon talked on the phone for nearly half an hour. She confessed to being fearful still, but she was reassured somewhat by the way the police kept contact, their knowing the current location of the car, and the presumed close proximity of its owner. Near the end of the conversation, Sky became warmly and openly expressive. She told Jon how close she felt to him and how, when all this settled down, she hoped they could spend some quality time with one another.

She then gave him a gift: "Jon, there are moments when I feel I've known you all my life. Those moments on the couch in the workshop, when you held me and we were breathing together, as shaken as I was I felt I never wanted that moment to end. In a way it was the first time I've ever felt peaceful with a man."

"I don't want this conversation to end, either, but I have to, Sky. I should have gone to the head before I called you. What a beautiful gift you just gave me! Now here I'm telling you I've got to go to the bathroom. Not exactly a Shakespeare moment. I'll call you when I get to the boat. I'll be there about seven-thirty. Until then, Love?"

"Until then, Love," she echoed.

Purposely, Jon parked his pickup in a place far from his gangway. In his mind, these three desperados would eventually seek him out. He needed to be vigilant and change his routines. He could walk to work by different routes, park in unusual places, swim earlier in the morning, and, generally, alter his habits to make their finding him more difficult. The boat was vulnerable, especially during the day. His office was vulnerable, especially at night, but at least they locked the building after ten.

The only comfort I have is knowing that they want me alive. They can't find the sunken Madonna *without Sky and me.*

As he thought further about this, he realized a secondary comfort. Sky had given them the wrong location for the sunken vessel. But, there were lots of questions, too. The main one had to do with how they had learned about this wrecked ship and why were they so interested?

It was dark, except for the sodium vapor parking lot lights and the lights along the gangway. He took his time walking to the boat, looking over his shoulder for anyone unusual. Unzipping the boom tent and climbing aboard, he felt relief that everything seemed to be the way he had left it. Once below he called Sky.

Early Tuesday morning, he returned from his swim in the pre-dawn light. As he climbed up the *Daimon's* stern ladder, Frank Martinez greeted him. He stood on the dock, having waited for him to return from swimming.

"Morning, Jon. I saw you swimming around the point. You do a good Australian crawl. I for sure couldn't keep up with you," he said, but without his usual smile.

Grabbing a towel, Jon said, "Looks like something's on your mind, Frank. Glad to see you."

"I've got a question. There's a description of a wanted car and possible dangerous occupants from yesterday afternoon. When my lieutenant called the Long Beach cops about it, a Detective Aubry called me back and spilled your beans, telling us to keep an eye out for you. Why didn't you say something, Jon? This looks not only serious, but could be life-threatening. The other news has to do with one of our patrolmen who saw this same car yesterday morning, cruising around Basins Two and Three. I reported the car, but I didn't know then that it was a wanted vehicle. When he stopped the two men in it, they told him they were trying to find a friend who had a boat in the marina, but they gave him a false name," Frank said. He concluded by telling Jon they had left right after the officer stopped them. "It's the same car. He took down the plate. We didn't get the info until about 1700 last evening, but the car he saw and stopped had been in the marina around 0600, that morning."

What a lot of activity and too close for comfort. Can't help but be intrigued with how many sightings of this vehicle in just twenty-four hours.

Frank interrupted his thoughts with one more item of curious information.

"We also have a report of a stolen Grand Banks from the San Pedro marina. It was reported stolen last evening by the owner. Apparently, according to the detective working on this, it was close to where they parked the Honda, near Ports O'Call, over there by that marina. Could be nothing, but, then, it could be related," he said.

"Keep in mind, Frank, I don't even know if these are the same people as the ones who attacked Dr. Rowan. I don't even know if it's the same car. I know I'm alert and super vigilant, watching my ass all the time since Sunday evening."

"Good. Keep watching. I'm convinced we have the right vehicle."

Jon admitted there were lots of Hondas and lots of blue ones, too. But, the two fellows stopped yesterday morning in the marina parking lot were up to no good.

Frank said, "I have hunches often and most often my hunches are right."

Jon reminded him of his own hunches and some of the times in the past when he had reported incidents in the marina, just on a hunch.

"You've been a good citizen, my friend. Wish we had more live-aboards like you. Thanks a bunch for the several times you've seen and reported something suspicious. At least three times your calls have resulted in our arresting thieves. Once, you gave us a heads-up which kept a valuable racing boat contender from being damaged just prior to the Congressional Cup race. Remember that one?"

Jon had forgotten that. The whole incident had happened about midnight with one of the Congressional Cup racers nearly being vandalized. He just happened to be walking on the gangway by the row of boats, all set for the next day's event, when he noticed a man on one of them and a van in the parking lot. He felt very good about his helping to thwart a theft that night. They had already damaged the compass in the boat's binnacle and had the cabin door lock broken when three patrolmen arrested the two of them.

"Frank, if these guys happen to be the ones who took the Grand Banks, and I value my hunches, I may know what they're up to and where we might find them," he said, mostly guessing.

"If you've got one of your hunches, let's have it."

"If these are the same guys who took all the stuff about the figurehead, they demanded to know where the boat sank.

Dr. Rowan told them exactly where it could be found," Jon said.

"Well ... where?"

"She gave them a false location, Frank. Guess she's a good liar. She told them it was on the northwest end of Catalina, not far from Shiprock. I think she said something about the depth of it, to be more convincing, but I can't recall that part," he said.

"I'll let the Coast Guard know about this possibility. Would that be a break! If we could catch them with the stolen boat, we'd have the whole package," he said.

"I'm going to call Dr. Rowan, Frank. She needs to know what we're up to. She might be relieved, because I know she's frightened they might return and follow up on their threats, not only to her but to her daughter. But first, I've got to get out of wet trunks, take a shower, and get ready for the office."

Frank arranged for a dive-boat, a fifty-foot Ocean Alexander Mark I Pilothouse. This powerful classic craft would do the job in style. Frank's friend, Dick Brophe, didn't ask him any questions about why he needed to charter the boat, which Frank appreciated. Brophe and Frank had gone on dives before. Both of them were certified divers and Dick Brophe, a man in his mid-seventies, held a Captain's license for up to six tons. He had an enviable seafaring history and would add greatly to the safety and success of a dive. Frank and Jon parted, agreeing to talk later that afternoon.

Jon had wondered if this would be a haphazard adventure, but now he felt reassured about it. Frank didn't want to tell anyone about this search, at least not yet. He admitted being already wary because of what had happened to Dr. Rowan. It made Frank wonder what might make this sunken boat such a glamorous find. They were both wondering about this. Jon kidded about their finding sunken treasures.

He said, "Nothing ventured, nothing gained. And, just maybe, there'll be nothing gained no matter what we venture. But, maybe all of us will come away with millions of dollars. Greed is a great motivator."

As Frank walked away, he said over his shoulder, "Greed! Ah, greed! I'm motivated, Jon."

Jon arrived at his office early enough to call Sky and they arranged to meet for dinner. Krystal had a play rehearsal at the high school, so she could not join them. The rest of the day went routinely: six clients, phone calls, a couple of professional letters to write, and preparation for an attorney's visit regarding a deposition for a client he would foil as best he could.

Sky and Jon met at their Japanese restaurant. They found this the best place for good food and conversation. Sky came from giving a lecture. She seemed preoccupied at first, still wrapped up in the mixed responses to a controversial subject. Her presentation focused on a study of ocean temperatures and the communication frequencies of whales. Sky gave some well-known, accepted theories about how whales transmitted their sounds within thermal zones for thousands of miles. A derivative of this knowledge pertained to how shipping lanes and the frequencies transmitted by certain Navy transmitters were disturbing and confusing some species of whales.

They discussed this as they ordered and began eating. Soon the subject changed. Jon told her about arranging for the dive-boat and Frank's coming up with figures for the two to three-day exploration. She relaxed a bit when Jon told her that Frank and the Long Beach Police Department were hot on the heels of her abductors. She admitted being terrified at the thought they would return. She feared for her own safety because of those three men, but Krystal's safety concerned her most. When Jon brought up the possibility of their having stolen the Grand Banks, she became intrigued. Speculations as to what they were doing led both of them to the same conclusion. They apparently had taken the misinformation Sky had fed them as bait. They would be looking for the sunken vessel near Shiprock, just northwest of Catalina Island. Most likely they would look first in the 150 foot depth she had given them. If they had the right scuba-diving apparatus and skill, they could go that deep.

"I'll get out my charts. I think we'll find all of them."

"What'll you bet we find that powerboat, too?" she asked, taking his hand and moving closer to him in the booth.

"I like sitting next to you like this, Sky. We communicate better while touching as we talk. Being close is getting easier and feels better to both of us. You haven't mentioned any fear the last several times we've been together. But, we haven't talked about that personal stuff for a while." Jon paused, then asked, "Are you feeling more comfortable?"

"All I know is I look forward to every one of your phone calls. Every time I'm going to see you for business or for pleasure, I look forward to it," she said. She turned a bit and moved closer so he could kiss her. He did.

"I think we can do both, the business and the pleasure. In fact, I wouldn't be surprised if we just keep on the way we seem to be going, we'll be able to do everything," he said.

"Everything?" She made an expression of coy excitement.

"Everything!" he lifted her hand to his mouth, kissing it while watching her intently.

There seemed to be no hesitancy in her response. They sat quietly for several minutes. In the silence, they became even more peaceful. He had no doubt Sky felt more trusting and at ease. "One more thing, Sky. This moment, right now, is sacred. We have a spiritual connection right now. Can you sense it?"

"I'm not sure of all that spiritual or sacred stuff, but there is a peace inside me along with feeling my whole body warming from deep inside. Is that a spiritual thing, Jon?"

"As far as I'm concerned, it is. Partly, for me, it is a matter of affirming certain experiences as sacred or spiritual that opens the door to realizing they are. It is deeper when we let ourselves open those windows inside ourselves, like right now. If you're uncomfortable with my words, let's just leave it alone and let the peace and warmth in without having to name it in any way. I'm okay without tags on things. I just know, right now, I don't want this to end and I want to be closer and closer to you."

She did not pull away, letting this feeling between them deepen. They lingered in silence. When they finished eating, they were suddenly interrupted by the waitress, who apologized for the intrusion.

"Excuse me. Seems like a bad time to give you your bill," she said.

Standing together beside her car, they embraced. The quiet stayed with them. They didn't want to lose the mood. He leaned against the fender of her Thunderbird and she leaned into him, their arms around one another. Jon bathed in the fragrance of her hair, the warmth of her body against his, breathing together, cherishing a few more minutes. As her breathing increased just a little, she began to stand up, holding his hands in hers; she looked up at him, smiling.

"Well, Jon, this is the moment of decision. Either I take you home with me or we bid farewell for tonight. I can't do another five minutes this way. Make up your mind. If I take you home, you're not leaving tonight," she said, suddenly looking away. "Oh my God! What am I saying?"

"You've just said what we're both thinking and feeling. But, I'm not going home with you. Not yet. We need more times like this. We're not that many days from the panic you experienced. We've got time, Love. We've got plenty of time. There is so much more to this than a fling, though it would not be just a fling for me with you. I know that to my toes."

"Now I'm embarrassed. You've got more control than I. Your saying no to an invitation makes you stronger. But, maybe this isn't a contest. Maybe you're right about how you see us and our having time. I won't be able to sleep tonight, though. What will I do?" She pressed against him and they hugged even more closely than before. They stayed this way as she gently moved her hips against his. They knew how complete they would be together. "Don't let go of me. Hold on right now. Stay just this way, Jon. Just this way..." Her breathing turned to a few deep sighs and her forehead became warm and moist against his neck. Several minutes went by and she relaxed in his arms. "Oh, Jon, that's a preview of coming attractions. I could sing that song, 'This is the Start of Something Big.' Remember that one? Just one thing I need right now, before we part."

"Anything. Anything, my Love."

"Tell me again you love me like you did the other night. Tell me just the way you said it the other night. I'll never forget how you said it." Without the Thunderbird holding them up, they would have been on the ground for sure.

"I love you. I love you, Sky," he declared, without an ounce of uncertainty - with no reserve.

"That's it. I can go home now. I can and will go to bed. I'm going to sleep well. You don't need to promise you'll call me tomorrow, but if I don't hear from you by about seven-thirty, after your swim, I'm either coming to find you or call the police," she said, smiling.

"You better answer! I'll call you the moment I get showered after swimming. I'll put clothes on before I call you," teasing her.

"That isn't necessary."

Within a few minutes, she was in her car, with the top going down. She looked very pretty and inviting in her convertible, even in the discoloring lights of the parking lot. The warm evening allowed her to drive home with the top down. She revved the engine a few times, tossing her hair, making it free for the breeze, all the while watching his reactions. Jon fully enjoyed the whole scene. The glass-packed mufflers of the Ford's twin pipes emitted a very distinctive, throaty resonant sound as she drove away into the night.

Wednesday morning's swim was a stressful, almost traumatic workout for him.

The captain of a large powerboat should have seen him in the early morning light. He swam close to the ends of the docks as the boat made a sudden turn directly towards him from about fifty feet away. With all his strength, he pushed away from the boat's starboard bow. It came too fast to an end-tie position. Jon thought the captain could see him from the flying bridge, but evidently not. He could not hear Jon's yelling at him, with his diesel engines revving up to governed speed in reverse to slow the boat. The propeller-driven current suddenly slammed Jon against the dock.

To keep from being crushed by the hull, he swam under the dock flotation, emerging in the waterway on the other side. The narrow escape took probably twenty seconds, but it completely broke the mood of his peaceful morning swim. Flooding adrenalin made his heart race. He swam fast for another fifteen minutes to quiet his reaction to the surprise event. He climbed up the stern ladder on the *Daimon*, continually shaking from the experience. He knew it would not be of any use to talk to the skipper. He was not paying attention, at least to a swimmer. His vessel was ahead of his control and his focus was on docking a boat beyond his skill-level in size and power. Later, Jon looked at the boat, moored at an end-tie; the craft flew a Marina Del Rey Yacht Club burgee. It was not a local boat.

About 7:30 Jon remembered to call Sky. The near miss while swimming had frozen his feelings for a while, but they came back the moment he heard her voice. He told her about the boat's coming at him and how he evaded it. She expressed concern and her response to his story touched him. He commented that her caring and tenderness were very helpful and loving. She thanked him for saying so. They hung up, planning to talk later in the day.

Wednesday afternoon he heard from Carlos Diaz. He wondered how things were progressing. Between sessions, they talked for just a few minutes and ended their conversation with his promising to get back to him on Thursday, when Jon hoped to have more definite information about a possible dive. Carlos dropped an alarming bit of information at the end of their talk.

"When I told my son, Michael, about what we were doing, he got very interested in going along."

Jon had specifically asked Carlos to keep this all to himself. Learning that Carlos had told one of his children about the planned exploration, Jon immediately wondered if this might have been the leak in their container of secrecy.

Perhaps this is connected with what happened to Sky and Krystal.

They had no time for discussion during this phone call, so Jon left it to Thursday's call. Then he confirmed his suspicion.

"Dr. Scott, I'm excited about going to look for the wreck," Carlos said.

"Well, Carlos, we've almost got a date. The divers and the dive-boat are secured. We're waiting for costs, details, and we need to confirm the area of exploration. Once we know those things, we are on our way," he said. Then, Jon could not contain his curiosity any longer, he asked, "How much did you tell your son about this, Carlos?"

"All I told him had to do with our going to look for the sunken boat his great-great grandfather had sailed here in 1849. He knows the story about Shuka's trip south from San Francisco. Our family has liked all that history. They don't care much about it, but they always act interested when I tell or retell them stories about the great escape their triple-great grandfather pulled off," he said.

"So they know we're out to find that boat, Carlos?"

"Only Michael really knows that. The other two kids don't care about this stuff; you know, they're girls. Michael is at that age where everything strange is interesting and an adventure. He likes weird adventure games, mysteries, science fiction, all that stuff. Sometimes, he pretends he's a macho hero out in the world of dangerous adventures. I get a kick out of his imagination. He's nineteen, but often acts like a kid playing cowboys and Indians. Of course, we're the Indians, but he still takes the cowboy part, because they always win."

"I'd like to meet and talk to Michael, Carlos. Is he around?"

"No. Not at the moment. In fact, I'm a little concerned. He left with his buddy the other night. He left a note about going hiking. He always tells me where he's going, but didn't tell me exactly where this time, but I know he likes to hike in the San Bernardino Mountains, around San Gorgonio, and they probably went there. All of his hiking gear is gone, so I know he's on a back-packing trip, like I said, probably there. It will be the last of the season, with weather changes soon. He's going to take a test for firefighter and paramedic school next week, but he's got nothing but time on his hands since high school," he said.

"When he gets back, let's the three of us get together. I'd like to meet him."

"That's a sure thing, Dr. Scott."

"Call me Jon, Carlos."

"Okay, Jon. I always think when a person has a degree or a title, they ought to be given respect."

"Carlos, we're in the same boat and equal in every way, as far as I'm concerned."

"Well, it's obvious, you've never been an Indian or a Mexican, but thanks for telling me how you feel. I can't wait to get going on this trip to find the *Madonna*."

Jon imagined Carlos rubbing his hands together, savoring the anticipation of this journey. His voice filled with excitement. Before hanging up, he put in one last comment, apologizing for having told Michael. Then, he tried and failed to reassure Jon, by claiming Michael would keep it to himself.

"Whatever, Carlos. But remember, this affair needs to be kept absolutely confidential for now," Jon said firmly. "No more talking to anyone, but me, Carlos! Understand?"

Friday morning the plan was set. They arranged for a dive in eleven days, on Monday morning, December 17th. The cost seemed reasonable to Sky and Jon. Frank arrived at an estimate of $4,500, if they took three days, all things considered. Including himself, there would be three divers, two of them students, volunteering their time for the experience. All they needed was their food, which would be simple cuisine. There would be about eleven of them on the trip; Frank, his three divers, the boat's skipper, Dick Brophe, Sky, Krystal, Carlos Diaz, and possibly his son, Michael, and Jon.

On a forty-six-foot powerboat, they had plenty of room. The intriguing name of Brophe's boat was the *Tiamat*. *Tiamat* means *Sea Monster, Goddess of the Deep,* or, *Sea Dragon.* From his Old Testament classes, Jon recalled how the professor made a big thing out of the root word, *tamdu* or *tamtu*, which meant *sea* or *ocean* in ancient Hebrew. He contended that the first line of Genesis indicated that the creation story was linked to a water culture in Mesopotamia. It occurred to Jon this Dick Brophe might be an interesting fellow to get to know, especially if he named his boat *Tiamat*. Indeed, this turned out to be true, adding a great deal to the trip. From the yacht club, Jon had known Dick for a few years, but only as an acquaintance. Dick had a powerboat and Jon had a sailboat; they had few reasons to associate. That changed in the weeks to come.

Jon arranged a dinner for nine of them at the yacht club in a private room for Friday evening, a memorable date, December 7th. Sky, Krystal, Frank and his wife, Lupe, Carlos and his wife, Laura, Dick, Dick's wife, Sharon, and Jon, made a large group, some of them meeting for the first time. Carlos told him his son wouldn't be able to join them. Jon specified that he wanted Bruce, his favorite and most entertaining waiter, to take care of their table that evening. Luckily for him, Sky insisted on putting half the bill on her budget, this being a pre-dive exploratory meeting. Also, the best news, her research grant would entirely cover the voyage bill.

After they all sat down and went through the introductions, they had a brief time to socialize and become more familiar with one another. The evening was one of Long Beach's best and the festive yacht club added to it.

Dick Brophe and Jon had a chance to talk about the name of his boat. It turned out Dick had been a layman scholar in theology and had kept it up as a hobby. At one time, he explained to Jon, he thought of going into the ministry, until he got realistic about how little money he'd make and how much politics he'd have to face in the church. They agreed to get together for lunch soon, just to talk.

Sky interrupted the happy chatter, their drinks having come and orders placed.

She clinked her spoon against her glass and introduced herself and reminded them of the reason for their being together. Jon liked her taking charge, so direct and with a gracious style. She shared most of the story of how it all came about, including Jon's finding her dismasted, floundering Cal-20 drifting with her dog, Schwartz, and herself aboard. The group sat spellbound with her story and the way she told it, including the describing the figurehead, which she named for them, Meri. Jon finished the story, adding a few details about the discovery and the complications with the Coast Guard. At the end of all this, he ordered them not to talk about the dive in any way with anyone. They all agreed on the need for secrecy. Only Brophe asked why the need. That's when Jon told him of a problem that had already occurred, including the threat to Sky and Krystal if they didn't tell the three thugs the location of the boat. He told them Sky had revealed it was at the northwest end of Catalina. He explained that Sky had told those jerks the wrong location and they bought it.

Carlos Diaz looked startled when Jon told of this event. It was the first he had heard about the three men attacking and robbing Sky, taking her papers and research, threatening her with death if she didn't tell them where the boat was. Then, he asked Jon to repeat the location. He told him the thugs thought the boat sank near Shiprock, near the Isthmus. He leaned back in his chair, looking pale. The group watched him, thinking he might be ill. Jon asked him if he were okay.

"No. I think I must tell you all something. My son, Michael's in jail. They picked him up at the Isthmus, trying to get someone to take him to San Pedro on Wednesday evening, last week. He's in jail for stealing a boat. How I wish he were innocent! If only this could all be a misunderstanding. A Grand Banks, a forty-two footer, was stolen about a week ago from a marina in San Pedro. They found Michael's Honda close by and someone tipped off the Coast Guard as to where the boat might be found," Carlos said, pausing to take Laura's hand to reassure her. She fiddled with her spoon, looking down as he told this story. He continued, "The boat went aground near Black Point, almost at the west end of Catalina. One man was on the boat when they found it. Later I learned that man's name was

Luís Jimenez. Michael knew him. They hung out together. Jimenez claimed he owned the boat, that he was waiting for the tide to come in so he could get the boat off the rocks. He's in jail, too. It turns out there's one other fellow who drowned scuba diving. This is too much for me. I'm very upset telling you all this. Perhaps I need to get out of the group. Jon told me not to say anything to anyone and I made the mistake of telling Michael.

"Michael knew the family stories about a lot of gold aboard the *Madonna* when it sank. He's heard me say things. I know I've said if we only had all that gold, we'd be able to pay our bills. We all thought it would be a fortune just waiting for someone to find. He's probably heard me talk about this gold in that sunken, lost ship dozens of times. Anyhow, our son's in jail because of me and Jon told me not to tell anyone. All this is my fault," he said. He sank down into his chair, his head glumly forward on his chest.

Frank's wife, Lupe, mentioned having seen something in the Long Beach Press Telegram about a scuba diver drowning and a boat on the rocks at Catalina. A photograph of the boat had been taken from a helicopter. No names were in the article, she reported.

The group sat awkwardly silent, until Frank spoke.

"No one said anything about any gold. I think we need to be sure what we're doing here. If there's some kind of treasure in this wreck, aren't we supposed to do all kinds of salvage documentation, all that complicated, legal stuff?"

Sky said, with authority, "Frank, we don't know anything at this point. There is a story Carlos has shared with us and it's validated by a scroll we've found indicating there was gold originally brought on the *Madonna*. We don't know how much or if any is there. We don't know if it had been taken ashore in 1849, before the ship sank. We know nothing about gold, except gold had been taken aboard when the ship sailed south from Yerba Buena in 1849."

"What happens if you find this wreck? Are you supposed to claim it or give it to the State or something?" Krystal asked.

Sky said, "There are all kinds of details having to do with wrecks and salvage laws. We'll have to cross that bridge if and when we come to it. I have some influence, being known in the oceanographic community and having been in on several discoveries of off-shore wrecks and some salvage. Everything we're doing is legal. Let me assure you all."

By this time Bruce had served coffee and deserts. Several times during the meal, Bruce and Jon had exchanged puns. He had teased Jon about their having a date after he got rid of all these people. He enjoyed kidding Jon about wanting a date. In his very funny, affected manner, Bruce asked him if he'd ever get over the notion that he was heterosexual.

Once Jon told Bruce he should have been born a beautiful woman.

Bruce queried, "You've not seen me in drag?" The group laughed. "That Geraldine Ferraro, the one on the ticket for Vice President. She's really a man in drag, you know!" Bruce insisted.

Bruce took care of the nine of them in fine style, never missing a detail, giving excellent service.

In the back of his mind, Jon wondered why the Coast Guard or Detective Aubry had not informed him about finding the stolen boat and the three men involved. He got angry about the matter all over again. He made a promise to himself to follow up on the story Carlos shared about his son, Michael, and how he came to be in jail, charged with stealing the Grand Banks. Several times after Carlos had told them about Michael, Sky, Krystal, and he exchanged questioning glances.

Sky leaned over to Jon, cupped her hand near his ear, and whispered, "We need to talk after the party breaks up." Jon mumbled an 'uh-huh,' squeezing her hand. Krystal had left early for another one of her high school play rehearsals. Jon savored Krystal's closeness as she bent over his shoulder and gave him a kiss on the cheek. She thanked him for dinner as she left. Sky watched this intently. She smiled and obviously approved.

The group dispersed about 9:00 PM. Sky and Jon walked out onto the club's veranda that overlooked the water and the marina. The night air was crisp. Thousands of lights reflected in the water, dancing on the ripples. He put his arm around her and mentioned they shouldn't stay out there long, having been in the warmth of the dining room for the last couple of hours.

"But, it's so romantic. Give us a few more minutes together, Jon."

A sailboat came in. It dropped the headsail as it turned into its docking area in the club's basin. A Cal-40, it was one of his favorite boats. This particular one held a good racing reputation, being fast and well-sailed. They watched the boat slide into its slip, the idling engine slowed it to a gentle berth. A man and woman were aboard. She jumped off and hooked the dock lines, displaying ease and skill with a maneuver she had done many times. Jon knew the couple and how they enjoyed sailing together, usually going to their mooring at Avalon. He told Sky about them. She said he sounded envious and just maybe there could be other couples who loved to be together to do things, like sailing.

Many of the boats in the marina displayed Christmas decorations and lights. Some of them were being prepared for the annual Christmas boat parade, scheduled for the next weekend.

They left the club and walked along the sidewalk above the gangways. Her T-Bird was parked next to his pickup. "Don't those two vehicles look happy together?" he said.

"Yes they do, now that you mention it. They'd like to stay together all night, just like they are right now, your pickup and my T-Bird, close to one another, side by side."

"Well, if they did stay together just like they are now, you'd have to either stay on my boat with me or take a taxi home."

"What do you think, Jon? Are we ready for that? We just had this conversation and agreed, being very rational and disciplined people, we were going to take our time. You reminded me of my recent panic. Remember?"

"It's up to you. I would love it, but it has to be your decision. If you want, just come to the boat and I'll give you a Bailey's Irish Cream. You could decide, while we talk about our dinner group and what we learned about Carlos and Michael. Strange. Laura had nothing to say about any of that. I suppose Laura is Michael's mother, but maybe not."

"Irish Cream?" she asked, licking her lips, making them glisten.

"Irish Cream," he confirmed. He took her hand and led her down to the dock. The high tide made the gangways nearly level with the sidewalk. All the boats seemed larger, riding high in the marina. They talked until midnight. Concerns about Michael took some of their time. They wondered how much damage he could still do, even though in jail. They were fading and they both had to rise early. Sky had an early morning Saturday lecture, starting at 8:00, and he had a lot to do, too.

He reluctantly walked her to her car where they embraced and kissed goodnight.

They were excited about the plan. But, there was a lot to do. Jon, Sky, and the others had just one week to finish all the preparations for the trip aboard the *Tiamat* to China Point, on the east end of San Clemente Island.

Saturday morning he had only a few professional commitments. That enabled him to be free by about eleven. After a light lunch, he cleaned the boat, changed his bunk sheets, and gave the boat a good deck and hull scrubbing. About three in the afternoon, he got the urge to sail, which he did for a couple of hours. The wind stopped as the sun hit the horizon. He came into the harbor entrance just as it died. The perfect timing with no wind allowed him to drift toward his marina basin. The diesel thumped in gear at idle, while he stowed the sails. The routine went well; the *Daimon* slipped into her berth, all put away.

Sky had arrived at the marina parking lot with Carlos right behind her. The timing was perfect. They watched him come in and walked down the gangway together as Jon was tying up. Earlier, Carlos had called her and asked if the three of them could talk this evening. By chance she told him to meet her in the marina parking lot, hoping Jon would be available. Her calls had not reached Jon as he had not checked messages since he had left his office that morning. They greeted one another as he cleated the last dock line.

"Ahoy, Skipper!" Sky called.

"This is my lucky evening. Good to see you, both of you. To what good fortune do I owe this visit?"

He invited them aboard and offered them a glass of wine, cheese, and crackers. Sky accepted, but Carlos refused.

"Dr. Scott, I've got to tell you! Michael is out of jail. He is mixed up, to say the least," Carlos said.

"Come on aboard, Carlos. Let's relax as best we can. We need to talk," Jon said.

It did not take much coaxing. Carlos did indeed need to talk. Jon could tell he was deeply conflicted about what he had been through with Michael. Having apologized earlier about telling Michael about the *Madonna*, he repeated the whole litany. He felt quite guilty.

"Carlos, what's done is done. But, I'm concerned for Sky and Krystal if Michael is free. As far as we know, he and two others are the ones who attacked, robbed, and threatened Sky. They took her papers and research, and threatened her with death."

"Nothing to worry about now," Carlos said. "There are charges against Michael and Luís, the other fellow with him - serious charges. Stealing an expensive boat and a death involved in the affair required a lot of bail money and we got an expensive attorney. The damned attorney wanted ten thousand dollars up front just to look at the case. On account of the bail, Laura and I are too strapped. We can't afford to do anything regarding the *Madonna*. Besides that, my involvement in this may have caused very serious harm to Dr. Rowan and, maybe, I've complicated the search for the vessel."

The three of them sat on the settee around the table. Jon poured port wine into three crystal glasses and sliced several kinds of cheese, which he arranged with crackers on a platter.

"Carlos, you can't be responsible for what Michael did. We're all okay and that is all that matters. Our priority is to find the vessel. We need your help to establish the history behind it. Your help is crucial. We don't need any financial help," Sky said.

He hesitated quietly, looking at the colorful wine in the ornate wine glasses. Jon weighed the feelings and the situation. In a few minutes, they began to thaw enough to enjoy the refreshments.

"Carlos and Sky, I hereby propose a sip of the nectar of the grape as a token of our communion. Let's also direct a prayer of forgiveness and mercy for Michael and his buddy, Luís," Jon said. Then, to be honest, he added, "Of course, I've got to confess, a few days ago I would have enjoyed wringing their necks, all three of them."

Sky clinked her glass to the others a second time, and said, "I would like to forgive, I guess. I would like to have the three of them as terrified as they made me feel. But, I suppose I just need to be thankful Krystal and I are okay. But, there's more to come. Krystal and I are caught up in the legal stuff, at least as victims, from what I gather. One day at a time, I guess," she said with resignation.

The conversation grew mellow and friendly. Wine and cheese helped. Carlos talked about his family and the differences between his children. Laura, his second wife, had tried to be a mother to his children, they having only one of the three children as their own. Michael had been in trouble many times during his teens. Carlos admitted he had probably bailed him out too often, but he always felt guilty about divorcing his mother. She had killed herself soon after they split up. Michael had been with her the night she died. He was twelve when she took the lethal dose of mixed pills. For a long time Michael blamed Carlos for her being so unhappy and for her suicide. Finally, a family doctor explained her manic-depressive disorder, telling Michael how much better it was for the family to find some stability with Laura's marrying Carlos. The doctor reminded Michael of the years of various kinds of abuse, from neglect to violent rages, which all of them had suffered prior to the divorce. Michael had not remembered any of that. He blocked out those painful times, until hearing the doctor tell and re-tell the descriptive, painful stories.

Soon Carlos got up to leave. He looked distant and sad.

"Goodnight, Carlos. God go with you. We'll be in touch about the trip in the next few days," Jon said.

Sky and Jon had listened intently. Carlos had not told this whole story to anyone before. He mentioned that several times during this two-hour evening on the boat. By the time he left, he agreed to come on the trip with them, to help all he could, and thanked them both several times for listening to him, for the refreshments and the time together. Carlos had tears in his eyes as he said goodbye at about eight o'clock. Sky and Jon sat for a while, recuperating.

"The night is young. Do you feel like going for a walk and talk?"

"It's a bit chilly, but I've got my big coat in the car. A walk and talk is just the thing for us right now. We could walk around the marina and back up to Second Street for a snack," she said.

"Or we could come back here and I'll fix us some chili, a few slices of tomato and lettuce, and another glass of wine, if you like," he offered. He reached over and brushed her hair back from her face.

"I liked that thing you just did. Maybe we better have our chili now and take a short walk later. Who needs a snack? Your chili sounds really good," she said, as she placed her hand on his.

He got up, stepped into the galley, and before fixing a salad he poured two glasses of Chardonnay. By the time they ate, talked, and walked for a while along the marina walkway, it was after 10:00 PM. They began to sag. The clear, chilly evening required Sky to bundle herself in a long, warm coat. As they walked, they held hands, keeping at least one hand warm. From time to time, they changed sides, to warm their other hands. She thought this was a fun game. Both of them mentioned how much they enjoyed the peace and closeness of this evening. They kissed and hugged goodnight with plans to talk in the early afternoon, after he finished at church. Letting go of one another was even more difficult this time.

Chapter Twenty-Three

After services on Sunday, Jon returned to the boat to change clothes. An official envelope from the Coast Guard was taped to the dock box. He opened it immediately. A form letter had a penned note at the bottom. Ensign Shabro's signature appeared on both the formal and the penned portions. Except on the part written in long hand, she gave her first name, Lore. The penned part of the note was friendly and, almost, apologetic.

To the Rev. Dr. Jon Scott: 30 November 1984

It is our pleasant duty to inform you of having been cleared of all matters under investigation by the U. S. Coast Guard, the Federal Bureau of Customs, and the the Long Beach Police Department. We must remind you, however, at any time, if there is further cause to reopen this matter, you will be apprized of our need to do so.

Regards, Lore Shabro, Ensign, U. S. C. G.

The first, formal note was typed. Then, in penned script there was the personal, bewildering note at the bottom that seemed surprisingly friendly:

Dear Dr. Scott,

Please give Dr. Rowan my regards. It was a pleasure to have met both of you and I must send along my regrets for any distress this matter may have caused either of you.

Sincerely, Lore Shabro

He read this with mixed emotions, relief and irritation. He could barely wait to share the missive with Sky, but wanted to do it in person.

They arranged to meet at her workshop. He offered to bring sandwiches and drinks, when he learned she was buried in a project there. But, before he left the parking lot, Frank Martinez drove alongside in his cruiser. He wore a big smile.

"Fancy meeting you here, Frank."

"I've never known what 'fancy' meant, Jon. Am I fancy? Tell me what fancy means," he said, looking serious.

"Fancy is the way Lupe looked each time you had your kids baptized and confirmed. Fancy is how she looked at dinner the other night at the yacht club," Jon said.

"Now I know what it means. Every time we meet I learn something really important. But I've got good news. Everything is set for next Sunday. Brophe's ready. The divers are ready and eager. The depth-finder's working. We have submersible lights and a good marine camera. I got us detailed charts from a Navy friend of mine. There's only one concern I have, Jon. Have you found out anything about what we have to do in the legal department if we find anything?"

"Not yet, Frank, but Sky may have more information. She has special privileges, being registered with the Ocean Archeological Society and being a university professor. She's also a certified diver. She may want to dive with you guys. I'm not certified, but I've got the gear. I've never been legally below twenty feet. I must confess, the figurehead was about thirty-five feet deep, though."

"Lupe is excited about this dive, too. She talked to me for a long time last night. She said she hadn't seen me in such a good mood for months. She's sure it is because we're going on this trip. Let me tell you, we've kept everything a secret and the divers know nothing yet, except we may go pretty deep," he said, reassuring Jon the best he could.

"Thank you for that. I want nothing about this trip out there for anyone else but you, the divers, Dick, Sky, and me. About Lupe, she's just excited because of all the gold you're going to bring back." Jon paused, giving himself time to choose his words. He wanted to be sure they were sharing this adventure for the same reasons. "I'm sure she's seeing your old bouncy self come back because of doing this. In fact, I'm feeling unusually good, too. I don't care what we find or if we find nothing at all. Just the fact we're taking a trip together and having an exciting adventure is all I need. We should talk about what to do about Michael, Frank, if anything. Sky and Krystal went through a lot because of him."

"I don't think there's much to be done, Jon. Let's just see how this shakes out with him. Carlos is on top of it now and that helps. I don't think Michael can cause any more trouble."

Frank's radio called him and he responded. He gave Jon a left handed handshake through the car window. "Gotta go. Some business in Basin Three. Let's stay in touch during week, Jon."

"Take care. We'll be in touch."

The cruiser backed up and sped out of the parking lot.

Weekends, especially Sunday afternoons, were the busiest times in the marina.

Marinas are little cities. Their citizenry changes day to day, but the boats remain fairly constant. People in charge of security become much more familiar with boats than people. They know how boats are maintained, which ones get used and which ones don't. The pulse of a marina's life is kept by the Harbor Patrol people. They are different than city police types. These professionals want to be by the water and have an affinity for everything to do with boating. They can sense when a boat is sitting low in the water, perhaps because of a hull leak. They know when a boat is listing in a slip. They notice when a dinghy is gone or in a strange place, having been used or perhaps stolen. Frank was one of the best in this marina's security crew. Jon could think easily of dozens of incidents in which he had detected a problem and initiated effective action. Living on a boat in this marina was one of the best situations he had ever experienced and Frank knew he felt this way.

Jon pulled the gate open and petted Schwartz, She danced at his feet and sniffed his sandwich bags. He called to Sky, who answered heartily from her bench in the shop. Since he hadn't been there for a while, he became immediately aware of Meri lying near the doorway, covered by the blue plastic tarp. He kissed Sky on the cheek and put the bags down on the workbench, out of her way. She kept her concentration, tenderly extracting a piece of cloth embedded in a chunk of mud or clay. She wore magnifying glasses. A strong Halogen-beam lamp strapped around her head illuminated her work. She told him to relax for just a few minutes. He watched her work intently on the cloth. She seemed to be counting the threads or, maybe, she was studying the pattern and the weave of the material. At last, she turned off her forehead lamp and looked at him. Even with her headlamp tightly strapped to her head, he took in her beauty. He told her so. She did just the right thing; she blushed.

"Can you believe how well this cloth is preserved? It has been embedded in this mud for at least 150 years. It was found in a graveyard near the San Luís Rey Mission. They want to know if it's clothing or a liturgical piece for some reason. I think it may have been both. It's definitely made for liturgical use, but there are seams sewn into it that may be evidence that it was later used for a shawl, veil, or, even, perhaps, a blouse. It is definitely older than they think, perhaps by 100 years. It matches some of the lace material from the seventeen hundreds that is still on display in mission museums," she said, with authority.

"That's fascinating, Sky. Aren't you hungry?"

"So, you're more interested in your stomach than in my old lace? Let me wash my hands. Yes, I'm famished," she said.

She slid from her tall stool and went to the bathroom. He unwrapped the sandwiches and put out paper towels as place mats on the workbench near her project. By the time he poured the drinks into the plastic cups, she stood beside him and tugged gently on his arm so he would lean down for a kiss. As they ate, Jon told her about Frank's visit just before leaving the marina and how he and Lupe were excitedly anticipating the dive next week. Sky was excited, too. Jon especially liked how openly Sky conveyed whatever feelings and thoughts she had. She also told him that she'd have her scuba gear with her and intended to join the divers if and when possible. She ignored his concerns about the safety questions and the unknowns of the whole adventure. Her determination to be in on every bit of the exploration was clear.

Along with her enthusiasm, she teased him about his becoming a certified diver by next Monday. Of course, he did not have enough time to do this, but he began to feel odd man out. He felt a bit of jealousy about her diving with the three or four male divers.

"Sky, I'm already twitchy about your diving with these guys. I don't know them, except for Frank. Frank I trust. But, I don't know the others."

"What are you worried about? You think I can't take care of myself? I've been on lots of dives," she said to reassure him.

"Do divers fall in love down there in that mystical medium?"

"Every time I dive I fall in love with the other divers. Luckily, there are too many of them to single out a real partner. So when I bob to the surface, if you're still there, you're the one I'll be wanting to see, to smoosh my mucky wet suit against, and rub all the slime off onto you," she said. She grinned and watched him for a reaction.

"Go ahead. Play your mind games with me. I can take it. Besides, if it's that easy for you to switch loves in your life, chances are this thing we have is doomed anyhow."

"Why, Jon! I think you're serious. I was just kidding."

"Oh, I know that. I'm surprised at my insecurity thinking about this. I know if we open up to the love we're experiencing, we'll feel vulnerable. After all, that's what love's all about … that's what makes it work." He attempted to be convincing and smart about the most complex of all matters - love.

"Something I must confess, Sky. I'm embarrassed to say this, but there are times I feel disloyal to Miriam. How can that be? It is completely irrational."

"That is so like you. What you just said to me about Miriam makes me feel even closer to you, Jon. I know there is more we need to talk about and I relish those conversations about you and your former lives. Miriam must have been a very special woman," she said. She looked at him intently and leaned closer.

As she finished her sandwich and taking a large swallow of her drink, she cleared her throat and turned face-to-face with him, taking his hand. "We have to talk about a lot of things, Jon. There are times, especially when we're not together, when I have anxiety about what we're doing. There are other times, usually at night, when I nearly panic, like I did that awful day I called you to end this. I remind myself that you are not my ex-husband. I remind myself that you are not like my father. If I have you clearly in focus, just the ways we've been together, I calm down. There are more times lately when I can even feel both in love with you and peaceful at the same time. I've never had that in my life. I love the whole thing, except for the panic and anxiety," she said, just inches from his face.

Tears welled up in his eyes. The warmth and honesty of what she said to him thawed out another one of his cold, empty inner spaces. He had no doubt Sky knew exactly what was happening. Their luncheon was finished, but they were at a new depth.

Suddenly, he remembered the letter in his pocket.

"Look at what we got from Ensign Shabro. I was surprised by how congenial she seemed. Couldn't help but wonder, too, if she was taking us in, perhaps setting us up for something. But, maybe she's sincere." He handed the envelope to her and she opened it.

"I had to read this twice. I can't tell you the relief I feel reading this. She's actually a human being. I think she's changed her mind about us," Sky said.

The week raced by. His clients and the matters of his practice kept him busy every hour. Her teaching schedule was heavy, too. Taking three or four days off from being a professor next week, there were extra things for her to do. Once in a while Sky and Jon talked and they had a couple of evening light meals together.

Several times, there were calls to make about the Sunday trip aboard the *Tiamat*.

Twice during the week he visited Brophe's boat, while Frank and Jon met there to take care of stowing charts and food for the trip. Frank checked out the scuba tanks, the regulators, and made sure the hydraulic stern dive platform functioned.

Jon enjoyed watching Frank work so methodically, as if he were going down an aircraft checklist, item by item. There were seven tanks, all charged, and five regulators. Of course, the other divers had their own equipment, but there needed to be extra tanks and regulators in case of difficulties. When divers get into trouble, it is essential other divers are able to descend to help them, even though all diving is done in teams of at least two divers, never separating from one another. On their last trip Frank had checked the equipment and it all worked and was deemed reliable. They parted, satisfied and eager for Sunday to arrive for their trip to China Point and the east end of San Clemente Island.

Krystal, Sky, and he met for dinner on Friday evening. Krystal had to depart early for another rehearsal at her high school. Sky and Krystal were having a disagreement about her going out later with Sean, because she would not be home until after midnight. Both of them looked to Jon to help them out of this difference, but he refused to be involved. He did ask Krystal if she would be in good shape for the trip on Sunday. Would she have her assignments done so she could miss up to three days of school? She had permission for the time off from school, given the opportunity to go on a mysterious archeological dive with Dr. Sky Rowan, who just happened to be her mother and a respected oceanographer, too. Sky and Jon emphasized the secret nature of what they were doing. They asked Krystal to continue to keep all this to herself. It was not difficult to persuade her, with the frightening adventure they had experienced just a couple of weeks before.

"After what we went through, do you think I would tell anyone? Even though we think the goons have been caught, we're not sure. Besides, there may be others interested in searching for this ship for some reason," Krystal said.

Sky and Krystal hugged goodbye, and Krystal left. Jon and Sky finished their dinner and left for the workshop. There they had to arrange freshly copied papers relevant to the *Madonna* and to the vicinity of where the *Madonna* probably sank. Sky accomplished some of the legal research and determined this would be under the category of a 'Find' and not 'Salvage'.

"We're lucky we're under the old salvage and find laws for this. There is work being done on a new 'Abandoned Shipwreck Act,' but it is at least a couple of years from being law. The only problem might be if we find treasure and whether that will be something we have to report to either the State of California or the Feds," she said.

"What determines that?"

"It may be a technicality related to the depth of what we find. I don't know enough yet, and we don't need to decide anything until after all the data are in from our trip. One thing I do know, I'm fascinated with this and haven't had this much fun in a long time. The last time I got to do something like this was on an expedition for wreckage in the Gulf of Mexico about five years ago. How wonderful that was! We found things that are still being excavated," she said.

In the background Pachelbel's *Canon in D* played, one of his favorite pieces of music. He took Sky by the hand and led her to the couch. They snuggled quietly and listened to the whole Canon and then the next pieces on the tape, Vivaldi's *Concerto for Two Trumpets in C* and Albinoni's *Adagio in G*.

When the tape clicked off, she said, "I've never felt so peaceful. What a mix of feelings. I'm feeling very turned on right now. I am swept along by a deep sense of being loved, safe, and emotional."

Their long kiss and embrace sealed the sacred time they shared. Once again, their parting was difficult, but necessary. It was after midnight and she had to give an early morning lecture for a nearly all-day Saturday seminar. He had lots to do, mostly paperwork, in order to take off part of the week. He would probably not get back to his office before Thursday. All of his appointments were re-scheduled to the next week and most of those clients were doing well enough to miss a week of therapy. Only two were on his mind as being in risky and stressful places. He had given them another therapist's phone number and briefed Dr. Watts about their possible calls to him during his absence.

Chapter Twenty-Four

After tucking Sky into her T-Bird, he got into his pickup and drove ahead of her down the alley. He turned right toward the marina and home, and watched her taillights in his rear view mirrors.

Heavy clouds and drizzle set the mood for his Saturday morning swim. He hoped the weather would be better for their trip tomorrow. However, they could dive in almost any weather except a rough sea, and they had an alternate date if the weather turned bad. But they were all so excited for the trip that a delay would have been frustrating. Besides, each of them would have had to change their different schedules: Frank's time off, Krystal's permission to miss school, the appointments Sky and he had changed, and rescheduling Brophe's boat. All would have to change their schedules. These thoughts roiled around in his mind while he swam, got dressed for the day, and went to The Omelette House for breakfast.

He arrived at his office about nine. There were five phone messages on his machine. One of them was from Carlos Diaz. He had several questions about the trip tomorrow, one having to do with the weather. He had heard the weather was going to worsen. Jon had heard that, too, but in checking further, he learned the forecast was mixed. When Jon returned his call, he reassured him the seas would be fairly smooth, even if they did have the rain and clouds. No high winds were forecast and in the current weather picture no storms were detected closer than the tip of Baja California. Also, there was one system off the Aleutian Islands, but it was moving so slowly down the coast it would probably not arrive before next Friday. Before they got off the phone, Carlos reassured Jon he had not mentioned this trip to anyone besides his wife. "Everybody else thinks it is a fishing trip with some friends." He didn't tell them for what they would be fishing.

"What's happening with your son, Carlos?" Jon asked, a bit uneasy about needing to ask the question.

"He's back in jail, Jon. He violated the conditions. He told me he got drunk and took my car to Long Beach to see a friend. But, I called the police and had him picked up. I'm not bailing him out of this one. When he took my car I thought of calling you and Dr. Rowan to let you know he was gone. He had strict rules to stay at home, not drive, and to check in with the court officer every Monday morning. He didn't do anything required of him and I'm pissed at him. He'll have to deal with this on his own now. I'm going to let the attorney go unless Michael makes some kind of radical change for the better. Why should I try to save Michael if he's just going to screw up again? He better learn something from this and shape up. But, I feel so guilty about his childhood. I think I'm to blame for all his problems," Carlos said.

"It won't help him for you to feel guilty, Carlos. That takes the pressure off him to straighten things out. If he knows you're guilty for what he's doing or not doing, it makes it harder for him to take responsibility. It's his life, Carlos. Deal with your guilt or anger, but don't let Michael know in any way you feel to blame for his screwing up his life," Jon said, with conviction. He confronted Carlos just enough to make his point.

"I know. I've tried some therapy for this stuff several times. Never thought I'd be nuts enough to go to therapy, but I did. Laura made me go. Still, if I'm not careful, the guilt and blame for his unhappy life can eat me up."

They ended the exchange and affirmed their meeting time, 1:00 PM Sunday, at the *Tiamat*. Before he hung up, he thanked Jon for talking about his feelings and Michael's responsibilities. A bond grew between them, it seemed to Jon. Jon felt a growing admiration for Carlos, probably because he was a teacher, well-liked at that, and because he'd made significant accomplishments in his community of San Juan Capistrano.

Sunday, after celebrating the Eucharist and giving the homily at the eight o'clock service, Jon returned to his boat to change clothes. Packing things in a seabag for the trip and eating breakfast, he listened to the NOAA marine weather broadcast on the shortwave radio. Although high clouds were expected through Monday, no precipitation was in the forecast and winds were expected to be mild. By afternoon, the winds should be out of the west southwest at five to ten knots in the outer waters. This is where the boat would be anchored.

Sky called and told him she was on her way. They arranged for her to leave her car at her workshop and Jon would pick her up, along with the charts, the legal code abstracts from the Admiralty Law books, and her seabag and diving gear. Krystal would be coming on her own.

They arrived at the *Tiamat's* gangway along with two other strangers, two of the divers joined them. Both were in their twenties, tanned and obviously in great physical shape.

"I'm Paul and this is Ian. We have another certified diver coming."

The group chatted as they waited on the dock for Dick Brophe to arrive and pipe them aboard. Next came Frank Martinez, pushing a dock cart loaded with gear and his seabag. He greeted them, making sure all had introduced themselves to Paul Snow and Ian McCleod. Paul's red hair, trimmed in a military butch, and his very blue eyes, even with freckles, made him a very good-looking man. With an expressionless face, he held out his hand to meet Jon and Sky. Ian, right beside him, had blond hair and brown eyes. His very tanned, tall body stood about six-feet-two inches, nearly Jon's height. He spoke with a thick Scottish brogue, adding color to a strong first impression. Ian asked where Sylvia was, which surprised Jon. It hadn't occurred to Jon the third diver would be a woman. Sky seemed surprised, too. Frank noted their reaction.

"Sylvia Matthews is one of the best divers on the west coast. She's got awards up the whazoo and holds several depth records. You'll like her. When I asked Paul and Ian about diving, they immediately requested I ask Sylvia, which I did. She's eager to do this dive."

As they talked about her, she walked toward them, carrying a large bag over one shoulder and dragging two scuba tanks in a dock cart. Her smile was contagious. She greeted them with 'Hi!' and extended her free hand. As she put down her gear, Jon could not take his eyes off of her. Her brown hair was cut in a butch, an efficient style for a diver. She was stunningly attractive. Probably a body-builder, Sylvia would surely be able to physically handle the job ahead. She radiated poise and confidence. Dick Brophe came right behind her. Carlos and Krystal were the only ones left. But it was before the 11:00 AM appointed time.

By the time they had things stowed and bunks picked out, Krystal and Carlos showed up. Krystal explained to Sky and Jon how she had taken Schwartz to puppy camp, but the owners weren't there. That made her late. Their neighbor agreed to take care of the dog until they returned.

Dick Brophe started the twin diesels, checked gauges, and prepared for the departure, as a good skipper needed to do.

"We'll get together for a briefing on the mission as we begin our journey. As soon as we're out of the Alamitos jetty, come into the cabin," Jon said.

Carlos and Jon had already agreed no mention of gold would be brought up until they found the *Madonna*, if they indeed could find the relic. Dick asked them all if they had forgotten anything, giving the group one last chance for any afterthoughts or necessities. Each one declared they were all set to go. Jon had three flashlights, with extra batteries, his portable RDF receiver, all kinds of sun block, some reading matter, and two charts of the area. Only Sylvia and Paul had not eaten anything this morning, so Jon fixed eggs, bacon, and toast for them, insisting also that they drink their orange juice. Frank put on a coffee pot and also heated water for tea. Tea and coffee would be provided for the whole trip. Frank sang an old sea chanty while he worked in the galley with Jon.

"*Blow ye winds westerly, westerly blow. We're bound for the southern, so steady she goes,*" he sang.

"What talent! Frank, I didn't know you could sing," Jon teased.

"You probably still don't know I can sing."

Sky said, "Let's plan on some times of singing or reading stories to one another on this trip. We won't be diving all the time, plus we've got about six or eight hours of cruising to our anchorage and back, lots of time for some fun."

When the briefing was over, the group began to get acquainted, telling adventure stories, asking questions. An easy congeniality grew. The afternoon was uneventful. At times, flying fish glided ahead of the boat. Twice, the *Tiamat* powered in the midst of dolphins for several miles. A gray ocean reflected high clouds as far as they could see. A mild swell came from the west southwest, but the *Tiamat* made an easy twelve knots at partial throttle with very little roll on their course. Jon slept for an hour or so, until Sky awakened him. She wanted him to come topside and sit with her on the foredeck, which he gladly did. Krystal came forward with them, after a while, and cuddled up on one side of her mother with Jon on the other. Sky and Krystal talked for a few minutes, getting drowsy. Before he could talk to either of them, they were asleep, Krystal leaning on Sky's shoulder and Sky leaning on his.

Life doesn't get much better than this, he thought.

About 1600, they could see Pyramid Point clearly, almost dead ahead. It was dusk, but they had another hour of enough daylight to find an anchorage. With Dick Brophe's excellent seamanship, he would have no difficulty finding an anchorage, day or night. The *Tiamat's* electronics provided a lot of help, too, with sonar, two depth finders. Dick's familiarity with the San Clemente cove, China Point, and Pyramid Point was a great help as well. Jon cautioned that he didn't want them to attract any attention from anyone on the island. He noted that the whole island was a U. S. Navy restricted zone. He gave them a briefing on their not being able to go on the island; they might be ordered to leave at any time, their anchorage being in an uncertain area.

"Most of the activity," Brophe explained, "would be on the west end and the central part of San Clemente Island. I've called for information on San Clemente and learned that nothing was scheduled on the island by the Navy until after the first of the year, in a couple of months or more."

Once the group learned where they were headed, Paul and Ian especially expressed doubts about being able to dive in this area because of the Navy's restrictions. Sylvia told them of several times she had dived in the cove and how beautiful the undersea environment is there. Paul and Ian had not dived here, but were getting excited about looking for a sunken vessel, especially one having gone down in 1849. Carlos told them all the family story, talking about Shuka, his great-great grandfather, the whole thing, but he didn't mention the gold. Jon whispered a thank you to him for leaving out that part.

At about 1800 hours, they dropped a large CQR anchor from the bow in about fifty feet of water, not more than 200 yards from the China Point rocks. The rugged rocks were foreboding, making it all but impossible to go onto the island at this point even if they were allowed to do so. Ian and Sylvia inflated two rubber Avon Redcrest dinghies and put them out of the way on deck, ready to launch them in the morning. Dick lowered the dive platform and let out a stern anchor from the starboard quarter. He pointed the boat into the very mild swell, which was rounding the point from the south.

They agreed to two-hour watches all night, just for safety's sake. Dick showed all of them how to use the depth finders, how to keep them located properly so as to detect any possible drag on the anchors. Jon pointed out from their stern, as best he could judge, where he had run into the kelp and where he found the figurehead, nearly 100 yards astern of their anchorage. The three newcomers wanted to know the story of the figurehead and how the *Daimon* had gotten caught in the kelp. This led to the story of finding Sky's Cal-20. Krystal then added some things about becoming such good friends. She teased them both about acting like teenagers. Frank picked up on this theme and broke into song, warbling a tune from *Anchors Aweigh* about falling in love too quickly and easily, acting like a crooner; he demonstrated impressive musical talent. Sky and Jon hugged during Frank's singing. They all clapped at the end.

Krystal, Paul, Ian, and Sylvia settled in at the galley table and began to play Hearts, talking all at once, it seemed. The four of them were getting along very well. Brophe, a pleased skipper, commented that the *Tiamat* had rarely, if ever, had a more cordial and spirited group than this one.

"If you all get along like this for this entire trip, we should plan on something else together soon,"Jon said.

Sky eagerly agreed, asking, "When? When?"

Frank took charge. "2130. Sack time! We'll be up at 0600. As we decided, I'm cutting the watches to two hours each, to conserve our energies. I take the first watch, from now to 2300. Jon takes second watch, from 2300 to 0100. Sky takes third watch, from 0100 to 0300. Carlos, you have fourth watch, from 0300 to 0500. Dick, your watch is the last one, a short one, 0500 through 0700, but we'll be all up and have eaten breakfast by then. Jon and I will cook breakfast," he said.

Jon interrupted: "Frank, one change in this schedule. Krystal will replace you on the first watch. You're diving tomorrow. All the divers get a full night's sleep with no watches, and that should include Sky. If you're going to dive tomorrow, you should not have a watch tonight."

"I don't know if I'm going to dive tomorrow," Sky said. "I think I'll wait until something is found worthy of a dive.

I'd like to dive, but will save my air for later on, unless Frank comes up and invites me down to see something. So, as Frank ordered, I take third watch."

"Anyone on watch, be sure to monitor the depth finders and keep a sighting on the rocks. Watch for any drift. That's the main purpose for the watches. We seem to have good holds on both anchors, but as the tide comes in, the scope will change enough to pull more on them. Remember, watch for drift," Dick warned, having the most at stake with their being aboard his boat.

Each said goodnight and turned in. Sky and Jon took separate bunks, using the quarter berths. Krystal took a bunk just below Sylvia's. Dick had his own skipper's berth, the aft cabin. Paul and Ian located their foam pads and sleeping bags on the foredeck, sleeping outside. Even though they had a cloudy sky, the warm air made them comfortable. Frank and Carlos had midship bunks. This boat would sleep about fourteen people, if everyone got along well.

Being a sailboat person, Jon was always impressed with how much room a powerboat provided compared to a sailboat of similar length. This forty-six foot powerboat had more room than the average sixty foot sailboat.

Sleep came fast for them, gently rocking with a slight swell. Taking to heart their mission, they needed rest. Tomorrow would be an exacting, perhaps challenging, day for all of them. Before climbing into his bag, Jon sneaked an embrace and several goodnight kisses with Sky, whispering in her ear how much he loved her. She held on tightly, teasing that she would not let him go. But, both knew there were other times ahead for them. Besides, Krystal had the first watch and watching both of them was her first priority. Jon gave Krystal a hug goodnight, too. She put on her coat for her watch and climbed the ladder to the deck.

Chapter Twenty-Five

The morning watch thumped on the deck, awakening the rest of the crew. Paul and Ian came into the main cabin, after they had rolled up and stowed their sleeping bags and pads. They took turns using the heads, there being two of them. Dick Brophe had briefed them on the protocol for head use and included the rule of not pumping overboard. His boat was one of the first to have a holding tank, except for gray water, which went overboard. Dick kept everything aboard the *Tiamat* state of the art, including a hot water system, electronics that all worked well, which is unusual on boats. Also, there were several radios, radar, sonar; and two generators, besides the engine generators, provided all the power they needed. He ran the engines out of gear to top off the batteries, while they fixed and ate breakfast. The swells continued about the same as the evening before, making for ideal diving conditions. The water temperature was sixty-two degrees, providing relative comfort in wet suits. The dive time approached. Early sun shone just for a few minutes below the cloud layer to the east; then the sun disappeared, climbing behind the clouds. They took that to mean the day might become sunny as the clouds thinned. But, the forecast called for continuing high clouds through Wednesday and rain by Thursday.

By 0730, they were all on deck, helping the four divers with final preparations.

They were to start from about where the figurehead had been found, astern the *Tiamat's* anchorage, and, staying close to one another, they would begin to swim back and forth, working an imaginary grid, along the forty-foot depth line. If necessary, they would then go deeper to the east, beyond China Point and back. This procedure began the search for what they hoped would be the remains of the *Madonna*.

Frank and Sylvia were the first into the water, then Paul and Ian. They all bobbed to the surface long enough to give a 'thumbs up' and down they went. Those on deck tracked them by their bubbles. The murky water limited visibility to not more than about fifteen feet, which might hamper their ability to discover anything, but that did not prove to be a problem.

The first dive ended by 0845, when the four of them came to the surface and climbed aboard the dive platform, all panting. With deft motions their faceplates were off. Each diver removed regulators, checked them, and inspected their equipment. Sylvia had several strands of seaweed wrapped around her and her tank. She had fun, wrapping her face with the seaweed and making barking noises. It was a good imitation of a seal. They got into the cockpit and sat in the deck chairs to refresh themselves. They had tea and some cupcake snacks the moment their hands were free.

"Well, what so far?" Sky asked.

"You won't believe this, Sky," Frank said. Then he paused and slowly sipped his tea and took a bite of his cupcake. "Uhmm, that's good,"! he said, stalling to raise their curiosity.

"Is anyone going to tell us what you've seen so far?" Jon whined.

Frank said, "Jon, we've found part of the bow of a ship. It lies nearly covered in mud. Sylvia saw it first. I thought it was rocks, but she pulled me back and swept some of the mud off it. It is a huge bow or prow … a port bow, I think. There's what's left of a bowsprit, too. I could see where it attached to the bow in the mud and the mound of mud covering it for some ten feet or more. It is in about sixty feet of water, not more than thirty yards from where you say you found your figurehead. That ocean bottom slopes fast there. There's a lot more to see before we know what we've got. The bow is not too far from our port beam right now, just sixty or seventy feet below us, Dick, I wonder if your sonar scanner might pick up any shapes on the bottom. Can you aim it in that direction?"

Paul and Ian added some detail. They had gone farther southeast, by about 400 yards, along the same depth line. They hadn't seen the bow until on their way back to find Frank and Sylvia. They found part of a large mast protruding from the mud, claiming it had lines attached, complete with all kinds of growth, barnacles, and seaweed. They had passed over it several times before recognizing it as a mast. Not many yards farther, they found pieces of railing in the mud. It appeared to be the stern of a large sailing ship.

Ian reported, "I swam in circles near the mast stump and saw a row of broken ribs that made parallel bumps in the mud every few feet. Using some imagination, I figured it could be the outline of part of the original ship. It was an eerie sight, especially in the murky, deep water. There were strong currents beginning about fifty feet deep. The current caused the cloudy water at that depth. Above there, it was quieter and clearer. Jon, you never would have seen the figurehead in the mud had there been strong currents at thirty-five feet. Where the currents are running the water's really cloudy."

All of them expressed disbelief that they could have located the *Madonna* this quickly, if it were truly the *Madonna*. If it weren't, they had certainly found something equally as interesting. The ship had broken into pieces and appeared to be mostly buried. This made sense, because of the strong ocean currents around the south side of the island. Carlos reminded them that the ship not only had been burned, but also had exploded.

"It might be in many pieces," he said.

"Is there a way of determining the area the wreckage covers?" Dick asked.

"We'll do some more dives, Dick. This is only a beginning. We're eager to go down again in a short while, this time perhaps taking some probes with us to see if we can find pieces in the mud we can't see," Frank said. "Actually, we can see down there better than we thought we could. We have a good ten to twenty feet of visibility. Until Sylvia swept away some mud, when we couldn't see anything for fully five minutes, we were doing fine."

"What was I to do, Frank?" Sylvia asked, defensively.

"Just kidding, Sylvia. You earned your pay today finding that bow. I don't know how you recognized a shape like that covered with mud," Frank said.

"It was easy. The smooth mud bulged for nearly thirty or forty square feet, like a big burial mound, right there. Besides, if the figurehead came from that hole where we swam at first, the bow couldn't have been too far away," she reasoned.

"If we have the wreck we think we have, the rest of her ought to be strewn all around here beneath us," Ian said. Jon looked at Sky and asked, "Is it going to be worth excavating for this vessel? Will it be worth it for them to want to raise the pieces that are left?"

"That is going way ahead of where we are now. Let's learn as much as possible from the few dives we have before us. I'll do the charting of what we find as best I can.

"I'm going down with you for the next dive," she said. She stood from her cushion and left to struggle into her wetsuit.

"I wish I were certified. Would I ever love to tag along on this dive! I wouldn't be much use, I guess, but I'd love the experience," Jon said.

"I won't tell if you won't. I'm a diver here, not a cop," Frank said.

"Sorry, Jon. No illegal or unsafe diving from this boat. I know you'd probably be okay with the scuba and snorkeling you've done, but you've got to be certified to dive from the *Tiamat*," Dick said, very seriously.

"I understand, Dick. I want nothing to jeopardize what we're doing today. I am still in shock we have found whatever we've found already. You people are terrific," Jon said, raising his coffee cup in a toast to the four divers. "You all have an added assignment on the next dive, though. Watch out for Sky. Don't let her swim off by herself. She'll get down there and start doing her mapping and forget about her air and her partners. I want nothing to happen to any of you, but do watch out for Sky."

"Don't worry, Jon. We'll bring your woman back alive," Frank said, bumping Jon with his elbow as he stood up to step back aboard the dive platform.

Sky emerged from the cabin, very shapely in her wetsuit. Paul lifted her tank and helped her on with it, arranging her gear and holding her faceplate so she could slip it on easily. She thanked him and winked at Jon, her smile revealing how very happy she was to be diving. This was her profession at its best. She looked about sixteen, younger than Krystal. Krystal gave her a bump with her hip and a quick hug, telling her mother to be careful and have a good time down there. Having waited barely the minimum time of two hours, the five of them repeated the first dive departure, rising, giving thumbs up and then, disappearing below, bubbles marking their courses as they headed off the starboard bow. Carlos and Jon went to the bow to watch their progress.

"I can't help but be excited, Jon. This is so incredible to me. I can hardly believe I'm here, doing this. The other thought, of course, has to do with the secret treasure lying below us somewhere. Of course, the chances of finding it are slim, I suppose, but wouldn't that be amazing if we found the 'g' word treasure?" he said, rubbing his hands together.

"Carlos, we better keep this quiet about the *Madonna*, if she is definitely the vessel we've found. I can't imagine there being two such ships here, but anything could be, I suppose," Jon said.

"I'll watch my greedy curiosity, Jon. I guess I should be embarrassed wanting also to find the treasure. To think all those years ago, Shuka got this very stuff, sailed perhaps on this very vessel embedded below us right now, and all of them rowed to San Juan in the dark, escaping the American brig chasing them. This should be a movie. Maybe this is a movie, Jon. It seems so unreal to me right now," Carlos said, gripping Jon's arm with intensity and colorful awareness. "I know I can't, but I want to call Laura and tell her all about what we've found," he added. "But, maybe it's not the *Madonna*."

"No matter what, Carlos, no telling anyone anything about this until we've decided on exactly what to reveal. This expedition is still top secret. Sky will be the only one to talk to about this ... the official spokeswoman," Jon said, making himself as clear and direct with Carlos as possible. He realized he harbored feelings about his having told Michael in the first place. The ordeal Sky and Krystal had gone through had been completely unnecessary. Carlos knew that and felt guilty for several things, including having breached confidence and secrecy.

Forty minutes went by before the five came up. Dick and Jon were getting worried because they were already five minutes longer than their safe time down. Paul and Ian came up first. They watched for the other three. Paul, sitting on the dive platform with his mask off, told the others they were still finishing up some probing and would be up in a few minutes. As he said this, the three emerged at the same time. Paul and Ian helped them aboard the platform. Their masks were off in seconds and they were breathing hard from the swim, but all three were obviously pleased with themselves.

"I can draw a map of the debris field." Sky paused, taking some deep breaths. She tossed her head, throwing her wet hair back and forth, the water flying in Frank's face as he sat beside her on the platform. "I need to do it soon, so I remember the dimensions and approximate locations of the items or the humps in the sand we detected with our probes," she said.

"I think we should all rest, have some lunch, and then decide on what to do next," Frank said. "In a way, we've accomplished most of what we have come to do, but there may be more we could explore, if you all want to do that."

"I planned to be out here for a while. I don't have to be back to school before Thursday. I don't want to go back until we have to," Krystal said.

"I might suggest we save more dives for another time, though," Frank said. "We could use more equipment and, perhaps, do some minor excavating." Then, looking at his watch, he said, "We can't dive again today to seventy feet until about 1500. That'll give us the required recovery time."

"Let's get some rest and lunch and talk about this later," Sky said.

Jon agreed with the plan and each went to take off wetsuits and get into comfortable clothes.

Frank and Jon began to fix lunches. They prepared a mammoth salad: shrimp, two kinds of lettuce, tomatoes, croutons, and several options for dressings. There were pita sandwiches, leaving a variety of sliced meat and cheeses on a large tray for each to have as they wanted. Four different kinds of juice were set out, along with coffee and teas. Jon offered beer and wine to anyone wanting some. Paul, Carlos, and Jon had white wine. Sky had a beer out of the can. Krystal wanted a beer, but Sky wouldn't let her, so she had a Pepsi.

With her beer and sandwich, Sky sat down at the galley table and drew out the debris field as best she could recall it. She started from the hole where the figurehead had been embedded, to the location of the probable stern of the vessel. This covered nearly 250 feet in total distance. Jon sat next to her, watching her do her figuring and notations on a large piece of paper.

"It's weird the wreck is stretched about 100 feet longer than the *Madonna*'s total length," she said. "She and the *Apostle* were about 127 feet long, including their bowsprits, a beam of nearly 30 feet. They drew about fourteen feet in depth, without cargos, judging from what I have been able to glean. The explosion might have broken the ship up so much that she sank in pieces and we're finding those sections, scattered apart on the bottom."

It sounded reasonable, even likely, to Jon. Dick agreed with her about the ship coming apart. The fire at first might have weakened the hull enough so when the explosion happened it literally blew apart. Or, maybe when it sank, it came against the rocks it had hit when rounding or doubling China Point.

"Are you going to register the wreck, Sky?" Jon asked.

"I've got to. Besides, we'll have more control over the site once it's registered than we have now. Now, if anyone finds out about this and it's not registered it will be subject to looters, curious divers, and lord knows what could happen to the remains of this find," she said.

"What about Carlos and his determination to find the treasure?" Jon whispered to Sky.

Quietly, she responded, "He'll have to be patient. Who knows where or if there is any treasure? But, no matter what, there will be a lot to do to find it in the mud of this site."

"We can't tell the others about the treasure. Or should we?"

"No! Not yet, Jon. Don't breathe a word about treasure at this point. Let's keep this just an interesting archeological find for now," she said, finishing her pita sandwich and taking a draw from her can of Coors Light.

"Sky, do you know how much fun it is to be doing this with you?"

"As a matter of fact, Jon, I've never enjoyed my work as much as I've enjoyed doing this. Along with that, no matter what we might do together, just being together makes it more fun," she said, whispering to him and snuggling against him at the table, drawing attention from three others around the table.

Frank sat across from them listening somewhat and reading a back issue of *Time* magazine. He pretended not to hear them, but he was obviously paying attention.

"You two are doing pretty well together. I think this was all meant to be, Jon. What do you think? You're a shrink and a minister. You're supposed to have a feeling about how fate works," he said.

"It isn't fate, Frank. It is the guidance of the holy."

"That's too deep for me. I'll just leave it to fate, if that's okay."

"I'm with you, Frank. This stuff about the holy is too much for my little brain or heart to get around," Sky said.

"Okay. That's settled. You pagans can call it fate and I'll call it the guidance of the holy. We'll never know which, but I'll get more out of my twist on this romance than you two will," said Jon.

With that exchange, Sky and Jon leaned back together against the cushion. Then she turned and stretched out on the seat. Lying down, she rested her head in his lap, soon dozing. Jon stroked her damp hair as she breathed very gently.

Dick sat down with them. He had ideas about more accurate ways of working with this wreck. Aboard the *Tiamat* he had a handheld, underwater metal detector that worked pretty well. Being a 1982 model, there were better ones available now, but Dick had used this unit and found things like anchors, and parts of ships. Once he found some silver bars in six inches of mud. The idea intrigued Jon. Dick suggested borrowing or renting a boat-towed unit. They could use the Avon dinghy, lower the unit to just above the mud and tow it back and forth over what they thought to be the whole debris field. Jon felt sure that using a magnetometer for this search or a side scan detector much could be found. Of course, the wood part of the ship, probably porous now from the teredo worms, would not be detected. But there were all kinds of metal pieces on the square rigged ships and those pieces, if not too deep in the mud, would render a signal to a good detection device.

Thinking Sky to be asleep, Jon asked Dick to bring this up to her later. But, she stirred in his lap and said, "That would be a good thing to do, Dick. We probably can't do too much more on this trip, but maybe, if there is enough interest in this find, funds could be found to explore the entire site."

"Can just anyone use these underwater metal detectors, Dick?" Carlos asked.

"It takes a good deal of skill and trial and error to learn how to read the sounds and the signals, but after enough time and use anyone can do it," he said.

"Would it pick up other metals besides iron?"

"Ferrous metals are the most easily detected, but if the other metals aren't too deeply buried, it will do well on them, depending on how much there is in any location," Dick said.

Jon became nervous about Carlos asking these questions. Giving him a look to remind him of their agreement about the possible treasure, Carlos caught on right away and asked nothing more about detecting metals. Sky sat up and stretched. Jon smoothed her hair and she excused herself to go to the head. The conversation went to one topic after another, and Dick and Frank told stories about having dived on various projects over their years of exploring. Carlos and Jon enjoyed the stories and conversation. Carlos got them all beer and a bag of pretzels to share as they chatted. The others were on deck. From topside, they could hear the muffled conversation and, especially, Sylvia's contagious laughter from time to time. Sky returned and sat down next to Jon, stretching out the map of debris she had drawn.

"What's next?" Frank asked.

"I'd like one more dive, perhaps tomorrow morning or even this afternoon. There are two areas where I didn't use the probe, because I was running low on air," Sky said.

"If you're up to it, let's do it this afternoon. We have about two hours left of good light. If you're too tired, we should wait until morning," Frank said.

Dick checked with the three divers on deck. Everyone grew eager to go down this afternoon. Clouds still covered most of the sky, but they were thinning.

Dick said, "The rain forecast is for Thursday, and possibly earlier. At best we have only one more day here before the front will move in. The swells should be increasing by noon tomorrow and we've already noticed some increase in swells out of the south-southwest."

All agreed to do one more thirty-minute dive this afternoon at 1530. Organizing for the dive began. Not more than a half hour later, the five divers were poised for their descent. The calm water had a slight swell out of the southeast. With a low tide, the kelp astern looked like a floating green garden. Two seals watched from a distance.

Cormorants, pelicans, and seagulls populated the rocks. Another two seals rested on a buoy far astern. Once in a while their barking could be heard.

Sky checked her regulator, wiped her faceplate glass with saliva, and placed it over her face as she pulled her hair back to make a good seal against her skin. She splashed into the water first, with the others right after her. Before going down, the five in a circle looked somewhat like the watching seals. They checked one another's gear, synchronized watches and checked depth gauges. All thumbs up, they disappeared in a mass of bubbles.

Within minutes, Krystal and Jon were in an Avon rowing in the direction of their bubbles. The cloudy water obscured their seeing more than about fifteen or twenty feet down, but they could track their bubbles. They positioned the dinghy over the place where the divers seemed to be.

Sky and Frank took down long probes to see if they could find more pieces of the wreckage. Paul took with him the handheld metal detector loop. A 300 foot length of coaxial cable linked the loop to the sensing unit Dick watched aboard the *Tiamat*. The plan was for Paul to swim slowly along one side of the wreckage and then back and forth along it, in a grid pattern, like plowing a field. The detector loop worked best about one foot above the mud, according to Dick's instructions. Dick would chart the course on a piece of paper, marking active places with circles. Jon would give each circle a magnitude indicator, from one to five. Five was the highest reading from the detector.

Ian's job was to be sure the coaxial cable didn't get caught on anything and to stay with Paul. Frank, Sylvia, and Sky were to stay together doing the probing.

"Look, Jon!" Krystal shouted, her mouth only two feet from him in the dinghy. "Look, a couple of dolphins over there! They're really close," she said, excited.

Two fins glided through the water not fifty feet from their starboard side. Jon noticed, too, that the seals had disappeared. For a moment, he didn't want to say anything to Krystal, but insisted they row toward the dolphins, which he urgently began to do.

"You'll scare them away, Jon," she said.

"I hope so, Krystal. Those two fins are on one large shark," he said, watching her reaction, which took only seconds.

"A shark! Jon, no! A shark? They're down there and here's a shark? Jon, do something!" she screamed.

Jon took the Avon paddle and began slapping the water as hard as he could, hoping the five divers below would hear it and look up, or, maybe, he could scare away the shark. There were Yellowtail all around this area. Pyramid Reef seemed to attract them. The shark probably came after them, but all divers are wary of sharks, to say the least. The shark immediately circled their Avon, swimming fast about forty feet around them. Then it dived.

The divers had not been down more than twenty minutes when Paul and Ian surfaced, swimming as fast as possible toward the *Tiamat*. Then came Frank, holding Sylvia under his right arm. Krystal and Jon rowed frantically toward him, Krystal shouting, "Where's mother? Where's mother?"

Frank grabbed onto the Avon with Sylvia limp alongside him. Flipping off his faceplate, he yelled, "Get her aboard! Someone call the Coast Guard for a rescue. Hurry. Get her aboard!"

With Frank's boost, Krystal and Jon pulled Sylvia aboard. She seemed unconscious and blood spurted from her torn right arm. Krystal yelled at Frank to get her mother.

Replacing his faceplate, he disappeared below. Within seconds, he returned with Sky by his side. They swam fast, racing to the dive platform a hundred yards from the dinghy. Jon rowed the Avon with all the strength he could muster. Krystal kept applying direct pressure through the torn wetsuit on Sylvia's right arm.

"Jon, she doesn't have some of her arm," Krystal said, almost calm. "Sylvia's arm is gone, or some of it! There's blood all over! I can't stop it enough!" she wailed.

They made it to the dive platform. Dick and Carlos were already helping Sky and Frank out of the water. Paul and Ian stood in the cockpit of the boat, breathing hard, tanks and gear lying at their feet.

Dick said, "I've called the Coast Guard for a rescue chopper. But, they haven't responded yet. I'll keep calling."

Ian said, "I tried to get the shark to come my way. It circled all of us, looking us over. Then, it went like a bullet for Sylvia. She was about fifteen feet from me. I didn't think it got any of us, until I saw the blood in the water around Sylvia. Frank grabbed her and came topside, coming up with his bubbles, holding her bleeding arm as best he could. Paul and I swam like hell, thinking the shark was chasing us. As deep as we were, we had to come up slowly. We left Sky alone. I can't believe we left her alone. I started to go back, but Paul grabbed me and turned me back toward the boat. We couldn't see Sky anywhere. Is everyone okay? We came up too fast, but I guess we're okay."

Having a hard time speaking, breathing hard and still in panic, Sky said, "I was right behind all of you. I used my probe stick, swinging it with all my might. The shark watched me from about ten feet away." She paused to take some deep breaths. "It just watched me. I swam slowly by it, swinging the stupid stick as fast as I could in the water. I was terrified. I knew Sylvia had been hit. I couldn't see what happened to her, but knew she had been hit hard by that thing." She took some more deep breaths.

Dick gave her orange juice, which she drank, then passed the bottle to Frank. They all drank, looking at one another, while they cut the wetsuit away from Sylvia's arm.

Tiamat, Tiamat, Coast Guard Radio Long Beach Channel 16. Come in.

"Coast Guard Radio Long Beach, this is the *Tiamat*, we have a shark-attack victim. Require helicopter transport immediately. Location China Point, east end San Clemente Island. Repeat, need immediate medical transport," he said.

Tiamat. Keep your position. Stay on the radio. Helicopter dispatched to you at 1552. Verify, China Point. Provide first aid to victims. Our medic is on the radio with us and will advise to help, came the reassuring word from the loudspeaker.

Dick had a tourniquet on Sylvia's upper arm, but the direct pressure was best in stopping all but a trickle of blood. She remained unconscious, probably from shock and having lost too much blood. Krystal and Sky wrapped her in blankets. Carlos attempted to get a bit of juice in her mouth, but it came right out again. She could not swallow.

Luckily, through everything, she had kept her regulator mouthpiece in her mouth. They didn't think she had taken in sea water, or they hoped that to be the case. Her heart rate was fast, but strong. Once in a while, she had a slight twitching, perhaps mild convulsions or spasms.

"It's taking that chopper a long time," Paul said.

"I'd put this in gear and start for the coast, but they told me to stay put," Dick said.

Sylvia's eyes opened. She winced with pain and moaned. They did their best to comfort her. Krystal held her head in her lap and stroked her wet head.

"Shark," Sylvia said. "I saw a shark down there," she repeated, very calmly.

"We have a chopper coming to take you to emergency, Sylvia. You're going to be okay," Frank said, attempting to reassure her.

"My arm hurts like hell."

"Where does it hurt?"

"My hand and wrist hurt the most, like they're broken," she said, grimacing.

It was nearly forty minutes until chopper blades sounded from around Pyramid Point and a large Coast Guard helicopter careened toward the *Tiamat*, dropping fast, skillfully coming to a hover just leeward, off the starboard side. A strapped basket hung from the chopper and rapidly descended even before it started to hover. The basket was nearly in the water and inched closer. The strong downdraft from the chopper added to Paul's difficulty, but he used the boat hook, grabbed the basket, and shoved it close to them on the deck. They all helped, carefully loading Sylvia into it, strapping her securely. The whole operation took less than two minutes. They watched, speechless, as the basket swiftly ascended and was carefully pulled into the helicopter. Another line dropped, with a boatswain's chair attached. Frank grabbed it and he was winched aboard the helicopter before any of the others could react. He still wore his wetsuit, minus flippers and diving gear.

"He's going to look funny waiting for the emergency docs to come out of the operating room in his wetsuit," Paul said, attempting to lighten up the catastrophe they had witnessed.

Jon said, "I want you to get changed into your clothes. We're pulling up stakes here, weighing anchors. We've done all we're going to do this trip."

Dick agreed with him. But, first, he had a detail to tend to.

"Look at this, Jon," he said quietly, gesturing for Jon to move close to his side.

Looking at the monitor, sitting alongside his sonar and depth finder scopes, the two saw a very strong pulse coming from the loop, lying on the bottom. Almost whispering to Jon, he said, "Jon, this loop is apparently next to a lot of metal. I can locate the loop with the sonar's image. See here, on my paper? It is right here, about eighty or ninety feet ahead off our bow where we sit right now, right at twelve o'clock."

Jon marked his improvised map, about one-half drawn from the scanning Paul and Ian had accomplished with the loop. When they escaped the shark, they dropped the loop. They could easily retrieve it, as they carefully pulled it up with the coaxial cable. He hoped it didn't get caught on anything. According to the sonar, nothing seemed in the way, unless it got caught sliding along the mud bottom. Jon decided to row out with the coaxial cable and pull it straight up into the Avon from above, instead of taking a chance on its getting caught on something. If it sank in the mud, there were lots of wreckage pieces that could catch it. It was too expensive to lose. Carlos went with Jon to get it. They retrieved the loop as they rowed back to the dive boat. Jon could hear Dick start his engines.

Krystal remained sitting with Sky. Sky held her on one side and Paul on the other side of her. Krystal wept softly. Sky kept hugging Krystal, kissing her hands, telling her what a good job she had done with Sylvia. Jon echoed Sky's praises. Krystal moaned, "I couldn't stop the blood, Jon. I couldn't stop it. We went all that way and her blood was in the dinghy. No matter what I did, I couldn't stop her bleeding. She lost too much blood. Is she going to live, Jon?" Krystal asked, her eyes begging for comfort.

"Everything's being done, Krystal. We all worked as a good team and you were right there with her, keeping her going," Jon said, doing his best to quiet her fears.

Dick ordered everyone to freshen up and change into clothes for dinner. Sky excused herself. She went to the stern of the *Tiamat*, hung her head over the railing and vomited. Jon ran to her and held her as she fed the fish. Carlos brought a damp washrag and gave it to Jon, who pressed it against her forehead, supporting her shaking body as she retched a few more times. Once through, Jon stretched her out on the cushion in the cockpit and put a blanket over her, sitting by her. Carlos handed them a glass of water.

"Wish I could sing something soothing to you right now, Sky."

"I don't think there are any good songs for me right now," she said, weakly.

"There are a bunch of hymns I could sing, but I think being quiet would be the best help."

She reached up and touched his face, smiling.

"This is the shits, Jon!"

"We're on our way home, Sky. Frank is with Sylvia and she's being cared for. We got all of you back alive. That shark could have killed any one of you."

"I heard something slapping on the water above us, she paused," her body taking some shaking breaths. "I guess you were trying to get our attention. When I looked up, there was that animal doing spirals down to where we were and I knew we were in for something awful."

Ian had the stern anchor up and stowed. Dick moved forward on the bow anchor and Ian ran to the bow to engage the electric windlass, pulling up the hook. With only about 150 feet out, they quickly secured the CQR in its bow anchor locker. Dick backed away from it as it came up, making a smooth operation. The mud and kelp were washed from the anchor as the boat towed it for a minute in the water, slowly going astern. Once the hook was secured, Dick began going forward, turning to port, to depart the anchorage. They pulled the Avon aboard the *Tiamat* and stacked it on top of the other one, lashing them both to the foredeck. The fore and aft anchors were stowed and the *Tiamat* maneuvered to head for the open sea and the trip home. Dick swung the bow to starboard while he powered up. The boat's stern dug into the churning water, to clear the east end of the island.

Chapter Twenty-Six

The sun descended behind the island. By the time they were clear of San Clemente Island's Pyramid Point, heading northerly at about three six zero degrees toward Long Beach, the sun again became visible, sinking beneath the clouds into the sea. Dick Brophe corrected ten degrees to port to compensate for the coastal current. But, one more problem suddenly arose.

A Coast Guard launch with five people aboard approached at full speed toward them as they headed north for the mainland from Pyramid Point. A loudspeaker hailed, *Tiamat! Tiamat! This is the United States Coast Guard ordering you to slow to five knots.*

Dick immediately cut his throttle to 700 rpm. The group, suddenly tense, did not know what to expect. The rubber launch came alongside and they secured their lines fore and aft. Jon secured the bumpers to protect from chafing. A Seaman Griffith introduced himself and handed Dick Brophe an envelope, wrapped in a plastic bag to keep it dry. Griffith told Dick he needed a receipt signed for the envelope, which Dick did. The other four Coast Guardsmen waited until finishing the business. Seaman Griffith told them they were not supposed to be diving in this area without permission. They needed to make a complete report regarding a shark attack involving a Miss Sylvia Matthews as well as an explanation of their business diving in this area.

Dick said to him, "We've had clearance to have a day's vacation here and diving in this cove is always inviting. What's the problem?"

"All I know is, you need to respond to the questions and fill out the document in the envelope. The officer dispatching us has reason to believe you were doing more than leisure diving here," Seaman Griffith said.

"I'll look over all this you've given me and will do what is required. Who do I report to about this?" Dick asked.

"Ensign Shabro is our dispatching officer. You will find her through the phone number in the envelope, Sir," he said.

"Are we free to go, Seaman Griffith?" Dick asked.

"Yes Sir," said Griffith.

Jon asked Griffith as they untied their lines, "Where'd they take Sylvia Matthews?"

"They flew her to Emergency at Good Samaritan Hospital, downtown Los Angeles!"

They pushed off from the *Tiamat*'s starboard beam, their big outboard churning the water as they left, heading west along the island's cliffs. Dick throttled up to two thousand rpm. The forty-six foot *Tiamat* accelerated on course toward Alamitos jetty, about sixty nautical miles ahead. Carlos, Krystal, and Sky stretched out on the cockpit cushions. Paul, Ian, Dick, and Jon found places to sit in the flying bridge. Dick turned the helm over to Paul, telling him to steer three five zero degrees and hold the speed at about twelve knots. The swell ran with them. Judging from the clouds, the wind, and the forecast, it was fairly certain there would be rain by tomorrow. But, they would be back in the *Tiamat*'s slip by midnight, with ease. Before all got too comfortable, Dick announced that Jon and Carlos would prepare dinner for the seven of them.

Jon said, "Aye-aye, Captain."

Jon and Carlos went below to make dinner for all, taking out a pre-cooked roast of beef to be heated up. Carlos placed the aluminum foil wrapped rolled roast into the oven. Jon cut vegetables to stir fry them. Carlos asked who wanted what to drink and they filled the orders all around. Sky obviously felt better. She said, "Do you have a good Merlot aboard or, perhaps, a gin and tonic?" "Sky, my love, we have both. You name it. If I can't be honest about it, I'll call what I give you anything you want," Jon said. He poured her a glass of Merlot. Along with it, he gave her a small plate of crackers and cheese. "Don't spoil your dinner, Sky, your wine should go well with the roast beef."

Krystal had her usual Pepsi. Carlos, Ian, and Paul insisted on Coors. Dick and Jon had Vodka martinis, two olives each. It would be about an hour before the roast was ready. The crew was getting sleepy as the resonant engines along with the rocking boat soothed them into the night. No lights on the coast were yet visible. They powered into black ocean. There were no stars and only phosphorous from the propellers and their reflected bow lights that added sparkle to the night. Jon wondered whether they would be awake enough for dinner - a foolish thought. As soon as the meal graced the galley table, the swarm of hungry mariners and divers were upon it. The meal obviously satisfied them, and they complimented the cooks. Dick had the *Tiamat* on auto-pilot, checking her heading every five or ten minutes.

Ian was the first on bow watch. Crossing the shipping lanes required a constant vigil. They were already into the coastal traffic lanes. There were lights from a container freighter far astern. Other lights appeared to be a tanker, at about their one o'clock position, just off the starboard bow. Though it appeared to be sitting still, Dick figured they were on a collision course if they did not pay attention as they drew closer. As the perspective changed, Dick announced the tanker would cross the bow in about fifteen minutes and head probably toward the Los Angeles harbor entrance. The visible red light blinking ahead marked that entrance.

He was within two minutes of his estimate. As they went within 100 yards astern of the tanker, into her churning wake, their presence probably was never detected. Its great, black mass towered above. Her lights were ablaze around the superstructure of the tanker. She flew a Liberian flag, illuminated by a soft stern light. Dick guessed the tanker, low in the water, probably carried crude. By the time they were clear of the ship they could see the first coastal lights, including an intermittent light at the distant Long Beach jetty entrance. It would be a little while longer before they recognized the flashing light at the end of the Alamitos jetty. That light marked the jetty access to their home slip.

Dick called out, "I've got the Alamitos light. Hard to see it with all the surrounding lights, but I've confirmed the flashing period and it's definitely Alamitos Bay jetty."

The crew settled in for the rest of the trip, about an hour left. Dishes done and all asleep, except for Ian at the helm, Sky and Jon snuggled together on the stacked dinghies on the foredeck. A surge of gratitude swept through Jon. He commented to Sky how close they had come to losing her. She moved even closer into his side.

Even with the strong, warm wind off the port bow, they maintained twelve knots. Wrapped in blankets and holding one another, they were warm on deck under the cloudy sky. Sky's frequent, delicate snoring told Jon she felt comfortable, safe, and peaceful. Krystal stayed below in her bunk, sound asleep since dessert. Dick and Carlos also slept. All in all, after what they had been through this Monday of all Mondays, they were relieved, peaceful, and on their way home having accomplished a great deal, but with a dreadful casualty. It looked as though Sylvia had lost her right arm just above her elbow. The thought sickened Jon. Quietly, he prayed for her and gave thanks for this collection of people, their skill, bravery, and the good fortune to be returning to the Long Beach slip with relative ease. The twin diesels throbbed out their steady thrust to Alamitos Bay.

Heading into the bay's entrance, they prepared to leave the *Tiamat*, each person gathering gear and personal items. Sky and the other divers bagged their wet suits and diving paraphernalia. The craft glided slowly into the slip, reversing the props skillfully for a full stop. Four of them cleated the dock lines, lowered the gangway, and prepared for departure.

As the first one on the gangway, Krystal excused herself. She said she had something important to do.

"I'll be back right away. I really need to make a phone call," she said.

"Okay, Krystal. But I'd like us all to have a brief talk before we depart," Jon said.

Sky added, "I'm glad you said something, I was going to tell them the same thing."

Though tired, they eagerly convened around the galley table, Sky next to Jon. In a few minutes, Krystal returned and quickly snuggled against her mother, squeezing herself between Carlos, Dick, Ian, and Paul. Quite cozy, they filled the settee seating area.

"I guess I'll start off with my concerns. The first thing I want to do is find out how Sylvia is doing," Jon said.

Krystal interrupted, "She's in Good Samaritan Hospital's critical care unit. I went to the dock phone and called the Coast Guard, that number on that guy's card. They didn't want to answer my questions, but I told them who I was and my being on the *Tiamat* and they told me they had helicoptered her to Good Samaritan Hospital. I want to go see her right away," she said, with tears in her eyes. Krystal reached out and gripped her mother's arm.

Jon said, "Thank you, Krystal. Sylvia is one of our first concerns and your learning all that and sharing it with us helps a lot. I want to go with you to Good Sam." "I'm going to go right now. You two come as soon as you can," Krystal said firmly.

"Can't you wait for us, Krystal? I know you're impatient, but we could all go together," said Sky.

"I can't wait, Mother. You and Jon finish what you need to do and come when you can."

Sky shrugged and said, "Okay, do what you need to do. It will take us a while here, then we'll come." Then she turned to speak to the others.

"We've got to keep everything we can secret at this point. The Coast Guard gave us a number of questions. I think we can answer them in such a way that will not reveal what we need to keep to ourselves for now. The location of what we found, the map Dick put together, everything has to be secret. I'm afraid, because of the shark attack, we will be besieged by the media searching for stories, the more sensational the better as far as they're concerned. Let me assure you all, we're on good legal ground so far for everything. We've done nothing illegal. There is an Abandoned Shipwreck Act that has been in the mill for several years, but it won't be a law for at least another couple of years," Sky said, folding pages of notes and putting them in a manilla folder.

"Political and jurisdictional things are being argued now. All the greedy hands are in the law that is being written. The State wants theirs, the Feds want theirs. Who knows what the salvage people will get in the end? But, finding the *Madonna* is exactly that, a 'Find.' I'm sure we've found our ship. When something is found that has clearly been abandoned, it doesn't come under the current salvage laws and the finders are the keepers. Of course, everything has to be registered with the State and the Federal Government, but this wreckage and the site will be credited to us. I will probably end up claiming it for the California State University Long Beach History Department and the Marine Archeological Society," she told them. She took a breath and turned the discussion over to the others.

"I think we're all agreed about keeping this quiet. The only things we should mention are those disclosed in the paper, mostly about Sylvia's close call, even if people pump us for more," Dick said.

Paul and Ian added their approval to the plan, but they wanted to be sure they would be asked along on any other dives and they hoped they could return soon to do some more exploring. Being in agreement, they all piled hands together into the middle of the table and Dick said, "Agreed! Jon, you're in charge of keeping us all informed."

After Paul and Ian had gone, Carlos asked, "What if we find some treasure?"

"That is the part we need to keep most secret, Carlos," Dick said. "Let's agree, we don't move on any possible treasure until we get together and devise a search and retrieval plan. It's obvious, from the three guys thinking they could find it first at Catalina, others would quickly start a treasure hunt if the location were revealed. It may already be conjectured, seeing as San Clemente's where we were diving when Sylvia was attacked by the shark. That for certain made the news. Someone might guess we were there looking for the *Madonna* and they could easily leap to thinking the wreck could contain treasure."

"Michael and Luís Jimenez are in jail, but they could have told someone else," Carlos said. "The one who drowned may have told people, too. His family lives close to us in San Juan Capistrano. Ray Cramer is the one who drowned. It's ironic, of the three of them, he was the only certified diver." Carlos paused, then added, "Michael had lessons, but never finished. Luís knows boats and probably talked them into stealing the Grand Banks. We don't know if anyone else was in on the plan when they stole the boat."

Reluctantly, they began departing, stepping onto the dock in the night air. Several dock carts were required to carry all the gear and luggage. Jon told Dick he would come back to help clean up the boat. He explained he had to coordinate with Sky as to when they were going to visit Sylvia at the hospital. Carlos also volunteered to clean. Dick let them know they had been a good crew and there wasn't a lot to do, reminding Jon of the leftover food to be removed. Krystal left for home right away. Dick wanted to have some time with Sky and Jon to go over the map of the ship's wreckage he'd constructed. Partly he needed to clarify things, but he also wanted to establish where the metal detecting loop had been lying just before it was pulled up.

It was nearly 10:00 PM when Sky and Jon talked about going to the hospital. Because of the late hour and their exhaustion, they decided to put the trip off until morning.

Jon went to the *Daimon*, unloaded his luggage, took a shower, and decided there was nothing to do until dawn. Just past midnight, his on-board phone rang.

"Jon, I'm sorry for calling you this late, but I had to talk to you and tell you about Krystal's going to the hospital. I'm so worried about her. I wish she had waited. She just had to get to Sylvia. I feel guilty. I should have gone with her. She's really attached to Sylvia somehow."

"Of course. They hit it off immediately when Sylvia came on board. Remember how they talked for several hours? Krystal helped Sylvia with her gear. Sylvia brushed Krystal's hair for a long while and they were laughing. I've not seen Krystal laugh like that in the short time I've known her."

"When Krystal left tonight, she seemed excited to be going," Sky said.

They talked for a few more minutes, then decided to have breakfast at seven at The Omelette House, in just six or so hours hence, and then drive to Los Angeles. Before hanging up, Sky said one more thing that left Jon warm and excited.

"Jon, I could come to the boat right now. We could hold one another until breakfast. Remember how we were breathing together lying on the dinghy coming back from the island? That was heavenly, Jon," she said.

"I'd love that. I also relish your saying that and wanting to come here. Think about it. If you're sure you will feel comfortable and safe, please come, Sky," Jon said.

A long pause followed. The seconds passed. "I guess I better not, not yet, Jon. But, I could almost come be with you and know it would be okay afterward. For me, that is quite a change," she said.

"Sky, I love you."

"Oh dear. I don't think you should say that to me right now. Take it back!"

"Nope. I'm leaving that right there in your ear. My love is going to work its way clear down to your beautiful heart and your terrified liver."

"Good night, *mon capitaine*. I'll see you at seven."

Chapter Twenty-Seven

Sky pulled up to the curb as Jon approached the café, greeting him with her smile.

When he opened the car door for her, she stepped out, taking his hand to gracefully arise from her T-Bird. Her hair was in a neat bun on the back of her head. She wore a blue sweat suit and running shoes.

"You look exquisite no matter what you're wearing, even in a sweat suit."

"I look exquisite to you because you love me. Remember, you told me you loved me?" she said. She was demure with a tincture of shy.

"Well, that explains it fully." He took her hand and they walked toward the café.

Julia put down two water glasses as she greeted them and bumped Jon's shoulder with her hip, "Where've you been hiding out? Haven't seen you in several weeks. Are you eating somewhere else these days?" Julia paused and reached for the coffee pot. "Men! No loyalty whatsoever. Can't live with 'em and can't live without 'em."

They bantered for a few seconds. Jon refreshed her memory as to Sky's name and the two of them talked easily to one another. Julia took their orders before leaving the booth. When she left, Sky got up and came to his side to sit next to him.

"There, that's better, she said."

"I think you're feeling safer with me. This is going well. This is really going well."

"I'm embarrassed to tell you how well this is going, Jon. I've not felt like this ever. I awoke about three o'clock this morning, so ready to make love and all of it from thinking of you. I kept thinking how I would not be able to admit this to you and then, driving over here, I decided to tell you. I'm sitting here like a well-socialized woman, but I'm throbbing and loving every moment of it," she said, taking his hand and placing it against her lower abdomen. "Feel that?"

"I feel that," Jon said, his body responding.

"Jon, what do we do with all this? Where are we headed? You're a priest and I don't know anything about religion, except in cultural anthropology terms. I can't get used to a priest being able to be romantic or even be married. Maybe, in time, I'll understand all of this stuff. I never thought I'd have to learn about priests, celibate or not."

"We've got a lot to talk about. I'm first of all a human being who happens to be a priest. My understanding of ministry is to always be authentic, to celebrate the sacredness of relationship. I must be true to myself first, true to God, of course, but also honest and true with those I love. I'm absolutely taken with you and how we are together, Sky. How can I deny that? I'll go with this as long and as far as the two of us can travel. There is a saying I like. 'Love is a journey; the journey's what it is. No matter where it leads, the journey is what love is.' We're on a journey and I'm loving it. You seem to be accepting this, too, which is quite a change from the terror you had some weeks ago. What's changed for you? By the way, remember, I'm not Roman Catholic. I'm Episcopalian. We don't have a Pope breathing down our necks." He took a sip of coffee before going on. "I know you escaped a very abusive marriage, survived a near catastrophe at sea, and I would expect you to be unsure - at least cautious. I've never seen a person come out of such trauma without emotional scars or reservations about intimacy. Actually, I'm surprised and so very pleased you are able to open up to what we have so far. It is wonderful, from my point of view. Let's keep it going," Jon said, giving her hand a gentle squeeze for emphasis.

At that moment, Julia brought orange juice. She faked confusion because they'd moved close together.

"I am still having moments of doubt and fear. They come at strange times. Some-times I think you're too good to be true. Are you too good to be true, Jon?" she asked, looking very serious.

"I have no idea how to answer that. All I know is that I never want to hurt or disappoint you. But, I will do my best always to be truthful with you. That includes being truthful about my feelings and responses. A good example of being truthful is telling you I've had an erection during this entire conversation."

"You do get right to the point. But, you have to admit, I set the pace for this, admitting I was throbbing and now even more turned on." She snuggled closer to him, smiling as Julia brought the food.

"I hate to interrupt you two with breakfast, but you've got to eat it while it's hot, if you get my meaning," Julia said. She winked at them and spun away to leave them to savor the *double-entendre.*

"Okay. We've passed the test. We're on the same page. Both of us knew what Julia was saying to us and we should take it to heart. 'Eat it while it's hot.' As corny as that sounds, let's use that as a reminder," Jon said.

"Well, that won't help me to finish this omelette. I'd like to forget breakfast and go to your boat. But, we've got to get to Good Samaritan. Krystal called just before I left the house and Sylvia is going through some procedures this morning, until about ten."

Julia brought the check, topping off the coffee cups. Teasing, she said, "You two have a good time today."

"Thank you, Julia. You've added greatly to our having a good start," Sky said.

They left and got into Sky's car for the trip to Los Angeles. Soon, as they headed onto the freeway northbound on-ramp, the conversation came alive.

"Again, we're on the same page, my love. If you're sure about that, let's go."

He could tell from the hesitancy, they were not ready for that, but they entirely enjoyed anticipating the event. They were for certain headed to bed together sooner than later, but both of them had a caution flag that could not be ignored.

"Mind if we talk while you're driving?"

"Go ahead. We've got so much to talk about, Jon."

"Sky, would it be too much this morning for me to talk about marriage? I feel that is a huge leap from our feeling turned on, but it has been on my mind, a lot on my mind. I decided some time ago never again to be married, knowing no one could ever replace Miriam. I also decided you and I probably wouldn't go anywhere really, because of your hurt and anger from your bitter divorce and miserable marriage.

Also, you seemed completely engrossed in your work and so was I," he affirmed.

"You're moving right along. I've thought of marriage a number of times since we've been together. I just throw the thought in the freezer. It is some kind of habit, I think, to think of marriage just because we love one another. What's wrong with just being in love with one another, doing what we're doing, until death parts us? Why mess it up with marriage?" she asked.

"Let's just see how we do, Sky. I have those thoughts, too. Marriage doesn't solve any problems, but it can sure amplify any that are there. We both know it doesn't make for security, either. Most of the people in my practice either dissolve their marriages, want to dissolve them, or are just sticking together in some kind of miserable conspiracy. Is it foolish to think you and I might be different?"

Sky headed north on the Harbor Freeway.

"I agree, at least for now, Jon. Let's just see how we do. But, I won't promise you I will close the door on marriage. It surprises me how quickly and how often the idea occurs to me with you. But, there's no hurry. There is some urgency, however, in my being able to sleep with you, so whatever it takes to allow that to happen, keep navigating toward that destination," she said, taking her hand away to undo her hair, letting it cascade to her shoulders. "That wasn't a symbolic gesture. I needed to loosen the bun. Got it too tight this morning in my haste," she said.

"I like your hair up, down, and would like it spread on a pillow," he said.

"Is now a good time to pose a burning question?" she asked, turning so she could glance at him and still watch the road.

"Of course, Sky. Sounds a bit ominous, but ask whatever's on your mind."

"How come you want to consider marriage at all right now? Your wife died not that long ago and you seem to be enjoying being a relatively free man."

"Sky, I can tell you've not noticed how happy I've been these past months with you. You seem to accept that I am able to be romantic and even get married. You're mostly right about my being relatively free. There are some ghosts I have to deal with at times. I'll tell you sometime about Ron, my adopted son, Miriam's boy. We had a really bad time and I have no idea where he is or how he is. That's a ghost, for sure."

Jon became defensive for a moment about how free and happy he felt. He wondered for a few minutes if he were moving too fast.

Sky stepped into his silence, saying, "I know you've had enough time since losing Miriam, but I need to know more about what I'd be getting in to with your being a priest and a psychotherapist. There's a lot to learn, I'm sure. Just mentioning your adopted son makes me want to know even more. Besides, I've got some studying to do, Jon. I've never taken the time to learn about denominations, much less all the machinations of various doctrines. I do remember Abraham Lincoln saying something about the North and the South reading the same Bible. I guess that sums up all the ways religious people can justify anything they want, even in their so-called sacred scriptures. But, thank you. I know we will have a lot more of these discussions down the line, but somehow your explanation removes a huge question mark about how I've regarded our relationship and, perhaps, our future. I still think marriage is a good way to destroy a great love life, but that is probably good for more discussion, too," she said.

"Just for the record, Sky, I'm not a paid priest. I work free for the church and there's a big word for that - 'non-stipendiary,' which means I'm kind of a volunteer priest, just doing it for the joy of it, I guess," he said. Immediately, having said this, he wondered to himself why he needed to add this information. But, it seemed important to do so and he felt some relief having explained this to her.

Jon told Sky what off-ramp from the 110 to take to reach the hospital and directed her to park in the space marked 'Clergy'. They got out, walked and held hands to the hospital entrance. They stopped at the lobby information counter. Charlotte, the day-time receptionist, was on duty. Jon introduced Sky to Charlotte. She had been at this information desk for about twenty years, never missing a day.

As they walked to the elevator, Jon said, "There are those salt-of-the-earth steady people in the world. They just make things work right day after day and Charlotte's one of those people."

Jon had put on his clergy shirt for the day, so he slipped in the white collar tab and then took the elevator to the third floor, to Sylvia Matthews' room. Wearing the clerical collar in the hospital usually made things easier with staff, patients, and families. A family of three occupied the family waiting room. The woman resembled Sylvia, so Jon guessed and he was right. After he introduced himself, he expressed his condolence to them.

Sylvia's father and brother talked almost at the same time to tell him about Sylvia's condition. She was now conscious and knew she had lost her arm, but still felt pain in the missing hand. She was still in some shock and had received several units of blood. Her father expressed how grateful they were that her life had been spared. They realized not much more could have been done to help after the shark attack. Along with all this came a quick story of two people who drowned recently on a dive where Sylvia had been a key diver; they knew how dangerous Sylvia's work could be. All this came so fast Jon could not be sure who contributed which thought, the father or the son. He could make no response. He just took it all in. When there was an opportunity he asked if they wanted a prayer together. They did. Jon prayed with them, all holding hands for a few moments before he and Sky left to go see Sylvia.

Krystal was in Sylvia's room. Only two visitors at a time were permitted, but no one said a thing to Jon and Sky. Krystal told them that Frank had just left. Sylvia seemed to recognize Jon. Krystal sat by her, holding her hand and stroking her hair.

"Sylvia, remember me? I'm Jon. Along with your family, Frank, Paul, Ian, and the others, I am so grateful you're going to be okay."

Her speech was slow and weak, but audible. "Thank you for coming, Jon," she said.

Sky stood by him, holding his hand. Both moved closer to the bed and he put his hand on Krystal's shoulder. Krystal did not look up. She continued to gently stroke Sylvia's hair. When she did turn to look at him, she had tears in her eyes.

"Jon, is she going to be alright, really?"

"I'm sure she will, Krystal. Ask her."

"Sylvia, do you think you're going to be okay? I know you're in pain, even with the pain medications, but do you think you're going to be okay?"

A long pause and Sylvia's eyes had tears in them, but a slow smile formed on her beautiful face. "Yes, Krystal. I'm going to be fine and soon. I'll have to learn how to do everything with the wrong hand, but I'm going to be fine," she said with conviction.

Krystal rose just enough to kiss Sylvia on the forehead and whispered something in her ear. Sylvia said, "I love you too. I like your being here. Please don't leave for a while," she said, very quietly.

"I'm not going anywhere," Krystal said, assuring her.

Sky and Jon held on to one another. He replaced his hand on Krystal's shoulder, whispering a prayer, "God's will be done in healing Your servant, Sylvia."

He felt Sky was in the prayer with him, though she said nothing and he knew praying was not something she would admit to easily.

"Krystal, while standing here with your mother, I want you to know I'm praying for Sylvia's healing and for the two of you, also giving thanks for the love and caring you've shown to your friend."

"Thank you," she said, pausing. "Who knows? It can't hurt and it might even help,|" she said.

They left the hospital for Long Beach to take on their commitments. On the way, they discussed what they had to do. Sky wanted to take care of some matters at her office and Jon needed to go to his office for mail and make phone calls. Then, as he had promised, he had to meet Carlos and Dick Brophe at the *Tiamat* in Basin Two.

It began to sprinkle as they hugged goodbye. Sky insisted she drive him to his office building as rain began. As they arrived in the parking lot, their kiss brought everything back to life again. It was just the right setting and time for their passion. The rain came heavier now. It drummed on the convertible top. A Long Beach FM station played just the right song, "You'll never know just how much I love you. You'll never know how much I care. Time after time ...

Sky said, between kisses, "Can you believe this moment?"

"Sky, the sooner we get our things done, the sooner we can be together. I've got to help clean up the *Tiamat* after I take care of things in the office. I'll call you this afternoon." Reluctantly they parted.

At his office, Jon checked his messages on the exchange and sorted through which ones had to be called sooner rather than later. One from Carlos told him he would be at the *Tiamat* at two-thirty to help clean up. He also mentioned he wanted to be there when Dick and Jon went over the map of the wreckage because of his interest in what they might find.

The next call was from Frank Martinez from The Hospital of the Good Samaritan.

Sylvia remained critical, but she had regained consciousness and could respond to questions with short answers. Frank had called around midnight, before Krystal had arrived. Also, his message conveyed having contacted Sylvia's family and that they were on their way to the hospital, too. The other four messages were from clients, including a new person wanting an appointment as soon as possible. He returned the calls, organized the mail, watered two plants, and locked the office door as he left.

Back on the *Tiamat*, Dick spread his self-made map out on the galley table. Carlos busily scrubbed the counter, having finished the forepeak and head. Jon began right away to empty the refrigerator. Dick stopped Jon and drew his attention to the map.

"Jon, let's leave the food on board for now. I've got a plan I want you both to hear," Dick said.

Carlos and Jon sat down at the table. Dick moved the map so they could see. The heavy rain on the cabin top required Dick to speak up.

"At the very last, just before we left, the detector started going crazy right here," he said, as he pointed to the spot on his map. He continued, "There is a concentration of metal at this location. It could be a binnacle and the navigator's balls, I suppose, but it just might be the gold Carlos is so eager to find. Either way, we really ought to find out soon. It isn't in the right place in the wreck to be a binnacle, but we know the boat exploded and pieces could have landed anywhere, like the figurehead so far from the bow," he said.

"When can we go?" Carlos asked.

"We have to have Frank. I think Ian and Paul would be eager to go, too, and the sooner the better. Did you read this morning's paper?" Dick asked.

"No. I didn't have a chance to read it, but I've wondered if there's been anything about the shark attack," Jon said.

"There is a two column story, naming my boat, the shark attack, Sylvia Matthews being taken by helicopter to Good Samaritan Hospital, and the fact we were diving near San Clemente Island. It has too much detail in it. Someone is going to be curious. A lot of people know my boat as a dive boat. I only do serious diving. Questions are going to be coming soon. So far, I've avoided the phone calls. I have two unanswered calls from *The Times*. Can you get away, Jon?" he asked.

"I could do one more day, as we planned, but I've got two family therapy things I cannot reschedule on Friday. If we went this evening, they could dive tomorrow. How's the weather? This rain is hard and steady now. Is it going to stay with us?"

"It's supposed to clear by this evening. It will be windy out of the northeast by tomorrow night, if the forecast is right. I think we should take a chance on the weather. Even if the Santana develops, it's not supposed to be a strong one, winds are forecast by tomorrow evening to be twenty to thirty out of the northeast below canyons and passes. Sometimes, as you know, they don't even get out to sea. I've seen Santanas where the sea stayed as flat as a lake, but then, I've been in those others with the forty-foot waves, too," he said.

"Dick, let's plan on going out there tonight. I'll be talking to Frank today. Last night I finished the report for Shabro, leaving out some things. Frank's going to pick it up and take it to her. Hope she's satisfied with the details I included. But, yes, let's go tonight. I know Paul and Ian will be eager to do it. Frank had originally scheduled time off through tomorrow, planning on giving us at least two full days of diving. If we were out there for dawn diving tomorrow morning, I'll bet we could get a lot done and be back in by Friday morning," Jon said.

"Do you think Sky can go, too?"

"I'm quite sure she scheduled the same time off, so I don't know why she couldn't. I'll be talking to her soon, too. Carlos, you're okay to go, right?"

"I can hardly wait. One thing about being a substitute teacher, along with my side business, I can make my own schedule nearly all the time. This is the most important thing on my date book," he said.

They planned on talking to one another concerning a firm plan for the trip by 4:00 PM that afternoon. With the food on board, they just needed to bring the diving gear back aboard, air the tanks, and they would be ready to go. Before leaving, Jon used Dick's phone to leave messages for Frank and Sky, neither of whom answered.

Chapter Twenty-Eight

A correct weather forecast was unusual, but the rain stopped at sundown as predicted. To the south and west clouds appeared to be thinning. In the east and north they hung heavily.

As Dick throttled the twin Cummins 320s to one-thousand revolutions per minute, the *Tiamat* slowly left the Alamitos channel heading into open water. Frank, Sky, and Carlos were still stowing their gear. Paul helped Jon prepare for a late supper. Dick sat at the helm, high up in the flying bridge. He briefed Ian on the layout of the instruments, the buttons, switches, so that Ian could take over the helm for the first watch. The sea was calm, with only five knots of wind out of the north-northeast. The gentle Huntington swells gave a slow roll to the *Tiamat* out to sea beyond the Alamitos jetty beacon.

When Dick came down to the galley, he told them he had corrected for current, steering 170 degrees, and they were cruising at twelve knots with a slight assist from the wind off their starboard quarter. Jon conjectured on their heading the swells would not slow them, if they remained as they were now, off their starboard beam. Dick gave an ETA of 2400 to 0100 for fetching China Point. He primarily used the Loran C navigation device to guess this arrival time. The plan was to anchor as nearly as possible where they had been anchored the day before. The Loran would not be that precise, but Dick felt he could tell visually once they were close to the earlier anchorage position, especially when the fathometer read seventy-foot depth, the same depth as before.

Conversation during supper included random things on their minds. It flowed from one subject to another, with philosophical insights thrown in from time to time. Of course, as usual, the constant quips, puns, and jokes sprinkled the conversation. Carlos and Ian stayed quiet. Frank told of the helicopter trip with Sylvia, the paramedics tending to her, the skillful landing on the pad on top of Good Samaritan Hospital. Frank mentioned the great Celtic cross marking the adjoining older building, a landmark to be seen from all around the hospital.

Frank said, "I wished that I had a rosary during the trip to the hospital. That was a very tense trip. The pilot got confused as to where to take Sylvia. He didn't get clearance until the last few minutes to take her to Good Sam's emergency facility. The pilot had been there before and recognized it by that beautiful Celtic cross. I had been there before, too, and was sure relieved when I saw that cross. The helipad is on the building right next to it."

Jon was very interested in Frank's comments. He thought, *Maybe there's a sermon in there somewhere.*

Paul told a story about a dive he'd made with seven others in the Gulf of Mexico, looking for La Salle's sunken boat. It was frustrating. They didn't find it on that dive. He knew a lot about La Salle, especially the stories about the *Belle*, the third of La Salle's ships supposedly lost in the 1680s in the Gulf during La Salle's search for the entrance to the Mississippi River. A group of archeologists was convinced that the wreck was to be found somewhere along the coast. They had explored various locations, but, at that time they had no luck.

"My dad bought a La Salle, in 1938, but maybe it was 1937. A great car. Kind of a jazzier version of the Cadillac. That car kept going through the war and I got to drive it when I was in high school," Paul said, as if that had anything to do with the subject.

Paul's knowledge and the history he shared held their interest. Ian asked Sky a couple of questions regarding finding shipwrecks and all the complications that arise when one is found. Sky launched into a dissertation on the procedures, the red tape, the disputes, and the difference between 'salvage' and a 'find'.

As the conversation meandered, each reluctantly admitted being tired. Sky and Jon cleaned up the galley. He urged her to go to bed to rest for her dive in the morning. Teasing, she pulled his arm, as if to take him with her. They both wanted to, but they also knew this was once again not the time nor place. She kissed him goodnight and went through the companionway to her bunk in the forepeak.

About 2200, with everyone asleep, except for Ian at the helm, the *Tiamat* suddenly, almost violently, turned to port. The engines just as suddenly accelerated, thrusting in reverse. Dick, in his skivvies, leaped up the ladder to the flying bridge. A huge, black wall was almost close enough to touch. A mound of white foaming water, churned up by the *Tiamat*'s own reversed propellers, created a mountainous watery chaos ahead, visible even in the darkness through the cabin windows. Their own running lights provided some reflected illumination. Jon heard Dick's angry voice reprimanding Ian.

"What the hell were you doing!" he shouted at Ian.

"She had no lights, Dick. Just by chance I saw the white foaming bow wave. The only light on the freighter was one on the bridge, a dim, reddish light in the window of the bridge. I wouldn't have known her to be a ship at all except for that. I was really watching, Dick," Ian explained loudly, which awakened some of those below.

"I guess we're just lucky as hell," Dick said. "No matter. A miss is as good as a mile, they say. You did the right thing, Ian, reversing, turning immediately to port, even though you knocked over everything that's loose," he said, beginning to find humor in the near catastrophe.

The massive black wall was nearly past, not fifty yards off the starboard beam. The *Tiamat* was all but dead in the water. She drifted in neutral. The twin diesels idled. Within a minute, the ordeal ended. Engines throttled up to their efficient revolutions, driving ahead at fifteen knots cruising speed, and Ian steered back on course, 170 degrees. The *Tiamat* rocked and rolled through the freighter's wake. Dick stayed on the bridge with Ian for a while. The two of them talked quietly, gradually bleeding off their adrenalin.

Through the fracas, Sky, Frank, Paul, and Carlos never stirred from their bunks. The rest of the trip to San Clemente Island, was uneventful. They rounded Pyramid Point at 0045. The *Tiamat* dropped anchors just off China Point. By 0130 both anchors were set. Carlos had the first anchorage watch. The next watch would be awakened at 0400.

Climbing to the bridge to relieve Carlos, Jon found him snoozing. Carlos, asleep on his watch, startled awake, embarrassed. Jon told him he would report him to the captain and he would be flogged at dawn. They could keel haul him, too, or what other punishments might amuse the crew.

Carlos didn't find this funny. His sense of humor was eclipsed by genuine irritation with himself for being asleep on watch.

"Jon, I once fell asleep on guard duty in Korea, resulting in seven Koreans stealing some of our patrol's food and a flame thrower. I lost a stripe because of that bad night."

Jon didn't kid him again about falling asleep. The two of them verified the *Tiamat*'s position and determined they had not dragged either anchor. Jon took a moment to soak up the peace of the early morning, with a subtle dawn's light blossoming in the east, beneath a blue, crystal-clear sky. All was well. He went below.

About 0530, Jon put on coffee. He hoped the aroma would arouse the sleepy crew. Sky appeared, stretched, yawned, and she embraced him as he put the filter in the coffee gadget.

"Don't turn around. I've got a bad case of morning breath. I think the Russian Army marched barefoot through my mouth this morning," she said.

Before she could move, he stole a kiss and flipped her wild hair around. "You always look and smell inviting to me, no matter when I see you or what you're wearing. This just gets better and better."

In the half-light of the galley, she smiled, thanking him, then left to get dressed for breakfast and the planned dive. Dick came next, also stretching and yawning. Jon flipped on the weather channel. They listened to the forecast. Nothing had changed since yesterday, with Santana winds below canyons and passes by early afternoon. Seas were to be mild throughout the day, with two to four foot waves at ten to fifteen second intervals, and winds light to variable from the west-southwest by 2100 (Coordinated Universal Time, 1300 local time). The twenty-four-hour forecast called for increasing northeast winds out twenty miles, seas rising to five to ten foot waves, choppy within five miles of the coast from Point Conception to the Mexican Border. Dick seemed satisfied that the good conditions would give them plenty of time to do what they hoped to accomplish.

"The gods are with us so far, at least weatherwise. Hope the sharks leave us alone today. I can't get Sylvia's losing an arm to that animal out of my mind. I dreamed about that last night. You're a shrink. Maybe I should lie down here and tell you my dream, doctor. But, first, that coffee is smelling pretty good," Dick said.

"I don't do dream analysis unless I'm being paid. I know you'll understand that, being a business man," Jon joked.

"That's a relief. I'm always wondering if you're analyzing us."

"All the time, Dick. I've got everyone figured out, except for myself. If I could just get someone to figure me out, I wouldn't have to analyze the rest of you."

"Too early for me to understand that. What's for breakfast?" he countered.

"Eggs, toast, hashbrowns, sausage, three different cereals, coffee, orange or cranberry juice. If all that doesn't satisfy, the fishing poles are hanging right over there on the bulkhead."

"Sounds better than what I have at home, Jon. No complaints from me. By the way, thank you for all the cooking you've done. I don't know when I've worried less about feeding people aboard my boat than on this trip, thanks to you and Carlos," he said.

Frank appeared. "I'll second that. We've had good food on this boat."

"You're sure welcome. I was only thinking of myself, of course. I figured if I had my choices and shared what I like, the rest of you wouldn't go hungry. So far it has worked." Jon poured some more juice and handed it to Frank.

Sky emerged from the companionway. She wore a bathrobe over her swim suit. She greeted Dick, who responded politely, suddenly shy. Then, he brightened. "I've got a realization to share with you, Dr. Rowan. I knew you when you were around twelve years old. I knew your parents, too, Doctor Glenn and Marilyn Rowan. It occurred to me just last night where I had met you, years ago. Your dad and I met in a geology class one summer on Santa Rosa Island. Then, later, we got together, your mom and dad, my wife and I all got to know one another pretty well. I'm guessing you were twelve and your brother was fifteen. Small world!"

Sky looked surprised and delighted too. "You knew my parents? I can't believe anyone alive now would remember or have known my parents. They've been gone eleven years and I think of them all the time. When daddy died, my mother was okay for a while. Then, nearly six months after his death, she was diagnosed with pancreatic cancer. She died three months after her diagnosis. But, when I was twelve? You must have known them in one of the best times of their lives. Daddy loved geology. He is the reason I became an archeologist. Mother was into physics, a Master's from Stanford. She worked on the linear accelerator. Did you know her that well? They were such fascinating and loving people. I just can't believe you knew my mom and daddy. Let's talk about them when we have time, Dick," she said, excited at the prospect.

"You bet, Sky. I'd love to share some stories of them. Sharon and I had a couple of years of doing things off and on with them after that class on Santa Rosa Island. That must have been 1958. What a long time ago! God, I'm older than fossil scat!" he exclaimed. "What's your brother doing?"

Paul and Ian came from their quarter-berths, dressed in swim trunks. "Where's the party?" Paul asked.

"Okay, y'all. Here's breakfast. I scrambled the eggs. A little spice in them. Hope you like whole wheat toast with apple butter. I used the last of the butter for scrambling the eggs. But, as I told Dick, if there are any complaints, over there are the fishing poles. Ian and Carlos, would you please pour the juice and coffee?" Jon handed them the tray with cups enough, hot and cold, for all of them.

Frank reached for the tray. "I'll handle the coffee and juice. These guys are too hairy. I'm better dressed in this colorful t-shirt and won't be getting my body hair in the drinks," he said, looking pleased with himself.

"Okay, we'll put on t-shirts too, if that's what it takes to eat breakfast with you old people. No shoes, no shirt, no service on this boat," Ian said.

In seconds they were back, pulling down t-shirts, with funny sayings on them.

Paul's read, 'Don't ever fight with ugly guys. They got nothing to lose'. Ian's read, 'If you can read this, you're too close'.

Later, while the four of them prepared for the dive, Dick rigged the metal detector, preparing the long coaxial cable attached to the loop for the descent. He explained to Frank how he should keep a very light tension on the coax. When Dick got a signal strong enough, he would give the coax a gentle tug and Frank and the others could stir around in the mud for what might be close to the surface. Paul hooked a small shovel to his weight belt. Ian took a large net, with fine mesh, in case they found something worthy of bringing up. A small crane positioned near the stern of the *Tiamat* would be used for lifting up to 500 pounds. Dick told them it had at least 500 feet of line on it, which would certainly be enough if they found something.

The four divers sat on the dive platform, checking out and adjusting their equipment. Sky already had her faceplate pulled down, her hair pulled back out of her vision. Dick, Carlos, and Jon were to watch for sharks. Frank and Paul had long knives with them, mostly for reassurance. They made sure they would all stay close to one another on this dive, presenting a formidable group to possible sharks. The long knives would also serve as probes in the soft, muddy bottom. Frank felt quite sure he could locate almost the precise place where the loop had been receiving strong signals when they so suddenly abandoned the dive on Tuesday afternoon. They agreed on this location as a starting point. Then, they all four of them were in the water. They bobbed to the surface, adjusted hoses, regulators, faceplates, and tugged here and there to make their wetsuits more comfortable. All thumbs up, they disappeared in a swarm of bubbles beneath the starboard beam. The three of them on board watched diligently for sharks. Their signal would be hard, repetitive thumps to the hull if something threatened them during the dive. They would be within range to hear that sound just seventy or so feet below.

Dick moved to the scope. He put on his metal detector earphones for any audible signals. The first signals came within a couple of minutes. They had not been down more than five minutes when Dick began giving small tugs to the coaxial cable. He said, "Look at this signal! The needle is almost pegged. There's something in the mud right below Frank right this instant."

Another ten minutes went by with no sign of sharks. The three of them impatiently wondered what those below were doing. The signal on Dick's monitor remained strong. Frank had not pulled out more cable. Apparently they remained in one spot on the bottom. Within a couple more minutes Paul came to the surface, very excited. He held up a small brick and a much smaller ingot. Paul's mask hung off to the side just enough for him to speak. "There are lots of these down there. Sky and Ian are putting as many as they can find in the net. Frank's got the loop. We'll need the line and hook. Except for the small ingots, the rest is heavy. They seem a lot heavier than iron," Paul said. Carlos climbed onto the dive platform and took the objects from him.

"They're gold!" Carlos exclaimed. "This is gold," he repeated. "We've struck gold!"

"Quiet, Carlos. Remember, this is a secret journey," Dick warned, half teasing.

"Paul, do you want me to suit up? I'm not certified, but I can certainly come down and help," Jon said.

"We can do it, I think. I'm going back down," he said. He installed his faceplate, peeled away, and went down into the opaque water.

They could see ten or fifteen feet, before he disappeared, dragging the hook and line from the stern crane with him. The spool whined as it played out the nylon line all the way to where they were on the bottom.

The crew scanned the water, looking for sharks. Large fish glistened from time to time, mostly yellowtail. The barracuda were in this area too, but they were deeper. Frank had seen several in the morning during the first dive, but they were gone during the second one. Yellowtail were plentiful, though. Thousands of silvery fish swarmed by from time to time, first one direction and then another. They determined as long as these fish were around, chances were there were no sharks close by, or, at least, thinking that gave them some needed relief.

The first tug on the crane line happened at nine minutes. Carlos pushed the button, taking in the strained line. Dick warned the limit was only 500 pounds. The line rating was 4,000 pounds, but the crane motor was rated for only 500 pounds. In three minutes of winding line back on the spool, the loaded net rose above the water enough to swing it onto the dive platform. The three men hurriedly unloaded it onto the cockpit deck, ingots and some unique coins, some with stamped marks on them and some with no marks. The ingots were not uniform in size. Some of them were larger by half than the others. They easily had more than 200 pounds with this load. Ian surfaced suddenly at the edge of the platform. He waited to take the line and net back down, which he did. He got a firm grip on it and immediately disappeared below.

Jon moved aside Dick's earphone to speak to him. "You know, Dick, they only have another ten or fifteen minutes at this depth. Total time at seventy feet is max thirty-five minutes, according to the table. I hope they're watching their time. When they come up, they can't go back down again for at least two or three hours working at that depth. Hope we can get this done today, whatever we're doing."

"We'll do as much as we can," Dick said. He concentrated on his monitor and put the right earphone back in place to listen.

At thirty-seven minutes all four came to the surface. Frank's faceplate came off and he asked the deck crew to bring up the net again, much heavier this time, but the groaning motor handled the weight. By the time they were all on the swim platform, the net was at the surface, bulging with its contents. Frank and Paul pulled it onto the platform. Raising it some more, they brought it into the cockpit, swiveling the crane. As they carefully opened the net, each of them in concert uttered a version of *Wow*!

Carlos began to finger through the muddy loot. He took an ingot and rubbed it vigorously on his pants to clean it. In seconds, a gold ingot almost shined, with a number embossed on one side. It looked like '833'. A few smaller ingots, half the size of the one Carlos had, were scattered through the mud-covered debris.

"We just scooped as fast as we could, running short of time down there. This is just part of it," Frank said.

"I've got a few coins and some ingots in my wetsuit," Paul said.

Sky had some coins and ingots, too. She took a towel and wiped the growth and mud off of several and handed them to Jon. "Here, Jon. Have some valuable history," she said. "I'm going to get out of this wetsuit." She began to peel it off with Jon's assistance.

The others helped each other struggle out of their wetsuits and they brought the tanks into the cockpit to exchange them for filled ones aboard. They babbled excitedly. But, the moment became serious when Sky spoke up.

"You fellows do know this find has created a serious set of difficulties for us all. We've got some talking and planning to do. I suggest we do one more dive in three or so hours, after everyone gets some rest for now and has a light brunch," she said. It took no argument. Sky seemed suddenly in charge.

Frank suggested they take time to nap for a half hour, then eat light, get some more rest, and dive again at 1500. It was a plan.

Frank, Paul, and Ian went below. Sky and Jon sat on a cockpit cushion, with Dick and Carlos across from them. They exchanged ideas and agreed to take all the found gold to Sky's workshop for sorting, inventory, and appraisal.

Paul said, "We've got to get that done before the Coast Guard finds us again. Wonder if they know we're here today?"

They felt uneasy having all this gold aboard, while they noticed how intense Carlos had become.

Jon said, "I would like us to give a significant amount of what we have to you, Carlos. And, Carlos, I would like you, too, to help us determine how we should handle this discovery."

"Thank you, Jon. It's a bit premature to talk of who gets what, though. We all ought to have a say," he said, being gracious.

"Your ancestor is the one who left this gold on the bottom, Carlos. It seems it is mostly yours," said Jon.

"Carlos is right. We all ought to have a say in it. We're all in this together. It's a joint venture," Sky said.

Dick became quiet. He looked deep in thought. Jon wiped off random pieces from the pile and put them aside in their brightened condition.

Dick said, "After our next dive, bringing up whatever we can in the thirty-five minutes we have down there, I would like us to get out of here. The sooner we have our load in Sky's workshop the better. I sure don't want the local Navy guys chasing us out of here again, or worse, coming aboard and seeing this pile of bullion."

That ended their time in the cockpit. Everyone agreed with him. He was the skipper, after all, and besides that, he was right to have the gold stowed somewhere safer than on the boat. Jon pulled some blue plastic sheeting over the pile and weighted it down with the scuba diving belts. They went below. Carlos and Jon prepared lunch. Sky went into the forepeak for a short nap, dressed only in her wet swim suit, very happy, giving Jon a quick squeeze and kiss on his cheek as he stood at the chopping board, cutting celery.

From the time they had left Long Beach, the sea had been almost flat, with only slow, gentle swells. Dick studied the weather. He knew the Santana winds were going to be kicking up in the afternoon, but not supposed to reach the outer waters before tomorrow. They were protected at China Point. They would proceed with the afternoon dive. To prepare, the four divers were awakened from their naps. As they appeared on deck, ready to put on their wetsuits, check their tanks and regulators, and discuss how to make the best use of their time on the bottom, Jon and Carlos rigged the net on the hook of the crane's line. Not a breath of wind stirred. The *Tiamat* sat almost motionless. Being at sea on an anchorage with such stillness felt eerie. Dick commented on it. But, then cautioned they would have winds enough returning to Long Beach if the forecast were correct. By 1300, earlier than scheduled, Sky, Frank, Paul, and Ian were on the dive platform ready to tumble into the ocean for their descent. Three seals far astern watched. One barked and Jon barked back.

"Pretty good imitation, Jon. You must have been a seal in your last life," Dick said.

"I'm going to be a dolphin in my next life," Jon declared.

"I'll watch for you," Dick said, guiding the line off the spool as the group descended with the net.

Dick moved to his monitor and put on the headphones to listen for signals. They had left the detector's loop in place on the bottom this morning. Dick held the earphone to his ear and then handed it to Carlos to listen. It emitted its sensing sound. As long as the seals were nearby, they figured no sharks were in the area, but watchful eyes scanned the water to be sure. A flying fish fluttered along the surface off the port beam. It was always an amazing sight. Far off beyond their port bow a pod of porpoises played, jumping, passing from south to north. Jon made a mental note to sail back to this place in the near future.

During their dive, they pulled up one more large load, heavier than the first ones from the morning. The winch crew, Jon and Carlos, had a system now, swinging the crane around and gently dumping the heavy contents alongside the other pile, being careful not to hurt the deck of Dick's boat. There were hundreds of various-sized ingots in this load.

By the time the net was emptied, all four of the divers were on the surface, their time had run to nearly forty minutes. This had Jon and Dick worried again. Even though obviously tired, they were excited as they were helped aboard, removed their tanks and stowed them in the rack. Sky unzipped her wetsuit. Another pile of ingots fell out onto the deck, thirty-seven of them, large and small. Paul had two small bricks tucked into his wetsuit, adding greatly to his ascending weight. He complained about having to swim like hell to make it to the top with his extra weight. Ian had one brick and Frank had a lot of little ingots that fell on the deck as he struggled out of his wetsuit. It was a rain of gold, even though the bricks and ingots were covered with mud and green slime.

"There's a lot more down there for sure," Frank said.

"I think we ought to leave it there. The more we leave the less problems we're going to have. When there is an authorized dive on this wreck, it would be well for them to find some of the treasure, as if they discovered it," Sky said.

"You're pretty shrewd. Have you been in on other conspiracies?" Jon asked.

"There is so much political nonsense in archeology, one has to be shrewd," she said.

"The metal clicker is weaker than before, but it's still clicking away," Dick said.

"Of course, there is a lot of metal to be found down there from the structure of the wreck itself. I think some hard-hat divers need to go down. They can spend hours at a time working on uncovering this wreck. We're too limited as scuba divers. Can you imagine how fun it would be to spend days excavating this site? Would I ever like to have that job!" Frank said.

"If there's a chance, Frank, count Ian and me in on that one. We're both hard-hat qualified, too. If we need to stay down longer or go deeper, we'll get hard hats," Paul said.

Ian said, "Yeah! Count me in on that one. The sooner the better. This is the most fun I've ever had on a dive, except when we were dragging corpses out of that train that went into the river three years ago. But, I'd rather do this kind of stuff any day."

"Sounds like gruesome work, Ian. I've unwrapped mummies, but dragging corpses out of a train wreck under water sounds like awful work. I'd have to go to a therapist to get over those images," Sky said. She bumped Jon with her hip, and threw her wet hair from side to side with her wetsuit peeled down to her waist.

Intrigued, they began to sort some of the gold pieces. Frank, Paul, and Ian used the fish scale to weigh the ingots or bricks. They did not appear to be a uniform weight, however. Dick called a halt to their curiosity. He told them to get ready to haul up anchors. Taking a skipper's command attitude, he ordered them to get ready to leave, with a sense of urgency in his voice. Their boat with a tired, happy crew, would be in the Long Beach slip by 2200, if all went well. The divers hosed off their wetsuits and regulators with fresh water. Frank wielded the hose, being sure to get Paul and Ian as wet as he could.

They went below to change into dry clothes. The galley team, Jon and Carlos prepared supper. It would take about an hour. The left-over roast they would heat in the propane oven. Dick started the twin diesels, setting them at idle. Jon and Carlos could leave the galley long enough to go topside and bring up the anchors; the *Tiamat* backed to free the stern anchor then forward for the bow anchor. By dragging the anchors and chains forward and back through the water the anchors and chains were clean enough to be stowed in their brackets. Dick made sure everything was secure before turning the boat around and headed for home. They rounded Pyramid Point at 1645. Then they headed for Long Beach, about 350 degrees, allowed for the westerly currents. It would be about fifty-five nautical miles distant. The coast was clear, every detail visible. Mt. Baldy, far to the north, had a crest of snow on it. The San Gabriel Mountains were clear, too. Blowing dust in the distant northeast gave evidence of a strong Santana wind.

Chapter Twenty-Nine

By 1715, the offshore wind began to blow. The northeast wind hit the *Tiamat* off the starboard beam, blowing about twenty-five knots, gusting to forty. Six to eight foot wind waves socked the hull abeam. With periods of fifteen to twenty seconds, each wave jolted the craft. They also had a westerly swell, providing a choppy sea. Had the *Tiamat* been a smaller, less powerful boat, the ride would have been much rougher and certainly slower. Still, they maintained ten to fifteen knots, with only a moderate roll.

Once in a while the waves from the northeast slapped the starboard hull like a hammer, but Ian did a good job at the helm. He softened the blows by steering into the approaching waves.

Sky and Carlos began to feel some nausea by 1740. She went forward to the bow and stretched out on the stacked Avon dinghies and let the wind help steady her stomach. Jon thought there might be too much pounding up there, but that was where she felt the best. Carlos made the mistake of going below to his bunk. He came topside fifteen minutes later and vomited over the leeward side. He headed for the starboard side, but Jon wheeled him around, guided him portside, and held onto him as he fed the fish.

Dick apologized for the rough ride. Jon told him he was probably not responsible for the weather, no matter how conscientious he tended to be. That got a smile out of him. Jon suggested that they head for San Diego to avoid this rough return to Long Beach. But, everyone agreed to tough it out. Only Sky and Carlos seemed to be having difficulties. The craft slammed and rolled, with some fore and aft pitching. Before going below to continue fixing supper, Jon went forward to join Sky and to check on her. She said she really didn't care about supper and neither did Carlos. But, by the time it was ready, at 1915, everyone was hungry and wanted to eat.

The waves had decreased considerably with the *Tiamat*'s position off Huntington Beach, about twelve miles from the Alamitos Bay jetty. They could already see the light flashing on the southeast end of the sea wall. As noted on the chart, it blinked every four-seconds. Their engines drowned out the jetty horn, which blasted every six seconds. Jon thought to himself, if he were sailing he would be able to hear the coastal horns. The *Tiamat*'s engine noise drowned out the otherwise audible horns. The five-second horn at the Long Beach entrance and the fifteen-second horn at the Los Angeles entrance were also marked by red and green lights, as in 'red-right returning'.

By suppertime, the *Tiamat* ran smoothly, with only a partial roll from the swells and the wind waves. The welcomed calm allowed them to enjoy the meat, potatoes, and vegetable supper. Each of them, except Sky and Carlos, had a glass of the Merlot. Jon had fun bragging about his culinary expertise, especially cooking well in a galley that had rolled and pitched as he hung on and cooked. The crew complimented him and thanked him, too.

Sky mentioned about how quickly she had recovered from feeling crummy. An hour before supper she knew she would not ever want to eat again, she said she would need to die to feel better. Dick filled in the conversational gaps with sea tales of high waves, storms, and even some catastrophes. Once he had lost a sailboat when it pitch-poled in forty-foot waves, drowning one of nine crew aboard in that storm.

By 2200, they were in Dick's slip, everything inboard cleaned, including the galley, and all the gear stowed. The Santana weather kept the evening very warm, nearly seventy-five degrees.

Sky said, "Can you believe it's December and still so warm?"

"Don't count on this weather staying warm for long. It will turn suddenly cold soon, so enjoy it while we've got it," Dick said.

The divers lugged the equipment to their cars in the dock carts. Carlos began to hose down the boat. When he got to the piles of treasure, he lifted the tarp and discreetly pressure-washed them off, which revealed the actual gold metal.

Dick brought topside five large canvas bags from below. "We'll use these old sail bags to carry the gold to our cars. If we use these bags, no one happening by will see what we're doing. It'll take several trips. We're lucky it is a week night. The marina is almost deserted."

From the boat they could see only a few cars in the parking lot besides their own. One lone couple walked by, obviously too involved with one another to notice the *Tiamat* or the group aboard. It was estimated they had at least 350 pounds in bricks and small ingots, about one-third of that weight being the ingots.

"I can't help but think there's a lot more down there where this came from," Carlos said. Then he reflected, "But, if all the gold old Shuka could carry on three or four mules was aboard the *Madonna*, there couldn't be too much more. How much could one donkey or mule carry, anyhow?"

Before they left, Sky suggested that each of them pick out two special ingots they liked to keep as souvenirs. She reminded them they would be able to share more later, after it was inventoried and Carlos had his part out of it. She explained that some of the gold would be the bait for obtaining interest in the wreck itself. Also, it would serve as evidence, proving that a wreck actually existed to be documented. The group agreed. The procedure for informing the authorities about this find needed to be done one step at a time. They should not give the location until all else had been established. Again, they were pledged to secrecy. Each ceremoniously shook hands with the others, promising to keep this to themselves until some final story became public. Jon told Carlos he would help him with his share of the gold, knowing he would not be able to carry it by himself. Then they began to fill the bags, in the near darkness, only a dock light for illumination. It would take about four trips. The old dacron bags would not hold more than forty or so pounds without tearing.

Dick and Sky exchanged their information. Sky thought the two of them should get together to document the trip and the find to make sure it agreed with the ship's log. Dick realized he would be implicated in everything having to do with this find, he agreed to work with Sky to help in any way he could. They also agreed to have exactly the same details of both of these trips, including the one where Sylvia and Frank had been evacuated and the second trip back to the site of the *Madonna*'s wreckage.

The work began in earnest. They used two dock carts. With the tide out, it took considerable effort to pull the loaded carts up the steep gangway. Jon put most of the gold into the back of his pickup, covering it with a plastic tarpaulin. He asked Frank to stay with it while he went for another load. Carlos quickly said he would do it, which he did. Carlos was excited about the entire operation, anticipating how they would divide it up once collecting it in the workshop. It occurred to Jon, the gold and the figurehead, his Lady, Meri, would be in the same space again, both treasures from the deep.

Frank said to Jon, "I need to go to the phone. I need to call Lupe and also the marina office to check in. Been too long out of touch."

That reminded Carlos he needed to call Laura. He told Jon and Frank how she never worried about him, but they played a game about her getting her lovers out of the house before he came home. He had to call her to let her know how much time she had left.

"It works great. We've been married seventeen years. I never catch her with her lovers," he said, with a smirk.

Dick Brophe came back to the parking lot. Before he could leave, they lavished praises on him. They thanked him exuberantly for all he had done, especially for his having the state-of-the-art metal detector and the expertise to use it. Jon reminded him of their plan to have everyone together soon for dinner again at the yacht club. Carlos left, waving goodbye under the sodium-vapor parking lot lights.

By 11:30 AM, Sky and Jon arrived at the workshop. Her T-Bird sat just inside the gated workshop yard, the chain-link gate locked against the back bumper. Carlos, Paul, and Ian, pulled up in back of them, in two cars. Frank had gone home. Sky opened the workshop's sliding door.

Jon entered and greeted Meri and told her they were bringing her treasures from the deep. The four of them set to work, using Sky's Radio Flyer wagon, moving the gold, a little at a time, to the floor of the shop. They piled up it as neatly as possible against the back wall, near the workbench, out of the way. The pile looked much smaller in the workshop than it had appeared in the cockpit of the *Tiamat*.

While they took care of the gold, Sky called home for Krystal. The answering machine took her message asking Krystal to call her at the shop. Then she called the Good Samaritan Hospital and asked for Sylvia's room. Krystal answered. The two of them talked, obviously very glad to be in touch. Krystal had worried about her mother's diving again. She asked her about sharks and the trip. She was relieved to learn all went well and the trip a success. Krystal told Sky that Sylvia had improved, but still suffered greatly from the pain, while struggling to accept the loss of her arm. When Sky got off the phone, she came to Jon. She took his hand and asked him to hold her for a moment. She cried softly, Jon guessed from relief and empathy for both Sylvia and Krystal. Krystal had told Sky she had something important to tell her, but she wanted to talk in person, not on the phone.

Just after midnight the little group dispersed. Carlos took 120 pounds of the gold with him, including 200 each mixed ingots, 100 of the large ones, 100 of the small. Carlos assured them he had a place to hide his stash and no one would know about it. They had no idea yet of the value of the gold. It did not matter at this point. Paul and Ian took two bricks each, along with ten of each size of the ingots. They, too, told Jon and Sky they would show no one until and unless they were given permission.

These two divers had worked together enough to trust each other completely. They also had unquestionable character. Jon told them what a privilege it had been to have met them. He described to them the pleasure he felt watching them: their skills in diving along with their teamwork, spirit, and easy friendliness. Especially, he emphasized to them how professionally and deftly they had helped save Sylvia, while protecting one another during that awful shark experience.

Before leaving, Paul gave Jon a big hug, then hugged Sky. Ian shook Jon's hand with warm emotion. He gave Sky a hug, bidding her goodbye for now. They told her to tell Krystal they would be in touch. They planned to see Sylvia the next day and maybe they would see Krystal then, too.

Jon said, "Don't forget I'm going to get everyone together for dinner at the Long Beach Yacht Club as soon as it will work."

Earlier, he said to Frank, "I can't thank you enough for getting Sylvia, Paul, and Ian together for this adventure. You couldn't have found a better team!"

Chapter Thirty

Early Friday morning, before Jon swam, a frantic call came from Carlos: "Jon, Michael and Luís Jimenez are indicted for manslaughter and for stealing the Grand Banks. Two felonies. I don't know what to do, Jon, but Laura and I talked endlessly about lawyers or not, helping or not. Both of us think they need the best attorney they could find. Jon, do you know any good attorneys who could help us with these serious charges? We don't know what to do. We're desperate. How can we help Michael? He screwed up, but he is our son, after all," Carlos pleaded.

"Carlos, I know several attorneys. But, I can't advise you on this. You've got to decide what's best. I'm still angry at those guys for what they've done and how they treated Sky. Let me know what you figure out and, if you want, I'll give you the names of three attorneys and you can pick one. I'll be sure I have their names and numbers and get back to you as soon as I can."

The Jimenez family did not have enough money. They wanted Carlos to help Luís along with his helping Michael. Apparently, the family of Ray Cramer, the one who drowned, was already suing Carlos and the Jimenezes, holding them responsible for Ray's death. They claimed that both Michael and Luís allowed Ray to be alone while diving, and Luís, having been the one who took the boat to Catalina in the first place, lured their son into the deal by promising him a lot of gold treasure. Ray had told his parents all about the gold and the sunken ship. Ray's father drove him to the place in San Pedro where he met up with Luís and Michael. Obviously, they thought they had good information for getting lots of money.

Carlos gushed out these details. At the end he asked again if Jon knew of a good defense attorney. The ones Jon knew were from the yacht club, but he didn't know their specialties. Jon volunteered to ask Frank Martinez, but the names he could give Carlos seemed sufficient. Laura got on the phone just before he hung up, thanking Jon for helping them. She apologized for what Michael had done to Sky and Krystal, asserting this was not like Michael, any of this. She blamed Luís and Ray for encouraging Michael to get into this mess in the first place. Then she gave the phone back to Carlos. Carlos hung up, sounding frustrated.

Nothing needed to be done now. Jon wanted to swim. Some of his time had been used up, so he would have a shorter time. Swimming felt good, but he was cold and needed the hot shower afterward. Though still tired, Jon had too much to do today to take time off. His practice had suffered some neglect this last week.

Calls were stacked up seven deep when he arrived at his office after breakfast.

After returning the calls, he left a message for Sky at her office at Cal State Long Beach. A secretary told him she would not be in until early afternoon. She would give the message to her that he had called, adding, "I know she'll be very glad to hear from you, Dr. Scott."

Following through for Carlos, Jon verified the three names and numbers of attorneys from the yacht club membership book, one in Long Beach, one in Los Angeles, and one in Corona Del Mar. He phoned the information to

Laura Diaz. Carlos was asleep when he called. Laura thanked him, asking if he had any advice as to which attorney would be best of the three. He had no suggestions, except to talk to them all, find out costs. Jon told her only that it would probably be a Los Angeles County Court procedure and a Los Angeles-based attorney would be better. That seemed to help her. Twice, before ending the conversation, she apologized for what Michael had done. She felt especially apologetic to Dr. Rowan and her daughter. Laura told Jon Carlos had put a lot of gold in their big freezer, under everything.

"Maybe there's enough gold here to pay for an attorney," she said.

Before the phone call ended, Jon said, "Whatever you do, keep the gold hidden and don't talk about it to anyone. I have a couple of precious-metal buyers in mind, if you decide to sell it."

"That would be very helpful, Dr. Scott. The sooner we get this out of here the better. Thank you so much."

Friday's *Los Angeles Times* had a long story about Michael Diaz and Luís Jimenez's being charged with manslaughter and felony theft. The article mentioned the drowning death of Ray Cramer, a mechanic, doing a recreational dive from a boat near Catalina Island.

There was another story in the Orange County paper about Sylvia Matthews, repeating some of the shark attack story. It told of the author's interview with Krystal Fitzpatrick, the daughter of Dr. Sky Rowan, noted archeology professor, residing in Long Beach. An unbecoming photograph of Krystal headed the column. She looked very tired. She wore a t-shirt and held a towel with 'Good Samaritan Hospital' printed on it. The article quoted Krystal's saying, 'Sylvia Matthews is the bravest person I have ever known.' She told the reporter she had seen the huge shark just before it struck Sylvia. She was in a rubber boat with Dr. Jon Scott at the time. The reporter added to the story how Krystal Fitzpatrick refused to tell her where the shark attack had happened. It confirmed that the helicopter had brought Sylvia Matthews from San Clemente Island. It stated that Ms. Matthews had been diving from a ship called the *Tiamat*, belonging to a Mr. Dick Brophe of Long Beach, a professional dive-boat owner and skipper. That was the extent of the Orange County newspaper article, written by a reporter named Megan Yoshioka.

Jon knew, along with the others, that everything would now be more complicated.

One by one, they checked in with one another. They decided Sky's Cal State Long Beach office would be the only source for the media to obtain information. They would all refer any calls or inquiries to the office of Dr. Sky Rowan. Sky provided her secretary with a printed information page, updating it a couple of times per day, in case media inquiries came into her office. The system was already working. Her secretary had nine calls on Friday from various media sources, including two television corporations, NBC and CBS news.

Sky and Jon met Friday evening at the Shogun Maru restaurant. She wore white slacks and a light-blue blouse, her hair up, tied with a ribbon matching her blouse. She already sat at a table when Jon arrived, the place completely filled with diners. As he approached, she smiled, but she seemed reserved, only reaching out her hand to greet him. He sat across from her. They were in a corner, a quiet booth for them to talk. Sky had a lot to talk about, beginning the moment he sat down. Their conversation flowed. Jon had his sake and Sky had her plum wine. They sipped and talked for at least a half-hour before they ordered. The waiter became obviously impatient.

"Krystal and Sylvia are an item, Jon. I don't know how you feel about homosexuality. It is the first time Krystal has declared her sexual identity, which she did at breakfast this morning. She is head over heels in love with Sylvia and says Sylvia feels the same way. Krystal's only seventeen, Jon. How can she be sure at seventeen? Sylvia is twenty-five. I guess Sylvia's an old hand at being a lesbian, but Krystal can't possibly know what she's doing, can she? What should I do, Jon? I thought I was open-minded. I have some lesbian friends, one in my department at Cal State, but not my own daughter. Just weeks ago, she had this guy on a string. He was nuts about her, calling her two and three times every night, pleading for dates, having long talks. He was the guy who drove her car. Remember Sean?" Sky unloaded all of this and became more agitated as she talked.

Jon reached across the table and took her hands in his. "Sky. You can't do anything about this. If you have a problem with Krystal's loving Sylvia, you'll lose her. She'll come to you if you accept this without blame or judgment. That is really accepting her feelings and her decision or compulsion to love Sylvia. She'll be watching you closely, Sky."

"Oh, shit, Jon! I know that! I just don't know how to get my innards around it. It knocked me for a loop. She's happier than I've ever seen her. She assured me she would finish high school and the play she's in, *Our Town*. Can you believe *Our Town*? It's next Friday night. By the way, she wants you to come to that performance, if you can. Krystal insists I have nothing to worry about. She went on and on about how wonderful Sylvia is, even while she's in agony in a hospital. She told me how they had talked about everything on the *Tiamat* that day we went to San Clemente Island. Remember how they sat together and talked and talked?" she said, taking a breath while Jon continued to keep her hand in his.

"Okay, Sky. I seldom talk about it, but I didn't do a good job with Miriam's son, Ron, who I adopted. He hasn't spoken to me ever since Miriam died. He is twenty-four and still blames me for his mother's death, I think. I think he's gay and won't or can't be open about that with me. Who knows? We have nothing together. When Miriam and I met, he was only eight. We had some good times, but he resented me from the beginning. But, this is about you and, of course, Krystal. I'm sorry for getting into my own crap."

"We've got so much to learn about one another, Jon. I still go through all this doubt about our being together. One day it's deliriously wonderful. The next it is miserably impossible. I feel like you're inside of me, taking me on a carpet ride to some magic place. Then, I panic. I feel I'm losing myself, don't know even who I am or how I feel about anything. I want to run, but know I can't get away from us," she said. Then she leaned back, pulled her hand from Jon's, and wrung her napkin as she spoke.

It was time to order. Jon ordered beef sukiyaki and Sky ordered the tempura with three items from the sushi bar, a small salad and their miso soup. Sky ordered another glass of plum wine. Jon ordered another sake. Sky waxed thoughtful and quiet.

"Come over here and sit next to me, Jon," she said.

"Boy! That's a relief. I was becoming very unsure of myself, and the evening is still young."

"Well, don't get too cocky." She paused a second. "That isn't a pun," she said, giving him a hint of a smile.

"I'll never be cocky with you, Love. I'll do my best always to at least fake confidence. I know men without confidence are a real turn-off to most women. So, I can always fake confidence, even when I'm trembling with terror inside."

"You? In terror? That's impossible."

"I'm only terrorized when I realize I'm in love with you, Sky. Otherwise, I'm cool. I can sit for hours with clients going through anything, always cool, but you reach into my trembling heart, especially when you're afraid of our love. How can I feel so confident most of the time and you become so fearful?"

Their food came. The waiter could not remember who had what, so they guided the plates to their appropriate destinations. Jon reminded him they both wanted chopsticks, napkins, and would like tea later. Before he could leave, Jon thanked him for his patience with them, telling him they would leave an extra tip knowing they had taken the table on a crowded Friday evening for too long a time. He seemed surprised by Jon's telling him this, but immediately acted more pleasant and attentive. The food was delicious, as usual. The sake and wine helped, too. Sky got more relaxed with her first bites. So did Jon.

During dinner, Sky talked more about Krystal. She slowly seemed more accepting of her relationship with Sylvia, but had misgivings that would take time for her to clarify. Sky talked about a girl she herself loved when she was nineteen. That relationship ended unhappily, but when it ended, Sky felt relieved. They had not been sexual, but in time it would have been inevitable. Jon admired Sky for her recalling this and telling him about it. They commented to one another how often they ended conversations affirming there would be more to talk about. They took this observation to be a positive sign.

After dinner, they went to the marina and walked and talked until nearly midnight, eventually admitting being tired. The week had been too eventful for both of them. Jon told her of having two family therapy sessions back to back, both of them highly charged. One family exploded over an affair. The other, a blended family, mixing seven teenagers, was reconciling. That family agreed to stay in therapy, all coming together for two-hour sessions every other week. Even the kids liked being able to talk. One of the sons told him before they left it was the first time his mother ever listened to him and he wanted Jon to come live with them. Jon gave him a hug and told him it would be expensive, but he would get a moving van and be right over.

It had been a stimulating day as a therapist, but now both of them were exhausted, feeling more so as their walk continued. Jon drove her back to her car in the restaurant parking lot and they kissed goodnight several times. She said, just before leaving, "Jon, I'm not scared right now. I love it when I'm not scared. Thank you for such a beautiful evening and for listening to me rant and rave. When I see Krystal, she's in for a loving hug, thanks to you." She started her V-8, easing out of her parking place, and disappeared into the night.

Jon's Saturday morning activities began early with a swim and breakfast at The Omelette House. He took his clothes to the Laundromat, then went back to the *Daimon*, washing her down, putting on clean sheets, taking some fuzzy, gray food out of his refrigerator, and making lines shipshape. The Santana's dirty deposits covered all the boats. Other skippers were on the docks washing off their boats, some getting ready for a weekend of sailing or powering, some into boat repair or maintenance projects. Good weather always helped make for a busy marina.

When he got back, Frank arrived to talk with him. He was on duty, looking handsome and military, complete with military pleats in his brown shirt. Jon teased him about ironing his own shirts, knowing his wife wouldn't put those pleats in so perfectly. They sat on the dock box to talk. Frank only had a little while before being interrupted by a radio call. Before he left, he told Jon there had been an investigator asking all kinds of questions about their dive at San Clemente. The investigator said he would be back.

"I was pissed. I wouldn't answer all his questions. I told him to call Dr. Rowan's office and gave him the number. He said he'd have my ass up for a deposition soon and I'd have lots of questions to answer. He said he'd be looking for you, too, Jon. He's an asshole. Watch out for him. You may want to have an attorney available. I don't know what he's up to, but it's like we have become suspicious, all of us, for nothing in particular. I felt the bastard was putting some kind of case together, but had no idea what the case would be about or even why he needed to pursue anything. I guess he's on a fishing expedition."

Jon assured Frank he would follow his lead, referring the police or attorney people to Sky's office for any information.

"I want nothing to do with the legal problems derived from the case against Michael Diaz. I sure don't want to deal with the flap about the figurehead and the crap that had happened with Ensign Shabro and her accusations. Frank, we've done nothing wrong. Sky is registering the wreck with the archeological people, the State of California, and the Feds. They know nothing of the gold, except for the little Sky kept for her evidence. Sky is insisting there's lots of treasure at the site and she will reveal the site, once it's registered. They're going to hound us, I'm sure. This is a big deal, especially in what is usually a dull place like Long Beach." Jon paused for a moment, then said, "I guess I'm worried about our having all that gold. But, you're right, they know nothing. Apparently, Michael Diaz told his attorney there is lots of gold to be gotten where this ship sank. Luís Jimenez told an attorney millions of dollars are there for the taking and anyone can have it, first come first served. That isn't true, but they don't know that. It takes someone well versed in Admiralty Law to know how to handle all that stuff. I'm sure whatever anyone finds there will be up for all kinds of litigation, disputes as to ownership, and we'll all be glad we stayed out of it with the small bit of what we retrieved.

"We'll see what we will see, Frank. I know you've gotta go, but let's stay in touch. Let's talk tomorrow or sometime soon. I'm getting everyone together at the yacht club probably two weeks from today, if you and your wife can make it and if the others can, too."

Frank said, "Sounds good to me. We'll be there anytime you say. Sure has been an exciting week."

He poked Jon in the stomach lightly with his radio, turned, and walked away, toward the gangway to his cruiser, the impressive Ford Crown Victoria.

Chapter Thirty-One

Sunday morning church services were nearly filled, being in the ecclesiastical calendar season of Advent. Jon had a sermon to preach next week, but only helped today by celebrating Eucharist at both services. Sky, Krystal, and he planned to go to Good Samaritan Hospital after church to see Sylvia, again meeting with her family there. Krystal had asked about coming to church, but overslept. Later she confessed she had been nervous about coming to church, especially wondering if lesbians were supposed to go to church. Jon assured her that she would be welcomed at Saint Paul's. He reminded her that, no matter what, she was a loved child of God. He made a point to tell her when Sylvia got out of the hospital, they would both be welcome. All this they discussed as they drove to the hospital. Once in Sylvia's room, Krystal and Sylvia hugged, gently. Then Sky gave Sylvia a kiss on the forehead, whispering something in her ear. Jon gave her a kiss on the forehead, too, inquiring about her pain level and telling her how good it was to see her. She looked much better, but still reported pain in her right arm and hand. She was bemused about having pain in an arm and a hand that was swimming around in a shark's belly out in the Pacific Ocean. Then she observed that this was the first time she could find humor in any of this.

"One of the nurses asked me if I were right-handed. I told her not any more," she said. "The nurse laughed and laughed. I could hear the nurse telling someone in the hall about this. Both of them had laughed. I've got a reputation here for being a comedian. Not a reputation for being a grumpy cripple, huh? I'd rather leave them laughing."

Sylvia's mother and father came into the room at that moment. They introduced themselves to Sky, Krystal, and Jon, having met before, but needing a refresher meeting. It seemed a long time since they had been together, but in reality it had been only a few days. A great deal lay ahead for Sylvia. She outlined the therapy facing her, along with what the doctors had told her about what to expect. She would be at least one more week in the hospital. That she had no infections helped cheer her up. Within a couple of months, if she wanted, she would be fitted for a prosthetic arm and hand. Sylvia expressed her discomfort with the need to do that, thinking she just might be better off with one arm and hand. Her candor, humor, and cool demeanor about her progress and the work ahead impressed all of them. Then she surprised them.

"Mom and Dad, I want you to know Krystal and I are going to be together a lot in the months to come. I want you both to get to know her. As you know, Margot is out of my life and has been for three years. I think she's gone, along with my arm, so I could be with Krystal," she said.

Her parents registered no surprise. They greeted Krystal. Both of them hugged her and told her she now belonged as part of the family.

"Who is Margot?" Krystal asked, stunned and uneasy.

"I'll tell you all about her, Krystal. We were together for four years, but she's gone and good riddance. We had a bad last year together. She's living now in New Zealand with an old broad with lots of money. I guess I still have left-over stuff about that time in my life," Sylvia said.

"That's no way to talk about Margot," Mrs. Matthews said, scolding Sylvia.

"Are you defending her? I can't believe you'd take her side after what she did. She lied to me for two years and left taking things that didn't belong to her. She caused me to lose two diving competitions. I'm glad that we had a couple of good years, but more glad that she's gone. Good riddance!"

Tension increased in the room. It dissolved quickly, however, when Sylvia introduced the nurse to them; the same nurse who had asked if she had been right-handed. They repeated the whole joke. Again, Cheryl, the nurse, laughed aloud, while she took Sylvia's blood pressure. Then she handed her a little paper cup with two pills in it. Sylvia swallowed the pills with a swig of water. Cheryl told her visitors they would have to step outside for a few minutes while she changed Sylvia's sheets and got her up to the bathroom. All, except for Krystal, left and went to the familiar family waiting room.

Krystal asked them to come back for her after they were through getting a late lunch. She said she was not hungry at all, wanting them to leave her alone with Sylvia for now. Sky and Jon said goodbye to Mr. and Mrs. Matthews, leaving for lunch at the Pacific Dining Car, across the street from the hospital.

As usual, Jon and Sky had a great deal to talk about. Some of it pertained to themselves, the rest had to do with documenting the wreck, reporting the finding of a portion of the gold Sky had kept, the irritation with all the media interruptions, and now the attorney and police questions. Sky's secretary had received calls on Friday, after the newspaper articles had been published. She also got calls at home from an attorney who wanted to find Dr. Rowan.

Monday promised to be a busy day for Sky and for her office. Her exchange had five calls about this. By the time they finished their meal, Sky and Jon were again close. Jon remarked about how natural it felt just to be together, to talk about anything and everything, and through it all, to be turned on by being with her. Sky responded by giving him a very deep, lingering kiss, which ended by the waiter's presentation of the bill. Walking back to the hospital, they held hands, cracking small jokes back and forth, mostly about finding a womanly wooden figure in the mud. Sky said she felt jealous until she realized the figurehead was only wooden and had a bad complexion from the worm holes.

Krystal and Sylvia seemed to have worked through the news that the woman, Margot, had been a big item in Sylvia's life. They didn't talk to others about this, but Krystal told Sky everything was settled about the 'bitch' who had hurt Sylvia.

The next two weeks became a blur of events: the holidays, the arraignments for Michael and Luís, and Sylvia's hospital release. There were countless phone calls, letters, for all of them, from Dick Brophe, Frank Martinez, Sky's office, and calls to Jon. They were besieged by the media and the legal people. Carlos called for support and advice almost every day. The only ones not bothered were Paul and Ian. Luckily, they had not been named anywhere. On several occasions, when Sky had arrived at her workshop, there were people waiting to ask questions. They wanted to see her workshop, and they even asked questions about Krystal. Sky let no one beyond the alley gate, which she kept locked. Schwartz barked furiously to help keep people out.

They had planned festivities for Christmas. Then they would be ringing in the New Year, 1985. These two special days raised issues for everyone, some glorious and others stressful. Some of Jon's clients found this time of year especially difficult. Jon was to help with the Christmas Eve late service at St. Paul's.

Surprising Jon, Krystal, Sylvia, and even Sky came to that festive Holy Communion service. Even though Jon had invited them to come, it surprised him when they were in the congregation. Sky stayed in the pew, but he was even more surprised and pleased when Krystal and Sylvia came forward for the bread and wine. It was an especially meaningful time for Father Jon, because he was able to serve bread and wine to the two of them, along with the annual throng. However, he was pleasantly surprised when afterward Sky told him the Communion service was beautiful.

Sky later said, "I felt out of place for a while, but I began to like being there and the whole thing makes me want to ask you a lot of questions. Is it okay to be a doubter?"

"Sky, Very few of us are free of doubts. That's part of the deal in religion."

They spent Christmas morning together, all of them at the home of Sylvia Matthews. Jon left early to have time alone at the marina, to read and relax. Sky understood Jon's need for time to himself. She needed time, too. Jon's memories of Miriam and sometimes Ron, their adopted son, crowded in on him during the Christmas holidays. He felt he was letting go even more deeply than before. Several client calls had interrupted the last couple of days, but otherwise, he had not seen clients since Friday and would not until the day after Christmas.

Krystal's having been in the high school play had also attracted media attention. She had done an outstanding job in her role. One reporter was intent on writing not only a review of the high school play, but also announcing to the world Krystal's affair with the shark attack victim, Sylvia Matthews. The gossip started while Sylvia was in the hospital and now, with this tabloid 'review', it was spice for the public. Krystal had difficulty going to school after the article appeared; even her best friends harassed her as a lesbian. Others, though, gave her support.

Two of her friends began to take on some of the others at her school. By the end of the third week of too much negative attention, things began to quiet down. Krystal's challenge would be to finish her senior year without being destroyed by those hostile girls, who had previously been her friends. In the end, her poise and popularity won out. Sky and a school counselor encouraged her not to react to things said. That helped to quell those who taunted and criticized her, calling her crude, insulting names, like 'lesbo' and 'faggot' and other more gross epithets. Krystal welcomed the Christmas vacation. Those two weeks gave her a reprieve from the biting, hurtful comments at school.

What a mixed time for her; from high acclaim for her leading part in *Our Town*, having performed well as Emily Webb, to being ripped apart on a daily basis by her homophobic, cruel, perhaps envious classmates. The biggest surprise came from a friend, Sean, who quickly came to her side, sticking with her, apparently confusing everyone. He was popular on campus, a football star fullback, also a senior this year. His being with her, supportive while not asking anything of her, became Krystal's major help. She thought how much he must care for her to stick by her without a hope of their being together. Sylvia's constant assurance helped, but Krystal was the more vulnerable of the two. She acted poised by day, crying at night. Along with Sylvia, Sky and Jon did their best to give her solace. Sky suggested she drop out this year, if she wanted, take the G.E.D. test for early departure from high school, and then go to a junior college or any college she wanted. But, Krystal seemed determined to weather the storm and remain living at home to graduate with her class. Within a couple of weeks after Christmas vacation, her courage won over many of her critical peers. Members of the high school faculty were supportive, which helped.

In spite of their professional commitments, Jon and Sky found times to do things together. With her time off from teaching for a few weeks, she had accomplished a lot, preparing for a major lecture for the archeological society in New York in late January. They enjoyed times working late together in her workshop. Jon got an education in archeology, helping her piece together fragments of a large Native American bowl. He compared marks on it with pictures of others similar to it. Sky called Jon's putting this broken bowl together 'his occupational therapy'.

Sky and Jon listened to a number of musical pieces: Holst's *The Planets*, Bach concertos, some country-western music, Willie Nelson, Merle Haggard, Patsy Cline, Brenda Lee, Waylon Jennings, the Beatles. The one they had on at this moment was Linda Ronstadt's new one, *What's New?* and *Lush Life*. Sky had a great collection of jazz tapes. They realized they both enjoyed all kinds of music. Along with their teasing, joking, and moments of intense affection, their bond joyfully deepened. But, they needed to be practical; there was much to do.

One of their ongoing projects was to determine the amount of gold they had and the varying values of that gold. They established the 1849 price of gold to be around $18.00

per ounce, often more, but much less when paid to those finding it. They could barely believe the 1984 price. Sky had done her homework. The current price of gold ran from $360.00 to about $320.00 per troy ounce. They just looked at one another in amazement. They'd given Carlos approximately 120 pounds, worth about $700,000 in today's fluid gold market. Some of that in coins, some in small ingots, a lot of one-ounce ingots and larger ones, and there were three large nuggets.

Apparently, according to Sky, the large nuggets were almost priceless, being of historical value plus the gold itself. Also, Sky determined that the coins were worth a lot more than the per-ounce price, especially because they were in such fine condition.

They discussed the history that had been uncovered along with the myriad questions. Why had that man, Vallejo, whom Shuka killed, so much gold in the first place? What was a lot of gold in 1849? How did Shuka and his terrorized band of escaping tribesmen manage to carry so much gold on just three or four mules? How did Shuka know he might escape capture by going to Mexico? They wondered and speculated about so much. But no matter how many questions, they had gold enough to choke Fort Knox. Even if they did not declare what they had picked up, there might be a million or more dollars in gold, in various forms, left in the wreckage of the *Madonna*, along with a great deal of other memorabilia.

From the looks of the figurehead, even some of the wood from the original ship might be in recognizable condition. Sky was excited about the future of this wreck and Jon enjoyed her enthusiasm. As she became more animated, she also became more lively, sensuous, and within minutes they were in an embrace, kissing, transported. Jon held her close, kissing her hair, and telling her he loved her, over and over again. She kept saying, "Say it again, Sam." So, he did.

They were still in the workshop when the sun rose that morning, having been knitted together all night on the couch. That night the tide turned, propelling them beyond the point of no return into a bond that would last. They now knew it would last. Even Sky, with all her doubts and fears, knew it would last. This wave had taken them onto a beautiful beach. Nothing could destroy what they'd found with one another.

Chapter Thirty-Two

They celebrated the New Year. During the rest of the week, they got back into their usual routines. Late Friday afternoon Sky phoned Jon from her office. She'd finished preparing her lectures for upcoming classes. She was excited, again, because her Department of Archeology at Cal State Long Beach had taken control of all the red tape for the 'finding' of the *Madonna*. She had received the cooperation of several agencies, as well as the State of California and a law firm that specialized in archeological 'finds'. The department had even accepted responsibility for the gold embedded in the wreckage. The department researchers accepted her guesses and shared her uncertainty about how much might be there. Sky had made a wild comment about there being a 'valuable treasure' of gold buried on the muddy bottom with the wreckage. At the current price, as of December, 1984, she computed a modest estimate. Without any margin for ingots, perhaps coins and nuggets, just taking the per-troy-ounce price, there had to be over half a million dollars in gold at the now registered and protected site.

Sky and Jon said nothing about what they had taken away, which might be computed later, at least some percentage of it. They kept a strict accounting of the gold, but decided to deal with the totals later, when everything was done that could be done. Of course, as the gold began to be sold here and there, those in the market would become intensely interested. But, when it comes to gold, rumors run the news. Few who know about the gold market tell the truth and even fewer believe all the stories. Sky and Jon decided not to mention anything of what had been given to Carlos Diaz, nor the small amounts they had given to Ian, Paul, Frank, and the part they had set aside for Sylvia. Sylvia's portion, alone, amounted to forty pounds, about $231.000, at December's price. What surprised both of them had to do with the absence of searching inquiries about the gold. As the stories became more public, both Sky and Jon anticipated lots of curiosity as to values and quantities. There were speculations, but no one seemed to demand precise information. Nearly all gold stories become fiction and few believe them. Their apprehensions about future inquiries gradually subsided.

Sky told Jon she was meeting Krystal for dinner in the late afternoon, but she wanted to work in her workshop to finish preparing for a paper she was writing. They agreed to meet at the shop that evening about eight.

Jon drove up and saw that her light was on and the door closed. Schwartz came running to her side of the fence to meet him. Using the key Sky had given him, he opened the chainlink gate. Schwartz wiggled and bounced up and down in frenzied glee, barking her friendliest bark. Jon picked her up and carried her to the sliding workshop door. Sky sat at her workbench with a legal-sized yellow pad covered with notes and dimensions and a small pile of shards and calipers under a strong, goose-neck lamp. She looked up and welcomed him. She wore her coveralls and a red bandana over her hair. After a hug and greetings, they began to talk. Her dinner with Krystal had been a good one, with Sky's avoiding any judgmental discussion about Sylvia and Krystal. She was proud of herself, asking for his compliments, which he gave with sincerity. Then they moved on to other matters, taking up from where they had been before regarding the gold.

A problem kept creeping into their thoughts. How would they deal with what had been stowed in the corner of Sky's workshop? How would they deal with the continuing news coverage, the media questions, and the many holes in their evasive explanations? What unforeseen complications lay ahead from the gold they had and even the gold they had shared? Rumors were already in the media, but, luckily, the rumors all collided and obviously became just speculation. There had been five newspaper stories during the last two weeks, some about the *Madonna* and others that spun off from Sylvia's shark attack. These newspaper reports were making a nuisance with which they had to cope almost daily. Astute journalists began to see between the lines of what they had said and did not say. They wanted to find a less than astute journalist, but it was really too much to hope for. Also, they must stay aware of the problems caused by Ray Cramer's family. These included the law suit against Carlos and the family of Luís Jimenez, and the demand for compensation for the Cramer son's drowning.

Gold, as was always the case with anyone who found it, had attracted and concentrated a complex of difficulties. Jon did not want to cope with the imminent avalanche. Sky, too, wanted to be a professor and a researcher, not someone answering questions from the State, the Federal Government, the U. S. Department of the Treasury, and on and on. Others wanted to consume their lives for their own journalistic ambitions. Jon and Sky were dedicated to their own lives with one another. They wanted to pursue their professions, their evening walks and love-making times without interruptions. They expressed mutual disgust at the thought of legal complications and harassing interviews with sensationalist media folks. They wanted their lives without being afraid of thieves breaking in and stealing. This situation was not simple.

"In most all cases of people discovering gold, the one finding it has not lived to benefit from it," Jon said.

"That's an unhappy thought, Jon. Is there a warning in this?" she asked.

Nothing involving the discovery of gold at any level had ever been simple. Their decision, after discussion, was to talk about everything in the original group get-together. They had to be sure this gold had not destroyed their trust and comradeship. There could not be any lingering suspicions or incipient envy of any one of them. Each one of them must be trustworthy. Trust was needed for them to agree on what had transpired about finding the wreck itself and, especially their finding the gold.

Gold, the discovery, the presence of it, the ownership of it, the dispersion of it, the eventual relinquishing of it, would challenge and captivate those who came to more thoroughly excavate the site of the *Madonna*. Gold was the transformational element, just as in ancient alchemy. This fascinated Jon, as a depth psychologist. He mused about Leonardo da Vinci's work with the alchemical beliefs regarding lead and gold. All the lives lived and spent in the acquisition and loss of gold were at least under-stories running through eons. Jon reflected on how gold motivated explorers, pirates, fomenting and intensifying battles on land and at sea.

These ideas also fascinated Sky. She had studied the role of gold in Egypt, Australia, Africa, and especially the role of gold in California's history, to say nothing of the hoards of gold mined in Mexico during the last thousand years. Since 1785, the United States had been on a bimetallic system, where silver and gold provided the value for the currency and coins. The sudden rise of golden wealth in the United States resulted in controversy and economic complications. The United States eventually adopted the Gold Standard as a basis for the value of money in 1900. Whether in Egypt, Africa, Mexico, California, or the United States as a new nation, the presence or lack of gold had complicated cultures, the lives of individuals, and has overturned whole political and economic systems. Sky and Jon talked about how unusual it was for all of the *Tiamat*'s group members to stay so trustful. Jon guessed that their finding the *Madonna*'s gold might completely change them. It might have immediately converted previously friendly, cooperative relationships into suspicious and uneasy ways of being with one another.

Sky and Jon did not want this to happen between them. But they were not sure how to manage the treasure lying on the workshop floor. Should they simply distribute it? Should they report it all or dump it back into the mud? Should they hide it, invest it wisely, secretly? No matter what, they had to deal with this pile of gold in the corner, near the workbench. It was under a stereo speaker, which was now playing George Frederick Handel's *Water Music.* This tape was just the right music for now. It included the *Alchymist*; with Christopher Hogwood conducting Jon's favorite version. Jon thought about the synchronicity. It was the strange musical joining of gold, alchemy, sky and water. And now, in the background, played this particular tape. Sky responded with immediate recognition, when he reminded her of the music she had put in the tape player. This brought her to him. Sinking onto the couch, she cuddled up on his lap. They bathed in the Water Music, breathing together, floating down into a peaceful, sensuous place – a place they had grown to treasure.

"Jon, is it possible the golden love we've found might replace the complications from having the chunks of that cold element over there in the corner?"

"It seems to me that's already happened. That gold does complicate things for us, but so far our love outweighs it and, if we stay on track, we'll keep our priorities in the love column."

Thursday, January 3rd arrived with three connected events. They began for Jon at 5:20 AM, with the phone ringing.

"Hello," he answered with a sleepy voice.

"Jon, this is Frank Martinez. I'm on duty this morning. We got a message that there's someone cruising around over in your basin. He's driving Michael Diaz's Honda. I'm on my way over, but the patrolman there said he's parked the car near the yacht club and is walking your way," Frank said, clearly giving Jon a warning.

Leaving his light off, Jon got up and dressed. He didn't want to be trapped in his boat. In the near darkness, he crept from under the boom tent on the side away from the parking lot, so as not to be seen. He squatted down, hidden by the hull of his boat. The row of dock lights prevented him from moving from this place. Jon waited and watched. Within minutes, he heard someone walking down the gangway toward his slip. The person moved very slowly. Under the second dock light, he saw a young man wearing a leather jacket, a golf cap, and Levis. He carried something in his right hand - a gun. Jon's heart raced now even faster. Car lights in the parking lot startled him. The intruder moved behind a large powerboat, just four slips beyond where Jon hid. Jon heard Frank's voice, talking to another person, probably another marina patrolman. The figure was visible from where Jon crouched, but they could not see him from the parking lot. Jon watched Frank walk toward the gangway to his right and the other man toward the one to his left. They had guns drawn. They converged at the end of Jon's gangway, walking slowly toward his slip. He knew they could not now surprise the armed man.

Without hesitation, Jon yelled, "Frank, he's in front of you! He's armed!"

Both patrolmen ducked behind boats, Frank to his right, the other to his left. The suspicious person looked in his direction. The man could not see Jon, but he now knew he was trapped. Jon heard a splash. Seconds later, he stepped out from behind the Spindrift, a forty-foot powerboat.

Frank abruptly accosted him, his bright flashlight beam in the man's face.

"Stand where you are! Hands over your head!"

The other patrolman moved in cautiously as Frank kept his gun on the man. He ordered, "Turn around! On your knees! Hands behind you!" He easily put handcuffs on the seemingly compliant man.

"Frank, I think he threw his weapon in the water."

"I heard the splash, too, Jon. The ripples and bubbles mark the spot," Frank responded, shining his light into the water by the boat bow beside him.

Once cuffed and frisked, they got the man to his feet. Frank began to look through his wallet under the dock light. The intruder was heavy, about five feet eight inches tall. His cap lay on the dock He had a butch haircut. Every time he began to say something, Frank told him to shut up. All his papers were out of his wallet on top of the dock box next to Frank. The other patrolman called the marina office to report the apprehension. Jon heard the answering voice on the radio telling him to proceed to the parking lot. The Long

Beach Police would meet them at their cars. The man did not take his eyes from Jon. Something he kept mouthing, but Jon could not understand him.

"Frank, he's wanting to tell me something," Jon said.

"Okay, Steven, if that's really your name, let's hear what you've got to say," Frank said to the man, again shining the light in his face.

"I don't got nothin' to say to you assholes," he said.

"Good start!" Frank said. "Some idiots don't have the brains God gave soda crackers, and you've just made your life harder. Sure you want to make it tougher on yourself? We're about to turn you over to the real cops. You think we're assholes. Wait till you get downtown with them. It won't be long before we have your gun out of the mud. Lucky you didn't use it, Steven," Frank said, beginning to walk him away on the gangway toward the parking lot.

The prisoner turned his head back over his shoulder and yelled at Jon, "You better watch your fucking back, Father Scott. You're number one on the list!"

It took a few seconds for the threat to soak in. Jon rehearsed his words in his mind. The trio reached the end of the dock. They turned to go up the gangway, illuminated by the gangway light just above them. The other patrolman came back. He shined his light into the dark, muddy water where the splash and circles had been. Of course, in twelve feet of water and soft mud below, nothing was visible, but he had the right place to look. Jon imagined that Frank, in his scuba gear, would be the one to find the weapon Steven had dropped. The patrolman introduced himself as Bill Schroeder. They talked for a few minutes, long enough for Jon to learn this was Bill's second night on the job as an Alamitos Bay Harbor Patrolman. He looked all of twenty years old, about Jon's height and build. He told Jon he would stay on the dock until Frank came back to dive for the weapon.

"Good idea. There's evidence down there. I can witness he had a gun as he came down the gangway. That's the only thing that would have made that splash," Jon said. He was suddenly embarrassed, sounding like a B-Grade movie actor in a corny crime flick.

Bill had the courtesy not to make any wise cracks. He sat down on the dock box, next to the splash point, offering Jon a cigarette as he put one to his own lips. Jon declined, being only a once-in-a-while pipe smoker. The lights on the cars in the parking lot reflected off the white masts around them. Jon watched with a clear view of the five officers talking. The secured prisoner was already in the Long Beach police cruiser. Their voices were muffled. They talked for nearly fifteen minutes before Frank called for Jon to come up to where they were parked.

As Jon approached the officers, Frank introduced him to them. Frank told them what the prisoner, Steven Cramer, had said to Jon. Frank suggested Jon might need some protection, at least until things were figured out. The Long Beach officers declined to obligate their department to do that, suggesting this was a marina jurisdictional matter. Jon quickly absolved them of any need for protection, insisting he could watch his own back. But, that did not quell their curiosity. They wanted to know how this guy knew Jon and why he would be his target.

"This is a long story, officers. I'll be glad to tell it, but I think the short part has to do with your prisoner's name being Cramer. You see, Ray Cramer drowned at Catalina a few weeks ago. I'll bet this is a close relative, a brother, perhaps. The whole Cramer family is suing anyone they can attach to Ray Cramer's death. I'm implicated in a very indirect way. I'm sure others are in danger, too."

"Okay, Dr. Scott. We're taking him downtown. We can hold him for about forty-eight hours or maybe less. He doesn't have a weapon. He also made threats, but that won't help us hold him long. The only charge we can put on him for now is loitering," one of the policemen said.

"I'll have the weapon shortly, Ben," Frank said to the officer with the sergeant stripes. "I know where it went in the drink."

Frank's radio called him. He took it from his belt, answering, "Frank here."

The scratchy radio voice said, *Frank, I got a man here at the desk who says he's George Cramer. He says his son is heading over to Basin Four.*

"Tell Mr. Cramer we've got a Cramer in custody, maybe his son. Keep him there. I'm coming in," Frank said.

Frank got into his Ford cruiser and the Long Beach police followed him out of the parking lot. Jon walked back to his boat, asking Bill Schroeder if he would like a cup of coffee. Bill gave Jon an enthusiastic 'You bet.' Jon told him it would take a few minutes to brew, inviting him aboard. Bill said he thought he should stay put for now, obviously keeping a responsible watch over the submerged evidence, lying in the marina mud.

"That gun's going nowhere. It's about four to six inches into the muddy silt. I've dropped things overboard, wrenches, an electric shaver once, a winch handle, and an expensive snatch block I had clumsily unhooked. Once in a while I've dived to pick things up, but usually I get the hull cleaning guys or Frank to pick up stuff," Jon said.

Schroeder lit another cigarette. Jon went below to put on the coffee. It was dawn, nearly 6:40. The dock lights went out on their own. Seagulls began to screech, following the smarter ones to early-morning glistening fish. Circles marked the rises here and there, all around the boat slips. A pelican crashed just astern of the *Charisma*, a beautifully-restored thirty-nine foot classic, built in the mid-1920s. One of Jon's joys was being able to look at this fine, old boat in the row of sterns just across from his slip. The pelican had a large fish flopping in its beak, with seagulls pulling at any exposed part they could snatch before it took it almost whole into its protective pouch, wagging its head and neck in a triumphant maneuver. The bird's wings stretched wide, scattering the seagulls as it kicked along into flight, until landing on top of the head building close to where the police had been just minutes before.

Chapter Thirty-Three

The morning's other two events were as dramatic, but only indirectly involved Jon. Sky called crying, as Jon, on the boat, was making coffee. She talked so fast he had to ask her to slow down. Jon could not understand her.

"Krystal got a phone call just a while ago, Jon. They have Sylvia. Someone kidnaped Sylvia. After they took her, they called the Matthews and told them Sylvia would not be harmed if they were given what they want," Sky said, her voice shaking.

"Where are you now, Sky?"

"Krystal and I are both home, but I don't think we're safe, Jon. We've had four phone calls and when we answer they hang up. The first one came at four-thirty this morning. I heard breathing on the other end, but they hung up right away."

"Sky, please call the police right away and report this."

"Eleanor Matthews said they were threatened. They came right into their house and took her. If the police are called, they said they would kill Sylvia. Then they said she would be returned unharmed back to them as soon as they knew the location of the shipwreck. They told Eleanor Matthews they know all about the shipwreck, except exactly where it is," Sky reported.

"How is anyone to get information to them, Sky?" Jon asked, thinking there might be a way to apprehend whomever had Sylvia.

"Eleanor wants me to tell her exactly where the wreck is, writing it on a piece of paper, putting it in a brown envelope, and dropping it under the slide in the park on Ocean Avenue by ten this morning."

"Sky, we've got to let the police know. No matter what, Sylvia needs her medical care still. We can't take any chances with her still healing. Let's give all the information to these people right away. We've got nothing to lose now."

Krystal took the phone. "Jon, Sylvia's got to be okay. Do something, Jon! Mom's been afraid to do anything! You've got to do something!" she shouted, crying.

"We'll do everything we can, Krystal. I've talked to Aubry. Detective Aubry informed me that they are already tapping the phones, yours and the Matthews's phones. It was their idea and a good one. If the kidnappers call again, see if you can keep them on the phone. Tell them anything that keeps them interested. Tell them Sylvia's a patient, just home from a hospital. If she doesn't have medications, she will be in severe stress. Tell them anything, Krystal. They'll call again. Tell Eleanor Matthews to do the same thing, to keep them on the phone if and when they call," Jon said.

Having done his best to assure Sky and Krystal, he said goodbye and called the Long Beach Police. The police took the information, including where one of them was to leave the brown envelope by ten o'clock this morning. They assured Jon there would be no uniformed police around the area, but three of their scruffiest plain-clothes officers would be not too far off. While on the phone, they told him Frank was heading over to dive for the weapon and should show up soon. Serving Bill his coffee, Jon explained to him the call he'd just gotten that delayed him.

"What the hell is this all about, Dr. Scott? This thing is growing like scum in my aquarium," he said.

"Bill, they think there's lots of gold down there with the wreck they think is there. They're probably right. I guess they're getting impatient. It has been a couple of weeks since this adventure got in the news. Obviously, the word has gotten out. There were originally three guys who went out looking. There may also be others they talked to, especially Steven Cramer and his family, who are going after this treasure, or what they imagine to be treasure. Greed is a powerful motivator."

Bill drank his coffee and ate a slice of the toast that Jon had made for him. Jon sat on his dock box, drinking coffee. Jon told more of the story about discovering the wreck, including the part when Sylvia Matthews lost an arm to a shark and how the whole thing had been in the local papers. Before he could finish the story, Frank came walking the dock toward them, dressed in his wetsuit, carrying a tank and regulator, his fins, and faceplate.

"You're used to swimming in the early morning, Jon. Why don't you go down and look for this gun?" he said, smirking.

"Frank, I'll be glad to go down. I don't even need a tank. I'll free-dive it. Just say the word."

"I know you'd do it, too. But, this is official business. If anyone heard I had you dive for the gun, I'd never hear the end of it," he said, sitting down next to Jon on the dock box to pull on his fins.

Jon helped him on with his tank, turning the valve on for him. Frank smeared his faceplate with saliva, pulled it down over his face, stuck the mouthpiece in his mouth, and walked a few steps to the edge of the dock. For a moment he stood beside the bow where the gun had been dropped. Squatting down, without hesitation, he rolled backward into the murky water, disappearing in a cloud of bubbles. Bill and Jon stood by, watching for him. He had been down no more than five minutes when he bobbed to the surface. He reached up and put a rusty pipe wrench on the dock, disappearing again. The next time he surfaced, he dropped a revolver at their feet, a 357 Ruger with a six-inch barrel. It had all six bullets in the chambers. Jon reached down to take Frank's tanks and dive belt from him. Once free of the weight, Frank used his fins to kick himself high enough in the water for them to help him back onto the dock.

"How's that for a day's work?"

"Not bad, Frank. But, if you'd now go below my boat, I think you'll find several tools I've dropped over the last few years. Remember when you found Dick Brown's radio and field glasses? Those guys had stripped his boat just before the Ensenada Race. They left so fast, they dropped winch handles, the radio, and Lord knows what else. I think you found most of what they tried to take." Jon uncoiled enough hose and turned it on. "Stand over there and I'll hose you off." Jon said.

"Yes. I remember that. That was a good day's work, too. Dick thanked me over and over. We got things to him in time for him to make the start of El Cinco de Mayo race that year," he said, puffing himself up and swaggering with pride.

"Here's your coffee, Frank," Jon said, having fetched it just before he rose with the gun. He also warmed Bill's cup and his own.

Frank and Bill walked to the head, pushing the dock cart loaded with his tank, lead dive belt, and flippers, so Frank could change into his uniform. He asked Jon to call Sergeant Sills at the Long Beach Police Department to tell him Frank had the weapon. Jon did as Frank asked.

Jon told the sergeant that Frank would bring in the weapon by 8:30 AM. Sergeant Sills thanked Jon for the news. He said to tell Frank that they could now make a charge with evidence and could hold Steven Cramer.

"Even if we can't trace the weapon to Cramer, we hope it might be enough to get a confession out of him," the sergeant said.

The rest of the morning was uneventful, until nearly noon. Sky called, excited. Sylvia had been found. Two men were in custody, having been picked up on Ocean Avenue with the brown envelope in their possession. One of the men eventually admitted that he knew George Cramer. He was the same guy who had come to the Harbor Patrol office this very morning to warn them about his son. So far, no one could make sense of the tangle. Encouraging for Jon was the indication that only a few people were involved. Explaining that to Sky relieved her. Jon asked how Krystal was doing. Krystal immediately had gone to Sylvia's home to meet her. Other than being shaken up, Sylvia seemed to be doing well under the stressful and frightening circumstances. She had required some first aid, because her injury had begun to bleed again.

The interesting twist came in early that afternoon when Dick Brophe called Sky. He told her he had been threatened at gunpoint by two men ordering him to take them to the wreck of the *Madonna*. That was just before midnight last night. They took Dick to his boat, holding him at gun-point in the back seat. When they got to Dick's boat, he agreed to take them, but he had to get diesel fuel. Dick explained to Sky that it was easy to delay, because the fuel dock did not open until 7:00 AM. They held him hostage until about 4:00 AM, when one of them had to go to the head. When he went into the head on the *Tiamat*, Dick told the other he would have to start warming the engines and get out his charts. Dick distracted his captor for a second, he got into the cockpit of his boat and from there slipped into the water off the dive step. Escaping the two of them on the boat, he swam under the docks to where he could get out of the water undetected. It was still dark when he made his way to the parking lot of Basin Two. He watched their car leave minutes after he reached the parking lot. He got their license number and a good description. The men were wearing stocking masks, so he could not describe them, except for their height and weight. He identified the taller one by his voice. He was the older one, for sure. Some of what Dick told Sky he read from the police report he was writing.

Later, when the pieces came together more clearly, it became apparent that these two men were George and Steven Cramer, the father and brother of Ray Cramer, the drowned man. Apparently, when George went to the marina office to inform them that Steven was out to get Jon, he was afraid Steven would somehow reach the wreck first. Steven knew two divers he had told about the gold. These two were ready to go the instant Steven called them. They did not know enough, though. They would have had difficulties at seventy-five feet. They realized, as did the police, that this wreck was a glamorous attraction. The 28th of December local newspaper story about the shipwreck, just the week before, made secrecy impossible. It had been on the front page, entitled, 'Gold Found in Local Shipwreck'. Much of the story was inaccurate.

When Sky and Jon discussed this story both realized with great relief, the whole matter was out of their hands. The rest of whatever happened to the *Madonna*, the gold, the credit for the find, all of it would be interesting, but their parts in the story would quickly fade, eclipsed by whatever drama unfolded at the site itself.

Friday evening, the Matthews invited Krystal, Sky, and Jon to come to their house for dinner. Krystal had driven her Datsun. She parked it in the circular driveway in front of the large, white, freshly painted, Colonial-style, two-story home. It was well-lighted for maximum effect. The Matthews, including Sylvia, greeted them at the door. Krystal came from the kitchen, wiping her hands with a dishtowel. The guests were greeted warmly and supper soon followed. Mr. Matthews asked Jon to say grace. Around the table they took hands and Jon prayed a thankful prayer, with grateful mention of Sylvia's survival and healing. He was careful to be brief.

After grace, he volunteered, "There are few things as annoying as a grace so long that the food gets cold."

Sylvia had Krystal's arm around her and Sky held Krystal's free hand. The ambience, the spirited conversation, along with a splendid home-cooked meal, could not have been more healing. Even among the comments, each one filling in parts of the story from the day before with relief and humor. Sylvia's account of being kidnaped was gripping. The salad and lasagna, along with a bottle or two of good Cabernet Sauvignon, left them relaxed. After dinner, Eleanor Matthews brought out a photograph album, featuring Sylvia's diving exploits and experiences.

The only point of tension came from Mr. Matthews as he carried on at length about Geraldine Ferraro's not being qualified to be president. Mondale, according to Mr.

Matthews, didn't have the strength nor the brains to fight even a cold war. He spoke with pointed irritation about how women should not be in politics or business. The thrust of his comment had to do with his intense approval of Ronald Reagan's election. Walter Mondale and Geraldine Ferraro would have led the country to ruin, he insisted. He had supported vice-president George H. Bush, telling them he would put Reagonomics on the map.

His only comment directed toward Jon criticized the Episcopal Church because of the ordination of women and the church's stand on Fair Housing. With polite restraint, Jon decided not to ruin an otherwise pleasant evening with his comments. Mr. Matthews enjoyed his monologues. Jon knew any protest or opinions of his own would not be well received and would destroy an otherwise splendid evening.

Eleanor finally told him to change the subject, which he soon did. The awkward moments for that transition were remedied by Krystal's telling them that she had been in the play, *Our Town*. She spontaneously recited a couple of her more dramatic lines.

Mr. Matthews said, "Krystal, you did well with those lines. I read that play some years ago. I would like to have come to the performance."

The party broke up by 10:00, with hugs all around for a good night. Sky reminded Krystal about having to be at school on time in the morning and Krystal responded with a mildly sarcastic, "Oh, Mom! You think I'm ten years old?" Jon and Sky left together. Krystal stayed there with Sylvia.

Sky and Jon were both tired from an emotional and strenuous week.

Jon said, "This New Year has gotten off to an adventurous start. I wonder if what's happened so far is an omen of what is to come. If so, we're in for quite a ride."

"If it brings us closer together," Sky said, "I don't care what more happens, Jon. I've been more comfortable daily with you. I think coming to church on Christmas Eve was some kind of breakthrough for me. Your being a priest has really bugged me. Somehow, now, it doesn't seem a problem. You're mostly a very special man to me. I think your roles were confusing me."

She moved closer to him in the pickup, saying how much more comfortable his pickup seat was than the bucket seats in her T-Bird. "In this Chevy I can snuggle. Look, I can just rest my left arm right here. Does my arm get in the way of your driving?" she said, teasing him.

"Just don't move away and I'll be okay driving, Love."

"I won't move away until we get to my house. But, I've arranged for an assayer to come tomorrow. I've got to get sleep and then get things together for him to appraise. Will you come when he's there tomorrow afternoon?" she asked, burrowing more closely into his side.

"I wouldn't miss that. I'm sure we'll learn a lot from him, if he really knows his stuff. He came highly recommended. Unless we've been given a bum steer, he ought to teach us a lot about what we've found."

Fred Emerson, a gold assayer from Huntington Beach, had agreed to come to Sky's home on Saturday afternoon to meet with them. Sky brought home a variety of pieces from the pile in her workshop, to see what value they might have. On Saturday Mr. Emerson came with three recommendations of other numismatists in the Long Beach area. He arrived on the dot of three o'clock, the appointed time. As Sky walked to answer the doorbell, she commented to Jon he had passed the first test of promptness. He walked with a cane, slightly stooped and unsteady and looked to be in his eighties. He spoke quietly, but clearly, with clipped precision. On her dining room table she had displayed about nine pieces, two small ingots, three larger bricks, two nuggets, and two coins.

Emerson sat at the table, setting up a small scale in front of him within easy reach. A monocular lens in his right eye completed the picture. Jon and Sky watched him as he handled each gold piece carefully. He wore white, soft, very clean gloves. He made notes on a scratch pad beside him, recording the numbers and letters embossed on each gold piece. He commented about the pieces having bits of mud stuck to them. They could be carefully cleaned. One of the bricks had nothing engraved on it. He showed them how each of the ingots and bricks had a tiny corner taken off, indicating they had been assayed. Twice he asked if this gold was from the archeological dig he had read about. Sky only confirmed they were part of that dig and there was more there, but it would be unavailable until certain determinations were made about ownership. Sky added that there were complications with the 'finders-keepers' salvage rules now in effect, but these would soon be clarified. That seemed to satisfy him for now. Weighing, measuring, making notes, he sat back in his chair and withdrew a large book from his canvas bag. It had countless lists of numbers and an appendix with photographs of gold items.

"I want you to know you have an assortment of great value here. The coins you have were not in distribution until 1850. They were minted by Moffat Company in San Francisco in 1849 and 1850. John Little Moffat is famous in the early days of Sutter's Creek gold. There was a Bavarian engraver named Kuner, I think. He and his partners, whom I can't recall right now, captured the assaying business in San Francisco and in Sacramento. Kuner was a johnny-on-the-spot fellow. There was also, besides these five and ten-dollar coins, a twenty-dollar gold piece. Do you have any of those?" he asked, pausing. "If you look closely, you will make out the words 'Moffat & Co.' and on the other side 'Liberty.' The letters 'S.M.V.' stand for 'Standard Market Value.' Even with the bits of mud on the coin, can you see how sharp the thirteen stars are on this side and the eagle is on the other? These are extraordinary. The date had been a marketing gimmick, because they were not distributed until 1850 and they're stamped 1849. They could not have been available to the public until early 1850," he said, looking over other pieces, and once referring to a list in his large book. Confirming Sky's research he continued by saying, "The other pieces are earlier, perhaps 1848 or 1849. These one-ounce ingots were valued in 1848 at $18.00 per ounce. Today, just considering their weight, they're worth about $361.00 each. These are not all the same weight, of course. They're close to one another by fractions, but each one must be valued separately to assay them correctly.

"The larger blocks vary in value, mostly because they seem to be twenty-two carat gold, which is not common in today's market. They weigh more than my portable scale can handle. But this one is easily five pounds. This one is perhaps seven or eight pounds. The markings will help. You have historic gold here, worth much more because of its antiquity. I wouldn't be surprised if, just here on this table, you have at least a couple hundred thousand dollars. These two coins are nearly perfect. They show some deterioration, perhaps from being buried at a shallow depth in water, probably salt water and mud. Even so, under magnification, they would go as very fine. There is usually less turbulence as depth increases, and, therefore, less water action on the gold surfaces. Often, gold found at great depths is nearly pristine, except for attached marine life, once cleaned. I know of no gold ingots in existence like these.

"I suspect Moffat's minted gold is extremely valuable, just because he was the first in the gold rush days to mint gold with very good molds. One problem with his gold pieces, like these, though, had to do with their not being reliable weights. For instance, this five-dollar gold piece here was valued at $4.98, because he shorted the weight. The ten-dollar gold piece, this one here, was valued at $9.98 in 1849. I made extensive studies of gold from the San Francisco area, but there isn't much to be found. You have found gold here worth a great deal. We know it by description, but to my knowledge no one owns gold from 1849 any more," he said, leaning back, tucking thumbs under his suspenders. Sky, impressed, refreshed his tea.

He became thoughtfully quiet for several minutes. Then he cautioned her, "I would say nothing about this gold right now. Absolutely nothing! Certainly, do not let anyone know you have these pieces. Some people would do anything to get their hands on this collection, especially if they knew what I know about it," he said, sipping the hot tea with approval.

Sky assured him she would say nothing for now. She managed to obtain an agreement that he would say nothing, assuring him whatever she did with the gold would be done through him and with his guidance. That seemed to satisfy him. He refused to take any money for his time and information, but he did insist on a note from Sky that he would be the only one with whom she would consult about this variety of pieces.

Intuitively he asked her, "How much more of this do you have?"

"There is more, but we will have to do some sorting. As I said, some of it cannot be taken from the site yet. As soon as we get it together, we'll call you, Mr. Emerson, if that's all right with you," she said. "By the way, you may have read about the site where this was found. It comes from the shipwreck, the *Madonna*, found recently off San Clemente Island. The specific island information is also secret, but the press has published too much for us to keep the general site unknown," she said, pouring him more tea.

"I've been following that story with great interest. Your name is already famous, Dr. Rowan. I don't know how coins distributed in 1850 could be on a ship that sank in 1849. Any ideas about that? Perhaps someone had access to the minted gold prior to its being distributed. The article in the paper is the reason I came this afternoon. I suspected you were in possession of some of the gold from the shipwreck you found. I also think others suspect you're in possession of some of this gold. Do be careful, Dr. Rowan. I thank you for trusting me with your information. I'll be silent," he said, seriously, for emphasis.

They said thank you and goodbye to Fred Emerson, letting him know he would hear from them by the end of next week. He left his card, writing on the back the name of his assistant, a man who could be trusted to keep any confidence. They were to talk to no one else about any of this, including his having come to Sky's home this afternoon to discuss these pieces. No one could know of his involvement.

They walked with him to his car, a 1963 Chevrolet sedan. It had a crumpled right fender, the chrome strip missing from the right side, a cracked windshield, and it was in need of a new head liner. As he got in, he said, "Don't laugh. It's paid for." They smiled. The door rattled closed, and he started the car. Looking up at them, he repeated, "Not a word to anyone!"

Chapter Thirty-Four

Sunday morning, a stormy wind began rocking the *Daimon* about midnight. Jon slept restlessly. He finally got up to tie off clanging lines on the sailboat next to his. The rain began by 4:30. He meditated about his sermon, listening to the rain, feeling the boat nudging against her dock lines. With the combined sounds of the rain and wind, he luxuriated in the warmth of his bunk.

At nearly dawn, he went for his swim in the rain, but the cold got to him. He cut the exercise short, took a hot shower, ate a light breakfast, and prepared for the eight o'clock Communion service. His sermon felt unusually good to him. Keeping it to a typical Christmas season sermon, he spoke of the Incarnation and the gift of grace for human beings who had the potential to love. In the sermon he gave some personal associations, describing his own sense of new life in recent weeks, emphasizing how new life for him came through being able to love and be loved. He knew of others in the congregation who would appreciate the message. One of them had found new life in remission from a severe cancer. Another was a couple that had just had fraternal twins. He realized new life partly with the developments between Sky and himself. He saw new life, too, in Sylvia's healing and the love Krystal and she found together.

Krystal and Sylvia came to the ten o'clock service. They both came forward to receive the bread and wine, too, as they had at the Christmas Eve service. In the greeting line, after the service, he gave them both hugs.

Sylvia said to him then, "Krystal likes it when I call her by her Vietnamese name, Vo Thanh Thuy. Father Scott, did you know her name until eight years old was Vo Thuy?"

"No, I didn't know her childhood name, but now you have learned it. You and Krystal have even more intimacy, just by using her original name." Krystal beamed happily through the whole interchange at the door of St. Paul's. Sylvia had grown up as a Roman Catholic, so her liturgical roots were familiar. But Krystal, except for her early Buddhist roots, had been raised in an agnostic family. She had a scientific mother, who thought of religion as a subject of cultural anthropology. Her father worshiped at the altar of business and finance; acquired things were the symbols of success. Not knowing him, Jon should not have prejudged. However, based on Krystal's hurt and anger about how her father had treated her and, ultimately, neglected her, Jon did not like him. Krystal knew him to be cold and abusive. It would not be her word, but 'narcissistic' and 'alcoholic' fit everything described to Jon about Robert Fitzpatrick.

Back aboard the boat, Jon changed his clothes for lunch and relaxation. He was eager to call Sky. She just as eagerly answered the phone.

"Sylvia and Krystal are with me, and the three of us are on our way to lunch. Krystal can't stop talking about having gone to St. Paul's, hearing your sermon, which she liked. It meant a lot to her, also, to have Communion with Sylvia. She surprised me with that. It never occurred to me Krystal would warm up to church stuff."

Jon listened to her intently. A strange feeling grew from sensing he was excluded from their plans. That feeling of exclusion caught him by surprise. He had no idea he would have that feeling as Sky almost gleefully told him about the three of them going to lunch and sharing so much conversation. It occurred to him he was feeling sorry for himself. By the end of the conversation, as Sky prepared Jon for the hang up, he told her he was going to an afternoon movie. Since the weather had improved, he would do some evening sailing afterward. He purposely did not invite her or intrude on their plans. He thought, because of his feelings of being left out, he needed to contain himself and not be so dependent or connected for now.

I can't believe I'm trying to teach Sky a lesson. Oh well. We'll see what comes of this.

A 1980 Cadillac El Dorado pulled up behind his pickup before he could leave for a movie. Carlos Diaz and his wife waved to him. He turned off the Chevy, got out, and walked around to say hello to them. Carlos asked him if they could talk for a minute. He didn't want to hold him up, but had something important to say to him. Instantly, the movie disappeared from Jon's agenda and he invited them to the boat to have a beer and to talk. They accepted. Carlos parked the car. Laura, Carlos, and Jon walked to the boat, chatting about the weather and the birds. Then Carlos introduced the subject.

"Michael has been arraigned, along with Luís Jimenez, on second degree manslaughter. But, that isn't the only thing, Jon. It turns out, Ray Cramer and Michael went to high school together. Ray is the one who drowned. Remember?"

Jon acknowledged that he not only remembered that, but he had even more to remember, having had a close call with Ray's brother, Steven, and his father, George. As they settled around the *Daimon's* galley table, getting comfortable, Jon served Carlos and himself Dos Equis, which they took from the bottle. Laura had a cold glass of grapefruit juice. Carlos had visited his son in jail and talked with him. Michael had told Ray about the gold on the bottom with the shipwreck, having known about the gold from family stories. Michael reminded his father about his having written a paper for California History class in high school, telling of the history of his ancestor, Shuka. In that paper Michael wrote about a square-rigger coming down the coast to southern California with lots of gold.

Carlos eagerly told Jon the news. He had, however, many mixed reactions to it. It bothered him that George Cramer was related to Wilfred Cramer, the *Madonna*'s ship's carpenter. Carlos did not know that Jon had already come across that name. It had slipped his mind, however, even though Jon remembered it from recently having read the scroll to Sky. He thought to himself how amazing this was, Carlos and George being connected in this way. Apparently, both families had carried the stories of how the *Madonna* came south with a large amount of gold. The amount probably grew through the several generations of telling the story. Laura remarked about a small world, but, Carlos added, there were probably other local people who shared the Pomo Indians' history.

Carlos said, "After all, San Juan Capistrano is a small area. Most likely about twenty Pomo Indians landed there. Also, the ship's original crew members had come ashore at the same time. They would have descendants, too. Just figuring the odds, there must be others close to San Juan Capistrano who are related to the original landing party. Who knows how many of these people might still be around who know their history?"

Jon's question now: *Why would Steven Cramer be gunning for me or want to kidnap me? Or, what did he intend to do when he came to find me that morning?* Jon shared his thoughts with Carlos.

Carlos explained to him, "Michael told me that Steven had asked him who could take him to the wreck. Michael knew of Dick Brophe, because I told him about Dick's owning the dive boat. Michael also knew that you knew the location of the boat and you had a boat that could take them there. Seeing as Dick Brophe, the dive boat captain, had escaped them, Steve and his father, George, were going to force you to take them to find the wreck and the gold.

"They had two divers all set up the morning Steven got caught looking for you. But, Steven's father got cold feet. When Dick Brophe escaped, George Cramer decided this plan would not work. I went to the Harbor Patrol to report that Steven was looking for you. I'm sure George Cramer still thinks he's going to win this big law suit against all of us. When he does, he'll not have to dive for the gold, because he'll be rich from winning the suit. He just might, too," Carlos said, sipping the last of his beer.

"Carlos, I know it's too late now, but I told you to keep this to yourself. I can't help but be angry with you. You've caused a lot of problems blabbing this stuff to Michael."

"I'm sorry, Jon. I know sorry doesn't solve anything, but, believe me, I'm very sorry I told Michael about this and even sorrier that he's done what he's done."

Jon got up to cool off and got Carlos another and moved to replenish Laura's juice.

He put out a dish of small pretzels and some cheese for the two of them. Laura readily changed from the juice to a glass of white wine. They talked for nearly two hours.

By the time they left, late that Sunday afternoon, Jon decided to go for an evening sail. He waved them a goodbye. Carlos and Laura held hands as they walked down the dock toward the parking lot. Laura had thanked Jon several times, obviously very relieved about revealing this history and information to Jon.

Jon needed to write this conversation down or he would not be able to keep it straight. For some reason, he felt no fear of Steven Cramer anymore. Steven had been charged with carrying a concealed weapon, but he was not in custody. It began to interest Jon how gathering all the stories together from the various people who might remember the odyssey of the *Madonna* would be a very interesting enterprise. It would make a good movie, perhaps. He wondered how many other descendants from people on that December 1849 trip south to the rocks off San Clemente Island could still be around southern California.

These thoughts occupied him while powering out of the channel into the evening twilight. Reaching the end of the jetty, he cut the engine and lazily sailed at about four knots with just the genoa headsail. He soaked in the peace. It was a spiritual way to gather himself, his thoughts and feelings. His boundaries and hard edges softened as he sailed aboard his floating home in the crisp evening. The breeze grew chilly, but he wore his flotation jacket, which was warm and comfortable. The sun had set and he headed out to sea for a couple of hours, as if he could follow the sun around the world. Thoughts tumbled through his relaxing mind.

Thoughts of Miriam came to him. He savored memories of the two of them. A soft easiness seemed to be taking over, where so much grief had been. He mused about having not been in as much pain about losing her for some time, really since getting close to Sky and Krystal. He thought about his Lady, Meri, lying under a blue tarpaulin on the cold floor of a fascinating workshop in an east Long Beach alley. He thought of Sylvia and Krystal and the complicated lives that might be ahead for them. He wondered about Sky and about himself with her and about her with him. Back and forth, the monkey mind played itself out as the water splashed pleasantly against the bow of the *Daimon* on this gratifying, reflective Sunday evening. He began to think they needed a party, getting everyone together at a planned reunion and wrapping up loose ends, finishing business, perhaps gaining some closure. Clearly, he needed to talk to Sky to arrange a party.

Jon gybed and headed back toward the Alamitos Bay's flashing beacon. He counted the period of four seconds for the light. He counted the horn's period from the southeast end of the sea wall, blowing once every six seconds. The countless lights along the coast made finding the jetty at night difficult, were it not for the definite periods of the sea wall horn and the green and red jetty marker lights. He rehearsed the sailor's axiom, 'red right returning', and altered his course just enough to fetch the entrance. About 22:15, he coasted slowly into his slip. He tied up, plugged in the phone and electric lines, put the boom tent back on, and crawled into bed by midnight, still watching his monkey mind play. All the mental monkeys swung from tree to tree as he drifted into a deep sleep.

Chapter Thirty-Five

Monday's very cold swim got him started on a busy week. Frank joined him for breakfast at The Omelette House, Jon's breakfast being Frank's lunch. They had lots to discuss. Frank brought Jon up to date on the legal problems the Diaz and Jimenez families were having. Frank was pleased when Jon suggested they all get together by the end of the week for a reunion. He and Lupe would like to help with the cost of a party, which Jon appreciated. He was beginning to feel too much the host. It had been his idea, but too often he tended to pick up the tab for these affairs. Regarding money, Jon and Sky had discussed expenses. She insisted on helping. They would together produce their next events, if he would let her do so.

Julia was in good form, joking with both of them. Frank gave her teasing back to her, being careful to show his respect for her. Frank had told Jon how much he admired her. Watching him with her this morning reflected that admiration and care. She said, as they paid the bill, "If you two were thirty years younger, I would ask you to date my daughters."

"Why, Julia, that's the nicest thing anyone has ever said to me," Frank said: "Here dear. That's worth another buck on the tip."

Clearing Monday's phone messages took about a half-hour. Jon left a message for Sky, letting her know he wanted to talk with her about a party for the whole crew, including everyone. His first client arrived a few minutes late, giving him time to go to the head, brush his teeth, and write a couple of checks. He closed the check book and moved a stack of paper, a reminder that he had a lot of mail and paperwork to do. These thoughts cleared instantly as his client walked in and parked himself in his favorite chair, talking even before he sat down.

The whole day went like that, with not a minute to spare. It ended late in the evening, with an angry couple shouting at one another all the way to the elevator. Jon felt relief as he closed the door and stood for a few moments. He breathed deeply. Then he wrapped up the day's details at his desk and left the office by 9:30 PM. The refreshingly cold night made for a pleasant walk to the boat. He felt drained and ready for a snack and bed.

Jon had just stepped onto the gangway when Sky's car turned into the parking lot, her lights fixing him near the railing. He waved to her as she pulled into the parking space in front of him, beside his pickup. On reaching the car, her door opened and she leaped out into his arms.

"You work too much, Jon. I saw the light on in your office when I drove by twice earlier and decided if you were in bed by now, I would wake you up. I have to see you," she said, keeping her arms firmly around his waist, her face aglow under the sodium vapor parking lot lights.

"Your lips are green."

"I love you too," she said, taking his hand and heading down the gangway with him toward the boat. "Now, don't get your hopes up. I'm going to talk to you for a few minutes, hug and kiss you, tuck you in, and leave," she said, firmly.

"We'll see."

She did leave, after a glass of Port, cheese, crackers, and two hours of holding one another while talking. They had endless matters to discuss, enjoying the flow between them, and his burying his nose in her fragrant hair from time to time.

"We are so ready for one another, Jon! We have to make some decisions, soon," she said.

"I've made my decision. It's like the old saying, 'I have all my solutions. I just don't know how to arrive at them'."

"That may say it all. Maybe arriving at the solution to what we're finding with one another is wordless. Hmm. Yes. I think it is wordless," she mused, smiling her enigmatic smile, so often an expression in moments such as this.

They talked about planning a reunion party. For a moment they changed the subject; they both agreed that they needed to make decisions about their relationship. Then, back to business, they finished by discussing the party. They decided it should be next Saturday night at the yacht club. She and Krystal would call and start inviting everyone tomorrow morning. Jon would make the reservations for the smaller of the banquet rooms at the yacht club. There would be enough privacy there, away from the Saturday-night dance band and revelry.

After a busy week, Saturday night came soon enough. The group assembled in the banquet room about 7:30 PM. A feeling of anticipation and excitement filled the air. Sylvia and Krystal changed their plans so they could be there, too. They had helped with place cards and Krystal had decorated the room with small arrangements at each place. In the small baskets at every setting, she had placed gold-wrapped chocolate coins. Sky and Jon were impressed with how real these coins looked, complete with an embossed American Eagle emblem. The raised letters on the other side read, 'In Chocolate We Trust'. Krystal and Sylvia had to leave for another engagement soon after the food was served. Exuberantly, everyone stood and toasted them before they could escape.

Also, all the little baskets contained a fortune cookie. No one was to know until after dinner that each fortune cookie had within it the same, small note. Krystal had hand-scribed tiny pieces of paper with all the names, informing the recipient that he or she had become an honorary, life-long member of The *Madonna* Society. Sky told the group there was a secret handshake that would be shown to everyone before the end of the evening.

As they opened the cookies, following an exceptional dinner of pork loin and an option of fish, Sky and Jon gave brief talks to the group. The intrigue added to the mood at the end of the meal, building up to the 'secret' handshake, which kept everyone curious to the very end. Jon requested Bruce for the official waiter. Bruce performed as usual. He entered into the party spirit, making funny comments and kidding with Sky and Jon. At one point, Bruce told Sky that had he met her some years ago, he would be straight now. At the end, Bruce took the group pictures with two cameras, one Jon's and one Sky's.

Part of what Jon and Sky had to say was to express their deep appreciation for what everyone had done, the roles they had played. They went through the list. They thanked Dick and Sharon Brophe, Ian and Paul, both having come with dates; Frank and Lupe, Laura and Carlos. In absentia, Jon thanked Sylvia Matthews and Krystal Fitzpatrick. Then,

Sky announced to the group that there would be a settling of accounts. The remainder of the gold needed to be assayed and a professional person had been found to do that task. Each person would be provided with a complete accounting of the final figures. Jon gave a date of February 28th for finalizing the accounting.

Sky made a special point of asking everyone if they had any concerns, questions, or problems with how things were being handled to be sure to talk to her. She explained about the unknown amount of treasure that remained at the shipwreck site and why it had been left there. She also reported that the site had been registered and that already a jurisdictional controversy was brewing between California and the Federal Government. Sky explained that no security guarded the shipwreck site. She added that tampering with anything there from the time it had been registered was a felony. Several people expressed uneasiness about leaving the wreck so vulnerable to robbers, but nothing could be done about that. Everyone felt as though the group owned the shipwreck, as if they had adopted it. They felt that they had obligations and rights of ownership over the archeological site itself. Because the Navy had tight security on part of San Clemente Island, there was a 'be on the lookout' notice given for any possible traffic around the area of the shipwreck.

Sky also provided a summary accounting of what the whole endeavor had cost so far. She gave everyone a brief cost sheet, which showed paying the divers, as well as Captain Dick Brophe and miscellaneous costs. Her list of these costs included: filling scuba tanks, food, fuel, insurance, and other details. Sky had previously given estimates to the attorney assisting with the project for the State of California and to her department at Cal State Long Beach. Thus far, her guesstimates had been accepted, including the probable amount of gold remaining at the site. Everyone polled in the group gave approval for how things had been handled. Several gave lavish praise to Dr. Sky Rowan for all she had done. The praises ranged from finding the information about the wreck in the first place to following through with countless details. They also thanked her for taking care of all the red tape, as well as for protecting identities and information about what had been brought back aboard the *Tiamat*.

The party ended by 11:00. Everyone left with warm feelings for one another.

There were hugs and joking and farewells, such as 'We'll be in touch', and 'See you soon'. Frank, Lupe, Sky, and Jon went into the main room and danced a couple of dances before the band played its sweetly sorrowful versions of *I'll Be Seeing You* and *Goodnight Ladies.*

They said goodbyes in the parking lot. Sky waited until Frank and Lupe left before throwing her arms around Jon, nearly knocking him over. Their goodnight kisses began to change the night's direction. She at first insisted on staying with him through the night. Then, pausing, she realized she had to feed Schwartz, because Krystal was spending the weekend with Sylvia and her family. They devised a plan, going to her home to bring the dog back to the boat, where they would spend the night together. A breakthrough had happened for both of them. They realized again how they felt close and safe enough to be together for an entire night. They were in a different and much better place with one another than that night in her shop on the sofa.

Jon rode with her in the T-Bird to get Schwartz. They were back to the boat just after midnight, having ended a full day with the grand party. As they were about to collapse into sleep, lying spooned with one another, fitting perfectly,

Jon said, "I told Frank and Lupe I was going to marry you." She became very quiet and intermittently held her breath.

Then she turned her face toward him with tears in her eyes, and said, "Oh, Jon, yes! Yes!" Her soft hair just touched his nose; his arm was wrapped around her. With her warm body pressed firmly against his, they were, within minutes, breathing together into a deepening sleep.

The next morning, during breakfast, the next steps in the *Madonna* adventure became clear to them. Jon could not recall who mentioned it first, but it was obviously a perfect thing to do. They planned advertising in various newspapers. They outlined the copy about wanting to meet anyone in the southland descending from the Pomo Indian tribe, tracing their ancestry back to the mid 1800s. Also, they would put in the advertise- ment: "We want to meet anyone whose ancestors or family came to the southland aboard the square rigger *Madonna* in 1849."

As they discussed this idea, Sky wrote the copy on a piece of legal-sized, yellow paper:

"Searching for anyone in Southern California who has Pomo Indian ancestry. Also, searching for anyone who may have ancestral stories related to the square-rigged ship, Madonna. If you or anyone you know has information of family ties to the Pomo Indian tribe or the ship, Madonna, please contact Dr. Sky Rowan at PO Box 1327, Long Beach Municipal Post Office, Long Beach, California 90801. Provide your address and a way to reach you. Please, also, if you are responding to this advertisement, keep Saturday, February 9th, 1985, free for a reunion to take place in Dana Point."

They read the copy several times, making a short list of which newspapers should run the advertisement. They chose the larger newspapers in San Diego, Orange County, Los Angeles, Long Beach, Sacramento, and San Francisco. They felt enthusiastic about this plan. Lots of details remained to be worked through, but they spontaneously shared excitement as ideas and plans developed. Like an ethereal puzzle, everything fell into place.

"After all, if we already know two people from the *Madonna*, Carlos Diaz and George Cramer, just in this local area, how many more could there be around here?"

"I'll bet people come out of the woodwork from all around here, Jon," Sky affirmed. "Can you imagine what an event this might become? Most of these people, whoever answers an advertisement like this, will probably never have known one another. If there were four or five people on the *Madonna*'s crew, they probably left some descendants here. Then, beyond those people, we know there were about twenty-six Indians who came south and rowed ashore with Shuka when the ship burned, exploded, and sank. What a story this is! We'll need an actuary to compute how many three or four of the off-sprung generations of people there might be from a beginning of twenty-six men. I imagine, too, they were all horny when they hit the beach in December of 1849. I wonder what their Christmas here might have been like that year," she said, reflecting with growing amusement.

Indeed, what a story! Four days after the item was published in eight newspapers, the first response arrived in Sky's postal box. It came from a woman, Theresa Marquez. Two hand-written pages introduced her family and explained that her ancestor, a Pomo Indian, had rowed from a sinking ship to San Juan around 1850. She lived in Huntington Beach, and the letter gave her address and phone number. In the next week came thirty-seven more responses, including one from Sacramento.

The festival began to take shape. The reunion party was set for the 9th of February, on the beach, just below the cliffs, at Dana Point Harbor. The clinching event had to do with Dr. Sky Rowan's being interviewed by two southland major television channels about their advertisement, the story behind it, and what was planned for this gathering at Dana Point. The television coverage included Sky's post office address, which yielded thirty-one more responses by the next evening following the television interviews. The most thorough interview surprised them. A Pasadena Public Radio station gave an entire segment to the story, inviting Sky, Carlos Diaz, and Jon to come for a live afternoon interview. Calls came from three more people, as the half-hour segment ended. Each one briefly shared stories related to the interview.

Along with making arrangements with the bureaucrats in Dana Point, Jon and Sky had to get permission for the affair and arrange for catering. Frank suggested locating a Mariachi group. They had a lot of things to work out.

But, prior to having this festival, one big thing had to be done. Jon did not know how to progress with finesse, but he needed to have an opportunity to meet with Carlos Diaz and George Cramer. There was still too much conflict with those two and Jon wanted that resolved, if possible. Of course, since they were in the midst of a law suit, this would be frowned upon by their attorneys. Jon, however, needed to give each of them a chance to make decisions to accept or reject his invitation.

On the phone to Carlos, after the initial greetings and comments about the yacht club party they had enjoyed, Jon simply asked him, "Carlos, if I set it up, would you be willing to meet with George Cramer? I'm thinking that just the three of us should meet for a conversation. Think about it. It might help you both with this ongoing rancor. At least that's my hope. The legal matters will do nothing to solve your problems."

"Jon, if you can pull this off, I'd be grateful. I would do anything to have this dissolved and for us to end this enmity. He's definitely a person who should be included. Our ancestors came here on the same ship," he said.

"I'll call him, Carlos. Any time you could not meet? If I just try to coordinate this for a breakfast, lunch, or dinner, is there a time you can't meet?"

Carlos was quiet for about a minute. He had a teachers' seminar to go to this coming Saturday and two nights the following week with scheduled meetings connected with his teaching. Lunches were out the days he taught, but he could meet Friday for lunch, which might be his best time. He liked the idea of meeting in the daytime. Jon thanked Carlos for giving this a try and ended the phone conversation.

Jon found George Cramer's number through Frank Martinez. Since his number was unlisted, Frank wanted to know why Jon wanted it.

!I've got this wild hair, Frank. There's a chance George Cramer and Carlos might be able to talk this matter out. I also have some incentive to offer. Sky and I agree on giving George Cramer some of the gold. He deserves it, too, after all. It was his great-great grandfather, I guess, Wilfred Cramer, who was the *Madonna*'s carpenter. If all this history is right, Wilfred deserved the gold payoff in the first place, that is if he had successfully reached Mexico with his fugitives." He paused, letting the whole story reconstruct in his mind as he talked to Frank.

"Do you really think this can happen? If so you'll be a celebrity in my book, even more than you are now. Jon, if there's anything I can do to help, let me know. I'd want to be at the meeting with you and those two guys. Maybe this will work. If I know you, it's a sure thing," he quipped, not losing a chance to remind Jon of his priestly role.

"It is my Lady, Meri, who's going to bring all this about. I'm going to ask them to meet me at Sky's workshop. I'll bring pizza and some Dos Equis. I'll have a predetermined amount of gold in a bag for George Cramer, if he'll accept the terms of a settlement and sign a gentlemen's agreement," Jon said. Then, as an afterthought, Jon added, "We've kept a strict accounting of everything so far, what's been found, spent, given, and used, including all those who have brought this to fruition. I'm sure we'll have to furnish someone with the whole saga. Maybe there'll be a book in the future."

At the end of their talking, Frank gave Jon his blessing, which encouraged him to make the phone call. Jon had scrawled George Cramer's number down on a note pad which had been recently mailed to him as a solicitation from the National Maritime Historical Society. As he put in the numbers, he viewed the logo of a stylized square rigger on the notepad. This somehow sealed his commitment. It seemed to him that divine intervention was assisting in bringing this plan to fruition - from the publishing of the advertisements to his making this phone call.

But, Jon got ahead of himself. The phone kept ringing with no answer. He looked at the pad again. He had put in the wrong number. The six looked like an eight, because of the way he had scrawled it. Unsure which number he had used, he dialed again.

A woman answered on the second ring. Jon told her his name and requested to speak to George Cramer. She told him he was at work and would not be home until about seven in the evening. When Jon told her he would call back, she responded sternly.

"We eat our evening meal between seven and eight. If you want to call about eight-thirty, that would be okay, but no earlier."

If their few minutes on the phone revealed anything, it indicated she did not know Jon, nor did she guess this call had anything to do with their law suit or the loss of her son, Ray.

The appointments that afternoon went well, except for one angry client who left slamming his door, shouting at him and convinced that he had encouraged her husband to end their marriage. Her anger was obvious from the moment the session started. She had accused him of taking sides, approving of her husband's immoral life. The worst part was that she left without paying. Jon rehearsed his frequent tape, *Can't win 'em all.*

His next client entered the waiting room as he picked up his mail. She said, "Is this a good time to have a session with you, Dr. Scott? I just passed your last victim in the hall. She was babbling to herself about someone's being a son-of-a-bitch. I presume that she was talking about you. Maybe I should re-schedule," she said, giving Jon the hint of a smile, which helped soften the episode. Her humor let him know they were okay and she was unafraid of having a session with him.

About 10:30 that evening, he moved some files out of the way, got a cup of water and settled into his desk chair for the call.

"Mr. Cramer?" Jon asked.

"Yes, this is George Cramer. Who is this?"

"My name is Jon Scott, Mr. Cramer. I have an invitation for you and would like you to listen carefully to me before responding. Is this a good time to call?"

"Depending on what this is about."

"It is about you, mostly. But, also, it is about a larger matter. It is about your loss of your son, Ray. It is about making things right," Jon said, purposely being quiet for a few seconds.

"What do you know about Ray?"

"Mr. Cramer, I am very interested in helping heal a lot of wounds along with getting people together who should be friends," Jon said. He felt his throat choke just a bit and needed a swallow of his ever-present water. His hands were cold, and he got even more nervous as the call progressed.

"No one can heal the death of Ray. He's dead because people he trusted let him drown, Mr. Scott. Nothing will heal our loss of Ray. He was a good boy. He didn't deserve to drown, Mr. Scott. You think you can make any of this nightmare go away? If so, you're full of shit," he said, with biting hostility.

"Please listen to me for a moment, Mr. Cramer. If you would rather talk in person, I will be glad to arrange that, but I have some information that will help you and your family," Jon said, trying to be as direct and convincing as possible.

"Nothing you can say in person you can't say on the phone. I'm tired, though. Worked since five this morning. It's nearly my bedtime; so make it quick, damn it! I'm not up for games," he said, his words hitting the earpiece like machine gun bullets.

"There is a large award of historic gold awaiting you, Mr. Cramer, if you will consider my invitation." Again, he purposely became quiet to let that information soak in.

"Gold? What kind of gold? What the hell are you talking about, Mr. Scott?"

"There was gold found in the shipwreck of the *Madonna*, Mr. Cramer, and your ancestor, perhaps a great or great-great grandfather, Wilfred Cramer, died never having gotten his share. That share is worth far more now than in 1849. Are you interested?" Jon said. He kept his hopes up and asked the Holy Spirit to stay involved in this call.

"Well, I don't have nothin' to lose. So what's this invitation you keep talking about?"

"Next Friday afternoon, at twelve-thirty, I would like you to meet with me and Carlos Diaz. If you are willing to do that, along with agreeing on some important matters, you will receive your share of the gold that has been recovered. I will pick you up and take you to the place myself, if you can take some time from your work. I guarantee, if you will say 'yes' to this, you will save yourself a lot of problems, come away with more than you can imagine, and become a part of a growing group of local people who share your history," Jon said. He was trying to sell the plan with his best efforts and enticements. "If you want your wife to come along, she would be welcome too."

"I gotta tell you that this won't be easy for me to do. There's too much that's happened for us to pretend to be friends. But, as I said, I guess I got nothin' to lose. Where can call you about this, Mr. Scott? I'll think about it. I have too much at stake right now, including the lawsuit problems, to agree to anything," George Cramer said.

"I understand. I would like you to give this meeting a chance, though. You think about it and leave your response on my answering machine. I'd like an answer tomorrow, no later. I gave my number to your wife earlier today, when I got her permission to call now." Jon wanted to add as much encouragement as possible without increasing the pressure too much, so he added, "My exchange takes messages around the clock."

The phone call ended with an agreement that Cramer would let Jon know one way or the other by tomorrow afternoon. Jon then called Carlos to update him on the talk. Both of them hoped he would decide to come to lunch, though Jon had not mentioned pizza nor the Dos Equis to Mr. Cramer. Carlos admonished Jon, "Not everyone likes cheap Mexican beer, Jon. Perhaps he's a martini fellow."

"Guess that remains to be seen, Carlos. I'll drop that into the offer if I detect he's unsure about coming. And, by the way, I offered to include his wife, too. Would Lupe like to be in on this with you?"

"No, Jon Maybe later, if it works out," he said, clearing his throat, hesitating to say more. "She's very bitter about all this. It wouldn't help to have her there at this point."

Clearly, Jon's suggesting this meeting had become problematical for Carlos and his wife. Sky and Jon talked later that evening as she worked in her shop. There was an uneasy feeling between them during the first part of the call.

"Sky, is something wrong?"

"Oh, Jon. Don't be so sensitive. I'm doing my paranoid dance number. You know that number? It starts off with all kinds of warm, fuzzy, juicy feelings, then moves to missing you, then to being pissed off because I'm missing you, then it goes to why should I give a damn anyhow and then to I don't give a damn and I'd be better off if I just stayed a professor and got away from all the complications you bring into my life, and then I start wishing you'd never found me on that boat and maybe I should have died the next afternoon ..." then there was a long pause.

Jon heard her uneven breathing. He realized she was not okay.

"I can be with you at the shop soon, Sky. I want to be with you."

"No, Jon. You can't fix me or get these thoughts and feelings to disappear. I'm depressed tonight, that's all. It helps just being in touch. I'm just screwed up tonight? One thing I did to your Lady that makes me feel better. I'll tell you later about that. It's really late."

"What did you do, Sky? I'd love to know what helped you feel better."

"I got your Lady injected with poison. I imagined I killed her. That seemed to help," she said and paused. "I guess I owe you an explanation. I'm jealous of her, your Meri, so, I poisoned her. A guy came from the termite company, the same guy that tented my workshop last year. I called him and said I had a lady lying on my floor who had worms in her. I described the dust that dropped out of the tiny holes. He said the dust from the lady is probably worm scat. He said he had just the medicine. So, I hired him to come poison Meri," she said, her words becoming less measured and her voice began to have a lighter tone. "It was worth the one-hundred bucks just to see her get wrapped in thick plastic and watch the man stick needles into her body. Somehow, after all that, I didn't hate her. For a few minutes, I even felt sorry for her. He left about an hour ago. He told me he needed to needle her again in a week to get the eggs or possible fledgling worms or any other critters living in her. He seemed quite taken by her, too. I began to be jealous about this guy I don't even know. He found her intriguing and that bugged me. Jon, I'm a sick woman," she said, giving Jon the hint of a giggle in her voice.

"Yes, Sky. I think I need to make a house call."

"Okay, if you insist, doctor." She consented without giving him any hope.

"I'll be there in a half hour, Sky. I know it's late, but I want to tell you about my phone conversations this evening with Carlos and George Cramer." He hoped she would become curious enough to keep the morbidity out of their relationship, even for a little while. He knew it would return from time to time, but he wanted them to have more of the good feeling they had shared these last few weeks. So much had transpired to bring them close and he wanted it to continue. He felt quite sure she wanted it to continue, too.

He called to her from the dark alley, outside her locked gate. Schwartz came bounding out of the lighted workshop, barking furiously. By the time she reached the gate, the dog recognized Jon, stopped barking and began dancing, doing a spaniel's wiggle with every joint in motion. He unlocked the gate and slid the door aside enough to enter. Sky glanced up from her notes, measuring tools, her wire brush and small picks, and looked serious.

"You're one brave man, Jon Scott. You too could have worms and need to be poisoned, you know?" she said, giving him the slightest hint of a smile. "When will I quit going nuts in this tunnel of love?" she asked earnestly.

"Maybe when you realize it isn't a tunnel. Maybe when you realize it's true love you're experiencing. Maybe when you know how much I love you and how frightened I become when you're coming apart. But, you know one thing?" he asked, giving her plenty of time to speculate what that one thing might be. "Each time we go through these things together, we come out the other side closer. So far, no matter how pissed or scared you get, we don't end this. We come out closer, somehow overcoming the demon who wants you all to himself." He said this while he approached her and extended his hands out to her.

She took both hands, as he wrapped his arms around her she buried her face in his chest. He moved so her head nestled in that pocket just below his left collar bone, that place designed in men to hold the head of a loved one. Just as at other times, her head fit perfectly, her ear next to his thumping heart. They held this embrace for at least five minutes without a word. She loosened her part of the embrace and lifted her lips to his. They merged in a kiss of peace. When she could talk again, she suggested they share some tea. The water was hot and the empty couch invited them, two tired lovers. She wanted then to know about the phone calls, reminding him of the late hour and that she had an early morning lecture at Cal State.

Jon dipped the bag of herbal tea into the hot water. On the cup were the words 'American Archeological Society - In Strata We Trust'. During the next fifteen minutes he related the story of the phone calls and the possibility that Carlos, George Cramer, and he would meet in this very workshop next Friday for pizza. He told her they needed to measure out a fair amount of gold from the pile. To his surprise, Sky became excited about the possible meeting. She assured him, being practical, they could find gold pieces that would more than appease George Cramer's desire to win a law suit. Buying him off may be shady, but it wasn't obviously illegal.

"Even if he won a million dollars suing Carlos and the rest of us, which he won't, he would quickly see the value of these historic gold pieces will be much more than he could make in winning a suit, especially after giving his attorney the forty or so percent," she said. She leaned back, away from him, with her expression softening. Her eyes came back to life.

"I love you, dear one," Jon said.

"That's all that matters. Don't give up on me, Jon. I'm just so unsure. I've not ever dealt with this stuff called intimacy before. I know you therapists talk about intimacy, reading and writing books about it, but most of us don't even consider it as something to be desired, much less experienced. If this roller coaster is because of intimacy, maybe it's best that regular human beings escape and just stay in their compromises and marital conspiracies.

"Besides, you and I have this religious dilemma to talk about, too. We've got so much to discuss, Jon. We keep saying we're going to talk about all this that concerns me, but we don't. Why don't we? How come I have all this to talk about with you, but we end up having too much fun, laughing too much? We need to work on the Pomo Indian history. We need to solve problems about people, too.

"How come we spend our time discussing people who don't even know one another? I'd rather talk about just our own stuff. I could go on all night. Is this my manic phase? Is this what 'manic' is all about?

"A couple of hours ago, I was sitting here, doing a project, writing notes for tomorrow, seething about us, feeling you've changed my life beyond repair. Now I'm all turned on, alive and glowing. I really am nuts. Do you go through any of this, Jon?" She suddenly became very serious, genuinely inquiring.

"I have my moments. I wonder how we're going to work things out. I wonder if we've really got what it takes to build and enjoy a life together. I wonder if I'm ready to give up some of my freedom and if you're ready to make a commitment. Then, I talk myself down a bit. I begin to realize we don't have any pressure. There's no hurry. We'll both know when the time is right.

"Maybe we'll decide just to be friends or lovers, or find some other identity together. Or maybe we'll part, with all kinds of feelings, memories, or … who knows where this journey is taking us? There's a quotation I've always liked. Maybe I've shared it with you before, 'Love is a journey. No matter where it ends. The journey's what love is.' Sometimes it helps me to rehearse this as a reminder. Maybe I don't quote it quite right, but that's the essence of it," he said. He moved his cup out of the way, so he could pick her up and maneuver her onto his lap.

"You just got me here without any effort. How'd you do that? Look where I am now. Just look at where I am! My whole body is alive with you, and it's no wonder I have problems when we're apart. Maybe if you kiss me I'll feel more secure. Let's try it," she said, moving into just the right place for a kiss. That sealed their doubts.

Chapter Thirty-Six

George Cramer left a message on Jon's exchange by 3:00, Wednesday afternoon, agreeing to have Jon meet him at Stater Brothers, the market where he worked in Cerritos. He asked Jon to pick him up at noon. He also would need a ride back to work, having only until three-thirty to be away that afternoon. Jon returned the call and agreed to pick him up, describing his red Chevy pickup. Though George sounded unfriendly and very business-like, Jon felt that they had progressed from the obvious distrust in last night's phone call. Carlos seemed relieved, perhaps excited. He assured Jon, if this worked out, he would have no hard feelings and Lupe, he felt sure, would eventually come around. The pending threat of the huge law suit frightened her, along with being upset about Michael's arrest and the continuance of the trial. Luís Jimenez and Michael were not allowed to communicate and their stories had remained essentially the same, but with different perspectives, each one holding fast to his particular version. This would become clearer later, because Luís Jimenez was the one being held most responsible for stealing the boat. Michael was accused only as an accomplice.

On Friday Jon met George Cramer in the parking lot, as they had planned. George came up to the driver's side. They talked for a few minutes. George's distrust was palpable. He had listened to Jon's phone exchange say, 'Dr. Jon Scott's

Office. Dr. Scott is not available at the moment, but leave a confidential message'. This left him with questions about Jon.

Jon sensed his questions. He explained to him that he was a therapist and gave him his business card. He told him he wanted to take him to meet Carlos Diaz at the workshop of Dr. Sky Rowan, a Cal State professor, the one who had located the *Madonna*. Cramer looked relieved, but still tentative. Then, Jon added some incentive.

"We're going to meet where the figurehead from your ancestor's boat is lying and where your part of the gold is waiting for you." Jon spoke as he gestured to shake George's hand. "My assumption is that all will go well between you and Carlos Diaz."

George walked thoughtfully, slowly around to the passenger's door. A few items were on the pickup's bench seat. Jon gathered up two books and papers. This gave him plenty of room. Then he opened the door for him. They drove in silence to Sky's workshop, heading down the back alley. Jon traveled to the workshop by an indirect route, so he was five minutes late. He realized he still felt mistrusting of George Cramer, and had gone out of the way to the gate. Carlos sat waiting in his car and stayed there until Jon unlocked the gate and called to him to join them. Then Carlos got out of his car. He towered easily two feet above the top of the car. At that moment, he looked formidable to Jon and George. Especially to someone who might be wary, Carlos appeared a possible threat. He had his hair pulled back into a braid and wore Levis and a blue denim shirt. If it were not for his bright, gold belt buckle, engraved 'Carlos', he could be mistaken for a prison trustee. George Cramer stood at least a foot shorter than Carlos and Jon. Jon imagined this increased his discomfort in meeting with them.

Attempting to disarm the wariness of both men, Jon said, "Come on in, gentlemen. I've got beer and can make any drink you might want inside. I've ordered two different pizzas to be delivered by one o'clock. We've got a good pizza place just four blocks from here. Dr. Rowan and I have used their services, and, I promise you, you will not leave hungry. By the way, she won't be able to join us because of a previous appointment."

Carlos broke the ice, extending his hand to George Cramer and introducing himself.

"Mr. Cramer, I am Carlos Diaz, and I'm very glad to finally meet you. I know we also have a lot to talk about, and I'm hoping Dr. Scott will help us."

His cordial attitude seemed to be working. George Cramer responded in an uneasy manner, but he did take Carlos' hand and returned the introduction. In the workshop, Jon moved a folding table in front of the couch, thinking he would sit on the couch and the two of them could be across from one another in the canvas director's chairs. Before they sat down, Jon asked them to come over to a mound of blue plastic tarpaulin.

"Gentlemen, you have not seen what I'm about to uncover. Before I let you see this object, I want you both to realize that your ancestors were very involved with the object itself and with how it ended up on this workshop floor." As he explained this, Jon gradually pulled back the blue plastic from the head all the way off the feet of Meri.

Both men stood motionless and speechless.

George Cramer spoke first. "That's a ship's figurehead! Is it from *Madonna*, the ship my great-great grandfather had been on? Am I actually looking at a part of his ship? This is unbelievable. That ship sank off the coast of San Juan Capistrano beach."

Carlos repeated nearly the same thing. "We're both great-great grandsons of men who had been on the same ship when it sank. I've got a bunch of written material passed down through my family describing Shuka, my ancestor, coming from Yerba Buena on this ship."

George Cramer interrupted, "My great-great grandfather had been the ship's carpenter. He wrote a diary, too, about the voyage to southern California, on their way to Mexico, when they had to abandon ship near an island south of San Juan Campistrano or, maybe, Capistrano. I read Dana's *Two Years Before the Mast*, and he referred to it as 'Campistrano.' I've always wondered what name is the right one."

From the moment Jon uncovered Meri, the feelings between these two began to thaw. They were already sharing their stories when the pizzas came. Jon set the food on the table, providing paper plates, utensils, and plenty of napkins. He replenished their drinks as they talked. For much of the next hour little was revealed. Ray Cramer's drowning, Michael's being in jail for manslaughter, or the enmity that had been generated by the impending lawsuit: these remained under the carpet, like the elephant in the living room. Sharing lunch definitely eased the tensions, but some topics were too sensitive to broach. By 2:30, knowing Jon needed to return George Cramer to his work in Cerritos, the true business emerged.

"How much gold is there with this figurehead, Dr. Scott?" George asked, making it very clear they had an agenda along with the reasonably friendly conversation and the history these two men shared.

"Not having had it thoroughly assayed, I can't report the value exactly. But there are various pieces in what we have to offer that will bring upwards to $30 and $50-thousand dollars. That's each one, depending on the market that day, on the evaluation of their worth as antiques, and other variables. Gold is running today about $370 per troy ounce." Jon paused and took from his pocket a notepad crowded with figures. He looked at the page for a few moments before proceeding. "A month ago, it was running about $320 and two months before that, about $360; up and down it goes like that." Jon paused. "In summary, just guessing at what is in the bag I'll show you, there is easily more than $150,000 worth of gold, all yours, undeclared, no questions asked. By the way, I request, no, I insist that nothing be said to anyone. I've spent some time cleaning up some of the gold and sorting it. I've got it in bags and soon we'll get into that part of our agreement. If your wife has to know, be sure to warn her it must be kept secret. The condition is, you drop your lawsuit, come to a festival on the beach at Dana Point the ninth of February, be able to shake hands, and talk in public with many who will want to meet you. Those are the conditions, Mr. Cramer.

"I would add, I hope a side benefit of all this has to do with helping to develop an anthology about this whole subject, the historical details, as much as we can put together. We have a scroll written in your great-great grandfather's own hand. Luckily this scroll was not with the stolen research papers. That would have been a great loss. We miraculously discovered this scroll in a small compartment he made in the head of this figurehead. What a craftsman he must have been! I'll show you exactly where it was, if you want to see. We found it quite by accident. The scroll validates much of what you both have had handed down to you in the written documents, Carlos from his great grandfather's writing and yours, from your great-great grandfather's. They clearly had the foresight to preserve the family history. But, we don't have time now. I'm making you late for work, George. It is obvious from other people we're finding that this story has been shared in one form or another by the descendants who were on the *Madonna* in December of 1849."

Both Carlos and George listened intently. By the time Jon finished, he knew he had accomplished more than he could have expected. Within two minutes of his being quiet, the agreement came, both men breathed easier, relaxing, sure signs of relief.

"As a witness to this, I would like you two gentlemen to shake hands on this agreement. Before you receive the gold, Mr. Cramer, I will need a document, an informal one is okay, signed by both of you as to the conditions and your agreement. I will be glad to word the document for you to sign, but it is necessary, especially because you will have to inform your attorney that you are dropping the suit." Jon looked back and forth at both men, doing his best to stay almost stern about the importance of documenting what he had just disclosed and their verbal agreement.

George Cramer spoke first. "I'm ready to sign anything to get over this nightmare. My attorney will be angry with me, but I am sick of this whole damned thing. No amount of money will help bring Ray back. I know, too, he drowned because he was diving with alcohol and a couple of other substances in his bloodstream. I know Michael Diaz and Luís Jimenez didn't make him drown. But, we couldn't just let this tragedy happen without doing something.

"My wife still can't accept that her boy could have done anything stupid. He'd been in three car accidents in the last eighteen months, but she still can't accept her boy could have been so screwed up. I'd tried for three years to get him to quit using and drinking. Nothing worked. I kept telling him he was headed for real trouble unless he straightened up. Two days before he went on the trip to Catalina with your son, Carlos, he told me to go to hell and his mother demanded I leave him alone, insisting he was a good boy and I should get off his back" he said.

Suddenly George became very quiet and pensive. Then he stood up and walked around the figurehead, sinking his hands deeply into his pockets. "I'm going to be an hour late getting back to work. I better call to tell them I'm on my way. It's been worth it, being late. But, it's time for me to get back to work, Dr. Scott. I'll sign any damned thing you write," he declared, visibly shaken from what he had just unloaded.

Jon walked over to him and stood beside him for a full minute. George stared at the figurehead saying nothing and not moving. Carlos came alongside him, on the other side. The three of them stood awkwardly together. With apprehension, knowing he still had the last step of writing the agreement and getting their signatures, Jon waited for the right moment.

"How does a man survive losing one of his kids, Dr. Scott? Got any good advice about that one?" George asked. He tearfully looked Jon straight in the eyes with obvious pain on his face.

"I'm sure, George, there will not be a moment of the rest of your life when you will be completely released from pain and anger. But, I also know, there are dimensions to your life you cannot imagine at this time. I'll be glad any time to talk about any of this with you and to share as much of what you've been through as I can," Jon said. He put his hand on George's shoulder. He felt some reservations.

George said nothing at that moment, but he did reach up and put his hand on Jon's for an instant. Suddenly, perhaps realizing his own softening for that instant, he took his hand away. Jon locked the door to the workshop and the gate. As they went to their vehicles, Carlos and George shook hands again. Jon told them the agreement would be ready to sign by tomorrow, Saturday. He would call them as soon as he could get it done in the morning. Both of them were subdued, perhaps emotional. Jon drove George Cramer back to the Stater Brothers market in Cerritos. Before he closed his door, George said, "Thank you, Dr. Scott. You've helped change some lives today. You're probably used to that, but I'm not. I'll be waiting for your call in the morning. Can't wait to get this finished. I must admit, that gold sounds very interesting, too. Guess this is all predestined, huh?"

"Could be. I'll call you just as soon as I get the agreement written, George. Carlos should be with us, so we sign and witness this together. I'll call him, too."

Jon drove back to his office, deciding to write the agreement late that afternoon, to get it off his mind. But first, he called Sky. Krystal answered warmly. He felt she would have talked non-stop the rest of the evening, had he given her the slack to do so. She got going about Sylvia, what they had done together this week, the fun they had, how Sylvia had several days with no pain, how much she liked Sylvia's family, and so it went.

"Oh, I guess you called for mother, didn't you?" she asked, with an affected voice.

"Oh, do you have a mother?" he asked wryly.

"Sometimes," she quipped. "She had a luncheon and a lecture after and is taking a nap. That's why I've had you all to myself for the last fifteen minutes, Jon. I began to hope you'd forgotten why you called. Maybe the four of us could have supper together soon," she offered.

"I'd like that, Krystal. I'd like that very much." There was a moment's silence before he said, "Tell your mother, when she wakes up from her nap, to give me a call at the office, if you would, dear. I'll be here probably until seven or so."

"Will do. I've liked talking to you. Thank you for caring. Do you mind if I pretend you're my real father? I'm sure no-one will notice," she said, with a happy voice.

"Krystal, I'll draw up the adoption papers as soon as I can. I've got another matter to tend to first and you'll hear all about that soon. By the way, we'll need your mother's permission for me to adopt you."

Jon drafted the agreement. He wanted Sky to check his wording prior to making a finished copy of it. It looked legal enough to him, but he wondered if he should have his attorney review it. Then, he decided to keep it just between the four of them. His Selectric II typewriter always came through with beautifully finished copy, even with three carbon copies he needed for this agreement. He liked typing on that machine. Being one who kept personal journals all the time, he used the typewriter to add pleasure to writing them.

This is an agreement negotiated this 26th day of January, 1985, between Carlos Diaz and George Cramer.

I, George Cramer, for $10.00 and other valuable considerations, do hereby agree to release Carlos Diaz, Michael Diaz, and all other associated parties, vis., Luís Jimenez and his family, from any liability regarding the accidental death of my son, Ray Cramer. This is a firm, binding agreement, precluding further actions of any kind *regarding the matter arising from his death and the legal procedures heretofore begun, now null and void.*

I have read and affirm this agreement and understand fully the terms agreed to above.

*Signed:*_____ *George Cramer*
*Signed:*_____ *Carlos Diaz*
*Witnessed:*_____ *The Rev. Jon Scott, Ph. D.*
*Approved:*_____ *Sky Rowan, Ph. D.*
Date: 26 January 1985

When he put the finishing touches on the document, he was pleased. It appeared legal and valid. Just then, the phone rang. Sky's sleepy voice was on the other end. He told Sky about his good conversation with Krystal and how happy Krystal seemed to be. He felt a change in mood on Sky's end of the phone.

"Jon, I can't listen to that right now. I feel I'm losing Krystal. She's just too involved with Sylvia and the Matthews' whole scene. She is over there nearly all the time, except for coming home, picking up clothes. Once in a while, she has breakfast or a snack in the evening here. I guess I'm just jealous."

"Sky, we need to get together, the four of us. Krystal wants us to have supper and I think we should do it soon. I can hear your distress and hurt. You two have been so wonderfully close and now Sylvia's captured Krystal's full attention. Let's have dinner tonight, Love. If you want Krystal and Sylvia to join us tonight, we can do that," he added.

"Krystal has already gone over there, Jon. Let's just you and I have some time together, but I won't dump all this on you. I know Krystal's growing up, nearly eighteen in March, and, even if Sylvia weren't in the picture, she'd be leaving for college soon. I've got to let go. It's just so damned hard to do!" She began to cry, which grew into sobs for a few minutes. Jon stayed on the phone with her, feeling helpless. As a therapist and in his priest role, he often had felt this way, but, still this was different. This was Sky. He wanted her to feel better. He restrained himself from saying everything that came to mind.

Instead, he listened to her sobs gradually decrease.

"I'm sorry, Jon. I guess I needed to cry. There's just so much changing. Maybe I should spend the evening alone, Jon," she said.

"If that's what you need to do, but I would rather we were together. You can cry all night with me, Sky. Letting Krystal go is going to be a long process. There's something I want to read to you, when you're in the mood for it, but how about your calling me back if you want to be with me this evening?" he said. He was giving her all the room she might need to gather herself together or to grieve this transition from her beautiful child's life with her.

A long pause followed. Though she was silent, he could hear her breathing, which he loved, together or on the phone. That sound gave him a sense of serenity that he had come to appreciate. Then, as if she popped back into the present with him, she said, "I'll meet you at your boat at eight o'clock, if that's okay. Maybe we could walk over the bridge to the Japanese place for dinner," she said. Her voice was still shaking. It gradually emerged from crying. He heard sniffles which added to the drama of the moment. "We'll talk. I'm feeling better, but I want some time just to talk."

Jon made two carbon copies of the agreement. He put the document into a manila folder to take to the boat, thinking they could read them over together, if she were in the mood. He had to finish this transaction, get the signatures, and move on to the next planned events. He very much hoped everyone would enjoy the fascinating and festive occasion on the beach on Saturday afternoon, the 9th of February. His head almost whirled with what they had been through these past weeks, even these past months.

Chapter Thirty-Seven

Sky approved the agreement and signed all four pages, one for each signer. She trusted him to get things right without her presence. By mid-morning the next day, Jon obtained all the signatures. George Cramer and Carlos had come to his office to sign the document. Jon wondered if Mr. Jimenez should be named on this document, but he was only implicated in the suit. The two of them shook hands. They agreed to use the *Madonna* festival as a time, if possible, to melt the residual ice with their wives, their children, and with the Jimenez family.

"Wish I had a cocktail here so we could toast this milestone," Jon said.

"That's all I need," Carlos said. "I'd be plastered before lunch on a Saturday. Laura's angry enough about the nightmare we've been trapped in recently, and now she's angry because we've finally resolved the matter, thinking why didn't we settle this in the beginning if we could do it so easily now? Hope I can reason with her before the celebration. Of course, nothing will make it right yet, but if I came home with alcohol on my breath, forget the rest of the weekend."

Jon went to a cupboard below his library and lifted from it a white canvas bank bag, too heavy to lift with one hand. He put it at George Cramer's feet. George took the heavy canvas bag. He opened it, looked in on an impressive assortment of ingots, a few coins, and three large bricks. In preparation for this moment, Jon had spent some time cleaning and even polishing the gold, hoping it would further impress George, which it did.

"I can't believe what I'm seeing here. I've never seen anything like this. I'm afraid to leave here with it," he said, registering genuine uneasiness about taking the bagged gold out of the building.

Jon offered him a small, weathered Gladstone satchel. George put the bag of gold into it for transport. He asked Carlos and Jon to walk to his car with him. He reached into the bag, before zipping the satchel and took out an ingot, studying it. Then, he took two of the coins, looking at them closely. "I have no idea how to get this much gold evaluated. I guess I should put it in a safety deposit box for now, don't you think?" he asked.

They agreed with him. Jon suggested the services of a reputable gold and silver assayer, scribbling his name and phone number on a card, "Mr. Fred Emerson, 714-960-8389." Not mentioning how he knew him, he recommended him for his expertise and professional stature. Jon planned to call Mr. Emerson and tell him about the referral and about his recommendation. George thanked Jon. They parted, expressing relief and satisfaction. Carlos had spent weeks wanting to find this man and deal with him, saved from violence only by his wife, Laura, holding him back. After Cramer drove off, Carlos also thanked Jon for helping to bring such a tense situation to a peaceful end.

"I hated to see him get all that gold, though," Carlos said. "If you'd given Cramer more than you gave me, I would have been upset. Guess I'm not above greed or envy. I'm confessing, Father Scott," he said, with some humor, but obviously reflecting on what they accomplished with the meeting and having the agreement signed.

"Now we can work on getting Michael and Luís out of the clutches of the law, Carlos. I think your attorneys will be able to use this document and what George Cramer has told us about Ray's drinking and irresponsible behaviors to get Michael and Luís released. I know there is the boat theft, and they'll have to do time or public service for that. But, the manslaughter charge will certainly come off the pile with this information and Cramer's willingness to let the law know about Ray's drinking and drug use. Seems like they'd already have all that from the autopsy, but there's no indication that evidence has been put in the case against them."

Carlos agreed and would see to it right away, contacting his attorney and Jorge Jimenez, Luís's father. "Will they ever be surprised and relieved! I'll call them when I get home. This has been an ugly mess for weeks. I know Michael isn't out of the stew with this, though. He and Luís have the matter with Sky Rowan on their record, too. Don't know what the court will do about what happened, even if she drops the charges. There's still a lot to deal with. He won't be released right away, especially if charges are kept active. No matter what Sky does about the charges, the owner of that stolen boat is still furious. He wants a big settlement. My attorney told me it cost $8,000 just to repair the damage from when it went onto the rocks at Catalina. I guess Luís over-revved the engines, too. We've got a ways to go, but we ought to get some relief from this, thanks to this agreement, Jon. I'm so grateful for your help," he said, first clutching his hand, then giving him a bear hug before settling into his spotless Lincoln.

Saturday afternoon Jon sailed for several hours, returning relaxed and doing an evening of cleaning the *Daimon*, then spending a quiet evening reading and journaling.

As he wrote in his journal, the idea occurred to him that Meri needed attention. A wave of enthusiasm swept over him as he imagined having her prepared for viewing, a center-piece at the February fiesta on the beach at Dana Point.

Arrangements had already been initiated with the city authorities. Sky made a deposit of $200, reserving the area, hiring two off-duty policemen for traffic and security management, and she made a liability insurance arrangement with them. All the details were ably handled by Sky's secretary, with Sky supervising the details. But, Jon wanted Meri to be there, too. In order to have her presentable, he needed to either clean her up and restore her himself, or find a genuine craftsperson to do the job. He decided on the latter, obtaining several names from people he knew.

The referral from the Marina Shipyard foreman proved to be just the right person. Manuél Padilla, an artist and a skilled wood-worker, both in one, was just the person. Padilla answered his home phone Saturday evening about eight o'clock. Jon told him what he needed to have done. They would meet to discuss the figurehead in the parking lot of Basin Four. Jon described his Chevy pickup and where it was parked as a place to meet. Manuél would come Monday morning, about 7:30, before his work.

Monday, he was painting a transom and the name on a boat at the shipyard, across from Jon's gangway. A week before his call, he had painted the name on another boat near Jon's. He thought he knew Jon's boat from the two days he had spent working close by. On Monday morning they would meet and Padilla would follow Jon to the workshop to see Meri and what he needed to do for restoration. To complete the plan, Jon informed Sky that they were meeting at her shop and he hoped it would be a good time for her to meet Mr. Padilla. Jon thought they would like one another and the artist would be very intrigued with her shop and the work she did.

He arrived early, just as Jon came out of the shower, refreshed from an early swim.

Jon invited Padilla to come to his boat with him, which he gladly did, chattering about all the familiar boats nearby, having painted boot tops, cove stripes, names, and a beautiful, sparkling dark-blue hull four slips from the *Daimon*. Jon dressed and the two proceeded to the workshop. Once inside, as Jon uncovered Meri, he described what he thought could be done to make her presentable. Padilla grasped his image immediately. He told Jon it should have a mounting base built for it, which he could do. The bronze bolts protruding from the rear end would work well to hold it in position. "I'll re-thread these corroded pins and use them to secure the figurehead to the mount," he said, as if it were easy. He suggested using two-by-ten-inch planks, one for a pedestal and another at an angle, like the bow of a ship, just enough to hold the figurehead firmly.

Gesturing with his hands, he said, "I'll place another of the planks crosswise at the base to make it more steady, making the base adequate to hold the weight. It'll be really sturdy and the figure will be well displayed that way."

Sky came into the workshop about twenty minutes after their arrival. Her morning lecture had been cancelled because of an academic testing schedule. Jon hugged her and introduced her to Manuél Padilla, who had read about her. He was excited being able to help restore this antique figurehead and he knew exactly what would work best for the colors, filling the worm holes, and helping to preserve it.

Manuél said, "I'll make a bronze plaque for the base, giving the name of the ship, the date it sank, the location, and maybe other small details about how and where it was discovered."

Jon pointed out to him the large glass eyes.

"Manuél, look closely at these eyes. They mesmerized me from the very first glance. Sky got hooked by them too. They magnified the scroll we found in the secret place in her head. The eyes are glass balls, called 'clearies', huge, clear marbles, very cleverly used for this figurehead. I'm guessing that was an innovation accomplished by the ship's carpenter, a master craftsman named Wilfred Cramer. That small cavern in her head, having held the scroll, captivated us. Somehow, Cramer managed to seal it and no moisture damaged it beyond restoration," Jon explained, perhaps telling him more than he cared to know, but he seemed interested.

Manuél rewarded Jon's detailed explanation by wanting to find a way to make a bronze copy of the scroll to be mounted alongside the figurehead on the base. His brother, a printer, could produce a bronze scroll-like facsimile of the original. The bottom line, if he were allowed to do it his way, the whole project would be $1,000 flat. Meri would look beautiful, he guaranteed, and assured her preservation, with the fillers and surfacing agents he would use. The price included the bronze facsimile of the scroll, even though he had not yet seen it. He guessed at how his brother would make it.

He bubbled with genuine enthusiasm and added, "I'll have the whole project finished easily two to three days before your fiesta, so you can display it there."

Jon wanted Meri to be the centerpiece of the fiesta decor. He had in mind dedicating her at that gathering and, later on, offering her to be an important part of a possible memorial to the Pomo Indians, to be located near Clearlake or, perhaps, in the Fort Ross area.

Sky thankfully seemed more than okay with all of this about Meri. Their imaginations were teeming with ideas and Manuél's expertise and creativity enhanced their ideas. Manuél had to go to work at the shipyard. That precluded them from planning to have lunch this Monday. However, they agreed they would have lunch together this coming Thursday. Manuél wanted to have a portrait of how she would look when mounted, painted. He also wanted to know how the plaque and scroll would be presented by Thursday's lunch.

Jon wrote a check for $100 earnest money. Manuél did not want the check, but Jon insisted he should have a good-faith deposit. All of this had taken no more than an hour. They arranged for Padilla to have help loading Meri, when he was ready to take the figurehead for restoration. As Padilla left, Schwartz followed him to the gate, begging for attention. He waved goodbye as his old Ford half-ton pickup's door rattled closed. A hole in the muffler added sound effects to his departure. Sky and Jon stood looking at the alley's empty space, suddenly quiet in his wake.

She turned to Jon and said, "I've just experienced a whirlwind of creativity. Have you ever met someone with so much energy, so willing to do everything, so much positive, accommodating 'can-do' spirit?"

"He's just the right person to do the job. I could feel good vibrations from the moment we talked on the phone. I hope we're not disappointed. He seems really to know what should be done, He talks like he knows how to accomplish the task."

Schwartz came bouncing back into the workshop. She stopped and sat, panting at Jon's feet, awaiting attention, her fragment of a tail vibrating about 280 cycles per minute.

Sky laughed at her, mentioning how she worshiped Jon and scolding him for having spoiled her. Then she added, "You've spoiled me, too."

"Love, bring Schwartz with you this evening to the boat. I'll fix supper and we can go for a walk. It will be chilly, but the weather is supposed to be mild. Will you accept?"

He held both her hands, begging with his eyes.

"I finish this afternoon's class about four-thirty, Jon. I've got some things to prepare for tomorrow, something which would interest you, by the way. I'll bring the drawing to the boat this evening, say, about six?" she said. "I'll feed Schwartz and leave her at home. Krystal's supposed to be home tonight, preparing for a test in history tomorrow. But, I'd love to have supper on the boat and a walk-and-talk with you."

Wrapping her arms around him, they kissed. He needed to leave to see his first client, but he left with her smiling and standing in her workshop watching him go.

Chapter Thirty-Eight

Jon needed some time to transition from his thoughts about his last client. This man had told him of how he'd recently met with his father: a father he had not seen since he was nine years old. He reported that the two of them were doing fairly well, getting acquainted and working through difficult abandonment, anger, and guilt matters. Then, however, it blew up. Jon suggested he call his father and invite him to a session. Surprising to both of them, the client's father accepted the invitation. Then, just as the client hung up, he began to cry. "Maybe he does give a shit, after all! Do you suppose, Dr. Scott, he'll really show up?" he asked, as if pleading for assurance.

Jon sat for a few minutes, after his client left. Then, he closed up the office and walked to the boat. His mood changed from dour to sunny the instant he saw the T-Bird parked beside his pickup. He looked for Sky. She walked slowly along the sidewalk, stopping from time to time, looking out over the forest of boats. She did not see him until he quietly walked right behind her, clearing his throat and hesitating to forewarn her of his approach. Anyone who had as much trauma in her life as Sky did not need to be startled.

Wheeling around, her smile and outstretched arms greeted him. In that instant, his reality changed, from being tired and drained to being responsive and filled.

How quickly everything changes when I'm with her.

They hugged briefly, leaning against the railing before they walked to the boat. But first she needed the key to the head, telling him she would be down in a few minutes. By the time she climbed aboard the boat, he had things opened up, the light on in the cabin, and had supper fixings out of the refrigerator. He poured her a glass of Chianti and spread rice crackers on a plate, along with a well-aged Brie.

"You sure know how to make a girl feel at home," she said, while lathering a cracker with the cheese and then she handed it to him for a starter.

Dinner done and the dishes stacked in the sink for later, they disembarked for a walk around the marina, heading toward the yacht club. Jon bundled her up in one of his sweaters and a scarf for the chilly night air, while he kept warm in his pea coat and knitted cap. The yacht club lights were mostly off. It was closed on Mondays. There was a large sailboat visible on a side tie, as they rounded the walkway on the dock side of the yacht club. It was a fine sloop, about forty-five feet in length. Her cabin lights were on. A faint sound of music came from a radio or tape aboard the boat. Having walked just past the boat, Sky suddenly stopped. She seemed startled. She stared intently at the bow in the illumination provided by the dock lighting, transfixed by the anchor. Jon too noticed a large CQR anchor on the bow.

"That's it!" she whispered, urgently, pulling hard on his arm to get him to look.

"This is the boat that hit me, Jon. I know it is. Even in this dim light, I know it is."

Jon turned and studied the boat. It occurred to him they might be able to see the occupants, if they went down the gangway and looked into the portholes. In the darkness, they could see in without those inside being able to see them, if they did not get right up to the ports. Silently, they walked down the steep gangway; steep because of a low tide. They sneaked alongside the sailboat. Sky was doing her best to look in the portholes to see who might be on board. Again, she grabbed Jon's arm firmly, pulled him back from the boat, and silently they walked fast past the stern and up the next gangway.

"It's Robert! Robert, my ex-husband. He's on board with another couple. I think the woman with him is the blonde who was at the helm that Saturday. I can't believe this. Why would he be here?" She began to tremble.

"He's flying the Marina Del Rey Yacht Club burgee, Sky. I suppose he has an arrangement to be here at this side-tie for tonight. I'm going to call and find out when Frank is on duty at the marina office. Let's go back to the boat and I'll call," he said, turning to walk toward his gangway.

"Slow down. My legs are about a foot shorter than yours. I can't believe this, Jon. What are you going to do? I know that is the boat. Krystal showed me pictures of his boat. Remember? I told you she had pictures. But, they didn't look like the boat that hit me.

"This is the boat, though. That is Robert, too. He's got a beard he didn't used to have, but it's Robert. I'd know that bastard anywhere. He must not know anything about you, Jon. He wouldn't come to this yacht club if he knew you and knew you were a member here. I thought Krystal had told him about you and your living on your boat here. But, he wouldn't come here, if he knew that," she said.

The Harbor Patrol office dispatcher answered. Frank would be coming on duty about 11:00 tonight, working graveyard shift this week. Jon asked to have him call as soon as he came on duty, no matter the time. He left his boat phone number. Turning to Sky after he made the call, he asked her if she wanted to stay tonight.

"Jon, how I'd love to, but I've an early-morning class and that's a priority right now. If I stay with you, I won't want to leave at six in the morning to get ready for it. I'll want to stay through breakfast, at least. God, how I want to stay! But, I also would not be able to rest knowing Robert Fitzpatrick is within spitting range all night," she said.

"I wish I were able to convince you to stay, but I understand. It makes me sick how understanding I am. How can you have any confidence in a lustful man, wanting you intensely, not wanting you to leave tonight, but who understands that your class in the morning is important?" he asked. Then he hoped they could get into a deep discussion about anything: anything at all that might keep her from leaving. It did not work. They hugged and kissed and walked to the parking lot. He opened her car door and she got in the driver's seat, looking up at him for one last kiss. As she swung her legs in, he closed the door and, in seconds, she drove away with the sound of those resonant twin pipes trailing from the parking lot.

Frank's call came at 1:15 AM. It took Jon a few seconds to awaken from a dream. At first he thought the phone was an alarm going off during a bank robbery.

"Sorry it's so late, Jon. What's up?"

"I've got something for you to do, Frank. I need you to find out anything you can about a sailboat on the side-tie in front of the yacht club. It's about forty-five feet long. The name on the transom is hard to read in shadow. I think it is something like 'Moonglow.' Underneath the name, the home port is Redondo Beach. I guess she's from King Harbor. She's flying a Marina Del Rey Yacht Club burgee. Can you find out about this for me? I'd like it if no one knew I'm asking you to do this; please keep it to yourself?"

"What's this about, Jon? Sounds ominous," Frank said, his intuition working well.

"Sky is very sure that this is the sailboat that rammed her that terrible weekend. She looked into the lighted cabin as we walked by it. She is convinced her ex-husband, Robert Fitzpatrick, is on board with another couple. Also, the woman she saw beside him looks like the woman at the helm that day. She realizes she got only a glance before the collision, but she's sure this is the boat. Just seeing him inside this sailboat upset her. She could not feel safe with him so close by. Not a word of any of this," Jon requested, and Frank agreed to keep it to himself.

"I'll get back to you as soon as I learn anything more."

They talked for a moment longer about what difference it made if this were the boat that hit hers. How could anyone prove it?

Jon said, "If Fitzpatrick didn't know who I am and didn't know where I lived, here in this marina, I think I have a plan that might flush him out."

Frank became intrigued. He warned Jon to be careful, though. "Jon, if this turkey tried to kill his ex-wife, he might be willing to do anything to save his ass. Watch your-self. I'll get back to you as soon as I learn anything. At least I can find out how long he's reserved a side-tie at the yacht club. We don't have any of the yacht club arrangements here in our office, usually, unless the boat is going to be staying more than a couple of days," he said.

"Anything you can learn will be useful, I'm sure, Frank. Thank you a bunch for looking into it."

The thumping on the hull of his boat awakened him at 05:30. Frank's muffled voice called to him. He opened the front hatch and stuck his head out, surprising Frank. Frank expected Jon to come from the cabin, emerging from the zippered boom tent.

"Want some coffee, Frank?" he asked, rubbing his sleepy eyes.

"No time for that, Jon. I've got some information. The Moonglow will be here through tomorrow. Tomorrow's already Wednesday? This week's gone so fast. Does that give you enough time to learn anything? Don't tell me your scheme, Jon. It is probably not a good idea, illegal, and might be fattening," he said, injecting humor to lighten Jon's possible prospects.

"I'm going to meet the captain of that boat, somehow. I'm going to get him to talk to me. I think I know how to tease out what I want him to say. I know it won't help, Frank, but I'm going to tape-record whatever we chat about," he said, feeling empowered about moving ahead on his plan.

Frank left. Jon would call him and give him anything he learned. He wanted credit for helping to bust this man, if it were possible. It would be an olive in his martini if he could help solve the matter of Sky's being hit not too far from King Harbor on that Friday afternoon, the day before he discovered her mangled boat.

Just barely dawn, at 6:30, he put on his trunks and braced for the cold bay, forcing himself to climb down the stern ladder for his morning constitutional; it just had to be done. He swam along the sterns of the boats on his gangway, heading into the channel, turning toward the yacht club. He swam by the Moonglow, just to get a better feel for what he would be doing later this Tuesday evening. In the early subdued morning light he noticed a man sitting in the cockpit of the sailboat, smoking a cigarette. He swam close by him, doing the Australian crawl. He paused for a moment near the transom and said, 'good morning'. The smoking fellow said something in return, but Jon stroked on, and whatever the fellow said did not matter. He had engaged Fitzpatrick. The enemy seemed unsuspecting, too, which is the best kind of enemy to have.

Before he went to breakfast, Jon called Sky. She was almost ready to leave for her first class. "I'll make it brief, Sky. I'm going to be talking to Robert this evening. He and his party have this side-tie reserved through tonight and into Wednesday."

"Jon, be very careful. I've warned you about his temper and also, if you're going to be talking to him after four or five in the afternoon, he will no doubt already be drinking," she said.

"Don't fret, dear. Talking to him may give me what I want. If he's drinking, he may even talk more easily. Don't worry."

"He's the kind of man who intimidates women, not men as much," she added, giving him some assurance.

"I only saw him from the water, just his head and shoulders. I could not size him up well, but I have no reason to suspect we will have a problem," Jon said.

Tuesday's appointments went well, two or three being near the end of their therapy sessions. Jon processed some of the backlog of paperwork during his noon hour, while trying to eat a crumbling BLT sandwich with his free hand. Phone messages complicated the day's schedule as usual, but all day he anticipated 'accidentally' meeting Robert Fitzpatrick aboard the Moonglow.

Sauntering down the gangway, like a tourist, Jon walked along the moored Moonglow, noticing the open cabin door. He could hear conversation aboard. He knocked on the hull. Within seconds, a bearded man in his late forties emerged from the companionway.

"Yes? Something you want?" he asked.

"I noticed your sloop and saw the Marina Del Rey Yacht Club burgee. Are you our guests here, just out cruising?" Jon hoped to establish some rapport.

"Yes. We're here for a couple of days. Leaving tomorrow afternoon," Robert offered.

"I'd like it very much if you'd join me for a drink at the yacht club bar. You'd be my guests. I'm one of the committee who welcomes guests here," Jon said, acting cordial and hospitable.

"We have reservations for dinner at seven-thirty, but I'm sure we would like to have a drink with you first. Never turn down a free drink. This is a fine club. Haven't been here for a couple of years, but we'd enjoy meeting you for a drink. Thanks for the invitation. What time?" he asked.

"I'll be in the bar in about fifteen minutes. Just come up any time you're ready," Jon said.

"I'll come up in a little while. My guests will probably take a few minutes longer, but they'll be along, too. Thank you. But, what is your name?" he asked.

"My name is Bill Bright," Jon said, watching his face intently, just in case there might be some kind of recognition. He saw no sign Fitzpatrick knew him, and he felt immediate relief. He would have to clue in the bar tender and perhaps some others in the bar that his name for this evening was Bill Bright and he was an official Long Beach Yacht Club hospitality host.

"May I have the honor of knowing your name, Captain?"

"Robert. Robert Fitzpatrick. I'll introduce my friends when we come up, shortly," he said.

Leon, the bartender, took Jon's five dollars in good humor, agreeing to call him Bill Bright and to tell the others at the bar his new name for the evening. Jon would later have to explain this to the curious and gossiping bar group.

About 6:45 the four guests came up the stairs to the bar of the club. Upon greeting them, they moved to sit in a circle around a table near the windows overlooking the marina. Jon purposely had chosen this table for privacy. The clear, calm night, with lights reflecting off the water just beyond the club's walkway railing made it a tourist's evening. The bar hostess came over for their drink orders.

"Cheryl, please put the drinks on my tab. I'll take care of it later. Remind Lenny I've got guests from an associate club and they deserve the best," Jon said.

"We'll treat them right, Mr. Bright," she said, helping Jon to relax with his identity.

The first part of the conversation had to do with sailing to Alamitos Bay from King Harbor, then sailing to Avalon, and then, tomorrow, back to King Harbor. Robert told Jon he often used a slip at King Harbor. His previous boat had been a thirty-six foot Columbia. He sold that after a recent divorce and bought this forty-three foot Camper & Nicholson sloop.

"I like King Harbor, but I've been a member of the Marina Del Rey club for a long time and keep a slip there for convenience," Fitzpatrick said. He leaned back in his chair to take the martini from the waitress.

The woman sitting next to Robert, was an attractive blonde, about thirty-five years old. Her tan, which had not yet leathered her skin, added to her healthy glow. Jon wondered how long it would take for the sun to begin to show its destructive powers on her blonde complexion. Robert introduced her as Heather, with no last name.

The couple with them, Charles and Louise Michelson, were new to sailing, but they would get a good introduction on this five-day jaunt aboard the Moonglow. Louise liked sailing more than Charles at this point, but admitted this was her first time since sailing with her father when she had been a little girl on a lake in Oregon. Charles seemed innocuously pleasant enough, but quiet. Jon decided not to try to draw him out.

A second round of drinks was ordered. Robert was drinking martinis. Heather was sipping a gin and tonic; the Michelsons drank Vodka Collins, two each in their first twenty minutes.

They may not be sailors, but they are definitely the usual yacht club landlubber veterans. Drinkers.

Jon said, "I know you have reservations for dinner in about twenty minutes, but I don't want you to feel hurried. They'll hold the table for you."

He decided to not waste more time and changed the subject to the matter on his mind. Deftly, he reached into his coat pocket and turned on the small tape-recorder he used sometimes in therapy sessions, only when clients gave their consent and promised to listen to the tapes he made. This time, he did not ask permission and no one noticed he had a recorder in his coat pocket.

"You know, Mr. Fitzpatrick, I've seen your boat before." Jon stayed purposely quiet for a few seconds, hoping the fly in his web would begin to think.

"Oh? Where?" Robert asked.

"Some weeks ago, I was sailing about an hour out, heading into King Harbor. I think it was on a Friday afternoon. I'm certain I saw your boat. Could it have been you, Heather, at the helm? On a starboard tack, as I recall. I was heading toward King Harbor, less than a quarter mile from your boat. You were heading out. I got past you quite a ways but it seemed there was a Cal-20 almost in your way," Jon said, watching Robert for reactions, giving time for his words to sink in.

"Wasn't my boat! You must be mistaken. I usually sail out of Marina Del Rey. Used to be at King Harbor, but for a year now, I've been at Del Rey. Besides, I'm an accountant and have office hours on Fridays. I'm seldom at King Harbor." He took a drink and then another swallow. He looked intently at Jon for a moment, the muscles in his jaw tensing. "Heather sailing? That's a laugh! Heather doesn't know the slightest thing about sailing, so she couldn't have been at the helm. It was someone else's boat, Mr. Bright. There are lots of sloops that look like mine from a distance," he said, as he drank the remainder of his martini. He gestured to the waitress for another.

"Maybe so, Mr. Fitzpatrick, but I don't think so. I'm sure it was your boat. There aren't many Camper & Nicholsons around. I know of only two in all of Alamitos Bay marina, and they have aft cabins. Yours is a sloop with a conventional cockpit - quite distinctive. A mighty fine boat, too, if I might add," Jon said. He continued watching Robert for a change in effect. Robert moved his chair back nervously.

"I think I'll have a cigarette before dinner, Mr. Bright. Do you mind if I excuse myself?"

385

"No, Mr. Fitzpatrick, it is about your dinner time. I'll just stay here with Heather and your friends. It's okay to take your drink out on the veranda here, if you wish to do so."

He wobbled ever so slightly as he left the table, carrying his drink in one hand while maneuvering for his cigarettes with the other. The moment Fitzpatrick left, the Michelsons excused themselves, saying they wanted to explore the club. They seemed to become uncomfortable during the exchange between Fitzpatrick and Jon. Now, alone with Heather, Jon turned to her and said, "He seems bothered that I think I saw you that Friday afternoon, Heather. Is everything okay? Is he okay? He reacted so quickly when I said I saw the two of you that afternoon, especially when I mentioned you had gotten very close to that little Cal boat," Jon repeated. He watched her for her reaction. He was not disappointed.

"I think he doesn't want to talk about that day, y'know. A really bad afternoon. I was upset, y'know, and we fought a lot, even while we were sailing. He got really mad at me that afternoon, y'know, and yelled at me to keep the boat heading this way and that. I think we hit that little boat, but he insisted we just skimmed it and everything was okay, y'know. Our boat was moving really fast, though. Someone on the little boat screamed at us. I didn't know what to do, except I turned the wheel as fast as I could at the last minute, y'know," she said. She took a drink and ate several of the little fish crackers.

"I'm sorry if I've upset him, Heather. I hope the rest of your evening is pleasant. I'll leave you all to a nice meal. Everything on the menu here is tops. Ask for Bruce. Tell him Bill Bright referred you. He's the most fun waiter," Jon said. He attempted to neutralize the moment.

As Jon arose from the table, Robert Fitzpatrick came hurriedly back, obviously three sheets to the wind; he asked where Jon was going.

"I'm glad to've had a drink with you. I'm especially grateful to Heather for our brief chat. Hope you all enjoy your dinner. The roast beef, of course, is always excellent," Jon said, moving toward the stairs.

Robert Fitzpatrick took Jon's arm in a firm grip. Jon stopped and stared into Robert's bloodshot brown eyes. Jon stood a bit taller and was definitely in better shape. But, for a moment, he wondered if they were going to have a problem.

Robert said, being emphatic, "Are you clear, Mr. Bright? Are you clear? We were nowhere near King Harbor that day you think you saw us?"

"I'm clear about what you think, Mr. Fitzpatrick. I'm sorry if you're troubled that I saw you that day. I thought, when I mentioned it, we would all just enjoy talking about a fine afternoon of sailing. I am very relieved you were able to avoid a collision with that Cal-20." Jon reached out to shake his hand. He thought, with increasing doubt, that they could still be cordial.

"Thank you for the drinks, Mr. Bright. You'll have to excuse Heather. When she has a few drinks, she has no accurate recall. I like that about her, most of the time, if you know what I mean." He said this in an attempt to imply humor.

Heather stood up and said, "Bob, y'know, I resent that! I'm not drunk now! I recall that afternoon like it was yesterday. From the time we left the dock, you were upset. You yelled at me to hurry up. Y'know, you got even more angry because your furling gear got hung up. Y'know, I do remember everything about that afternoon," she said, as she backed away from him a couple of steps.

As Jon left the bar to go to his boat the Michelsons returned. He relaxed a bit with their return. Heather would be safer with them there. He was eager to listen to the tape in his coat pocket. He also wanted to call Sky and needed to leave a message for Frank. The last thing to be done was to make notes about this encounter.

The tape came out clearly. Not having Heather's last name for the record bothered him. He had no idea what use all this might be, however he called Frank and left a message for him to call back. Frank was off duty this Tuesday. He would be back on graveyard shift tomorrow night. Jon calmed himself and thought there was no hurry. He felt good; he was certain that the charade had worked for him. Robert Fitzpatrick had used his boat to try to eliminate all of his problems, namely, Sky Rowan, his ex-wife. She had an ongoing law suit against him for years for back child support, health insurance payments for Krystal, and credit card debt he had abandoned. He left over $20,000 for Sky to pay. All of these expenses had been incurred by Robert during the last year of their marriage.

Maybe, it occurred to Jon, if they could nail him for the collision, satisfying the Coast Guard's 'want' for the person who rammed Sky's Cal-20, Fitzpatrick would feel more inclined to comply with the provisions of the law suit Sky kept going.

Sky had told Jon she was working late at the shop that evening and to please let her know what happened while having drinks at the club. Jon drove to Sky's shop to tell her about meeting with Robert Fitzpatrick and his woman friend. After talking to Sky about the experience in the yacht club bar, Jon felt a deep sense of relief. Sky, too, seemed appreciative of what he had learned. She asked him questions about how he had gotten this to happen. He told her about alcohol and yachting. "When you find someone with a boat, you generally know they will never turn down a drink, which was certainly true with these four people last evening, Sky. By the way," sticking out his hand to her, "meet Mr. Bill Bright." Then he explained the name change for the evening and how everyone cooperated.

"I got a tape-recording full of helpful talk, costing me only about thirty bucks for drinks and five bucks to Leon, the bartender. Heather nearly spilled the entire load about colliding with your boat," he said. He felt successful as an undercover agent.

"That would be his current bimbo, Heather Fenton. Krystal has gotten to know her a little bit. She told me about her bra size, about her blonde hair, and how she can't finish a sentence without saying 'ya know.' I think he's got what he deserves. She probably sees the dollar signs and is willing to fulfill all his fantasies for those bucks. How I ever got connected with Bob Fitzpatrick only a shrink could explain. But, I'd have to go for the long term analysis. I must admit, sometimes I wish we could have stayed with the fun. We had some laughs for a while. I met him not realizing how little I knew about fun. He was a barrel of monkeys the first two years," she said. She paused and told Jon she was sorry that she had dumped on him. She told him he didn't deserve to hear about this unhappy history.

"And you certainly don't need to hear me make my sarcastic judgments about him or Heather," she added.

"Sky, you need to do some dumping. You still have reactions from time to time from that marriage and the pain it caused you, maybe both of you. But I don't care about Robert. I care about you. The wonderful part of all this has to do with your being free of him. The other wonderful part, besides my knowing and loving you, has to do with your not being killed, drowned, or whatever might have happened when the Moonglow attempted to sink you and your little boat. I'm sure he thought he had accomplished his mission.

"Consider this: a broken mast, your having been knocked down and probably out, no working rudder, adrift on the high seas an hour out of King Harbor. All he had to do was read the papers the next day or so. He probably figured he would never have to worry about back child support again, the bastard. He didn't even care what happened to Schwartz. Actually, I think his girl friend will be the most use in the future legal matters ahead for you and Robert. I think she may have had her fill of this turkey, too," Jon said. He felt optimistic and, perhaps, overly confident, especially having the tape-recording of the brief conversation.

Wednesday, while Jon was in his office, Sky called him. He put the receiver to his ear and turned to look out the picture window. He listened to her and enjoyed his bay view.

"Jon. Thank you for all you've done. I've never in my life known a man to stick with me. You just stay right here. I feel better than I have for a long time. You even say the right things. How will I ever lump you into my thing about male jerks? You've been so different from other men with me," she said. She became quiet on the phone, breathing deeply. "How can you do therapy all the time and then be involved with me, Jon? You must feel you've got to be a therapist with me too. I think so often I need to stay with science and teaching. This personal world, love, intimacy, sex, all of it is just too crazy-making."

"No, Sky, I don't feel that way. What we have is completely different than what I do for a living. Besides, I'm completely in this with you and Krystal. You two have helped me let go of grief that I thought would imprison me for the rest of my life. I feel freer with you than I have felt since losing Miriam. You've given me very little reassurance about our future, but it doesn't matter. You're in every moment of my life. Can't help lovin' this gal of mine," Jon said, misquoting and half singing to her the Hammerstein *Showboat* ballad of yesteryear. "You just don't stop. You burrow deeper and deeper into me with your words, your love, and I have no defenses left," she affirmed, obviously feeling overly exposed and vulnerable.

"I'll watch my step. I'm beginning to hear your self-protective other side emerge. Before you go to sleep tonight, I want you to concentrate on feeling safe, in control of your life and feelings. I want you to know this Jon Scott character is in your life for good, not for pain and destruction." Jon hoped that she would let these thoughts soak into those places of wariness, traumatic memories, and her years of playing games to survive in a parched, painful marriage.

"I'll work at it, Jon. I really will. Maybe if we just remember we love one another and take some of the seriousness out of where we're heading, maybe then I could just enjoy all this and bathe in the light and warmth of your love. When I'm snuggling with you, in your arms, feeling your body spooned against mine, like we were the other night, there isn't a doubt or ounce of fear and no holding back. It's just when we aren't together that I begin this crazy thinking, doubting my feelings, everything. Left to myself I just want to be left alone to do my work and die safely like an old maid should." She added how tired she was and that she hoped they could talk tomorrow.

Jon's dreams that night were filled with boats, storms, rocks, and a sunken vessel with natives dancing on the ocean floor. There was one long dream about his not being able to find the altar in a huge church. He wandered through passageways, sometimes he called for someone to help. In that dream, he was late for celebrating the Eucharist, but the church became a huge labyrinth.

I must be seeking my soul or the holy. That's what labyrinth dreams are about. I wish I could talk to Carl Jung tonight.

The dream images stayed with him throughout the next day. Reflecting on them helped him realize how deeply the events of these past many weeks had become embedded in his psyche. His thoughts and feeling about clients and the lives they shared with him were familiar. These dreams, however, and these times with Sky and what she meant to him had become a whole new level of involvement. He reflected that this new life started with finding Meri at the bottom of the bay. Somehow his finding the figurehead had started a profound healing process. He began to contemplate about going back into therapy for himself. The thought of returning to therapy suddenly seemed important. He put Dr. Ann Tucker's card in his pocket before leaving the office that evening. He would call her at the right time. It had been two years since they had worked together, most of that had to do with the loss of Miriam. He knew he would not have made it through those months without Dr. Tucker's assistance.

When he returned to his boat, he noticed an envelope pinned to the boom tent. He opened it and read the note. 'Jon, the Moonglow left early this afternoon, ahead of their planned departure time. See you soon, Frank.'

About 8:30, he finished his light supper and a glass of Cabernet Sauvignon. He felt cozy and relaxed aboard his safe, warm boat. She seemed like a very protective, peaceful womb tonight. The stereo gave him a Duke Ellington medley, the current one being *Embraceable You*. He felt like writing in his journal and reminiscing for a while, but the telephone shattered the mood. It was Frank Martinez.

"Jon, I've got some more news about our Robert Fitzpatrick. Get my note? Also, I must tell you. I've talked to that Coast Guard ensign woman, Lore Shabro. Remember her?" he asked, probably in jest.

"How could I forget her? You're kidding, of course."

"Seriously, Jon, she was very helpful when I told her what we suspected, giving her the name of Robert Fitzpatrick and the Moonglow as likely suspects in the collision at sea with Sky Rowan's Cal-20. She took the CF numbers you left for me. It is interesting what she found. She knows the Harbor Master in Santa Barbara and the one in Marina Del Rey. What I've learned is probably a clincher for his being the jerk who ran over Sky's boat. Right after that day, the following Wednesday, the 7th of November, his boat went to dry dock in Santa Barbara to repair four stanchions on the port side, a deep scrape along the port side of his hull, and a main stay that had been kinked severely on the port side.

"The shipyard there confirmed this stuff with Ensign Shabro. She said they sent her a copy of the repair order. His boat was there six days, returning to his slip in Marina Del Rey on Tuesday, the 17th of November. Of course, we can't use the taped conversation you had for anything legal, but it will help us know how to confront him about it.

"It's my impression, as you suggested, that the Heather Fenton woman hates him or is afraid of him. Just the way she acts, I guess. She'll help us hang him. One thing this does, Jon, is to completely clear you of suspicion. I thought all that had been settled, but the way Shabro talked, there's still some question about your boat having collided with Sky's boat that afternoon. These people don't get over their first impressions or suspicions easily. However, finding Fitzpatrick and Fenton could clear everything up, if we handle it right," Frank said.

"I'm glad you've pursued this, Frank. I left all that information hoping it would help move things along. When you didn't call, I thought it might have been a useless exercise. You found all this out just today?"

"I was off duty last night. The office called me with what you had left early this morning. I did some homework before I came on duty this afternoon. It was surprisingly easy. That Shabro woman knows how to get right to the bones," he said, with obvious admiration. "I know she's been a pain in the ass to you, but she got immediately involved and helpful. Maybe you'll forgive her now," he suggested, releasing a shallow, probably fake laugh on the phone.

"Thanks, Frank. I owe you a breakfast soon. You'll be sleeping off your graveyard shifts this week and next. You go on days soon or do you then go to swing?" Jon was contemplating when they would have some free time together to talk.

"My schedule changed. Some guys are out sick. They've got me on afternoons to midnight for a few days. We could have breakfast any time soon."

Jon phoned Sky at her office. She listened intently to Jon as he relayed Frank's

report. It made her even angrier at her ex-husband. Halfway kidding, she suggested getting the Mafia to break his knees. He listened to her ranting. When there was an opportunity, Jon commented, "Now, Sky, you'll get all the back child support and all the rest of what has been rightfully yours. Plus you'll have the satisfaction that he will be charged with a hit and run on the high seas, a felony. If we can prove Heather Fenton steered the boat at the time, under orders, she'll have some time to do, too," Jon said. He offered Sky all the possible chances to change her anger to glee. At last, she could get even. "Ah, revenge is sweet!" he said. She agreed without a second's delay.

Chapter Thirty-Nine

During the next several days, having run the advertisements in the eight newspapers and their having already collected letters and phone calls in response, finishing arrangements for the fiesta at Dana Point rapidly became a priority. So far, Jon and Sky had received seventy-three responses. Three came from people who could trace their ancestry to several crewmen, besides the carpenter, Wilfred Cramer. The descendants of Thomas Hedge and William Brooks were also among those signing up for the Dana Point fiesta. This was promising to be an exciting and historic event. Anticipating the tales from these people, they decided to have some time and a way for people to sign up for articles and stories, Their own life stories and the stories that had come down to them from *Madonna*'s misadventure would be worthy of a grand book. Sky thought, perhaps, even a movie. She had already told the two reporters, Megan Yoshioka and Sandra Wells, because they were the reporters who had been involved from the very beginning.

Jon reminded Sky they had not appreciated their coverage, how the articles had caused them a lot of worry. She seemed more forgiving than Jon. The very next day, both reporters called her office for all the details they could collect regarding the newspapers' advertisements, the responses they had gotten, and the developing fiesta. Both reporters expressed appreciation for being given the lead stories on this affair. They would be at the party on the ninth of February, bringing along camera people. Two days later, an Orange County television news channel called to gather more information about the Dana Point 'beach party' or 'reunion'. Having gotten their names from the published guest list, with permission, a Pasadena Public Radio station interviewed two Pomo Indian descendants. The interviewer luckily found a certain Miguél Rodriguez, a native American tracing roots to the Pomo tribe at the 1850 massacre site at Clearlake. He had inherited diaries and journals from several ancestral sources. His great-great grandmother had been raped and made the property of a Russian fur trader sometime around 1830.

Her eldest son had sailed the *Madonna* south, escaping from the vigilantes who pursued them after the revenge murder of Jesús Vallejo. He had re-constructed a rich history of the Kashaya Pomo, along with his own heritage. Having accomplished his undergraduate work at the University of California at Los Angeles in 1958, he went on for graduate work at The University of Southern California, finishing in 1966. He had his Ph.D. from U.S.C., in history, writing his dissertation on the history, language, religion, and the unique basketry of his peaceful ancestors. Currently, he was a professor at California State University, San Diego.

He wrote about the Pomo Indians becoming enslaved, raped, murdered, and hundreds had died of diseases given to them by the white man. He included a long segment about the Bloody Island Massacre of about 200 men, women, and children, by the American Army dispatched to destroy the tribe in 1850. The one-hour interview was publicized and notice of it was provided to the list of guests, many of them writing in. Some called the station afterward, thanking the station's host for the excellent, informative interview with Dr. Rodriguez.

The scholar made a special point about the Pomo Native Americans having escaped to the San Juan Capistrano area in 1849 and 1850, quickly adopting Mexican and Spanish names. Dr. Rodriguez told the audience they had picked their names from the local, more successful Mexicans in the area around Oceanside, Escondido, San Diego, and San Clemente. They felt the need to blend into the local populace as much as possible, knowing they were wanted by the American authorities. But, after a time, their fear diminished and they began to feel secure with their adopted Mexican identities. He speculated about the fact that the *Madonna*'s burning and sinking was recorded by a pursuing ship, adding to the assumption the crew and passengers had been killed or drowned.

That first generation of Pomo tribesmen escaping Northern California in 1849 had to lose their identity as Indians to survive. Many of them were indeed wanted by the authorities. Some were known by their Pomo names to those who had enslaved them in the Sacramento, Fort Bragg, and Fort Ross centers of cruel power over their tribe.

Needless to say, this matter of changing identities invited even more curiosity to the anticipated gathering. Jon and Sky received lots of calls, some from other tribes in Northern California and others local to the southland. They wanted to come to show their interest and support at this beach fiesta. Comments about this major southland powwow spread rapidly.

Chapter Forty

Dr. Rowan, this is Mark Rinehart. We have a lucky break. A Heather Fenton wrote a long letter to me. I'd like to share it with you as soon as you have a chance. Call me back. The phone call came in on Sky's answering machine.

Mark Rinehart was Sky's attorney and had been for some years. He had helped her through the ongoing divorce complications. Now, again, he was on the job. He had told Sky he was going to have an investigator help him with details of the collision incident along with the probable problems related to finding the *Madonna*.

Rinehart used the recent events to further his advantage in Sky's suit against Robert Fitzpatrick. Apparently, Robert and Heather were parting company, an acrimonious end of their affair. Heather wanted to tell all, probably to get even. Sky asked Jon to join her to read the letter, but he had clients all afternoon. Mark Rinehart agreed to meet with them in the evening in the bar at Hof's Hut. On Monday evening it would not be too noisy, especially with football season over.

Before hanging up, Attorney Rinehart said, *There's a full moon tomorrow night, February 5th. Maybe that's what got Heather Fenton to talk. She seems eager to bring the nearly-lethal collision at sea out in the open. Plus, I think she wants to cook her boyfriend's goods . There's no limit to what a woman can accomplish, especially when she's been scorned.*

Sky and Jon arrived a few minutes before the attorney, giving them time to catch up on the day's events. She excitedly told Jon about her lecture, which was coming together for next Friday. Saturated with her new learning, mostly about typing and dating fossil blood, she was eager to give the talk. She thought that subject would attract the most interest for this particular group of archeologists and anthropologists. They were still discussing the fossil blood typing and dating technology when Mark arrived. Sky introduced him to Jon and told him they had been talking about fossil blood residues, inviting him to her lecture next Friday at the Archeological Society meeting in Los Angeles.

Mark said, "I'm fascinated by the fossil blood stuff. Very interesting, but I'd rather have scotch on the rocks, if it's all the same to you."

He was short, with a bulbous, red nose. A shining large forehead ended in a line of newly implanted hair. A scar ran from the edge of his mouth to the corner of his right eye, adding intrigue to his face. He breathed hard as he approached, just from having walked to the booth.

Jon studied his face. *Mark's been through a lot. Guess he's tough enough to handle the job. I hope he'll live long enough to finish the legal action for Sky and Krystal.*

Jon's usual cautious response to attorneys melted in a short time with Mark Rinehart. He found Mark to be very funny and the three of them laughed together. He told them about a court appearance he had that day. The other attorney showed up late and unprepared. He enjoyed telling them how his advantage, being well-prepared and on time, left the defending attorney in a heap. The bailiff had to scrape him up off the floor in a dust pan. At the end of the story, he told

Sky he would charge her less than his usual forty percent for her suit, because he easily had won much more in today's court matter than he thought he would get. "Besides, the Heather Fenton letter makes everything easy as pie," he declared.

The letter consisted of four hand-written pages, addressed to 'Mr. Mark Rinehart, Attorney at Law'. Sky and Jon shared the letter, reading it silently together. Mark sipped his scotch. He waited for them to finish. Sky slowly folded the letter and handed it back to him, smiling.

"Robert's head is on a plate. I think the creep has met his match. He must have beaten her up or something. She's probably realized what a jerk he is, no matter how much money he seems to have. I think she really hates his guts, which makes me like her," Sky said, leaning back, taking a swallow of her gimlet and counting out a few peanuts.

Her attorney said, "Keep in mind, this is going to help us, but her story will be difficult to prove, if it comes down to that. Fitzpatrick won't know that, though. I will let him know we have a full accounting of his attempt to murder his ex-wife. This Fenton woman claims she was just along for the ride on the Moonglow that afternoon. It doesn't matter what her role in the near catastrophe might have been. He's accountable. He's the skipper of the boat. He's responsible for everything that boat does. And, I'm sure, he did not count on your surviving this, Sky. You're going to get every buck you've got coming to you and then some. My fee will be a nice piece, too, and you won't even miss the chunk I'm going to make out of winning this suit for you. Consider these claims: six years of back child support, the bills he left for you when you two split, gambling debts you had to pay or lose your house; and the mental anguish he's caused you. You've got this sewn up, Sky." As he spoke, his face became rosier, noticeable even in the subdued light of the bar. Mark appeared contagiously pleased with himself. Sitting between them, quietly attentive, Sky squeezed Jon's hand and then Mark's.

"Mark, your estimate, after your percentage is out of this, was $60,000. Is it still this amount?" Sky asked.

"It's more now, Sky. Fitzpatrick has a felony hit and run on the high seas against him. You suffered physical and emotional trauma. Plus, we'll demonstrate attempted murder. He's going to be faced with charges, unless you refuse to press them. My suggestion is to let him quake in his shorts until we've got this in the bag. This letter from Fenton isn't notarized, but it is clearly in a handwriting, probably her own. I think she'll testify against him, too, if we need her to do so. She may ask for protection from him, if she feels threatened. I think we should go for $200,000, at least, plus, my fee. I want you to come out of this with $200,000. He'll have no problem paying that. I've done a TRW on him. He's got plenty. Then, he'll exhaust the rest of what he has defending himself against the felony hit and run action. The only concern I have," Mark said, pausing to take the last gulp of scotch, "has to do with his being a dangerous man. I wouldn't put anything past him, Sky. If you think your safety is a concern, we need to factor that in and find a way to keep him far away from you and Krystal." He said this sternly to alert her to a worst-case scenario.

"I'm still afraid of him. I've lived in fear of him for the last six years. I was often terrorized by him for a couple of years before that. He was especially mean when he drank. He broke furniture, wrecked cars, and had goons knock on our door to collect gambling debts. So, what's new?" she said. She took a deep breath and looked relieved, most likely realizing her long ordeal was now in the past.

"There's one thing I'm sure of. He cares about Krystal. He doesn't care enough to pay child support and health insurance, but he won't hurt her. He also knows, if she knew he did anything to hurt me, anything more, she would have nothing more to do with him. Now we've got him as the one who hit me that Friday afternoon. It will be interesting how all this turns out, really interesting.

"Somehow, I'm not as afraid of him now, right this minute. Maybe it's because I'm sitting here with a drink in me between two tough guys," she said, reviewing the dark prospects under discussion. She looked reflective. Then she said, smiling, "There'll be enough money to pay for an excellent college career for Krystal. That's what I care most about."

Mark was confident as he anticipated the meeting with Robert Fitzpatrick and his attorney. Giving him a copy of the letter from Fenton would nudge him into surrender, and then there would be little more to do than collect the check. The rest would be left up to the Coast Guard and the Los Angeles County legal system. Mark reminded Sky that he had all the information he needed, including: her stay in the hospital, the photographs of her boat after the collision, and the documentation of Fitzpatrick's boat repairs in Santa Barbara. He said that even the tape Jon had recorded might be useful. Also there were available Coast Guard records, the log of the matter, accusations directed toward Jon Scott, and details of saving Sky. There would be no wiggle room for Robert Fitzpatrick, no matter how much he paid his attorney.

Mark finished by saying, "I've got a rumor about who he's got as his attorney. A piece of cake. Yep! A piece of cake! Of course," he cautioned, "you must be aware that the legal system may go after him for the felony, no matter what you decide to do about it. But, don't fret, Sky. I've won three cases where his attorney thought he was running the show. He's a blundering amateur. He'll be blown away by the case we have, especially with Fenton's letter in our pocket. Get 'em by the balls and their hearts and minds will follow. We've got 'em," he said, a large grin spread over his bulbous nosed, red face. For a few seconds, he looked almost cute, like one of the Seven Dwarfs. The three had little more to talk about, so they parted. Mark would get in touch with Sky as soon as he could craft his next step.

The next day, Tuesday, Carlos Diaz called Jon. Carlos had given the information to Frank Martinez, but wanted to tell Jon himself. His son, Michael, and Luís Jimenez had been given a major break. They both were to serve six months in prison, two years' probation with weekend public service. They also had to pay $10,000 each as recompense for the damage done to the Grand Banks which they stole and punitive payments to the court.

Carlos seemed very relieved. He and Laura were almost rejoicing. Carlos explained how dropping the manslaughter charge had simplified things for both Michael and Luís. It was determined that Ray Cramer's drowning was caused by his own carelessness.

Also, the fact that Sky might not press charges for her being gagged and bound, along with the fact they had not physically removed her from her own property, lessened the legal problems for them considerably. Had they removed her or hurt her, they obviously would have had more serious charges against them. But, Jon reminded Carlos how angry Sky had been, especially about the threats ob harming Krystal. Sky had told him that it didn't seem right for Krystal not to see justice done. This was especially true because of the emotional trauma Michael and Luís had caused them, no matter how lucky everyone was for not going through even more. Sky also was emphatic in telling Carlos that the papers must be returned, or she would for sure press charges. Sky had been assured most of the papers were in police custody as evidence and they would be returned. Carlos told Jon that Michael and Luís were both writing letters to Sky, asking forgiveness and thanking her for not having pressed charges. It would have been better had they done this on their own, but they had been pressured into writing those letters by Michael's parents. Clearly, the matter was not settled, but Carlos and Laura of course hoped for an end to the ordeal. They could not face more legal complications, charges, testimonies, and the endless time these matters took to go through the court system.

Carlos expressed relief when Michael told him exactly where the rest of the stolen papers were located. They were under Michael's bed. Sky and Jon had a small argument about this issue, Jon's thinking she should definitely make them accountable for what they did to her that afternoon. Sky explained she had lived with a man just as abusive as these two had been to her. With her definite refusal to press charges, for sure another loose end from the past few months of adventure was tied up. Actually, she felt grateful not more had happened to her.

With these matters coming to closure, Sky, Krystal, and Jon could look forward to the 9th of February party at Dana Point, which promised to be a very successful, healing, and reuniting festival. Also, Sylvia now occupied a firm place within the family circle. Sky had come to a tentative understanding and acceptance of the love between Krystal and Sylvia.

Chapter Forty-One

The police blocked off the Dana Point beach access road. Parking attendants handled traffic from about ten o'clock that eventful Saturday morning in February. The weather could not have been better, an Indian Summer day, which brought jokes from some of the punsters. A large tent occupied the grass area below the majestic sandstone cliff. Folding tables and chairs were set up inside. A small stage, a public address system, and a generator were already working by eleven o'clock, two hours prior to the planned beginning of the grand affair.

Just to stage right stood Meri, exquisitely restored to what they imagined she looked like in 1849 - except for her being then attached to a barque sailing ship. Padilla had done his homework and returned Meri to her probable original appearance - very white skin, gold and black flowing dress, and reddish brown hair. Her large, polished, glistening eyes reflected light from a mirror placed at her base with two small spotlights trained on her voluptuously proud form. No one could imagine this figurehead had been deep in the mud since December, 1849. Looking very closely one could see hundreds of tiny worm holes that had been filled.

Manuél Padilla had done an excellent job, a work of art. The bronze scroll was prominently displayed alongside, about waist high to the viewer, illuminated with another light so it could be easily read. Adding to the clarity of the writing, Padilla had enlarged it to twice the size of the original scroll, about twelve inches wide by thirty-six inches long. The writing was a facsimile of the scroll's original script, penned by Wilfred Cramer.

Sketches of what they thought the *Madonna* looked like were on easels to the left of the Lady. The way she looked now, Meri no longer seemed an appropriate name for her. She seemed now to be definitely Jon's Lady of the deep, a life-changing archetype from the depths of the Pacific Ocean.

The table for the dignitaries was beside the stage, with eight chairs, including one for Dr. Miguel Rodriguez, several local politicians, Dr. Sky Rowan, and Dr. Jon Scott. A separate, reserved table for the diving crew and those in on the planning for the afternoon awaited them close to the stage. A Mariachi band would begin playing their vibrant, exuberant music, beginning at two in the afternoon. Signs indicated alcohol was not allowed. Of course, that could not be stringently policed, some of the guests having discreetly brought their own supply.

The portable barbecue trailer had arrived at about 11:00 AM and the catering people had the fire going for beef, ribs, or chicken by 4:00 in the afternoon. They could only guess how many would show up, having only seventy-four confirmed guests the week prior to the fiesta. But, there was abundant food, as it turned out, even with 107 people finally packing the reserved area. The buffet-style setup made it easy for people to pick their salads, vegetables, whatever kind of meat they wanted, and their drinks. The Mariachis played their joyous music. During their breaks, two Native American drummers put on a fine display of various drumming styles. It all came together with seemingly very little effort. Sky and Jon could not get over how the details of this magical, joyous afternoon coalesced into an historical reunion of *Madonna*-related people.

One enterprising man brought his own label of what he claimed to be aged whiskey. The man confided in Jon, without realizing Jon was a host, that his so-called 'Twelve Year Old Whiskey' was made in about two weeks. He was proud of his process.

He kept giving sips to those who wanted a taste to the point Jon thought they would have some trouble with the law. Luckily, his brew was not that good and most of the people were turning down his offer for samples.

One table held paper, pens, and crayons for people to write stories, notes, and maybe draw pictures. These were gathered by several workers at that table, filing the items in a large book that eventually would become published. Each person was given a program for the afternoon, complete with a copy of a printed facsimile of Wilfred Cramer's scroll. On the front of the program glowed a color photograph of the figurehead, known only to a few as Meri or Jon's Lady, but to the rest, as the caption stated, 'The *Madonna*'s Figurehead', then, 'She brought us to San Juan Capistrano and Dana Point in 1849'.

When Jon first read these words, he thought, *And she brought me both Sky Rowan and Krystal, and she brought me through my grief of losing Miriam to my new ability to love.*

After several hours of lively conversations, some guests went swimming in the designated area at the beach. The children present played on the bay beach nearby. The crowd gathered in the tent area for introductions of the key players in finding the ship and getting this afternoon's event to happen. Then came several brief talks, including one by Dr. Sky Rowan about the plans for a northern California memorial for the Pomo Indians. She explained the memorial would inform visitors about the tribe, their years of having been victimized by the Russians and later the Americans who came to the Fort Ross and Clearlake areas from 1812 on.

Dr. Miguel Rodriguez took time at the microphone to relate the little-known history of the Kashaya Pomo tribe, mentioning also the Tlingit, Yuupik, Alaskan Aleut, and other coastal tribes. All these native people had suffered, being exploited by the Russians and the Americans, especially during the Nineteenth Century.

When it came Jon's turn to speak, he simply told about discovering the figurehead in about thirty-five feet of water off the east end of San Clemente Island. He also explained how there was a bit of gold found that enabled them to find and purchase a memorial site in northern California, once they had all the suggestions from those present and other Pomos who might be interested in helping. Jon suggested Fort Ross, Fort Bragg, or a beautiful place at the north end of Clearlake for the memorial. The figurehead would be a centerpiece for that memorial, along with a Kashay Pomo Indian Information Center to be developed there. If they could collect the names of those massacred on Badonnapoti Island (later known as 'Bloody Island') and others of those dreadful years, their names would be engraved on a wall of native stone.

Frank Martinez came to the microphone and greeted everyone. He took a few minutes to acknowledge Sylvia, Ian, and Paul. His brief explanation of the dives they had done and how they first found the relics on the ocean floor captivated the audience. Jon and Sky were impressed with his ease in presenting the story. To Jon's knowledge, Frank had never talked to a group like this. His sincerity, knowledge, and delivery added greatly to the good feelings shared. Jon felt he would burst with affection and gratitude for Frank's role in the adventure, along with the gift of his friendship.

By the time the evening wound down, Jon and Sky watched how those present resisted leaving. They took names and addresses from one another. They heard comments about doing this again, perhaps an annual event somewhere in the southland.

Dr. Rodriguez offered on the public address to be the key person for any eventual times for their assembling, freely handing out his business cards, and writing his name and address on a large poster near the figurehead.

Sylvia and Krystal mingled and met one person after another interested in the shark attack and Sylvia's losing her arm, giving consolation as best they could.

Dick Brophe and Sharon managed to get some business for the *Tiamat* out of the afternoon, with two different media people wanting to shoot documentaries, not related to the *Madonna* or the Pomos.

The spirit and excitement of the afternoon made it a healing event and a complete success. Most of those present had never thought they would meet anyone else with a similar history. Their stories blended and augmented one another. At one point Jon and Sky felt they could actually be witnessing the resurrection of a southern California Pomo Indian Tribe, right then, in 1985. Clearly, these people belonged together.

Even the descendants from the crew members felt a part of the tribal unity. They were accepted into the warmth and congenial bond of these people. One man, dressed in a leather coat with long leather fringe hanging from the sleeves, stood and toasted with a beer he had brought, yelling to the Cramer, Brooks, and Hedge families, "My people are your people!"

At the beginning of the afternoon, Jon noticed the Jimenez and Diaz families sticking to themselves, but by the end of the afternoon, they were all getting along well with the Cramers. Apparently they had smoked the metaphoric peace pipe.

By eight in the evening, the last guests were leaving, but not before helping to load the figurehead into Jon's trailer, on top of a mattress in the bed. One of the elders began to sing, *The Party's Over.* He was singing solo, but the others who did not know the song, enjoyed listening. Gradually, the group thinned out as the last people backed away into the darkness, shaking hands, and walking toward their cars.

By ten o'clock, the tent and all the rented tables and chairs were gone, the barbecuing caterers completed cleaning up, and no trace remained from the fiesta, except for Meri, covered with a blue tarp Jon had made for her, tied prone in the back of the trailer. Sky and Jon walked to the surf side, sitting down at a picnic table near the jetty, feeling exhausted, but very close and quiet together. They were riding on the magic carpet of this Saturday's odyssey, neither wanting to change the mood that brought them so close and filled them spiritually and romantically. The ocean breeze grew to a penetrating wind which gave her reason to snuggle even closer, his coat wrapped around both of them.

"Well, Love, what do we do now? From the experience we had today, it's clear you and I together can accomplish wonders. I know the Holy Spirit had a glorious part in this, too, though," Jon said, venturing into a dimension of his life usually questionable to Sky.

"I am just sitting here astounded by this day we've shared, Jon. The images of those people, meeting, hugging, talking all at once it seemed, the pages of written material they enjoyed leaving, some with art, some with poems, some with biographical stories, their openness, the dancing they did, the drumming, perhaps authentic Pomo dancing, and, then, at the last, those four who brought us the baskets their grandparents had woven.

"Did you get a look at those baskets? They are exquisite. I've never seen such fine basketry work and I've looked at countless baskets. And look at this necklace of beads, the little disks and the beads. What a precious gift! They explained how the disks were of clamshells, the silver crafting is exquisite, and the beads were of Magnesite, which was their gold. Aren't they beautiful?

"Look," she said, leaning toward him and holding up a fine, handcrafted necklace. "I couldn't stop crying when that woman handed me those two baskets and wrapped a shawl around us both, saying something in a language I didn't understand. We both were crying. We didn't know what we were crying about, I guess, but I felt the warmth of her love or appreciation flood through me. A complete stranger! But, I would join her any time for anything. I felt like I had experienced an instant bond with her and a community. I'm not used to community, Jon. I'm the Lone Ranger, in a way. But, I could see living with these people - all of them. I didn't want them to leave," she said, bundling more tightly into him.

The surf's rhythm and the brilliant stars kept them on that bench by the sea probably too long. Shivering, they decided to go to their vehicles and back to Long Beach.

As Jon approached his pickup, parked near the place the barbecue had been, he saw several people standing beside the trailer. His immediate concern for Meri put him on guard. He saw she was exposed, her cover having been peeled back on one side.

"Excuse me, but I must ask who you are. This is a private property," he said, feeling wary and inarticulate. He still lingered a bit in the softness of the time Sky and he had just shared. Sky got right to the point.

"Who lifted that cover? This is valuable private property!"

"We just had to have another look at her, Dr. Rowan. We didn't want to leave without another look. She's a magical wooden woman to us. My wife and I are very interested in helping you and Dr. Scott accomplish this memorial you're planning. I'm an architect. We came back here, wondering if you might still be here. There were so many people we didn't get to meet you earlier. Let me introduce ourselves, and these two with us. I'm Bill Sanchez and this is my wife, Mary. Our friends, Michael and Joyce Thompson are also interested in making this memorial dream come true. We know there will be others, too, but we would like to help in any way we can. I have some ideas as to how the memorial shelter or building might look, especially if it is to be near Clearlake. We have a cabin near Clearlake. We didn't even know why we wanted to have a place there, until I learned my family's history. I am Pomo. Mary traces some roots back to Tlingit stock," he said, convincing them he was authentic and legitimately wanting to participate in making the dream come true.

They exchanged phone numbers, making a tentative time to talk in the next two weeks. Bill Sanchez offered at that time to have some drawings of an adequate building that could house the information center and protect the figurehead. They parted company for the evening. Sky and Jon were the last to leave, embracing and kissing goodnight, vowing to talk early Sunday morning, before he had to be in church. He closed the door to her T-Bird and she cranked down her window, "One kiss for the road, Jon. Drive carefully. You're precious enough, but you have your precious woman in that trailer, Saint Irene. That was funny when they dubbed our figurehead, 'Saint Irene'." She paused and laughed.

He recalled the moment when the remnant on the beach sang *Goodnight Irene* to Meri. He said, "Another thing I love about you is how you pick up on those small events and we can cherish them together."

"That was so much fun when they sang at the end," she said, smiling and puckering for her kiss, a bonding, long kiss, with Jon on his knees to kiss her through the car's open window. She used that opportunity to point out his being on his knees to her. "When you get on your knees to me, you will always win my heart."

They drove from Dana Point, heading up the coast route all the way back to Long Beach. She chose to follow him, he imagined to protect Meri from late Saturday night drunk drivers. She pulled off when he headed for the workshop. He planned to leave the trailer and Meri locked up in the secure fenced area for the time being.

Tomorrow afternoon, he would unload her and return the trailer to the rental yard. Once he dropped the trailer, Meri well-covered, and the gate locked, he headed home to the *Daimon* and a short night's sleep.

Chapter Forty-Two

Sky's call came early, waking him.

"Jon, I haven't slept much. Guess I'm too excited, still. But, I need to talk to you. Can we meet after you finish at Saint Paul's, maybe around noon?" she asked, arousing in him a feeling of concern.

"Of course, Sky. But, there's something in your tone that is troubling. Are you okay?" he pleaded.

"I just need to talk with you, soon. So much I need to understand. Maybe, if you think about it, you could pray for me, Jon. I know you believe in that stuff. Maybe it will help. That probably sounds funny coming from me. But, I really do want to learn more about you and this religion stuff is part of the deal. I've accepted that. I'll come to the boat about half-past noon, if that's okay."

"Why don't I just come to the workshop, Sky. I've got to unload the figurehead and take the trailer back. We can talk there, if that's okay. But, Sky, I'm really in a knot inside with the tone of what you're not saying to me now. Maybe I should phone Saint Paul's and leave a message about my not helping this morning," he said, thinking they needed to talk right away; his anxiety already detracting from feeling present in church. "I'll be anxious all through church, which isn't good for me or the parishioners."

"No, Jon. You need to do the church thing. I just need to know we're going to see one another soon. I'll get some sleep and then go to the shop. I'll see you there when you are free," she said. Then, she gave him a gift he desperately needed. "Oh, by the way, Jon. I love you incredibly. I love you!" she declared, hanging up instantly.

The two services went well, but Jon did feel distracted, wondering about Sky's need to talk. The urgency in her voice really bothered him. His imagination ran from things having to do with Krystal to things having to do with the two of them. He knew it was personal, but had no hint of what might be coming out of the dark tunnel. He kept repeating to himself, along with his prayers this morning, *Jon, stay in the present. Jon, be not concerned with foolish imaginings. Remember Saint Francis de Sales and his prayer you love. 'Do not look forward to what might happen tomorrow ...' and all the rest of that prayer. Remember the last line, Jon, 'Be at peace then, and put aside all anxious thoughts and imaginations'.*

A bit late, a half-hour after noon, he pulled up to the workshop gate in the alleyway, behind Sky's car. His heart rate was fast, but he could see no obvious reason to be feeling afraid. Still, he felt apprehensive, not knowing what fed Sky's urgency.

Schwartz met him, every part of her dancing, wiggling, jumping, with a few gleeful barks. He picked her up and carried her into the shop as she licked his face and neck. Sky sat on the couch, beneath a pile of papers and manila folders.

"I'm sorting through this stack of papers. Can't stand up to hug you, but I'm so glad to see you," she said, full of warmth, slowly quieting his fears.

"Before I sit down for our talk, if now's a good time, do you want me to get you something to drink? Looks as though you've been buried by paperwork for a while," he said.

"Yes. Thanks. I'd like some of that fruit juice in the fridge. Didn't know I was thirsty until you asked," she said, mumbling with a ballpoint pen between her lips, using both hands to separate sheets of paper into two piles.

Jon put her juice on the table beside the couch and sat down with his glass, again, beginning to feel his apprehension growing.

"When I get through with this last folder, Jon, I'll put this stuff aside. I've found the three things I thought I'd lost. I was really upset about not finding these two files. My talk to the Society next Friday night is based on what's in them. I'm talking on Carbon Dating and problems in stratigraphy. Of course, they want to know more about fossil blood typing and dating. I've got a wealth of information from a Thomas Roy on dating and typing fossil blood, which is fascinating," she said, handing Jon a file to occupy him during his moments of impatient waiting.

A few minutes later, as he perused her collected technical information on fossil blood, Sky looked up from the last file on the pile between them and turned toward him. She sat quietly, looking him over. He imagined her searching where to begin to express whatever occupied her mind.

Diving right into her turmoil, she said, "It's this marriage business we keep bringing up, Jon. That magical evening with Frank and Lupe was a turning point for me, and, I guess for you. I know I said yes that night, but I've not been completely honest. I'm still so wary about marriage. You keep mentioning it, as though we have a plan. I realize I don't say a real 'yes' or 'no', just letting you keep on as if we're headed down the chute for that altar."

She took a long draw from her juice, watching his reaction. Schwartz came over to him and climbed up on the couch beside him, seemingly to give him support and comfort.

"Sky, it's just something that is right for us. Perhaps I've just thought it was right for us because it is right for me with you. But, you have let me know several times there are problems with our being so close, especially when we are not together. It seems we have the most difficulty when we're too busy to get together. I thought, if we married we would be together and you would not have problems with us. When we're not together, that's when you get the most scared of marriage, isn't that so?" he said, being very aware of feeling inarticulate and clumsy with this subject.

"Jon, I would have no problems knowing we would be together for the rest of our lives. I just have something about this marriage idea. Then you said something about the Holy Spirit, which shook me. I know nothing about spirits, Jon. It seemed spooky. As you know, I don't understand the need for religion or the formal things that you priests do. I respect you for your commitment to the church, but I just don't have the interest in it, except for the history, the digs I've been on having to do with various religions, the evolution of religious practices, along with all the pagan practices. Humans are capable of fabricating or projecting all kinds of icons to worship, to make us feel more secure in our obvious insecurity.

"I think the pagan concepts, the fertility rites, and the sacrificial rites having to do with perpetuating life, crops … all that interests me a lot. I'm aware of some of the dying and rising gods, especially the Egyptian mythologies, Isis,

Osiris, and Horus. I know that Christianity absorbed all kinds of ideas and practices from surrounding religions as it developed from Judaism along with Mithraism, Zoroastrianism, and those other religions of those days in the Middle East," she said, stopping and looking down on the paper pile beside her, fidgeting with the pages. "I don't know why I'm getting off onto all that. It is easier to talk about that than about us, I guess. One thing that does bug me about Christianity is how it all started by the oppression and catastrophes from Emperor Constantine. Then, I meet an Episcopalian, who's in a church started by King Henry the Eighth, who was a jerk of the first order."

"Sky, there's no pressure. Of course, I'm troubled by what you might be deciding. I've come to realize I want you in my life. I want you, Sky. I love you. I have a full life and can live without you and Krystal and this goofy dog, but I have not felt this alive or this much love for years. I won't just give up, marriage or no marriage.

"No matter what happens to us, I'll never be without you in my heart from what we've shared in the past four months - only four months? It seems a lifetime to me," he said, feeling insecure. Schwartz nuzzled his hand and he began scratching her behind her ears. She put her head in his lap, looking up at him with those amazing doggie eyes of hers.

After a tense pause, Sky continued. "I don't want you to go away. Please don't even think such a thing. All I need is for you to love me just like you do, be patient with me, just as you have been, and please don't talk about getting married. Remember, I've been married. I don't do the marriage thing well, Jon. I need to feel free, which I do around you now, freer than I've ever felt with a man. Why can't we just have what we have without ruining it with marriage? Maybe, just maybe in time I'll feel some other way, but you mention marriage and I feel joy and existential dread all at once. I can't explain it. I love what we have. Can't we just have this, love one another, sleep with one another when we can, share our lives as we have?

"Look at the married people, Jon. Most of them seem dead as nails to me. They don't talk. They don't seem to have a sex life or romance. They envy us, the ones we've come to know together. That isn't true with Frank and Lupe. But Carlos and Laura, they seem to envy us. Dick Brophe and Sharon have some vibes going, I guess, but most people I know, the married ones, are like the walking dead to me. I remember when I was with Robert, we were the walking dead, too. We had about six months of good times, but I just did everything he wanted and let my own life go to hell during that time and we went downhill from there," she said, tears beginning to slide down her cheeks.

Jon reached over to move the pile of papers from between them onto the floor.

Stretching out his right arm to her, she curled herself into his embrace, squeezing Schwartz between them. The next thing he knew, she was sobbing uncontrollably, her head buried in his chest.

At least five minutes later, she began to speak, apologizing, blowing her nose like the air horn on a Peterbilt, then apologizing for that. "For the love of Isis, I never knew I was headed for this one, Jon. Now you'll just be relieved about my refusing to ever marry. Who'd want a woman who blows her nose like a steamboat horn and gets her snot all over your good clergy shirt?" she said, blowing her nose again, using his handkerchief.

Handing her the remaining juice, he insisted she take some swallows, when she stopped her shaking. He felt welded to her, holding her closely as she began to settle into a more relaxed breathing. The fragrance of her hair always captivated him and this moment was no exception. Burying his nose in her hair, he took deep breaths. With her in his arms, her fragrance, and the tenderness consumed both of them. They slid into a down, close position on the couch, with her on top of him. Their clothes almost magically disappeared, and suddenly they were in a timeless merging, lost, moving together, swept away into enchanted space - more deeply connected than ever before. They stayed that way together for nearly an hour, quietly and deeply grafted together. After a time, they both awakened, slowly, smiling, caressing, whispering, penetrating deep, hungry caverns within each of them.

At nearly 4:00 PM, Schwartz suddenly began to bark. Sky quickly rolled off of him, pulling on her clothes and helping him to dress, between hurried kisses. They heard the gate scrape open and a young woman's voice called out, "Mother! Jon! We're warning you! We're coming in, ready or not!" It flashed through his mind he would not be returning the unloaded trailer this afternoon, but what an afternoon they had together!

Sylvia and Krystal knocked on the shop door and began to open it slowly. The two of them were there, standing. Sky stood in front of Jon with his arms around her, both smiling at the two of them, looking conspicuously innocent.

"Looks like our timing was okay," Krystal said, a curious expression on her beautiful face.

"Your timing was perfect.

"May I offer you something to drink?" Jon asked, turning toward the refrigerator.

Both of them accepted orange juice. Sylvia told them they had gone hungry since breakfast, hoping they would find Sky and Jon so they could take them to dinner.

"It would be a celebration dinner, Mother," Krystal said. "I want to share exciting news. I just found out yesterday I've been accepted to USC, thanks to Sylvia. I wanted to surprise you at dinner, but now I've let the cat out of the bag. What a bag it's been!"

"No thanks to me. Your good grades, good reputation, and your immediate action when I told you about early application for the Fall of 1986 made it all work for you," Sylvia said, stroking Krystal's long, shining, black hair, gently moving each strand into place.

"What wonderful news, Krystal! I think this is worthy of a royal dinner for the four of us. Where would you like to go or should we make a decision for you?"

"The yacht club would be our preference. I hope Bruce is working tonight. He makes a fuss over us now that we've come out of the closet. Remember how he acted that night when we were together, having so much fun? Bruce knew we were together," Krystal said, putting her arm around Sylvia.

"This orange juice has pulp in it, Jon. Yuk! I can't drink orange juice with pulp, unless I'm dying of thirst. Got anything else?" Sylvia asked, making a prune face.

"Got some apple cider with no pulp. How 'bout that?" Jon said, going back to the refrigerator and pouring a glass of the cider, drinking the rest of her orange juice himself.

"By the way, before you two leave, would you help us put Meri back to bed on the floor over there? I've got to unload the trailer so I can return it sometime soon."

"Let's do it now, if you want. Then we might have more time to talk? I think the four of us can manage lifting her, sliding her out of the trailer, at least," Krystal said.

After putting Meri to bed on the floor, Sky and Jon pulled up the two director's chairs, facing the couch, and the four sat down to talk. They talked for over an hour about all sorts of things, from the fiesta to Krystal's going to college this very next Fall and where the two of them would live, if Krystal did not stay at home. At one point, Jon excused himself to make a reservation at the club for seven o'clock. He asked if Bruce were working that evening. Luckily, Bruce would be there to serve them. He requested a table in Bruce's section, near the northeast corner, where they could see the harbor lights.

Sylvia and Krystal carried most of the dinner conversation. Once in a while Sky had a comment, but they were both riding a wave of enthusiasm. Sylvia let Krystal cut her meat for her.

"I'm usually a vegetarian, but this center-cut pork is irresistible. I do feel a bit sorry for the poor piggy, but not eating this won't help him now," Sylvia said, adding drama by her expression.

Krystal had the lasagna with a Caesar Salad, prepared at the table by Bruce, entertaining with his talent and comical pomp. As he mixed the dressing, Bruce said, "This Caesar salad is being served with ham and I'm the ham."

By dessert, the subject of marriage came up. Sky immediately squelched any thoughts on the topic, letting both of them know they had no plans, besides their intention of staying together.

Sky assured Krystal. "You can count on our being with one another for the immediate future. In fact, the way we've been going, we might be together for a long, long time. Keep it a secret, but that's what I'd like."

Krystal surprised them with their plans. She seemed hesitant to share, but she could not hold back her excitement. USC had granted her request to enter in the Fall of 1986, a year after high school graduation. She and Sylvia were going to travel together next Fall, going to Sylvia's relatives in Maine in August, from there to Europe for three months, visiting Sylvia's uncle in Spain and then going to Italy, where she knew some divers, friends of hers from several dives in the Mediterranean about five years ago. If they could make it happen, Sylvia expressed interest in going to Vietnam with Krystal, perhaps in the Spring of next year.

Krystal said, "I've wanted to visit Vietnam for a long time. I'd like desperately to have better memories of the place of my childhood. But, I haven't wanted to go alone. I don't ever want to be alone again, especially with those memories in Vietnam."

Jon and Sky were taken by surprise with this sudden revelation. Krystal frankly said she had been afraid to bring it up, thinking her mother would refuse to let her go. On their way, driving to the yacht club, Sylvia convinced her she would be of age, able to determine for herself where and what she would be doing, and, besides, her mother would approve. Sylvia reminded Krystal how much her mother had traveled during her own childhood and teenage years, Sky's parents having been scientists and having taken her on many adventures. Sylvia was right. Sky was very happy for both of them, giving them her blessing, offering to do anything she could to add to their trip. Her only concern had to do with Krystal's putting off school and having too much fun, not wanting to take on the burden of an academic program after all the freedom of traveling. Sky was quiet for a few moments, then said, "Krystal, you have no idea how hard this has been and continues to be to realize you're so mature and leaving me. But, I know this has to be and Jon is helping me through letting you go."

"Mother, I promise that won't happen. I'm definitely going to finish school. Sylvia will help me stay on track. Also, I'm never going to leave you, really. I know USC is a terrific opportunity and Sylvia supports my going there. I'll be more ready for school after a year off. Don't worry."

Bruce gave Jon the ticket to sign for dinner, reminding him the tip should be more than usual because he had forced himself to be polite and not make any moves on him. "You look ravishing, Jon. But, I've got to warn you, that Bill Bright fellow was really cool," he said, bill in hand, turning to go. Bruce suddenly wheeled around and sneered, "Are you sure you won't change your mind, Sir?"

"Off with you!" Jon insisted, winking. "We'll talk later. Can't you see I'm surrounded by beautiful women tonight? Catch me when I'm lonely."

Sky's laughter topped the banter. Krystal and Sylvia enjoyed the show, too, at first having been startled by how easily Bruce and Jon quipped together. They left the yacht club, stepping into a very cold February evening. Sharing hugs and saying goodnight, Sky and Jon walked to the boat, talking about the evening with Krystal and Sylvia. Sky admitted how difficult it was to realize Krystal was making such grown-up, independent decisions. She suddenly seemed a woman. Krystal and Sylvia were clearly a match, showing their appreciation, respect, and deep affection for one another with confidence and a charming easiness. Opening the boat, Jon turned on the light, the electric heater, and he asked her to stay the night, promising to get her up early for her first class. Everything about them tonight was a 'yes'. They undressed, slid into bed, spooning, a brief time sharing mutual desires, then talking for a short while, and falling asleep by 11:00.

Monday morning came all to soon. Jon put on his swimming trunks. They hugged and kissed goodbye. They would talk again about lunch time. Sky walked the gangway to her car. He waved to her in the dim dawn and, cringing in anticipation, he plunged off the dock into the cold water for a half-hour swim.

Through his morning's sessions, a small storm brewed within him. He had a right to give Sky his thoughts on their relationship, too. At least a right to state his wishes and feelings. He phoned her secretary and left a brief message. "Please tell Dr. Rowan that Jon Scott needs to talk to her in person, when she has time." He left his office phone number with the secretary and went to The Omelette House for a light luncheon.

When he returned to his office, there were several messages, one being from Sky. She sounded anxious, not having reached him. Her message requested he call her just as soon as possible, which he did. Between his sessions, about three in the afternoon, he had fifteen minutes. She answered her office phone on the first ring. "What's wrong, Jon? Is there something wrong? You left a message you want to talk to me," she said.

"Not on the phone, Sky. I need to tell you what I've been feeling and thinking when you've got some time."

"How about right now?"

"I've got two more sessions before I can leave, Sky. Don't worry. It will wait. I want enough time to say what's truly on my mind," he said, bargaining for her full attention.

"You name the time and place, Jon. I'll be there. I have a few things to wrap up for tomorrow's classes, but mostly I'm prepared. Where do you want me to meet you?" she asked, sounding eager, perhaps a bit pensive. "Is it something bad, Jon? Are we just trading our misgivings, going back and forth with our doubts? Is this about doubts?" she asked.

"No. How about meeting at the boat? I just need to say some things to you about us. Nothing bad. Oh, by the way, Sky, I love you."

She came to his boat at 6:30 PM. He had poured two crystal glasses of Dry Sack, cut slices of several cheeses, put out an assortment of crackers, and a new, deep blue table cloth laid out on his galley table. As she stepped into the cockpit of the *Daimon*, she called to him, "Permission to come aboard, Sir?"

"Permission granted. The skipper is awaiting thy presence."

Stepping down the several steps of the companionway into the cabin, she took his breath away. Her hair down, flowed to her shoulders. Removing a shawl, a low-cut, blue blouse with billowy, elbow-length sleeves framed her graceful neck. Her brown eyes were moist and soft. She had on a long skirt, all the way down to her sandaled feet. She knew, just seeing him stunned, that her appearance had its desired effect. They embraced. Her head burrowed into that hollow between his shoulder and chest. He held her, breathing in the lovely fragrance of her hair. A few minutes later, giving them time for intermittent kisses, they sat down together at the table. She approved heartily of the table cloth and the displayed refreshments. "Well, Dear One, what is this you must say to me? I'm about as unraveled by your call as I can get. Talk to me! You talked to me before. Is this more of that? Are you getting even for some of those unhappy calls I've given you?" she asked, moving away just enough so they could see one another face to face.

"I sat without any argument when you gave me your dissertation on marriage. But, I've got something to say on the subject, too. I'm not going to get religious, because I know that won't matter much to you. But, there is one thing I need to tell you I believe deeply. True love makes everything new, Sky. We have here true love. Nearly all the time now, I don't think of Miriam when we're together or, even, when we're going to be together. We've just begun. We have just gotten together and the time has not been long enough, I realize. We've got a lot to learn about one another. I'm not in any hurry, but what we have is nothing like what you've had before. I never thought I could love after losing Miriam, but this is a whole new experience for me. It's all new! My proposal of marriage still stands, but I will do anything it takes for us to be together and grow with one another, eventually celebrating our comfort, the security you feel with me, and the healing you need to have. I need some time, too. I've gotten impatient, but I need time too," he said. After a brief pause, he gestured for a toast of their sherry glasses to seal what he had just declared.

She picked up her glass. They touched glasses, her eyes filled with tears. With his free hand, he drew her close and they sat quietly for a time.

A few deep breaths came before her response. "Jon, thank you. Thank you, Love. You've got whatever you want with me. We've a lot ahead of us. Both of us are independent and complex people, but at this very moment, our lives seem scored on the same musical page. I cannot imagine our ever being apart."

The rest of the evening included his fixing supper, Sky's reading part of a paper to him she would be delivering soon. She liked his suggestions, offering some editorial remarks for clarity, admitting he'd been a layman and she would be talking to experts in her field. The deepening of their felt commitment with one another became palpable. By the time they parted near midnight, they confirmed their bond, parting with, 'I love you'. And, not just a reflex response, but an emotion-filled 'I love you', too.

An Epilogue

Thursday morning, Saint Valentine's Day, Sky and Jon were given another gift. Fred Emerson completed the assay on Sky's remaining gold. The State of California and the Federal Government had both given him the assurance the gold remaining at the shipwreck site would be exclusively his to assay, seeing as he knew more about these Moffat-produced coins and ingots than anyone on the west coast. Emerson told Sky marketing the secret amount of gold she had remaining in the workshop would be an easy thing for him to do. Already, he had three people interested in the antique coins and ingots. The small bricks were not as valuable, but they would bring around $370 per ounce, the floating gold price in February and March of 1985.

The next good news that came to them that same morning had to do with locating the site for the Kashaya Pomo historical memorial, commemorating the Pomos. The combined education and museum building was given enough adjacent space on level ground adequate for a parking lot. It overlooked the lake: a beautiful location on donated land. The prospective structure would house the figurehead, the bronze scroll, and an educational display. The display would include Pomo money - various beads and clamshells - some of their baskets, only a few old ones, but all representing Pomo styles; showing the development of their craft and weaving skills.

With what Fred Emerson could bring in from the remaining gold, there was plenty to build the fascinating structure architect Bill Sanchez had rendered for them. Adding to the donated land, enough property for parking and a picnic area easily could be obtained, just off Highway 20, adjacent to the hill that was once Badonnapoti Island - the original name for Bloody Island. The water of Clearlake had receded from this hill site, about 1920, but the undeveloped land made possible the dedication of an entire half acre overlooking the site. It was already registered as an historic site, an obsidian marker, with a bronze plaque attached having been in place for some years. Future expectations, however, were that Clearlake levels might rise again, making the hill just to the west of Highway 20 an island once more.

An endowment was discussed that would be dedicated to maintaining the memorial itself, but also, in case the facility needed to be moved from the path of higher water levels, there would be enough money to do that. The whole plan would be placed in the hands of the local descendants of Pomos, some of whom had already been identified. A large surplus of cash could establish a scholarship for young Pomos who could go to college. Of course, many details needed to be worked out, but everyone who learned what was taking place took immediate, affirmative interest. Some of the local more militant Native Americans, one man especially, Milton Xasis Duncan, was eager to work with Dr. Miguél Rodriguez and the developing committee to help authenticate the artifacts and the historical details.

During Sky's Spring break, she and Jon arranged to take the Lady, her mounting, and the bronze scroll to a storage facility near Kelseyville. They made reservations at a beautiful place near the north end of Clearlake, called the Blue Fish Inn. When the local people learned about their coming and what they intended to do, they could not do enough to make the adventure memorable in every hospitable way. To Jon's surprise, Sky was excited about their driving north in his pickup, pulling a rented trailer, his Lady securely bundled up and riding behind them.

Later, during their stay near Nice, close to Clearlake, they found two places they wanted with a good view of the water of Clearlake, not far from Highway 20. They made an offer on one of them, a buildable view lot. Bill and Mary Sanchez, already having a place near there, generously offered to work with them to build their dream cabin, guaranteeing it would be a place they would never want to leave. After seeing what Bill had designed for their home, Jon and Sky knew it would be exactly what they wanted. Bill Sanchez had a good friend, a Danielle Howard, who arranged an evening where her friends, some of the local Pomos and interested people could meet them. In the snow, Jon and Sky were able to feel the natural, abundant beauty, and the spirit of the area, as they grew even closer to each other and more at home in northern California. The whole adventure was wrapped in a ceremonial Indian blanket that had been given to Sky earlier, further bonding them to the archeological history, the Pomos themselves, and to a place close to where their Lady would spend the rest of her 'life'. She would become the centerpiece of a memorial to the Pomos, especially for those who lost their lives to the brutal American army in 1850, up until now an atrocity that had been forgotten by too many.

Whether they waited to move permanently until retirement or not, they would find themselves spending restorative times in this enchanted place. The Lady of the Deep had led them to new spiritual, sensual, loving dimensions. She had led them, too, into a community of wonderful people, the kind of people who would become abiding friends.

There were teaching possibilities for Sky at several institutions, from Humboldt State University to the College of the Redwoods. Jon's Los Angeles Bishop gave him a letter of introduction to the Episcopal Bishop of Northern California, in case he chose to establish a connection with that diocese. There were several marinas with available slips, including Clearlake itself, if Jon brought the *Daimon* north. They rode a wave of new possibilities from the depths to heights of their lives together. Krystal's announcing that she had already thought about wanting to go to Stanford Medical School after finishing her undergraduate work at USC, became the frosting on a splendid future cake. Sky asked, partly in jest, "Why not Harvard or some Eastern school?"

"Sylvia and I don't ever want to be that far away from you, Mother," Krystal, declared, giving her mother a big smile and a hug.

Together, in the years ahead, there would be journeys as unimaginable as what Jon and Sky had been through since November. They agreed, too, that they would not want to lose their roots and friends in Long Beach, no matter where Meri and her spirit would lead. Jon's Lady of the Deep had become Their Lady. Her feminine spirit arising from Pacific Ocean sediments and having once graced the prow of a proud vessel, would now be the *Madonna*'s presence in these sacred surroundings of the Kashaya Pomo. Powerfully leaning into her new life from her impressive mount, the *Madonna*'s figurehead would be a reminder of survival, courage, and a renewed sense of identity and dignity for the Kashaya Pomo along with remnants of other coastal tribes.

Maybe, just maybe, the ancestral spirits would also find peace with the *Madonna*'s figurehead present: her spirit manifest; her translucent eyes gleaming; hair and dress flowing in an imagined breeze; providing peace and eternal rest to the departed Pomo Indians and their recently found descendants.

~o~

Thank you for taking the time to read Lady of the Deep. If you enjoyed it, please consider telling your friends or posting a short review. Word of mouth is an author's best friend and much appreciated.

~~o~~

Made in the USA
San Bernardino, CA
10 March 2016